THE BEST AMERICAN

HUMOROUS SHORT STORIES

THE BEST AMERICAN
Humorous Short Stories

Edited, with an Introductory Note by

ROBERT N. LINSCOTT

THE MODERN LIBRARY

To CLIFTON FADIMAN

who added and subtracted

Introductory Note

An introduction to an anthology should tell something about the book that follows and explain the principles of selection and arrangement. This book is adequately described by the title (with the modest qualifying phrase "in the editor's judgment" implied after the word "best"); the selection is personal rather than representative; and the arrangement is roughly chronological, with authors' dates given in the index at the end.

Of the forty-three stories included, ten were written before 1900 and twenty after 1930. The high proportion of contemporary writing is an indication of how quickly most humor goes sour. It is a sobering experience to reread the favorites of yesterday.

The reader will observe that the broadest possible interpretation has been given to the last word of the title. Even so, there were additional selections by Thurber, Perelman, Benchley and others which were omitted only with the deepest regret as falling on the wrong side of the tenuous line that divides stories and sketches.

The New Yorker deserves special mention as the original source of many of the stories here included. Thanks are also tendered to all those who have offered advice and suggestions, and in particular to the following holders of copyright who have permitted the inclusion of the material listed below.

A. & C. Boni, Inc., for a selection from *The Crazy Fool* by Donald Ogden Stewart.

Mrs. Ida Butler for *Pigs Is Pigs* by Ellis Parker Butler.

Marc Connelly and *The New Yorker* for "The Guest."

Doubleday, Doran & Company, Inc., for "The Ransom of Red Chief" from *Whirligigs* by O. Henry, copyright, 1910, by Doubleday, Doran & Company, Inc.; for "Gendarmes and the Man" from *A Villa in Brittany* by Donald Moffat, copyright, 1929, 1930, 1931, by Donald Moffat, reprinted by permission of Doubleday, Doran & Company, Inc. and *The*

                                            R. N. Linscott

Contents

THE BEST AMERICAN

HUMOROUS SHORT STORIES

SWALLOWING AN OYSTER ALIVE

By JOHN S. ROBB

———

AT A late hour the other night, the door of an oyster-house in our city was thrust open, and in stalked a hero from the Sucker State. He was quite six feet high, spare, somewhat stooped, with a hungry, anxious countenance, and his hands pushed clear down to the bottom of his breeches-pockets. His outer covering was hard to define, but after surveying it minutely we came to the conclusion that his suit had been made in his boyhood, of a dingy yellow linsey-woolsey, and that, having sprouted up with astonishing rapidity, he had been forced to piece it out with all colors in order to keep pace with his body. In spite of his exertions, however, he had fallen in arrears about a foot of the necessary length, and, consequently, stuck that far through his inexpressibles. His crop of hair was surmounted by the funniest little seal-skin cap imaginable. After taking a position, he indulged in a long stare at the man opening the *bivalves,* and slowly ejaculated, "Isters?"

"Yes, sir," responded the attentive operator, "and fine ones they are, too."

"Well, I've heard of isters afore," says he, "but this is the fust time I've seed 'em, and *pre-haps* I'll know what *thar* made of afore I git out of town."

7

Having expressed this desperate intention, he cautiously approached the plate, and scrutinized the uncased shellfish with a gravity and interest which would have done honor to the most illustrious searcher into the hidden mysteries of nature. At length he began to soliloquize on the difficulty of getting them out, and how queer they looked when out!

"I never seed anythin' hold on so: takes an amazin' site of screwin', hoss, to git them out, and ain't they slick and slip'ry when they does come? Smooth as an eel! I've got a good mind to give that feller lodgin', just to realize the effects, as Uncle Jess used to say about speckalation."

"Well, sir," was the reply, "down with two bits, and you can have a dozen."

"Two bits!" exclaimed the Sucker. "Now, come, that's stickin' it on right strong, hoss, for *isters*. A dozen on 'em ain't nothin' to a chicken, and there's no gittin' more'n a picayune apiece for *them*. I've only realized forty-five picayunes on my first ventur' to St. Louis. I'll tell you what, I'll gin you two chickens for a dozen, if you'll conclude to deal."

A wag who was standing by, indulging in a dozen, winked to the attendant to shell out, and the offer was accepted.

"Now, mind," repeated the Sucker, "all fair,—two chickens for a dozen: you're a witness, mister," turning at the same time to the wag: "none of your tricks, for I've heard that your city fellers are mighty slip'ry coons."

The bargain being fairly understood, our Sucker squared himself for the onset,—deliberately put off his seal-skin, tucked up his sleeves, and, fork in hand, awaited the appearance of No. 1. It came,—he saw,—and quickly it was bolted! A moment's dreadful pause ensued. The wag dropped his knife and fork, with a look of mingled amazement and horror,—something akin to Shakespeare's Hamlet on seeing his daddy's ghost,—while he burst into the exclamation,—

"Swallowed alive, as I'm a Christian!"

Our Sucker hero had opened his mouth with pleasure a moment before, but now it *stood* open. Fear,—a horrid dread of he didn't know what,—a consciousness that all wasn't right, and ignorant of the extent of the wrong,—the uncertainty of the moment was terrible. Urged to desperation, he faltered out,—

"What on earth's the row?"

"Did you swallow it alive?" inquired the wag.

"I swallowed it jest as he gin it to me!" shouted the Sucker.

"You're a dead man!" exclaimed his anxious friend. "The creature is alive, and will eat right through you," added he, in a most hopeless tone.

"Git a pizen-pump and pump it out!" screamed the Sucker, in a frenzy, his eyes fairly starting from their sockets. "Oh, gracious! what'll I do? It's got hold of my innards already, and I'm dead as a chicken! Do somethin' for me, do!—don't let the infernal sea-toad eat me afore your eyes."

"Why don't you put some of this on it?" inquired the wag, pointing to a bottle of strong pepper-sauce.

The hint was enough. The Sucker, upon the instant, seized the bottle, and, desperately wrenching out the cork, swallowed half the contents at a draught. He fairly squealed from its effects, and gasped, and blowed, and pitched, and twisted, as if it were coursing through him with electric effect, while at the same time his eyes ran a stream of tears. At length becoming a little composed, his waggish adviser approached, almost bursting with suppressed laughter, and inquired,—

"How are you now, old fellow? Did you kill it?"

"Well, I did, hoss! Ugh! ugh! o-o-o! my innards! If that *ister* critter's dying agonies didn't stir a 'ruption in me equal to a small arthquake, then 'tain't no use sayin' it. It squirmed like a sarpent when that killin' stuff touched it. Hu!" And here, with a countenance made up of suppressed agony and present determination, he paused to give force to his words, and slowly and deliberately remarked, "If you get two chickens from me for that live animal, I'm d—d!" and, seizing his seal-skin, he vanished.

HOW DADDY PLAYED HOSS

By George W. Harris

"Hole that ar hoss down tu the yeath." "He's a fixin' fur the heavings." "He's a spreadin' his tail feathers tu fly. Look out, Laigs, if you ain't ready tu go up'ards." "Wo, Shavetail." "Git a fiddil; he's tryin' a jig." "Say, Long Laigs, rais'd a power ove co'n, didn't yu?" "Tain't co'n, hits redpepper."

These and like expressions were addressed to a queer-looking, long-legged, short-bodied, small-headed, white-haired, hog-eyed, funny sort of a genius, fresh from some bench-legged Jew's clothing store, mounted on "Tearpoke," a nick-tailed, bow-necked, long, poor, pale sorrel horse, half dandy, half devil, and enveloped in a perfect net-work of bridle, reins, crupper, martingales, straps, surcingles, and red ferreting, who reined up in front of Pat Nash's grocery, among a crowd of mountaineers, full of fun, foolery, and whisky.

This was SUT LOVINGOOD.

"I say, you durn'd ash cats, jis keep yer shuts on, will ye? You never seed a rale hoss till I rid up; you's p'raps stole ur owned shod rabbits ur sheep wif borrerd saddils on, but when you tuck the fus begrudgin' look jis now at this critter, name Tarpoke, you wer injoyin' a sight ove nex' tu the bes' hoss what ever shell'd nubbins ur toted jugs, an' he's es ded es a still wum, poor old Tickytail!

7

"Wo! wo! Tarpoke, yu cussed infunel fidgety hide full ove fire, can't yu stan' still an' listen while I'se a polishin' yer karacter off es a mortul hoss tu these yere durned fools?"

Sut's tongue or his spurs brought Tearpoke into something like passable quietude, while he continued:—

"Say yu, sum ove yu growin' hogs made a re-mark jis now 'bout redpepper. I jis wish tu say in a gineral way that eny wurds cupplin' redpepper an Tarpoke tugether am durn'd infurnal lies."

"What killed Tickeytail, Sut?" asked an anxious inquirer after truth.

"Why, nuffin, you cussed fool; he jis died so, standin' up et that. Warn't that rale casteel hoss pluck? Yu see, he froze stiff; no, not that adzactly, but starv'd fust, an' froze arterards, so stiff that when dad an' me went tu lay him out, an' we push'd him over, he stuck out jis so" (spreading his arms and legs), "belike ontu a carpenter's bainch, an' we hed tu wait ni ontu seventeen days fur 'im tu thaw afore we cud skin 'im."

"Skin 'im?" interrupted a rat-faced youth, whittling on a corn-stalk. "I thot yu wanted tu lay the hoss out."

"The ——, you did! Ain't skinin' the natral way ove layin' out a hoss, I'd like tu no? See a yere, soney, yu tell yer mam tu hev yu sot back jis 'bout two years, fur et the rate yu'se a climbin' yu stan's a pow'ful chance tu die wif yer shoes on, an' git laid hoss way, yu dus."

The rat-faced youth shut up his knife and subsided.

"Well, thar we wer—dad, an' me" (counting on his fingers), "an' Sall, an' Jake (fool Jake we calls 'im, fur short), an' Jim, an' Phineass, an' Callimy Jane, an' Sharlottyann, an' me, an' Zodiack, an' Cashus Clay, an' Noah Webster, an' the twin gals (Castur and Pollox), an' me, an' Catherin Second, an' Cleopatry Antony, an' Jane Barnum

Lind, an' me, an' Benton Bullion, an' the baby what hain't nam'd yet, an' me, an' the Prospect, an' mam hersef—all lef in the woods alone, wifout ara hoss tu crup wif."

"Yu'se counted yerself five times, Mister Lovingood," said a tomato-nosed man in ragged overcoat.

"Yas, ole Still-tub, that's jis the perporshun I bears in the famerly fur dam fool, leavin' out dad, in course. Yu jis let me alone, an' be a thinkin' ove gittin' more hoops ontu yu. Yus leakin' now; see thar." Ha! ha! from the crowd, and "Still-tub" went into the doggery.

"Warn't that a devil's own mess ove broth fur a 'spectabil white farmerly tu be sloshin' about in? I durned ef I didn't feel sorter like stealin' a hoss sumtimes, an' I speck I'd a dun hit, but the stealin' streak in the Lovingoods all run tu durned fool, an' the onvartus streak all run tu laigs. Jis look down the side ove this yere hoss mos' tu the groun'. Dus yu see em?

"Well, we waited, an' wished, an' rested, an' plan'd, an' wished, an' waited agin, ontil ni ontu strawberry time, hopin' sum stray hoss mout cum along; but dorg my cats, ef eny sich good luck ever cums wifin reach ove whar dad is, he's so dod-dratted mean, an' lazy, an' ugly, an' savidge, an' durn fool tu kill.

"Well, one nite he lay awake till cock-crowin' a-snortin', an' rollin', an' blowin', an' shufflin', an' scratchin' hissef, an' a whisperin' at mam a heap, an' at breckfus' I foun' out what hit ment. Says he, 'Sut, I'll tell yu what we'll du: I'll be hoss *mysef*, an' pull the plow whilst yu drives me, an' then the "Ole Quilt" (he ment that fur mam) an' the brats kin plant, an' tend, ur jis let hit alone, es they darn pleze; I ain't a carein'.'

"So out we went tu the pawpaw thicket, an' peel'd a rite smart chance ove bark, an' mam an' me made geers fur dad, while he sot on the fence a-lookin' at us, an' a studyin' pow'rful. I arterards foun' out, he wer a-studyin' how tu play the kar-acter ove a hoss puffectly.

"Well, the geers becum him mitily, an' nuffin wud du 'im but he mus hev a bridil; so I gits a umereller brace—hit's a litil forked piece ove squar wire bout a foot long, like a yung pitchfork, yu no—an' twisted hit sorter intu a bridil bit snaffil shape. Dad wanted hit made kurb, es he hadn't work'd fur a good while, an' said he mout sorter feel his keepin' an' go tu ravin' an' cavortin'.

"When we got the bridil fix'd ontu dad, don't yu bleve he sot in tu chompin hit jis like a rale hoss, an' tried tu bite me on the arm (he allers wer a mos' complikated durned ole fool, an' mam sed so when he warn't about). I put on the geers, an' while mam wer a-tyin' the belly-ban', a-strainin' hit pow'rful tite, he drapt ontu his hans, sed 'Whay-a-a' like a mad hos wud. I shoulder'd the gopher plow, an' tuck hole ove the bridil. Dad leaned back sulky, till I sed cluck cluck wif my tongue, then he started. When we cum tu the fence I let down the gap, an' hit made dad mad; he wanted tu jump hit on all fours, hoss way. Oh, geminy! what a durn'd ole fool kin cum tu ef he gins up tu the complaint.

"I hitch'd 'im tu the gopher, a a-watchin' him pow'ful clost, fur I'd see how quick he cud drap ontu his hans, an' kick, an' away we went, dad leanin' forard tu his pullin', an' we made rite peart plowin' fur tu hev a green hoss, an' bark geers; he went over the sprowts an' bushes same as a rale hoss, only he traveled on two laigs. I mitily hope up bout co'n; I cud a'mos' see hit a cumin' up; but thar's a heap ove whisky spilt twixt the counter an' the mouf, ef hit ain't got but two foot tu travil. 'Bout the time he wer beginin' tu

break sweat, we cum tu a sassafrack bush, an' tu keep up his
kar-acter es a hoss he buljed squar intu an' thru hit, tarin'
down a ball ho'nets nes' ni ontu es big es a hoss's hed, an' the
hole tribe kiver'd 'im es quick es yu cud kiver a sick pup wif
a saddil blanket. He lit ontu his hans agin, an' kick'd strait
up onst, then he rar'd, an' fotch a squeal was nur ara stud
hoss in the State, an' sot in tu strait runnin' away jis ez
natral es yu ever seed any uther skeer'd hoss du. I let go
the line an' holler'd, Wo! Dad, wo! but yu mout jis es well
say woa! tu a locomotum, ur Suke cow tu a gal.

"Gewhillitins! how he run! When he cum tu bushes,
he'd clar the top ove em wif a squeal, gopher an' all. P'rraps
he tho't thar mout be anuther settilment ove ball ho'nets
thar, an' hit wer safer tu go over than thru, an' quicker dun
eny how. Every now an' then he'd fan the side ove his hed,
fust wif wun fore laig an' then tuther; then he'd gin hissef
a roun-handed slap what soundid like a waggin' whip ontu
the place whar the breechbands tetches a hoss, a-runnin' all
the time, an' a-kerrin' that ar gopher jis 'bout as fas' an es
his frum the yeath as ever eny gopher wer kerried, I'll swar.
When he cum tu the fence, he jis tore thru hit, bustin' an'
scatterin' ni ontu seven panils wif lots ove broken rails.
Rite yere he lef the gopher, geers, close, clevis, an'
swingltress, all mix'd up, an' not wuf a durn. The balance
on em, ni ontu a gallun, kep' on wif dad. He seem'd tu run
jis adzactly es fas, es a ho'net cud fly; hit wer the titest race I
ever seed, fur wun hoss tu git all the whipin'. Down thru a
saige field they all went, ho'nets makin' hit look like thar
wer smoke roun' dad's bald hed, an' he wif nuffin on the
green yeath in the way ove close bout ima, but the bridil, an'
ni ontu a yard ove plow line sailin' behine, wif a tir'd out
ho'net ridin' on the pint ove hit. I seed that he wer aimin'

fur the swimin' hole in the krick, whar the bluff am over-
twenty five foot pupendiculer tu the warter, an' hits ni ontu
ten foot deep.

"Well, tu keep up his karacter es a hoss, plum thru, when
he got tu the bluff he loped off, ur rather jis kep on a runnin'.
Kerslunge intu the krick he went. I seed the warter fly plum
abuv the bluff from whar I wer.

"Now rite thar, boys, he over-did the thing, ef actin'
hoss tu the scrib wer what he wer arter; fur thars nara hoss
ever foaldid durned fool enuf tu lope over eny sich place; a
cussed muel mout a dun hit, but dad warn't actin' muel, tho'
he orter tuck that karacter; hits adzactly sooted tu his
dispersion. I crept up tu the aidge, an' peep'd over. Thar
wer dad's bald hed, fur all the yeath like a peeled inyin, a
bobbin' up an' down an' aroun', an' the ho'nets sailin' roun'
tuckey buzzard fashun, an' every onst in a while one, an'
sumtimes ten, wud take a dip at dad's bald head. He kep'
up a rite peart dodgin' onder, sumtimes afore they hit im,
sumtimes arterard, an the warter wer kivered wif drownded
ball ho'nets. Tu look at him frum the top ove the bluff, hit
wer pow'ful inturestin', an' sorter funny; I wer on the bluff
myse'f, mine yu.

"Dad cudent see the funny part frum whar he war, but
hit seem'd tu be inturestin' tu him from the 'tenshun he wer
payin' tu the bisness ove divin' an' cussin'.

"Sez I, 'Dad, ef yu's dun washin' yersef, he hes drunk
enuff, less go back tu our plowin', hit will soon be powerful
hot.' 'Hot—hell!' sez dad; 'hit am hot rite now. Don't (an
onder went his hed) yer see (dip) these cussed (dip) infun
—(dip) varmints arter me?' (dip) 'What,' sez I, 'them ar
hoss flies thar, that's nat'ral, Dad; you ain't raley fear'd ove
them is yu?' 'Hoss flies! h—I an (dip) durnation!' sez dad,
'theyse rale ginni— (dip) ball ho'nets, (dip) yu infunel

ignurant cuss!' (dip). 'Kick em—paw em—switch em wif'
yure tail, dad,' sez I. 'Oh! soney, soney, (dip) how I'll
sweeten yure—(dip) when these (dip) ho'nets leave yere.'
'Yu'd better du the levin' yursef Dad,' sez I. 'Leave yere!
How (dip) kin I, (dip) when they won't (dip) let me stay
(dip) atop (dip) the warter even.' 'Well, Dad, yu'l hev tu
stay thar till nite, an' arter they goes tu roos' yu cum home.
I'll hev yer feed in the troft redy; yu won't need eny curyin'
tu-nite will yu?' 'I wish (dip) I may never (dip) see to-
morrer, ef I (dip) don't make (dip) hame strings (dip)
outer yure hide (dip) when I dus (dip) git outen yere,'
sez dad. 'Better say yu wish you may never see anuther ball
ho'net, ef yu ever play hoss again,' sez I.

"Them words toch dad tu the hart, an' I felt they mus' be
my las, knowin' dad's onmollified nater. I broke frum them
parts, an' sorter cum over yere tu the copper mines. When I
got tu the hous', 'Whar's yer dad?' sez mam. 'Oh, he turn'd
durn fool, an' run away, busted every thing all tu cussed
smash, an's in the swimin' hole a divin' arter minners. Look
out Mam, he'll cum home wif a angel's temper; better sen'
fur sum strong man body tu keep him frum huggin' yu tu
deth.' 'Law sakes!' sez mam; 'I know'd he cudent act hoss
fur ten minutes wifout actin' infunel fool, tu save his life.'

"I staid hid out ontil nex' arternoon, an' I seed a feller
a-travelin'. Sez I, 'How de do, mister? What wer agwine on
at the cabin, this side the crick, when yu pass'd thar?' 'Oh,
nuthin' much, only a pow'ful fat man wer a lyin' in the yard
wif no shut on, an' a 'oman wer a greasin' ove his shoulders
an' arms auten a gourd. A pow'ful curious, vishus, skeery
lookin' cuss he is tu b' shure. His head am as big es a wash
pot, an' he hasent the fust durned sign ove an eye—jist two
black slits. Is thar much small pox roun' yere?' 'Small pox!'
sez I, 'no sir.' 'Been much fightin' in this neighborhood

lately?' 'Nun wuf speakin' ove,' sez I. He scratched his head
—'Nur French measils?' 'Not jis clost,' sez I. 'Well, do yu
know what ails that man back thar?' 'Jist gittin' over a
vilent attack ove dam fool,' sez I. 'Well, who is he eny
how?' I ris tu my feet, an' straiched out my arm, an' sez I,
'Strainger, that man is my dad.' He looked at my laigs an'
pussonel feeters a moment, an' sez he, 'Yas, dam ef he ain't.'

"Now boys, I hain't seed dad since, an' I dusent hev much
appertite tu see im fur sum time tu cum. Less all drink!
Yere's luck tu the durned old fool, an' the ho'nets too."

THE SHAKERS

By Artemus Ward

THE Shakers is the strangest religious sex I ever met. I'd
hearn tell of 'em and I'd seen 'em, with their broad brim'd
hats and long waistid coats; but I'd never cum into immejit
contack with 'em, and I'd sot 'em down as lackin intelleck,
as I'd never seen 'em to my Show—leastways, if they cum
they was disgised in white peple's close, so I did n't know
'em.

But in the Spring of 18—, I got swampt in the exterior
of New York State, one dark and stormy night, when the
winds Blue pityusly, and I was forced to tie up with the
Shakers.

I was toilin threw the mud, when in the dim vister of the
futer I observed the gleams of a taller candle. Tiein a hor-
net's nest to my off hoss's tail to kinder encourage him, I
soon reached the place. I knockt at the door, which was
opened unto me by a tall, slick-faced, solum lookin indiv-
dooal, who turn'd out to be a Elder.

"Mr. Shaker," sed I, "you see before you a Babe in the
Woods, so to speak, and he axes shelter of you."

"Yay," sed the Shaker, and he led the way into the house,
another Shaker bein sent to put my hosses and waggin under
kiver.

A solum female, lookin sumwhat like a last year's beanpole stuck into a long meal bag, cum in and axed me was I athurst and did I hunger? to which I urbanely anserd "a few." She went orf and I endevered to open a conversashun with the old man.

"Elder, I spect?" sed I.

"Yay," he sed.

"Helth's good, I reckon?"

"Yay."

"What's the wages of a Elder, when he understans his bizness—or do you devote your sarvices gratooitus?"

"Yay."

"Stormy night, sir."

"Yay."

"If the storm continners there'll be a mess underfoot, hay?"

"Yay."

"It's onpleasant when there's a mess underfoot?"

"Yay."

"If I may be so bold, kind sir, what's the price of that pecooler kind of weskit you wear, incloodin trimmins?"

"Yay."

I pawsd a minit, and then, thinkin I'd be faseshus with him and see how that would go, I slapt him on the shoulder, bust into a harty larf, and told him that as a yayer he had no livin ekal.

He jumpt up as if Bilin water had bin squirted into his ears, groaned, rolled his eyes up tords the sealin and sed: "You're a man of sin!" He then walkt out of the room.

Jest then the female in the meal bag stuck her hed into the room and statid that refreshments awaited the weary travler, and I sed if it was vittles she ment, the weary travler was agreeable, and I follered her into the next room.

I sot down to the table and the female in the meal bag pored out sum tea. She sed nothin, and for five minutes the only live thing in that room was a old wooden clock, which tickt in a subdood and bashful manner in the corner. This dethly stillness made me oneasy, and I determined to talk to the female or bust. So sez I, "marrige is agin your rules, I bleeve, marm?"

"Yay."

"The sexes liv strickly apart, I spect?"

"Yay."

"It's kinder singler," sez I, puttin on my most sweetest look and speakin in a winnin voice, "that so fair a made as thou never got hitched to some likely feller." [N. B.— She was upards of 40 and homely as a stump fence, but I thawt I'd tickil her.]

"I don't like men!" she sed, very short.

"Wall, I dunno," sez I, "they're a rayther important part of the populashun. I don't scacely see how we could git along without 'em."

"Us poor wimin folks would git along a grate deal better if there was no men!"

"You'll excoos me, marm, but I don't think that air would work. It would n't be regler."

"I'm fraid of men!" she sed.

"That's onnecessary, marm. You ain't in no danger. Don't fret yourself on that pint."

"Here we're shot out from the sinful world. Here all is peas. Here we air brothers and sisters. We don't marry and consekently we hav no domestic difficulties. Husbans don't abooze their wives—wives don't worrit their husbans. There's no children here to worrit us. Nothin to worrit us here. No wicked matrimony here. Would thow like to be a Shaker?"

"No," sez I, "it ain't my stile."

I had now histed in as big a load of pervishuns as I could carry comfortable, and, leanin' back in my cheer, commenst pickin my teeth with a fork. The female went out, leavin me all alone with the clock. I had n't sot thar long before the Elder poked his hed in at the door. "You're a man of sin!" he sed and groaned and went away.

Direckly thar cum in two young Shakeresses, as putty and slick lookin gals as I ever met. It is troo they was drest in meal bags like the old one I'd met previsly, and their shiny, silky har was hid from sight by long white caps, sich as I spose female Josts wear; but their eyes sparkled like diminds, their cheeks was like roses, and they was charmin enuff to make a man throw stuns at his granmother, if they axed him to. They commenst clearin away the dishes, castin shy glances at me all the time. I got excited. I forgot Betsy Jane in my rapter, and sez I, "my pretty dears, how air you?"

"We air well," they solumnly sed.

"Whar's the old man?" sed I, in a soft voice.

"Of whom dost thow speak—Brother Uriah?"

"I mean the gay and festiv cuss who calls me a man of sin. Should n't wonder if his name was Uriah."

"He has retired."

"Wall, my pretty dears," sez I, "let's have sum fun. Let's play puss in the corner. What say?"

"Air you a Shaker, sir?" they axed.

"Wall, my pretty dears, I have n't arrayed my proud form in a long weskit yit, but if they was all like you perhaps I'd jine 'em. As it is, I'm a Shaker pro-temporary."

They was full of fun. I seed that at fust, only they was a leetle skeery. I tawt 'em Puss in the corner and sich like plase, and we had a nice time, keepin quiet of course so the old man should n't hear. When we broke up, sez I, "my pretty dears, ear I go you hav no objections, have you, to a innersent kiss at partin?"

"Yay," they sed, and I yay'd.

I went up stairs to bed. I spose I'd bin snoozin half a hour when I was woke up by a noise at the door. I sot up in bed, leanin on my elbers and rubbin my eyes, and I saw the follerin picter: The Elder stood in the doorway, with a taller candle in his hand. He had n't no wearin appeerel on except his night close, which flutterd in the breeze like a Seseshun flag. He sed, "You're a man of sin!" then groaned and went away.

I went to sleep agin, and drempt of runnin orf with the pretty little Shakeresses, mounted on my Californy Bar. I thawt the Bar insisted on steerin strate for my dooryard in Baldinsville and that Betsy Jane cum out and giv us a warm recepshun with a panfull of Bilin water. I was voke up arly by the Elder. He sed refreshments was reddy for me down stairs. Then sayin I was a man of sin, he went groanin away.

As I was going threw the entry to the room where the vittles was, I cum across the Elder and the old female I'd met the night before, and what d'ye spose they was up to? Huggin and kissin like young lovers in their gushingist state. Sez I, "my Shaker frends, I reckon you'd better suspend the rules, and git marrid!"

"You must excoos Brother Uriah," sed the female: "he's subjeck to fits and hain't got no command over hisself when he's into 'em."

"Sartinly," sez I, "I've bin took that way myself frequent."

"You're a man of sin!" sed the Elder.

Arter breakfust my little Shaker frends cum in agin to clear away the dishes.

"My pretty dears," sez I, "shall we yay agin?"

"Nay," they sed, and I nay'd.

The Shakers axed me to go to their meetin, as they was to hav sarvices that mornin, so I put on a clean biled rag and went. The meetin house was as neat as a pin. The floor was white as chalk and smooth as glass. The Shakers was all on hand, in clean weskits and meal bags, ranged on the floor like milingtery companies, the mails on one side of the room and the females on tother. They commenst clappin their hands and singin and dancin. They danced kinder slow at fust, but as they got warmed up they shaved it down very brisk, I tell you. Elder Uriah, in particler, exhiberted a right smart chance of spryness in his legs, considerin his time of life, and as he cum a dubble shuffle near where I sot, I rewarded him with a approvin smile and sed: "Hunky boy! Go it, my gay and festiv cuss!"

"You're a man of sin!" he sed, continnerin his shuffle.

The Sperret, as they called it, then moved a short fat Shaker to say a few remarks. He sed they was Shakers and all was ekal. They was the purest and seleckest peple on the yearth. Other peple was sinful as they could be, but Shakers was all right. Shakers was all goin kerslap to the Promist Land, and nobody want goin to stand at the gate to bar 'em out, if they did they'd git run over.

The Shakers then danced and sung agin, and arter they was threw, one of 'em axed me what I thawt of it.

Sez I, "What duz it siggerfy?"

"What?" sez he.

"Why this jumpin up and singin? This long weskit bizness, and this anty-matrimony idee? My friends, you air neat and tidy. Your lands is flowin with milk and honey. Your brooms is fine, and your apple sass is honest. When a man buys a kag of apple sass of you he don't find a grate many shavins under a few layers of sass—a little Game I'm sorry to say sum of my New England ancestors used to practiss. Your garding seeds is fine, and if I should sow 'em on the rock of Gibralter probly I should raise a good mess of garding sass. You air honest in your dealins. You air quiet and don't distarb nobody. For all this I givs you credit. But your religion is small pertaters, I must say. You mope away your lives here in single retchidness, and as you air all by yourselves nothing ever conflicks with your pecooler idees, except when Human Nater busts out among you, as I understan she sumtimes do. [I giv Uriah a sly wink here, which made the old feller squirm like a speared Eel.] You wear long weskits and long faces, and lead a gloomy life indeed. No children's prattle is ever hearn around your harthstuns—you air in a dreary fog all the time, and you treat the jolly sunshine of life as tho' it was a thief, drivin it from your doors by them weskits, and meal bags, and pecooler noshuns of yourn. The gals among you, sum of which air as slick pieces of caliker as I ever sot eyes on, air syin to place their heds agin weskits which kiver honest, manly harts, while you old heds fool yerselves with the idee that they air fulfilin their mishun here, and air contented. Here you are, all pend up by yerselves, talkin about the sins of a world you don't know nothing of. Meanwhile said world continers to resolve round on her own axeltree onct in every 24 hours, subjeck to the Constitooshun of the United States, and is a very pleasant place of residence. It's a unnatural, onreasonable and dismal life you're leadin here. So it strikes me. My Shaker frends, I now bid you a welcome adoo. You hav treated me exceedin well. Thank you kindly, one and all."

"A base exhibiter of depraved monkeys and onprincipled wax works!" sed Uriah.

"Hello, Uriah," sez I, "I'd most forgot you. Wall, look out for them fits of yourn, and don't catch cold and die in the flour of your youth and beauty."

And I resoomed my jerney.

MRS. MCWILLIAMS AND THE LIGHTNING

By Mark Twain

WELL, sir,—continued Mr. McWilliams, for this was not the beginning of his talk,—the fear of lightning is one of the most distressing infirmities a human being can be afflicted with. It is mostly confined to women; but now and then you find it in a little dog, and sometimes in a man. It is a particularly distressing infirmity, for the reason that it takes the sand out of a person to an extent which no other fear can, and it can't be *reasoned* with, and neither can it be shamed out of a person. A woman who could face the very devil himself—or a mouse—loses her grip and goes all to pieces in front of a flash of lightning. Her fright is something pitiful to see.

Well, as I was telling you, I woke up, with that smothered and unlocatable cry of "Mortimer! Mortimer!" wailing in my ears; and as soon as I could scrape my faculties together I reached over in the dark and then said,—

"Evangeline, is that you calling? What is the matter? Where are you?"

"Shut up in the boot-closet. You ought to be ashamed to lie there and sleep so, and such an awful storm going on."

"Why, how *can* one be ashamed when he is asleep? It is unreasonable; and man *can't* be ashamed when he is asleep, Evangeline."

"You never try, Mortimer,—you know very well you never try."

I caught the sound of muffled sobs.

That sound smote dead the sharp speech that was on my lips, and I changed it to—

"I'm sorry, dear,—I'm truly sorry. I never meant to act so. Come back and—"

"MORTIMER!"

"Heavens! what is the matter, my love?"

"Do you mean to say you are in that bed yet?"

"Why, of course."

"Come out of it instantly. I should think you would take some *little* care of your life, for *my* sake and the children's, if you will not for your own."

"But my love—"

"Don't talk to me, Mortimer. You *know* there is no place so dangerous as a bed, in such a thunderstorm as this,—all the books say that; yet there you would lie, and deliberately throw away your life,—for goodness knows what, unless for the sake of arguing and arguing, and—"

"But, confound it, Evangeline, I'm *not* in the bed, *now*. I'm—"

(Sentence interrupted by a sudden glare of lightning, followed by a terrified little scream from Mrs. McWilliams and a tremendous blast of thunder.)

"There! You see the result. Oh, Mortimer, how *can* you be so profligate as to swear at such a time as this?"

"I *didn't* swear. And that *wasn't* a result of it, anyway. It would have come, just the same, if I hadn't said a word; and you know very well, Evangeline,—at least you ought to know,—that when the atmosphere is charged with electricity—"

"Oh, yes, now argue it, and argue it, and argue it!—I

don't see how you can act so, when you *know* there is not a lightning-rod on the place, and your poor wife and children are absolutely at the mercy of Providence. What *are* you doing?—lighting a match at such a time as this! Are you stark mad?"

"Hang it, woman, where's the harm? The place is as dark as the inside of an infidel, and—"

"Put it out! put it out instantly! Are you determined to sacrifice us all? You *know* there is nothing attracts lightning like a light. [*Fzt!—crash! boom—boloom-boom-boom!*] Oh, just hear it! Now you see what you've done!"

"No, I *don't* see what I've done. A match may attract lightning, for all I know, but it don't *cause* lightning,—I'll go odds on that. And it didn't attract it worth a cent this time; for if that shot was levelled at my match, it was blessed poor marksmanship,—about an average of none out of a possible million, I should say. Why, at Dollymount, such marksmanship as that—"

"For shame, Mortimer! Here we are standing right in the very presence of death, and yet in so solemn a moment you are capable of using such language as that. If you have no desire to—Mortimer!"

"Well?"

"Did you say your prayers tonight?"

"I—I—meant to, but I got to trying to cipher out how much twelve times thirteen is, and—"

[*Fzt!—boom-berroom—boom! bumble-umble bang-SMASH!*]

"Oh, we are lost, beyond all help! How *could* you neglect such a thing at such a time as this?"

"But it *wasn't* 'such a time as this.' There wasn't a cloud in the sky. How could *I* know there was going to be all this rumpus and pow-wow about a little slip like that? And

I don't think it's just fair for you to make so much out of it, anyway, seeing it happens so seldom; I haven't missed before since I brought on that earthquake, four years ago."

"MORTIMER! How you talk! Have you forgotten the yellow fever?"

"My dear, you are always throwing up the yellow fever to me, and I think it is perfectly unreasonable. You can't even send a telegraphic message as far as Memphis without relays, so how is a little devotional slip of mine going to carry so far? I'll *stand* the earthquake, because is was in the neighborhood; but I'll be hanged if I'm going to be responsible for every blamed—"

[*Fzt!—BOOM beroom-boom! boom!—BANG!*]

"Oh, dear, dear, dear! I *know* it struck something, Mortimer. We never shall see the light of another day; and if it will do you any good to remember, when we are gone, that your dreadful language—*Mortimer!*"

"WELL! What now?"

"Your voice sounds as if—Mortimer, are you actually standing in front of that open fireplace?"

"That is the very crime I am committing."

"Get away from it, this moment. You do seem determined to bring destruction on us all. Don't you *know* that there is no better conductor for lightning that an open chimney? *NOW* where have you got to?"

"I'm here by the window."

"Oh, for pity's sake, have you lost your mind? Clear out from there, this moment. The very children in arms know it is fatal to stand near a window in a thunderstorm. Dear, dear, I know I shall never see the light of another day. Mortimer?"

"Yes?"

"What is that rustling?"

"It's me."

"What are you doing?"

"Trying to find the upper end of my pantaloons."

"Quick! throw those things away! I do believe you would deliberately put on those clothes at such a time as this; yet you know perfectly well that *all* authorities agree that woollen stuffs attract lightning. Oh, dear, dear, it isn't sufficient that one's life must be in peril from natural causes, but you must do everything you can possibly think of to augment the danger. Oh, *don't* sing! What *can* you be thinking of?"

"Now where's the harm in it?"

"Mortimer, if I have told you once, I have told you a hundred times, that singing causes vibrations in the atmosphere which interrupt the flow of the electric fluid, and— What on *earth* are you opening that door for?"

"Goodness gracious, woman, is there any harm in *that?*"

"*Harm?* There's *death* in it. Anybody that has given this subject any attention knows that to create a draught is to invite the lightning. You haven't half shut it; shut it *tight,*— and do hurry, or we are all destroyed. Oh, it is an awful thing to be shut up with a lunatic as such a time as this. Mortimer, what *are* you doing?"

"Nothing. Just turning on the water. This room is smothering hot and close. I want to bathe my face and hands."

"You have certainly parted with the remnant of your mind! Where lightning strikes any other substance once, it strikes water fifty times. Do turn if off. Oh, dear, I am sure that nothing in this world can save us. It does seem to me that—Mortimer, what was that?"

"It was a da— it was a picture. Knocked it down."

"Then you are close to the wall! I never heard of such imprudence! Don't you *know* that there's no better con-

ductor for lightning than a wall? Come away from there!
And you came as near as anything to swearing, too. Oh, how
can you be so desperately wicked, and your family in such
peril? Mortimer, did you order a feather bed, as I asked you
to do?"

"No. Forgot it."

"Forgot it! It may cost you your life. If you had a feather
bed, now, and could spread it in the middle of the room
and lie on it, you would be perfectly safe. Come in here,—
come quick, before you have a chance to commit any more
frantic indiscretions."

I tried, but the closet would not hold us both with the
door shut, unless we could be content to smother. I gasped
awhile, then forced my way out. My wife called out,—

"Mortimer, something *must* be done for your preservation.
Give me that German book that is on the end of the mantel-
piece, and a candle; but don't light it; give me a match; I
will light it in here. That book has some directions in it."

I got the book,—at the cost of a vase and some other
brittle things; and the madam shut herself up with her
candle. I had a moment's peace; then she called out,—

"Mortimer, what was that?"

"Nothing but the cat."

"The cat! Oh, destruction! Catch her, and shut her up
in the wash-stand. Do be quick, love; cats are *full* of electricity. I just know my hair will turn white with this night's
awful perils."

I heard the muffled sobbings again. But for that, I should
not have moved hand or foot in such a wild enterprise in
the dark.

However, I went at my task,—over chairs, and against
all sorts of obstructions, all of them hard ones, too, and
most of them with sharp edges,—and at last I got kitty

cooped up in the commode, at an expense of over four hundred dollars in broken furniture and shins. Then these muffled words came from the closet:—

"It says the safest thing is to stand on a chair in the middle of the room, Mortimer; and the legs of the chair must be insulated, with non-conductors. That is, you must set the legs of the chair in glass tumblers. [*Fzt!—boom—bang! smash!*] Oh, hear that! Do hurry, Mortimer, before you are struck."

I managed to find and secure the tumblers. I got the last four,—broke all the rest. I insulated the chair legs, and called for further instructions.

"Mortimer, it says, 'Während eines Gewitters entferne man Metalle, wie z. B., Ringe, Uhren, Schlüssel, etc., von sich und halte sich auch nicht an solchen Stellen auf, wo viele Metalle bei einander liegen, oder mit andern Körpern verbunden sind, wie an Herden, Oefen, Eisengittern u. dgl.' What does that mean, Mortimer? Does it mean that you must keep metals *about* you, or keep them *away* from you?"

"Well, I hardly know. It appears to be a little mixed. All German advice is more or less mixed. However, I think that that sentence is mostly in the dative case, with a little genitive and accusative sifted in, here and there, for luck; so I reckon it means that you must keep some metals *about* you."

"Yes, that must be it. It stands to reason that it is. They are in the nature of lightning-rods, you know. Put on your fireman's helmet, Mortimer; that is mostly metal."

I got it and put it on,—a very heavy and clumsy and uncomfortable thing on a hot night in a close room. Even my night-dress seemed to be more clothing than I strictly needed.

"Mortimer, I think your middle ought to be protected. Won't you buckle on your militia sabre, please?"

I complied.

"Now, Mortimer, you ought to have some way to protect your feet. Do please put on your spurs."

I did it,—in silence,—and kept my temper as well as I could.

"Mortimer, it says, 'Das Gewitter läuten ist sehr gefährlich, weil die Glocke selbst, sowie der durch das Läuten veranlasste Luftzug und die Höhe des Thurmes den Blitz anziehen könnten.' Mortimer, does that mean that it is dangerous not to ring the church bells during a thunderstorm?"

"Yes, it seems to mean that,—if that is the past participle of the nominative case singular, and I reckon it is. Yes, I think it means that on acount of the height of the church tower and the absence of *Luftzug* it would be very dangerous (sehr gefährlich) not to ring the bells in time of a storm; and moreover, don't you see, the very wording—"

"Never mind that, Mortimer; don't waste the precious time to talk. Get the large dinner-bell; it is right there in the hall. Quick, Mortimer dear; we are almost safe. Oh, dear, I do believe we are going to be saved, at last!"

Our little summer establishment stands on top of a high range of hills, overlooking a valley. Several farm-houses are in our neighborhood,—the nearest some three or four hundred yards away.

When I, mounted on the chair, had been clanging that dreadful bell a matter of seven or eight minutes, our shutters were suddenly torn open from without, and a brilliant bull's-eye lantern was thrust in at the window, followed by a hoarse inquiry:—

"What in the nation is the matter here?"

The window was full of men's heads, and the heads were full of eyes that stared wildly at my night-dress and my war-like accoutrements.

I dropped the bell, skipped down from the chair in confusion, and said,—

"There is nothing the matter, friends,—only a little discomfort on account of the thunderstorm. I was trying to keep off the lightning."

"Thunderstorm? Lightning? Why, Mr. McWilliams, have you lost your mind? It is a beautiful starlight night; there has been no storm."

I looked out, and I was so astonished I could hardly speak for a while. Then I said,—

"I do not understand this. We distinctly saw the glow of the flashes through the curtains and shutters, and heard the thunder."

One after another of those people lay down on the ground to laugh,—and two of them died. One of the survivors remarked,—

"Pity you didn't think to open your blinds and look over to the top of the high hill yonder. What you heard was cannon; what you saw was the flash. You see, the telegraph brought some news, just at midnight: Garfield's nominated, —and that's what's the matter!"

Yes, Mr. Twain, as I was saying in the beginning (said Mr. McWilliams), the rules for preserving people against lightning are so excellent and so innumerable that the most incomprehensible thing in the world to me is how anybody ever manages to get struck.

So saying, he gathered up his satchel and his umbrella, and departed; for the train had reached his town.

JOURNALISM IN TENNESSEE

By Mark Twain

The editor of the Memphis *Avalanche* swoops thus mildly down upon a correspondent who posted him as a Radical:— "While he was writing the first word, the middle, dotting his i's, crossing his t's, and punching his period, he knew he was concocting a sentence that was saturated with infamy and reeking with falsehood."—*Exchange*.

I was told by the physician that a Southern climate would improve my health, and so I went down to Tennessee, and got a berth on the *Morning Glory and Johnson County War-Whoop* as associate editor. When I went on duty I found the chief editor sitting tilted back in a three-legged chair with his feet on a pine table. There was another pine table in the room and another afflicted chair, and both were half buried under newspapers and scraps and sheets of manuscript. There was a wooden box of sand, sprinkled with cigar stubs and "old soldiers," and a stove with a door hanging by its upper hinge. The chief editor had a long-tailed black cloth frock coat on, and white linen pants. His boots were small and neatly blacked. He wore a ruffled shirt, a large seal ring, a standing collar of obsolete pattern, and a checkered neckerchief with the ends hanging down. Date of costume about 1848. He was smoking a cigar, and trying to think of a word, and in pawing his hair he had rumpled his locks a good deal. He was scowling fearfully, and I judged that he was concocting a particularly knotty editorial. He told me to take the exchanges and skim through them and write up the "Spirit of the Tennessee Press," condensing into the article all of their contents that seemed of interest.

I wrote as follows:—

"SPIRIT OF THE TENNESSEE PRESS.

"The editors of the *Semi-Weekly Earthquake* evidently labor under a misapprehension with regard to the Bally-hack railroad. It is not the object of the company to leave Buzzardville off to one side. On the contrary, they consider it one of the most important points along the line, and consequently can have no desire to slight it. The gentlemen of the *Earthquake* will, of course, take pleasure in making the correction.

"John W. Blossom, Esq., the able editor of the Higgins-ville *Thunderbolt and Battle Cry of Freedom*, arrived in the city yesterday. He is stopping at the Van Buren House.

"We observe that our contemporary of the Mud Springs *Morning Howl* has fallen into the error of supposing that the election of Van Werter is not an established fact, but he will have discovered his mistake before this reminder reaches him, no doubt. He was doubtless misled by incomplete election returns.

"It is pleasant to note that the city of Blathersville is endeavoring to contract with some New York gentlemen to pave its well-nigh impassable streets with the Nicholson pavement. The *Daily Hurrah* urges the measure with ability, and seems confident of ultimate success."

I passed my manuscript over to the chief editor for acceptance, alteration, or destruction. He glanced at it and his face clouded. He ran his eye down the pages, and his countenance grew portentous. It was easy to see that something was wrong. Presently he sprang up and said—

"Thunder and lightning! Do you suppose I am going to speak of those cattle that way? Do you suppose my subscribers are going to stand such gruel as that? Give me the pen!"

I never saw a pen scrape and scratch its way so viciously, or plough through another man's verbs and adjectives so relentlessly. While he was in the midst of his work, somebody shot at him through the open window, and marred the symmetry of my ear.

"Ah," said he, "that is that scoundrel Smith, of the *Moral Volcano*—he was due yesterday." And he snatched a navy revolver from his belt and fired. Smith dropped, shot in the thigh. The shot spoiled Smith's aim, who was just taking a second chance, and he crippled a stranger. It was me. Merely a finger shot off.

Then the chief editor went on with his erasures and interlineations. Just as he finished them a hand-grenade came down the stove pipe, and the explosion shivered the stove into a thousand fragments. However, it did no further damage, except that a vagrant piece knocked a couple of my teeth out.

"That stove is utterly ruined," said the chief editor.

I said I believed it was.

"Well, no matter—don't want it this kind of weather. I know the man that did it. I'll get him. Now, *here* is the way this stuff ought to be written."

I took the manuscript. It was scarred with erasures and interlineations till its mother wouldn't have known it if it had had one. It now read as follows:—

"SPIRIT OF THE TENNESSEE PRESS.

"The inveterate liars of the *Semi-Weekly Earthquake* are evidently endeavoring to palm off upon a noble and chivalrous people another of their vile and brutal falsehoods with regard to that most glorious conception of the nineteenth century, the Ballyhack railroad. The idea that Buzzardville was to be left off at one side originated in their own fulsome brains—or rather in the settlings which *they* regard as brains. They had better swallow this lie if they want to save their abandoned reptile carcasses the cowhiding they so richly deserve.

"That ass, Blossom, of the Higginsville *Thunderbolt and Battle Cry of Freedom,* is down here again sponging at the Van Buren.

"We observe that the besotted blackguard of the Mud Spring *Morning Howl* is giving out, with its usual propensity for lying, that Van Werter is not elected. The heaven-born mission of journalism is to disseminate truth; to eradicate error; to educate, refine and elevate the tone of public morals and manners, and make all men more gentle, more virtuous, more charitable, and in all ways better, and holier, and happier; and yet this black-hearted scoundrel degrades his great office persistently to the dissemination of falsehood, calumny, vituperation, and vulgarity.

"Blathersville wants a Nicholson pavement—it wants a jail and poorhouse more. The idea of a pavement in a one horse town composed of two gin mills, a blacksmith's shop, and that mustard-plaster of a newspaper, the *Daily Hurrah!* The crawling insect, Buckner, who edits the *Hurrah*, is braying about this business with his customary imbecility, and imagining that he is talking sense."

"Now *that* is the way to write—peppery and to the point. Mush-and-milk journalism gives me the fantods."

About this time a brick came through the window with a

splintering crash, and gave me a considerable of a jolt in the back. I moved out of range—I began to feel in the way.

The chief said, "That was the Colonel, likely. I've been expecting him for two days. He will be up, now, right away."

He was correct. The Colonel appeared in the door a moment afterward with a dragoon revolver in his hand.

He said, "Sir, have I the honor of addressing the poltroon who edits this mangy sheet?"

"You have. Be seated, sir. Be careful of the chair, one of its legs is gone. I believe I have the honor of addressing the putrid liar, Col. Blatherskite Tecumseh?"

"Right, sir. I have a little account to settle with you. If you are at leisure we will begin."

"I have an article on the 'Encouraging Progress of Moral and Intellectual Development in America' to finish, but there is no hurry. Begin."

Both pistols rang out their fierce clamor at the same instant. The chief lost a lock of his hair, and the Colonel's bullet ended its career in the fleshy part of my thigh. The Colonel's left shoulder was clipped a little. They fired again. Both missed their men this time, but I got my share, a shot in the arm. At the third fire both gentlemen were wounded slightly, and I had a knuckle chipped. I then said, I believed I would go out and take a walk, as this was a private matter, and I had a delicacy about participating in it further. But both gentlemen begged me to keep my seat, and assured me that I was not in the way.

They then talked about the elections and the crops while they reloaded, and I fell to tying up my wounds. But presently they opened fire again with animation, and every shot took effect—but it is proper to remark that five out of the six fell to my share. The sixth one mortally wounded the

Colonel, who remarked, with fine humor, that he would have to say good morning now, as he had business up town. He then inquired the way to the undertaker's and left.

The chief turned to me and said, "I am expecting company to dinner, and shall have to get ready. It will be a favor to me if you will read proof and attend to the customers."

I winced a little at the idea of attending to the customers, but I was too bewildered by the fusilade that was still ringing in my ears to think of anything to say.

He continued, "Jones will be here at 3—cowhide him. Gillespie will call earlier, perhaps—throw him out of the window. Ferguson will be along about 4—kill him. That is all for today, I believe. If you have any odd time, you may write a blistering article on the police—give the Chief Inspector rats. The cowhides are under the table; weapons in the drawer—ammunition there in the corner—lint and bandages up there in the pigeon-holes. In case of accident, go to Lancet, the surgeon, down-stairs. He advertises—we take it out in trade."

He was gone. I shuddered. At the end of the next three hours I had been through perils so awful that all peace of mind and all cheerfulness were gone from me. Gillespie had called and thrown *me* out of the window. Jones arrived promptly, and when I got ready to do the cowhiding he took the job off my hands. In an encounter with a stranger, not in the bill of fare, I had lost my scalp. Another stranger, by the name of Thompson, left me a mere wreck and ruin of chaotic rags. And at last, at bay in the corner, and beset by an infuriated mob of editors, blacklegs, politicians, and desperadoes, who raved and swore and flourished their weapons about my head till the air shimmered with glancing flashes of steel, I was in the act of resigning my berth on the paper when the chief arrived, and with him a rabble of charmed and enthusiastic friends. Then ensued a scene of riot and carnage such as no human pen, or steel one either, could describe. People were shot, probed, dismembered, blown up, thrown out of the window. There was a brief tornado of murky blasphemy, with a confused and frantic war-dance glimmering through it, and then all was over. In five minutes there was silence, and the gory chief and I sat alone and surveyed the sanguinary ruin that strewed the floor around us.

He said, "You'll like this place when you get used to it."

I said, "I'll have to get you to excuse me; I think maybe I might write to suit you after a while; as soon as I had had some practice and learned the language I am confident I could. But, to speak the plain truth, that sort of energy of expression has its inconveniences, and a man is liable to interruptions. You see that yourself. Vigorous writing is calculated to elevate the public, no doubt, but, then I do not like to attract so much attention as it calls forth. I can't write with comfort when I am interrupted so much as I have been today. I like this berth well enough, but I don't like to be left here to wait on the customers. The experiences are novel, I grant you, and entertaining too, after a fashion, but they are not judiciously distributed. A gentleman shoots at you through the window and cripples *me;* a bomb-shell comes down the stove-pipe for your gratification and sends the stove-door down *my* throat; a friend drops in to swap compliments with you, and freckles *me* with bullet-holes till my skin won't hold my principles; you go to dinner, and Jones comes with his cowhide, Gillespie throws me out of the window, Thompson tears all my clothes off, and an entire stranger takes my scalp with the easy freedom of an old acquaintance; and in less than five minutes all the blackguards in the country arrive in their war-paint, and proceed to scare the rest of me to death with their toma-hawks. Take it altogether, I never had such a spirited time in all my life as I have had today. No; I like you, and I like your calm unruffled way of explaining things to the cus-tomers, but you see I am not used to it. The Southern heart is too impulsive; Southern hospitality is too lavish with the stranger. The paragraphs which I have written today, and into whose cold sentences your masterly hand has infused the fervent spirit of Tennessean journalism, will wake up another nest of hornets. All that mob of editors will come—and they will come hungry, too, and want somebody for breakfast. I shall have to bid you adieu. I decline to be present at these festivities. I came South for my health, I will go back on the same errand, and suddenly. Tennessean journalism is too stirring for me."

After which we parted with mutual regret, and I took apartments at the hospital.

BROTHER RABBIT TAKES SOME EXERCISE

By Joel Chandler Harris

ONE night while the little boy was sitting in Uncle Remus's cabin, waiting for the old man to finish his hoe-cake, and refresh his memory as to the further adventures of Brother Rabbit, his friends and his enemies, something dropped upon the top of the house with a noise like the crack of a pistol. The little boy jumped, but Uncle Remus looked up and exclaimed, "Ah-yi!" in a tone of triumph.

"What was that, Uncle Remus?" the child asked, after waiting a moment to see what else would happen.

"News fum Jack Fros', honey. W'en dat hick'y-nut tree out dar year 'im comin' she 'gins ter drap w'at she got. I mighty glad," he continued, scraping the burnt crust from his hoe-cake with an old case-knife, "I mighty glad hick'y-nuts aint big en heavy ez grinestones."

He waited a moment to see what effect this queer statement would have on the child.

"Yasser, I mighty glad—dat I is. 'Kaze ef hick'y-nuts 'uz big ez grinestones dish yer ole callyboose 'ud be a-leakin' long 'fo' Chris'mus."

Just then another hickory-nut dropped upon the roof, and the little boy jumped again. This seemed to amuse Uncle Remus, and he laughed until he was near to choking himself with his smoking hoe-cake.

39

"You does des 'zackly lak ole Brer Rabbit done, I 'clar' to gracious ef you don't!" the old man cried, as soon as he could get his breath; "dez zackly fer de worl'."

The child was immensely flattered, and at once he wanted to know how Brother Rabbit did. Uncle Remus was in such good humor that he needed no coaxing. He pushed his spectacles back on his forehead, wiped his mouth on his sleeve, and began:

"Hit come 'bout dat soon one mawnin' todes de fall er de year, Brer Rabbit wuz stirrin' 'roun' in de woods atter some bergamot fer ter make 'im some h'ar-grease. De win' blow so col' dat it make 'im feel right frisky, en eve'y time he year de bushes rattle he make lak he skeerd. He 'uz gwine on dis a-way, hoppity-skippity, w'en bimeby he year Mr. Man cuttin' on a tree way off in de woods. He fotch up, Brer Rabbit did, en lissen fus' wid one year en den wid de yuther.

"Man, he cut en cut, en Brer Rabbit, he lissen en lissen. Bimeby, w'iles all dis was gwine on, down come de tree —*kubber-lang-bang-blam!* Brer Rabbit, he tuck'n jump des lak you jump, en let 'lone dat, he make a break, he did, en he lipt out fum dar lak de dogs wuz atter 'im."

"Was he scared, Uncle Remus?" asked the little boy.

"Skeerd! Who? *Him?* Shoo! don't you fret yo'se'f 'bout Brer Rabbit, honey. In dem days dey wa'n't nothin' gwine dat kin skeer Brer Rabbit. Tooby sho', he tuck keer hisse'f, en ef you know de man w'at 'fuse ter take keer hisse'f, I lak mighty well ef you p'int 'im out. Deed'n dat I would!"

Uncle Remus seemed to boil over with argumentative indignation.

"Well, den," he continued, "Brer Rabbit run twel he git sorter het up like, en des 'bout de time he makin' ready fer ter squot en ketch he win', who should he meet but

Brer Coon gwine home atter settin' up wid ole Brer Bull-Frog. Brer Coon see 'im runnin', en he hail 'im.

"'W'at yo' hurry, Brer Rabbit?'

"'Aint got time ter tarry.'

"'Folks sick?'

"'No, my Lord! Aint got time ter tarry!'

"'Tryin' yo' soopleness?'

"'No, my Lord! Aint got time ter tarry!'

"'Do pray, Brer Rabbit, tell me de news!'

"'Mighty big fuss back dar in de woods. Aint got time ter tarry!'

"Dis make Brer Coon feel mighty skittish, 'kaze he fur ways fum home, en he des lipt out, he did, en went a-b'ilin' thoo de woods. Brer Coon aint gone fur twel he meet Brer Fox.

"'Hey, Brer Coon, whar you gwine?'

"'Aint got time ter tarry!'

"'Gwine at' de doctor?'

"'No, my Lord! Aint got time ter tarry.'

"'Do pray, Brer Coon, tell me de news.'

"'Mighty quare racket back dar in de woods! Aint got time ter tarry!'

"Wid dat, Brer Fox lipt out, he did, en fa'rly split de win'. He aint gone fur twel he meet Brer Wolf.

"'Hey, Brer Fox! Stop en res' yo'se'f!'

"'Aint got time ter tarry!'

"'Who bin want de doctor?'

"'No'ne, my Lord! Aint got time ter tarry!'

"'Do pray, Brer Fox, good er bad, tell me de news.'

"'Mighty kuse fuss back dar in de woods! Aint got time ter tarry!'

"Wid dat, Brer Wolf shuck hisse'f loose fum de face er de yeth, en he aint git fur twel he meet Brer B'ar. Brer B'ar he

ax, en Brer Wolf make ans'er, en bimeby Brer B'ar he
fotch a snort en run'd off; en, bless gracious! 'twa'n't long
'fo' de las' one er de creeturs wuz a-skaddlin' thoo de woods
lak de Ole Boy was atter um—en all 'kaze Brer Rabbit year
Mr. Man cut tree down.

"Dey run'd en dey run'd," Uncle Remus went on, "twel
dey come ter Brer Tarrypin house, en dey sorter slack
up 'kaze dey done mighty nigh los' der win'. Brer Tarrypin, he up'n ax um wharbouts dey gwine, en dey 'low dey
wuz a monst'us tarryfyin' racket back dar in de woods.
Brer Tarrypin, he ax w'at she soun' lak. One say he dunno,
n'er say he dunno, den dey all say dey dunno. Den Brer
Tarrypin, he up'n ax who year dis monst'us racket. One
say he dunno, n'er say he dunno, den dey all say dey dunno.
Dis make ole Brer Tarrypin laff 'way down in he insides,
en he up'n say, sezee:

"'You all kin run 'long ef you feel skittish,' sezee. 'Atter I cook my brekkus en wash up de dishes, ef I gits win'
er any 'spicious racket maybe I mought take down my
pairsol en foller long atter you,' sezee.

"W'en de creeturs come ter make inquirements 'mungs
one er n'er 'bout who start de news, hit went right spang
back ter Brer Rabbit, but, lo en beholes! Brer Rabbit aint
dar, en it tu'n out dat Brer Coon is de man w'at seed 'im
las'. Den dey got ter layin' de blame un it on one er n'er, en
little mo' en dey'd er fit dar scan'lous, but ole Brer Tarrypin, he up'n 'low dat ef dey want ter git de straight un it,
dey better go see Brer Rabbit.

"All de creeturs wuz 'gree'ble, en dey put out ter Brer
Rabbit house. W'en dey git dar, Brer Rabbit wuz a-settin'
cross-legged in de front po'ch winkin' he eye at de sun.
Brer B'ar, he speak up:

"'W'at make you fool me, Brer Rabbit?'

" 'Fool who, Brer B'ar?'

" 'Me, Brer Rabbit, dat's who."

" 'Dish yer de fus' time I seed you dis day, Brer B'ar, en you er mo' dan welcome ter dat.'

"Dey all ax 'im en git de same ans'er, en Brer Coon put in:

" 'W'at make you fool me, Brer Rabbit?'

" 'How I fool you, Brer Coon?'

" 'You make lak dey wuz a big racket, Brer Rabbit.'

" 'Dey sholy wuz a big racket, Brer Coon.'

" 'W'at kinder racket, Brer Rabbit?'

" '*Ah-yi!* You oughter ax me dat fus', Brer Coon.'

" 'I axes you now, Brer Rabbit.'

" 'Mr. Man cut tree down, Brer Coon.'

"Co'se dis make Brer Coon feel like a nat'al-born Slink, en 't wa'n't long 'fo' all de creeturs make der bow ter Brer Rabbit en mosey off home."

"Brother Rabbit had the best of it all along," said the little boy, after waiting to see whether there was a sequel to the story.

"Oh, he did dat a-way!" exclaimed Uncle Remus. "Brer Rabbit was a mighty man in dem days."

HOW BROTHER RABBIT FRIGHTENED
HIS NEIGHBORS

By Joel Chandler Harris

"In dem days, de creeturs wuz same lak folks. Dey had der ups en dey had der downs; dey had der hard times, and dey had der saf' times. Some seasons der craps 'ud be good, en some seasons dey'd be bad. Brer Rabbit, he far'd lak de res' un um. W'at he'd make, dat he'd spen'. One season he tuck'n made a fine chance er goobers, en he 'low, he did, dat ef dey fetch 'im anywhars nigh de money w'at he 'speck dey would, he go ter town en buy de truck w'at needcesity call fer.

"He aint no sooner say dat dan ole Miss Rabbit, she vow, she did, dat it be a scannul en a shame ef he don't whirl in en git sevin tin cups fer de chilluns fer ter drink out'n, en sevin tin plates fer'm fer ter sop out'n, en a coffee- pot fer de fambly. Brer Rabbit say dat des zackly w'at he gwine do, en he 'low, he did, dat he gwine ter town de comin' We'n'sday."

"Brer Rabbit wa'n't mo'n out'n de gate 'fo' Miss Rabbit, she slap on 'er bonnet, she did, en rush 'cross ter Miss Mink house, en she aint bin dar a minnit 'fo' she up'n tell Miss Mink dat Brer Rabbit done promise ter go ter town We'n'sday comin' en git de chilluns sump'n'. Co'se, w'en Mr. Mink come home, Miss Mink she up'n 'low she want ter know w'at de reason he can't buy sump'n' fer his chilluns same ez Brer Rabbit do fer his'n, en dey quo'll en quo'll des lak folks. Atter dat Miss Mink she kyar de news ter Miss Fox, en den Brer Fox he tuck'n got a rakin' over de coals. Miss Fox she tell Miss Wolf, en Miss Wolf she tell Miss B'ar, en 't wa'n't long 'fo' ev'ybody in dem diggin's know dat Brer Rabbit gwine ter town de comin' We'n'sday fer ter git his chilluns sump'n'; en all de yuther creeturs' chilluns ax der ma w'at de reason der pa can't git *dem* sump'n'. So dar it went.

"Brer Fox, en Brer Wolf, en Brer B'ar, dey make up der mines, dey did, dat ef dey gwine ter ketch up wid Brer Rabbit, dat wuz de time, en dey fix up a plan dat dey'd lay fer Brer Rabbit en nab 'im w'en he come back fum town. Dey tuck'n make all der 'rangerments, en wait fer de day.

"Sho' nuff, w'en We'n'sday come, Brer Rabbit e't he brekkus 'fo' sun-up, en put out fer town. He tuck'n got hisse'f a dram, en a plug er terbarker, en a pocket-hank-cher, en he got de ole 'oman a coffee-pot, en he got de chil-lun sevin tin cups en sevin tin plates, en den todes sundown he start back home. He walk 'long, he did, feelin' mighty biggity: but bimeby w'en he git sorter tired, he sot down und' a black-jack tree, en 'gun to fan hisse'f wid one er der platters.

"W'iles he doin' dis a little bit er teenchy sap-sucker run up'n down de tree en keep on makin' mighty quare fuss. Atter w'ile Brer Rabbit tuck'n shoo at 'im wid de platter. Seem lak dis make de teenchy little sap-sucker mighty mad, en he rush out on a lim' right over Brer Rab-bit, en he sing out:

"'Pilly-pee, pilly-wee!
I see w'at he no see!
I see, pilly-pee,
I see w'at he no see!'

"He keep on singin' dis, he did, twel Brer Rabbit 'gun ter look 'roun', en he aint no sooner do dis dan he see marks in de san' whar sum un done bin dar 'fo' 'im, en he look little closer en den he see w'at de sap-sucker drivin' at. He scratch his head, Brer Rabbit did, en he 'low ter hisse'f:

"'Ah-yi! Yer whar Brer Fox bin settin', en dar de print er he nice bushy tail. Yer whar Brer Wolf bin settin', en dar de print er he fine long tail. Yer whar Brer B'ar bin squattin' on he hunkers, en dar de print w'ich he aint got no tail. Dey er all bin yer, en I lay dey er hidin' out in de big gully down dar in de holler.'

"Wid dat, ole man Rab tuck'n put he truck in de bushes, en den he run 'way 'roun' fer ter see w'at he kin see. Sho' nuff," continued Uncle Remus, with a curious air of ela- tion,—"sho' nuff, w'en Brer Rabbit git over agin de big gully down in de holler, dar dey wuz. Brer Fox, he 'uz on one side er de road, en Brer Wolf 'uz on de t'er side; en ole Brer B'ar he 'uz quiled up in de gully takin' a nap.

"Brer Rabbit, he tuck'n peep at um, he did, en he lick he foot en roach back he h'ar, en den hol' his han's 'cross he mouf en laff lak some chilluns does w'en dey t'ink dey er foolin' der ma."

"Not me, Uncle Remus—not me!" exclaimed the little boy promptly.

"Heyo dar! don't kick 'fo' you er spurred, honey! Brer Rabbit, he seed um all dar, en he tuck'n grin, he did, en den he lit out ter whar he done lef' he truck, en w'en he git dar he dance 'roun' en slap hisse'f on de leg, en make all sorts er kuse motions. Den he go ter wuk en tu'n de coffee- pot upside down en stick it on he head: den he run he galus thoo de han'les er de cups, en sling um crosst he shoulder; den he 'vide de platters, some in one han' en some in de yuther. Atter he git good en ready, he crope ter de top er de hill, he did, en tuck a runnin' start, en flew down like a harrycane—*rickety, rackety, slambang!*"

The little boy clapped his hands enthusiastically.

"Bless yo' soul, dem creeturs aint year no fuss lak dat, en dey aint seed no man w'at look lak Brer Rabbit do, wid de coffee-pot on he head, en de cups a-rattlin' on he gallus, en de platters a-wavin' a-shinin' in de a'r.

"Now, mine you, ole Brer B'ar wuz layin' off up de gully takin' a nap, en de fuss skeer 'im so bad dat he make a break en run over Brer Fox. He rush out in de road, he did, en w'en he see de sight, he whirl 'roun' en run over Brer Wolf. Wid der scramblin' en der scufflin', Brer Rabbit got right on um 'fo' dey kin git away. He holler out, he did:

"'Gimme room! Tu'n me loose! I'm ole man Spewter-Splutter wid long claws, en scales on my back! I'm snaggle-toofed en double-j'inted! Gimme room!'

"Eve'y time he'd fetch a whoop, he'd rattle de cups en slap de platters tergedder—*ricktey, rackety, slambang!* En I let you know w'en dem creeturs got dey lim's ter-gedder dey split de win', dey did dat. Ole Brer B'ar, he struck a stump w'at stan' in de way, en I aint gwine tell you how he to' it up 'kaze you won't b'leeve me, but de nex' mawnin' Brer Rabbit en his chilluns went back dar, dey did, en dey got nuff splinters fer ter make um kin'lin' wood all de winter. Yasser! Des ez sho' ez I'm a-settin' by dish yer h'ath."

HOW MR. ROOSTER LOST HIS DINNER

By Joel Chandler Harris

"One time, 'way back yander," said Uncle Remus, "dey wuz two plan'ations right 'longside one er 'ne'r, en on bofe er deze plan'ations wuz a whole passel of fowls. Dey wuz mighty sociable in dem days, en it tu'n out dat de fowls on one plan'ation gun a party, w'ich dey sont out der invites ter de fowls on Je 't'er plan'ation.

"W'en de day come, Mr. Rooster, he blow his hawn, he did, en 'semble um all tergedder, en atter dey 'semble dey got in line. Mr. Rooster, he tuck de head, en atter 'im come ole lady Hen en Miss Pullet, en den dar wuz Mr. Peafowl, en Mr. Tukkey Gobbler, en Miss Guinny Hen, en Miss Puddle Duck, en all de balance un um. Dey start off sorter raggedy, but 't wa'n't long 'fo' dey all kotch de step, en den dey march down by de spring, up thoo de hoss-lot en 'cross by de gin-house, en 't wa'n't long 'fo' dey git ter whar de frolic wuz.

"Dey dance, en dey play, en dey sing. Mo' 'speshually did dey play en sing dat ar song w'ich run on lak dis:

> "'Come under, come under,
>   My honey, my love, my own true love;
>   My heart bin a-weepin'
>   Way down in Galilee.'

"Dey wuz gwine on dis a-way, havin' de 'musements, w'en, bimeby, ole Mr. Peafowl, he got on de comb er de barn en blow de dinner-hawn. Dey all wash der face en han's in de back po'ch, en den dey went in ter dinner. W'en dey git in dar, dey don't see nothin' on de table but a great big pile er co'n-bread. De pones was pile up on pones, en on de top wuz a great big ash-cake. Mr. Rooster, he look at dis en he tu'n up he nose, en bimeby, atter aw'ile, out he strut. Ole Miss Guinny Hen, she watchin' Mr. Rooster motions, en w'en she see dis, she take'n squall out, she did:

"'*Pot-rack! Pot-rack!* Mr. Rooster gone back! *Pot-rack! Pot-rack!* Mr. Rooster gone back!'

"Wid dat dey all make a great ter-do. Miss Hen en Miss Pullet, dey cackle en squall, Mr. Gobbler, he gobble, en Miss Puddle Duck, she shake 'er tail en say *quickity-quack-quack*. But Mr. Rooster, he ruffle up he cape, en march on out.

"Dis sorter put a damper on de yuthers, but 'fo' Mr. Rooster git outer sight en year'n dey went ter wuk on de pile w'at wuz 'pariently co'n-bread, en, lo en beholes un'need dem pone er bread wuz a whole passel er meat en greens, en bake' taters, en bile' turnips. Mr. Rooster, he year de ladies makin' great 'miration, en he stop en look thoo de crack, en dar he see all de doin's en fixin's. He feel mighty bad, Mr. Rooster did, w'en he see all dis, en de yuther fowls dey holler en ax 'im fer ter come back, en he craw, w'ich it mighty empty, likewise, it up'n ax 'im, but he mighty biggity en stuck up, en he strut off, crowin' ez he go; but he 'speunce er dat time done las' him en all er his fambly down ter dis day. En you neenter take my wud fer't, ne'r, kaze ef you'll des keep yo' eye open en watch, you'll ketch a glimse er ole Mr. Rooster folks scratchin' whar dey 'specks ter fine der rations, en mo' dan dat, dey'll scratch wid der

rations in plain sight. Since dat time, dey aint none er de
Mr. Roosters bin fool' by dat w'at dey see on top. Dey aint
des' twel dey see w'at und' dar. Dey'll scratch spite er all
creation."

COLONEL STARBOTTLE FOR THE PLAINTIFF

By Bret Harte

It HAD been a day of triumph for Colonel Starbottle. First, for his personality, as it would have been difficult to separate the Colonel's achievements from his individuality; second, for his oratorical abilities as a sympathetic pleader; and third, for his functions as the leading counsel for the Eureka Ditch Company *versus* the State of California. On his strictly legal performances in this issue I prefer not to speak; there were those who denied them, although the jury had accepted them in the face of the ruling of the half-amused, half-cynical Judge himself. For an hour they had laughed with the Colonel, wept with him, been stirred to personal indignation or patriotic exaltation by his passionate and lofty periods —what else could they do than give him their verdict? If it was alleged by some that the American eagle, Thomas Jefferson, and the Resolutions of '98 had nothing whatever to do with the contest of a ditch company over a doubtfully worded legislative document; that wholesale abuse of the State Attorney and his political motives had not the slightest connection with the legal question raised—it was, nevertheless, generally accepted that the losing party would have been only too glad to have the Colonel on their side. And Colonel Starbottle knew this, as, perspiring, florid, and panting, he rebuttoned the lower buttons of his blue frock-coat, which had become loosed in an oratorical spasm, and readjusted his old-fashioned, spotless shirt frill above it as he strutted from the court-room amidst the hand-shakings and acclamations of his friends.

And here an unprecedented thing occurred. The Colonel absolutely declined spirituous refreshment at the neighboring Palmetto Saloon, and declared his intention of proceeding directly to his office in the adjoining square. Nevertheless the Colonel quitted the building alone, and apparently unarmed except for his faithful gold-headed stick, which hung as usual from his forearm. The crowd gazed after him with undisguised admiration of this new evidence of his pluck. It was remembered also that a mysterious note had been handed to him at the conclusion of his speech—evidently a challenge from the State Attorney. It was quite plain that the Colonel—a practised duellist—was hastening home to answer it.

But herein they were wrong. The note was in a female hand, and simply requested the Colonel to accord an interview with the writer at the Colonel's office as soon as he left the court. But it was an engagement that the Colonel—as devoted to the fair sex as he was to the "code"—was no less prompt in accepting. He flicked away the dust from his spotless white trousers and varnished boots with his handkerchief, and settled his black cravat under his Byron collar as he neared his office. He was surprised, however, on opening the door of his private office to find his visitor already there; he was still more startled to find her somewhat past middle age and plainly attired. But the Colonel was brought up in a school of Southern politeness, already antique in the republic, and his bow of courtesy belonged to the epoch of his shirt frill and strapped trousers. No one could have detected his disappointment in his manner, albeit his sentences were short and incomplete. But the Colonel's colloquial speech was apt to be fragmentary incoherencies of his larger oratorical utterances.

"A thousand pardons—for—er—having kept a lady waiting—er! But—er—congratulations of friends—and—er—courtesy due to them—er—interfered with—though perhaps only heightened—by procrastination—pleasure of—ha!" And the Colonel completed his sentence with a gallant wave of his fat but white and well-kept hand.

"Yes! I came to see you along o' that speech of yours. I was in court. When I heard you gettin' it off on that jury, I says so myself that's the kind o' lawyer *I* want. A man that's flowery and convincin'! Just the man to take up our case."

"Ah! It's a matter of business, I see," said the Colonel, inwardly relieved, but externally careless. "And—er—may I ask the nature of case?"

"Well! it's a breach-o'-promise suit," said the visitor, calmly.

If the Colonel had been surprised before, he was now really startled, and with an added horror that required all his politeness to conceal. Breach-of-promise cases were his peculiar aversion. He had always held them to be a kind of litigation which could have been obviated by the prompt killing of the masculine offender—in which case he would have gladly defended the killer. But a suit for damages!—*damages!*— with the reading of love-letters before a hilarious jury and court, was against all his instincts. His chivalry was outraged; his sense of humor was small—and in the course of his career he had lost one or two important cases through an unexpected development of this quality in a jury.

The woman had evidently noticed his hesitation, but mistook its cause. "It ain't me—but my darter."

The Colonel recovered his politeness. "Ah! I am relieved, my dear madam! I could hardly conceive a man ignorant enough to—er—er—throw away such evident good fortune—or base enough to deceive the trustfulness of womanhood—matured and experienced only in the chivalry of our sex, ha!"

The woman smiled grimly. "Yes!—it's my darter, Zaidee Hooker—so ye might spare some of them pretty speeches for *her*—before the jury."

The Colonel winced slightly before this doubtful prospect, but smiled. "Ha! Yes!—certainly—the jury. But—er—my dear lady, need we go as far as that? Cannot this affair be settled—er—out of court? Could not this—er—individual —be admonished—told that he must give satisfaction—personal satisfaction—for his dastardly conduct—to—er—near relative—or even valued personal friend? The—er—arrangements necessary for that purpose I myself would undertake."

He was quite sincere; indeed, his small black eyes shone with that fire which a pretty woman or an "affair of honor" could alone kindle. The visitor stared vacantly at him, and said, slowly:

"And what good is that goin' to do *us?*"

"Compel him to—er—perform his promise," said the Colonel, leaning back in his chair.

"Ketch him doin' it!" said the woman, scornfully. "No —that ain't wot we're after. We must make him *pay!* Damages—and nothin' short o' *that.*"

The Colonel bit his lip. "I suppose," he said, gloomily, "you have documentary evidence—written promises and protestations—er—er—love-letters, in fact?"

"No—nary a letter! Ye see, that's jest it—and that's

where *you* come in. You've got to convince that jury yourself. You've got to show what it is—tell the whole story
your own way. Lord! to a man like you that's nothin'."

Startling as this admission might have been to any other
lawyer, Starbottle was absolutely relieved by it, The absence of any mirth-provoking correspondence, and the appeal solely to his own powers of persuasion, actually struck
his fancy. He lightly put aside the compliment with a wave
of his white hand.

"Of course," said the Colonel, confidently, "there is
strongly presumptive and corroborative evidence? Perhaps
you can give me—er—a brief outline of the affair?"

"Zaidee kin do that straight enough, I reckon," said the
woman; "what I want to know first is, kin you take the
case?"

The Colonel did not hesitate; his curiosity was piqued.
"I certainly can. I have no doubt your daughter will put
me in possession of sufficient facts and details—to constitute
what we call—er—a brief."

"She kin be brief enough—or long enough—for the matter of that," said the woman, rising. The Colonel accepted
this implied witticism with a smile.

"And when may I have the pleasure of seeing her?" he
asked, politely.

"Well, I reckon as soon as I can trot out and call her.
She's just outside, meanderin' in the road—kinder shy, ye
know, at first."

She walked to the door. The astounded Colonel nevertheless gallantly accompanied her as she stepped out into
the street and called, shrilly, "You Zaidee!"

A young girl here apparently detached herself from a tree
and the ostentatious perusal of an old election poster, and
sauntered down towards the office door. Like her mother,

she was plainly dressed; unlike her, she had a pale, rather refined face, with a demure mouth and downcast eyes. This was all the Colonel saw as he bowed profoundly and led the way into his office, for she accepted his salutations without lifting her head. He helped her gallantly to a chair, on which she seated herself sideways, somewhat ceremoniously, with her eyes following the point of her parasol as she traced a pattern on the carpet. A second chair offered to the mother that lady, however, declined. "I reckon to leave you and Zaidee together to talk it out," she said; turning to her daughter, she added, "Jest you tell him all, Zaidee," and before the Colonel could rise again, disappeared from the room. In spite of his professional experience, Starbottle was for a moment embarrassed. The young girl, however, broke the silence without looking up.

"Adoniram K. Hotchkiss," she began, in a monotonous voice, as if it were a recitation addressed to the public, "first began to take notice of me a year ago. Arter that—off and on——"

"One moment," interrupted the astounded Colonel; "do you mean Hotchkiss the President of the Ditch Company?" He had recognized the name of a prominent citizen—a rigid ascetic, taciturn, middle-aged man—a deacon—and more than that, the head of the company he had just defended. It seemed inconceivable.

"That's him," she continued, with eyes still fixed on the parasol and without changing her monotonous tone—"off and on ever since. Most of the time at the Free-Will Baptist church—at morning service, prayer-meetings, and such. And at home—outside—er—in the road."

"Is it this gentleman—Mr. Adoniram K. Hotchkiss—who —er—promised marriage?" stammered the Colonel.

"Yes."

The Colonel shifted uneasily in his chair. "Most extraordinary! for—you see—my dear young lady—this becomes —a—er—most delicate affair."

"That's what maw said," returned the young woman, simply, yet with the faintest smile playing around her demure lips and downcast cheek.

"I mean," said the Colonel, with a pained yet courteous smile, "that this—er—gentleman—is in fact—er—one of my clients."

"That's what maw said, too, and of course your knowing him will make it all the easier for you," said the young woman.

A slight flush crossed the Colonel's cheek as he returned quickly and a little stiffly, "On the contrary—er—it may make it impossible for me to—er—act in this matter."

The girl lifted her eyes. The Colonel held his breath as the long lashes were raised to his level. Even to an ordinary observer that sudden revelation of her eyes seemed to transform her face with subtle witchery. They were large, brown, and soft, yet filled with an extraordinary penetration and prescience. They were the eyes of an experienced woman of thirty fixed in the face of a child. What else the Colonel saw there Heaven only knows! He felt his inmost secrets plucked from him—his whole soul laid bare—his vanity, belligerency, gallantry—even his medieval chivalry, penetrated, and yet illuminated, in that single glance. And when the eyelids fell again, he felt that a greater part of himself had been swallowed up in them.

"I beg your pardon," he said, hurriedly. "I mean—this matter may be arranged—er—amicably. My interest with —and as you wisely say—my—er—knowledge of my client —er—Mr. Hotchkiss—may affect—a compromise."

"And *damages*," said the young girl, readdressing her parasol, as if she had never looked up.

The Colonel winced. "And—er—undoubtedly *compensation*—if you do not press a fulfilment of the promise. Unless," he said, with an attempted return to his former easy gallantry, which, however, the recollection of her eyes made difficult, "it is a question of—er—the affections?"

"Which?" said his fair client, softly.

"If you still love him?" explained the Colonel, actually blushing.

Zaidee again looked up; again taking the Colonel's breath away with eyes that expressed not only the fullest perception of what he had *said,* but of what he thought and had not said, and with an added subtle suggestion of what he might have thought. "That's tellin'," she said, dropping her long lashes again. The Colonel laughed vacantly. Then feeling himself growing imbecile, he forced an equally weak gravity. "Pardon me—I understand there are no letters; may I know the way in which he formulated his declaration and promises?"

"Hymn-books," said the girl, briefly.

"I beg your pardon," said the mystified lawyer.

"Hymn-books—marked words in them with pencil—and passed 'em on to me," repeated Zaidee. "Like 'love,' 'dear,' 'precious,' 'sweet,' and 'blessed,'" she added, accenting each word with a push of her parasol on the carpet. "Sometimes a whole line outer Tate and Brady—and *Solomon's Song,* you know, and sich."

"I believe," said the Colonel, loftily, "that the—er—phrases of sacred psalmody lend themselves to the language of the affections. But in regard to the distinct promise of marriage—was there—er—no *other* expression?"

"Marriage Service in the prayer-book—lines and words outer that—all marked," said Zaidee. The Colonel nodded naturally and approvingly. "Very good. Were others cognizant of this? Were there any witnesses?"

"Of course not," said the girl. "Only me and him. It was generally at church-time—or prayer-meeting. Once, in passing the plate, he slipped one o' them peppermint lozenges with the letters stamped on it 'I love you' for me to take."

The Colonel coughed slightly. "And you have the lozenge?"

"I ate it," said the girl, simply.

"Ah," said the Colonel. After a pause he added, delicately: "But were these attentions—er—confined to—er—sacred precincts? Did he meet you elsewhere?"

"Useter pass our house on the road," returned the girl, dropping into her monotonous recital, "and useter signal."

"Ah, signal?" repeated the Colonel, approvingly.

"Yes! He'd say 'Kerrow,' and I'd say 'Kerree.' Suthing like a bird, you know."

Indeed, as she lifted her voice in imitation of the call the Colonel thought it certainly very sweet and birdlike. At least as *she* gave it. With his remembrance of the grim deacon he had doubts as to the melodiousness of *his* utterance. He gravely made her repeat it.

"And after that signal?" he added, suggestively.

"He'd pass on," said the girl.

The Colonel coughed slightly, and tapped his desk with his pen-holder.

"Were there any endearments—er—caresses—er—such as taking your hand—er—clasping your waist?" he suggested with a gallant yet respectful sweep of his white hand and bowing of his head;—"er—slight pressure of your fingers in the changes of a dance—I mean," he corrected himself, with an apologetic cough—"in the passing of the plate?"

"No;—he was not what you'd call 'fond,'" returned the girl.

"Ah! Adoniram K. Hotchkiss was not 'fond' in the ordinary acceptance of the word," said the Colonel, with professional gravity.

She lifted her disturbing eyes, and again absorbed his in her own. She also said "Yes," although her eyes in their mysterious prescience of all he was thinking disclaimed the necessity of any answer at all. He smiled vacantly. There was a long pause. On which she slowly disengaged her parasol from the carpet pattern and stood up.

"I reckon that's about all," she said.

"Er—yes—but one moment," said the Colonel, vaguely. He would have liked to keep her longer, but with her strange premonition of him he felt powerless to detain her, or explain his reason for doing so. He instinctively knew she had told him all; his professional judgment told him that a more hopeless case had never come to his knowledge. Yet he was not daunted, only embarrassed. "No matter," he said, vaguely. "Of course I shall have to consult with you again." Her eyes again answered that she expected he would, but she added, simply, "When?"

"In the course of a day or two," said the Colonel, quickly. "I will send you word." She turned to go. In his eagerness to open the door for her he upset his chair, and with some confusion, that was actually youthful, he almost impeded her movements in the hall, and knocked his broad-brimmed Panama hat from his bowing hand in a final gallant sweep. Yet as her small, trim, youthful figure, with its simple Leghorn straw hat confined by a blue bow under her round chin, passed away before him, she looked more like a child than ever.

The Colonel spent that afternoon in making diplomatic inquiries. He found his youthful client was the daughter of a widow who had a small ranch on the cross-roads, near the new Free-Will Baptist church—the evident theatre of this pastoral. They led a secluded life; the girl being little known in the town, and her beauty and fascination apparently not yet being a recognized fact. The Colonel felt a pleasurable relief at this, and a general satisfaction he could not account for. His few inquiries concerning Mr. Hotchkiss only confirmed his own impressions of the alleged lover —a serious-minded, practically abstracted man—abstentive of youthful society, and the last man apparently capable of levity of the affections or serious flirtation. The Colonel was mystified—but determined of purpose—whatever that purpose might have been.

The next day he was at his office at the same hour. He was alone—as usual—the Colonel's office really being his private lodgings, disposed in connecting rooms, a single apartment reserved for consultation. He had no clerk; his papers and briefs being taken by his faithful body-servant and ex-slave "Jim" to another firm who did his office-work since the death of Major Stryker—the Colonel's only law partner, who fell in a duel some years previous. With a fine constancy the Colonel still retained his partner's name on his door-plate—and, it was alleged by the superstitious, kept a certain invincibility also through the *manes* of that lamented and somewhat feared man.

The Colonel consulted his watch, whose heavy gold case still showed the marks of a providential interference with a bullet destined for its owner, and replaced it with some difficulty and shortness of breath in his fob. At the same moment he heard a step in the passage, and the door opened to Adoniram K. Hotchkiss. The Colonel was impressed; he had a duellist's respect for punctuality.

The man entered with a nod and the expectant, inquiring look of a busy man. As his feet crossed that sacred threshold the Colonel become all courtesy; he placed a chair for his visitor, and took his hat from his half-reluctant hand. He then opened a cupboard and brought out a bottle of whiskey and two glasses.

"A—er—slight refreshment, Mr. Hotchkiss," he suggested, politely. "I never drink," replied Hotchkiss, with the severe attitude of a total abstainer. "Ah—er—not the finest bourbon whiskey, selected by a Kentucky friend? No? Pardon me! A cigar, then—the mildest Havana."

"I do not use tobacco nor alcohol in any form," repeated Hotchkiss, ascetically. "I have no foolish weaknesses."

The Colonel's moist, beady eyes swept silently over his client's sallow face. He leaned back comfortably in his chair, and half closing his eyes as in dreamy reminiscence, said, slowly: "Your reply, Mr. Hotchkiss, reminds me of—er—sing'lar circumstances that—er—occurred, in point of fact—at the St. Charles Hotel, New Orleans. Pinkey Hornblower—personal friend—invited Senator Doolittle to join him in social glass. Received, sing'larly enough, reply similar to yours. 'Don't drink nor smoke?' said Pinkey. 'Gad, sir, you must be mighty sweet on the ladies.' Ha!" The Colonel paused long enough to allow the faint flush to pass from Hotchkiss's cheek, and went on, half closing his eyes: "'I allow no man, sir, to discuss my personal habits,' said Doolittle, over his shirt collar. 'Then I reckon shootin' must be one of those habits,' said Pinkey, coolly. Both men drove out on the Shell Road back of cemetery next morning.

Pinkey put bullet at twelve paces through Doolittle's temple. Poor Doo never spoke again. Left three wives and seven children, they say—two of 'em black."

"I got a note from you this morning," said Hotchkiss, with badly concealed impatience. "I suppose in reference to our case. You have taken judgment, I believe." The Colonel, without replying, slowly filled a glass of whiskey and water. For a moment he held it dreamily before him, as if still engaged in gentle reminiscences called up by the act. Then tossing it off, he wiped his lips with a large white handkerchief, and leaning back comfortably in his chair, said, with a wave of his hand, "The interview I requested, Mr. Hotchkiss, concerns a subject—which I may say is—er—er—at present *not* of a public or business nature—although *later* it might become—er—er—both. It is an affair of some—er—delicacy."

The Colonel paused, and Mr. Hotchkiss regarded him with increased impatience. The Colonel, however, continued, with unchanged deliberation: "It concerns—er—a young lady—a beautiful, high-souled creature, sir, who, apart from her personal loveliness—er—er—I may say is of one of the first families of Missouri, and—er—not—remotely connected by marriage with one of—er—er—my boyhood's dearest friends." The latter, I grieve to say, was a pure invention of the Colonel's—an oratorical addition to the scanty information he had obtained the previous day. "The young lady," he continued, blandly, "enjoys the further distinction of being the object of such attention from you as would make this interview—really—a confidential matter—er—er—among friends and—er—er—relations in present and future. I need not say that the lady I refer to is Miss Zaidee Juno Hooker, only daughter of Almira Ann Hooker, relict of Jefferson Brown Hooker, formerly of Boone County, Kentucky, and latterly of—er—Pike County, Missouri."

The sallow, ascetic hue of Mr. Hotchkiss's face had passed through a livid and then a greenish shade, and finally settled into a sullen red. "What's all this about?" he demanded, roughly. The least touch of belligerent fire came into Starbottle's eye, but his bland courtesy did not change. "I believe," he said, politely, "I have made myself clear as between—er—gentlemen, though perhaps not as clear as I should to—er—er—jury."

Mr. Hotchkiss was apparently struck with some significance in the lawyer's reply. "I don't know," he said, in a lower and more cautious voice, "what you mean by what you call 'my attentions' to—any one—or how it concerns you. I have not exhausted half a dozen words with—the person you name—have never written her a line—nor even called at her house." He rose with an assumption of ease, pulled down his waistcoat, buttoned his coat, and took up his hat. The Colonel did not move. "I believe I have already indicated my meaning in what I have called 'your attentions,'" said the Colonel, blandly, "and given you my 'concern' for speaking as—er—er mutual friend. As to *your* statement of your relations with Miss Hooker, I may state that it is fully corroborated by the statement of the young lady herself in this very office yesterday."

"Then what does this impertinent nonsense mean? Why am I summoned here?" said Hotchkiss, furiously.

"Because," said the Colonel, deliberately, "that statement is infamously—yes, damnably to your discredit, sir!"

Mr. Hotchkiss was here seized by one of those important and inconsistent rages which occasionally betray the habitually cautious and timid man. He caught up the Colonel's stick, which was lying on the table. At the same moment the Colonel, without any apparent effort, grasped it by the handle. To Mr. Hotchkiss's astonishment, the stick separated in two pieces, leaving the handle and about two feet of narrow glittering steel in the Colonel's hand. The man recoiled, dropping the useless fragment. The Colonel picked it up, fitting the shining blade in it, clicked the spring, and then rising, with a face of courtesy yet of unmistakably genuine pain, and with even a slight tremor in his voice, said, gravely:

"Mr. Hotchkiss, I owe you a thousand apologies, sir, that—er—a weapon should be drawn by me—even through your own inadvertence—under the sacred protection of my roof, and upon an unarmed man. I beg your pardon, sir, and I even withdraw the expressions which provoked that inadvertence. Nor does this apology prevent you from holding me responsible—personally responsible—*elsewhere* for an indiscretion committed in behalf of a lady—my—er—client."

"Your client? Do you mean you have taken her case? You, the counsel for the Ditch Company?" said Mr. Hotchkiss, in trembling indignation.

"Having won *your* case, sir," said the Colonel, coolly, "the—er—usages of advocacy do not prevent me from espousing the cause of the weak and unprotected."

"We shall see, sir," said Hotchkiss, grasping the handle of the door and backing into the passage. "There are other lawyers who—"

"Permit me to see you out," interrupted the Colonel, rising politely.

"—will be ready to resist the attacks of blackmail," continued Hotchkiss, retreating along the passage.

"And then you will be able to repeat your remarks to

me *in the street,*" continued the Colonel, bowing, as he persisted in following his visitor to the door.

But here Mr. Hotchkiss quickly slammed it behind him, and hurried away. The Colonel returned to his office, and sitting down, took a sheet of letter paper bearing the inscription "Starbottle and Stryker, Attorneys and Counsellors," and wrote the following lines:

Hooker *versus* Hotchkiss.

DEAR MADAM,—Having had a visit from the defendant in above, we should be pleased to have an interview with you at 2 P.M. tomorrow. Your obedient servants,

STARBOTTLE AND STRYKER.

This he sealed and despatched by his trusted servant Jim, and then devoted a few moments to reflection. It was the custom of the Colonel to act first, and justify the action by reason afterwards.

He knew that Hotchkiss would at once lay the matter before rival counsel. He knew that they would advise him that Miss Hooker had "no case"—that she would be nonsuited on her own evidence, and he ought not to compromise, but be ready to stand trial. He believed, however, that Hotchkiss feared that exposure, and although his own instincts had been at first against that remedy, he was now instinctively in favor of it. He remembered his own power with a jury; his vanity and his chivalry alike approved of this heroic method; he was bound by the prosaic facts—he had his own theory of the case, which no mere evidence could gainsay. In fact, Mrs. Hooker's own words that "he was to tell the story in his own way" actually appeared to him an inspiration and a prophecy.

Perhaps there was something else, due possibly to the

lady's wonderful eyes, of which he had thought much. Yet it was not her simplicity that affected him solely; on the contrary, it was her apparent intelligent reading of the character of her recreant lover—and of his own! Of all the Colonel's previous "light" or "serious" loves none had ever before flattered him in that way. And it was this, combined with the respect which he had held for their profes- sional relations, that precluded his having a more familiar knowledge of his client, through serious questioning, or play- ful gallantry. I am not sure it was not part of the charm to have a rustic *femme incomprise* as a client.

Nothing could exceed the respect with which he greeted her as she entered his office the next day. He even affected not to notice that she had put on her best clothes, and, he made no doubt, appeared as when she had first attracted the mature yet faithless attentions of Deacon Hotchkiss at church. A white virginal muslin was belted around her slim figure by a blue ribbon, and her Leghorn hat was drawn around her oval cheek by a bow of the same color. She had a Southern girl's narrow feet, encased in white stockings and kid slippers, which were crossed primly be- fore her as she sat in a chair, supporting her arm by her faithful parasol planted firmly on the floor. A faint odor of southernwood exhaled from her, and, oddly enough, stirred the Colonel with a far-off recollection of a pine-shaded Sun- day school on a Georgia hillside and of his first love, aged ten, in a short, starched frock. Possibly it was the same re- collection that revived something of the awkwardness he had felt then.

He, however, smiled vaguely and, sitting down, coughed slightly, and placed his fingertips together. "I have had an —er—interview with Mr. Hotchkiss, but—I—er—regret to say there seems to be no prospect of—er—compromise." He paused, and to his surprise her listless "company" face lit up with an adorable smile. "Of course!—ketch him!" she said. "Was he mad when you told him?" She put her knees comfortably together and leaned forward for a reply.

For all that, wild horses could not have torn from the Colonel a word about Hotchkiss's anger. "He expressed his intention of employing counsel—and defending a suit," returned the Colonel, affably basking in her smile. She dragged her chair nearer his desk. "Then you'll fight him tooth and nail?" she said eagerly; "you'll show him up? You'll tell the whole story your own way? You'll give him fits?—and you'll make him pay? Sure?" she went on, breathlessly.

"I—er—will," said the Colonel, almost as breathlessly.

She caught his fat white hand, which was lying on the table, between her own and lifted it to her lips. He felt her soft young fingers even through the lisle-thread gloves that encased them and the warm moisture of her lips upon his skin. He felt himself flushing—but was unable to break the silence or change his position. The next moment she had scuttled back with her chair to her old position.

"I—er—certainly shall do my best," stammered the Colonel, in an attempt to recover his dignity and composure.

"That's enough! You'll *do* it," said the girl, enthusiastically. "Lordy! Just you talk for *me* as ye did for *his* old Ditch Company, and you'll fetch it—every time! Why, when you made that jury sit up the other day—when you got that off about the Merrikan flag waving equally over the rights of honest citizens banded together in peaceful commercial pursuits, as well as over the fortress of official proflig—"

"Oligarchy," murmured the Colonel, courteously

"Oligarchy," repeated the girl, quickly, "my breath was just took away. I said to maw, 'Ain't he too sweet for anything!' I did, honest Injin! And when you rolled it all off at the end—never missing a word—(you didn't need to mark 'em in a lesson-book, but had 'em all ready on your tongue), and walked out—— Well! I didn't know you nor the Ditch Company from Adam, but I could have just run over and kissed you there before the whole court!"

She laughed, with her face glowing, although her strange eyes were cast down. Alack! the Colonel's face was equally flushed, and his own beady eyes were on his desk. To any other woman he would have voiced the banal gallantry that he should now, himself, look forward to that reward, but the words never reached his lips. He laughed, coughed slightly, and when he looked up again she had fallen into the same attitude as on her first visit, with her parasol point on the floor.

"I must ask you to—er—direct your memory—to—er—another point; the breaking off of the—er—er—er—engagement. Did he—er—give any reason for it? Or show any cause?"

"No; he never said anything," returned the girl.

"Not in his usual way?—er—no reproaches out of the hymn-book?—or the sacred writings?"

"No; he just *quit*."

"Er—ceased his attentions," said the Colonel, gravely. "And naturally you—er—were not conscious of any cause for his doing so." The girl raised her wonderful eyes so suddenly and so penetratingly without reply in any other way that the Colonel could only hurriedly say: "I see! None, of course!"

At which she rose, the Colonel rising also. "We—shall

begin proceedings at once. I must, however, caution you to answer no questions nor say anything about this case to any one until you are in court."

She answered his request with another intelligent look and a nod. He accompanied her to the door. As he took her proffered hand he raised the lisle-thread fingers to his lips with old-fashioned gallantry. As if that act had condoned for his first omissions and awkwardness, he became his old-fashioned self again, buttoned his coat, pulled out his shirt frill, and strutted back to his desk.

A day or two later it was known throughout the town that Zaidee Hooker had sued Adoniram Hotchkiss for breach of promise, and that the damages were laid at five thousand dollars. As in those bucolic days the Western press was under the secure censorship of a revolver, a cautious tone of criticism prevailed, and any gossip was confined to personal expression, and even then at the risk of the gossiper. Nevertheless, the situation provoked the intensest curiosity. The Colonel was approached—until his statement that he should consider any attempt to overcome his professional secrecy a personal reflection withheld further advances. The community were left to the more ostentatious information of the defendant's counsel, Messrs. Kitcham and Bilser, that the case was "ridiculous" and "rotten," that the plaintiff would be nonsuited, and the fire-eating Starbottle would be taught a lesson that he could not "bully" the law—and there were some dark hints of a conspiracy. It was even hinted that the "case" was the revengeful and preposterous outcome of the refusal of Hotchkiss to pay Starbottle an extravagant fee for his late services to the Ditch Company. It is unnecessary to say that these words were not reported to the Colonel. It was, however, an unfortunate circumstance for the calmer, ethical consideration of the subject that the church sided with Hotchkiss, as this provoked an equal adherence to the plaintiff and Starbottle on the part of the larger body of non-church-goers, who were delighted at a possible exposure of the weakness of religious rectitude. "I've allus had my suspicions o' them early candle-light meetings down at that gospel shop," said one critic, "and I reckon Deacon Hotchkiss didn't rope in the gals to attend jest for psalm-singing." "Then for him to get up and leave the board afore the game's finished and try to sneak out of it," said another. "I suppose that's what they call *religious*."

It was therefore not remarkable that the courthouse three weeks later was crowded with an excited multitude of the curious and sympathizing. The fair plaintiff, with her mother, was early in attendance, and under the Colonel's advice appeared in the same modest garb in which she had first visited his office. This and her downcast modest demeanor were perhaps at first disappointing to the crowd, who had evidently expected a paragon of loveliness—as the Circe of the grim ascetic defendant, who sat beside his counsel. But presently all eyes were fixed on the Colonel, who certainly made up in *his* appearance any deficiency of his fair client. His portly figure was clothed in a blue dress-coat with brass buttons, a buff waistcoat which permitted his frilled shirt front to become erectile above it, a black satin stock which confined a boyish turned-down collar around his full neck, and immaculate drill trousers, strapped over varnished boots. A murmur ran round the court. "Old 'Personally Responsible' had got his war-paint on," "The Old War-Horse is smelling powder," were whispered comments. Yet for all that the most irreverent among them recognized vaguely, in his bizarre figure, something of an honored past in their country's history, and possibly felt the spell of old deeds and old names that had once thrilled their boyish pulses. The new District Judge returned Colonel Starbottle's profoundly punctilious bow. The Colonel was followed by his Negro servant, carrying a parcel of hymn-books and Bibles, who, with a courtesy evidently imitated from his master, placed one before the opposite counsel. This, after a first curious glance, the lawyer somewhat superciliously tossed aside. But when Jim, proceeding to the jury-box, placed with equal politeness the remaining copies before the jury, the opposite counsel sprang to his feet.

"I want to direct the attention of the Court to this unprecedented tampering with the jury, by this gratuitous exhibition of matter impertinent and irrelevant to the issue."

The Judge cast an inquiring look at Colonel Starbottle.

"May it please the Court," returned Colonel Starbottle with dignity, ignoring the counsel, "the defendant's counsel will observe that he is already furnished with the matter—which I regret to say he has treated—in the presence of the Court—and of his client, a deacon of the church—with—er—great superciliousness. When I state to Your Honor that the books in question are hymn-books and copies of the *Holy Scriptures*, and that they are for the instruction of the jury, to whom I shall have to refer them in the course of my opening, I believe I am within my rights."

"The act is certainly unprecedented," said the Judge, dryly, "but unless the counsel for the plaintiff expects the jury to *sing* from these hymn-books, their introduction is not improper, and I cannot admit the objection. As defendant's counsel are furnished with copies also, they cannot plead 'surprise,' as in the introduction of new matter, and as plaintiff's counsel relies evidently upon the jury's attention to his opening, he would not be the first person to distract it." After a pause he added, addressing the Colonel, who remained standing, "The Court is with you, sir; proceed."

But the Colonel remained motionless and statuesque, with folded arms.

"I have overruled the objection," repeated the Judge; "you may go on."

"I am waiting, Your Honor, for the—er—withdrawal by the defendant's counsel of the word 'tampering,' as refers to myself, and of 'impertinent,' as refers to the sacred volumes."

"The request is a proper one, and I have no doubt will be acceded to," returned the Judge, quietly. The defendant's counsel rose and mumbled a few words of apology, and the incident closed. There was, however, a general feeling that the Colonel had in some way "scored," and if his object had been to excite the greatest curiosity about the books, he had made his point.

But impassive of his victory, he inflated his chest, with his right hand in the breast of his buttoned coat, and began. His usual high color had paled slightly, but the small pupils of his prominent eyes glittered like steel. The young girl leaned forward in her chair with an attention so breathless, a sympathy so quick, and an admiration so artless and unconscious that in an instant she divided with the speaker the attention of the whole assemblage. It was very hot; the court was crowded to suffocation; even the open windows revealed a crowd of faces outside the building, eagerly following the Colonel's words.

He would remind the jury that only a few weeks ago he stood there as the advocate of a powerful company, then represented by the present defendant. He spoke then as the champion of strict justice against legal oppression; no

less should he today champion the cause of the unprotected and the comparatively defenseless—save for that para-
mount power which surrounds beauty and innocence—even
though the plaintiff of yesterday was the defendant of today. As he approached the court a moment ago he had
raised his eyes and beheld the starry flag flying from its
dome—and he knew that glorious banner was a symbol of
the perfect equality, under the Constitution, of the rich and
the poor, the strong and the weak—an equality which made
the simple citizen taken from the plough in the veld, the
pick in the gulch, or from behind the counter in the mining
town, who served on that jury, the equal arbiters of justice
with that highest legal luminary whom they were proud to
welcome on the bench today. The Colonel paused, with
a stately bow to the impassive Judge. It was this, he continued, which lifted his heart as he approached the building.
And yet—he had entered it with an uncertain—he might
almost say—a timid step. And why? He knew, gentlemen,
he was about to confront a profound—aye! a sacred re-
sponsibility! Those hymn-books and holy writings handed
to the jury were *not*, as his Honor surmised, for the purpose
of enabling the jury to indulge in—er—preliminary choral
exercise! He might, indeed, say "alas not!" They were the
damning, incontrovertible proofs of the perfidy of the defendant. And they would prove as terrible a warning to him
as the fatal characters upon Belshazzar's wall. There was a
strong sensation. Hotchkiss turned a sallow green. His
lawyers assumed a careless smile.

It was his duty to tell them that this was not one of those
ordinary "breach-of-promise" cases which were too often
the occasion of ruthless mirth and indecent levity in the
courtroom. The jury would find nothing of that here. There
were no love-letters with the epithets of endearment, nor

those mystic crosses and ciphers which, he had been credibly informed, chastely hid the exchange of those mutual
caresses known as "kisses." There was no cruel tearing of
the veil from those sacred privacies of the human affection—
there was no forensic shouting out of those fond confidences
meant only for *one*. But there was, he was shocked to say,
a new sacrilegious intrusion. The weak pipings of Cupid
were mingled with the chorus of the saints—the sanctity of
the temple known as the "meeting-house" was desecrated
by proceedings more in keeping with the shrine of Venus—
and the inspired writings themselves were used as the medium of amatory and wanton flirtation by the defendant in
his sacred capacity as Deacon.

The Colonel artistically paused after this thunderous de-
nunciation. The jury turned eagerly to the leaves of the
hymn-books, but the larger gaze of the audience remained
fixed upon the speaker and the girl, who sat in rapt admiration of his periods. After the hush, the Colonel continued
in a lower and sadder voice: "There are, perhaps, few of us
here, gentlemen—with the exception of the defendant—who
can arrogate to themselves the title of regular church-goers,
or to whom these humbler functions of the prayer-meeting,
the Sunday-school, and the Bible class are habitually familiar. Yet"—more solemnly—"down in your hearts is the
deep conviction of our short-comings and failings, and a
laudable desire that others at least should profit by the teach-
ings we neglect. Perhaps," he continued, closing his eyes
dreamily, "there is not a man here who does not recall the
happy days of his boyhood, the rustic village spire, the lesson shared with some artless village maiden, with whom
he later sauntered, hand in hand, through the woods, as the
simple rhyme rose upon their lips,

Always make it a point to have it a rule
Never to be late at the Sabbath-school.

He would recall the strawberry feasts, the welcome annual picnic, redolent with hunks of gingerbread and sarsaparilla. How would they feel to know that these sacred recollections were now forever profaned in their memory by the knowledge that the defendant was capable of using such occasions to make love to the larger girls and teachers, whilst his artless companions were innocently—the Court will pardon me for introducing what I am credibly informed is the local expression 'doing gooseberry'?" The tremulous flicker of a smile passed over the faces of the listening crowd, and the Colonel slightly winced. But he recovered himself instantly, and continued:

"My client, the only daughter of a widowed mother—who has for years stemmed the varying tides of adversity—in the western precincts of this town—stands before you to-day invested only in her own innocence. She wears no—er—rich gifts of her faithless admirer—is panoplied in no jewels, rings, nor mementos of affection such as lovers delight to hang upon the shrine of their affections; hers is not the glory with which Solomon decorated the Queen of Sheba, though the defendant, as I shall show later, clothed her in the less expensive flowers of the king's poetry. No! gentlemen! The defendant exhibited in this affair a certain frugality of—er—pecuniary investment, which I am willing to admit may be commendable in his class. His only gift was characteristic alike of his methods and his economy. There is, I understand, a certain not unimportant feature of religious exercise known as 'taking a collection.' The defendant, on this occasion, by the mute presentation of a tin plate covered with baize, solicited the pecuniary contributions of the faithful. On approaching the plaintiff, however, he himself slipped a love-token upon the plate and pushed it towards her. That love-token was a lozenge—a small disk, I have reason to believe, concocted of peppermint and sugar, bearing upon its reverse surface the simple words, 'I love you!' I have since ascertained that these disks may be bought for five cents a dozen—or at considerably less than one half-cent for the single lozenge. Yes, gentlemen, the words 'I love you!'—the oldest legend of all; the refrain, 'when the morning stars sang together'—were presented to the plaintiff by a medium so insignificant that there is, happily, no coin in the republic low enough to represent its value.

"I shall prove to you, gentlemen of the jury," said the Colonel, solemnly, drawing a *Bible* from his coat-tail pocket, "that the defendant, for the last twelve months, conducted an amatory correspondence with the plaintiff by means of underlined words of sacred writ and church psalmody, such as 'beloved,' 'precious,' and 'dearest,' occasionally appropriating whole passages which seemed apposite to his tender passion. I shall call your attention to one of them. The defendant, while professing to be a total abstainer—a man who, in my own knowledge, has refused spirituous refreshment as an inordinate weakness of the flesh, with shameless hypocrisy underscores with his pencil the following passage and presents it to the plaintiff. The gentlemen of the jury will find it in the *Song of Solomon*, page 548, chapter II, verse 5." After a pause, in which the rapid rustling of leaves was heard in the jury-box, Colonel Starbottle declaimed in a pleading, stentorian voice, "'Stay me with—er—*flagons*, comfort me with—er—apples—for I am—er—sick of love.' Yes, gentlemen!—yes, you may well turn from those accusing pages and look at the double-faced defendant. He desires —to—er—be—'stayed with flagons'! I am not aware, at present, what kind of liquor is habitually dispensed at these meetings, and for which the defendant so urgently clamored; but it will be my duty before this trial is over to discover it, if I have to summon every barkeeper in this district. For the moment, I will simply call your attention to the *quantity*. It is not a single drink that the defendant asks for—not a glass of light and generous wine, to be shared with his inamorata—but a number of flagons or vessels, each possibly holding a pint measure—*for himself!*"

The smile of the audience had become a laugh. The Judge looked up warningly, when his eye caught the fact that the Colonel had again winced at this mirth. He regarded him seriously. Mr. Hotchkiss's counsel had joined in the laugh affectedly, but Hotchkiss himself was ashy pale. There was also a commotion in the jury-box, a hurried turning over of leaves, and an excited discussion.

"The gentlemen of the jury," said the Judge, with official gravity, "will please keep order and attend only to the speeches of counsel. Any discussion *here* is irregular and premature—and must be reserved for the jury-room—after they have retired."

The foreman of the jury struggled to his feet. He was a powerful man, with a good-humored face, and, in spite of his unfelicitous nickname of "The Bone-Breaker," had a kindly, simple, but somewhat emotional nature. Nevertheless, it appeared as if he were laboring under some powerful indignation.

"Can we ask a question, Judge?" he said, respectfully, although his voice had the unmistakable Western-American ring in it, as of one who was unconscious that he could be addressing any but his peers.

"Yes," said the Judge, good-humoredly.

"We're finding in this yere piece, out of which the Kernel

hes just bin a-quotin', some language that me and my pardners allow hadn't orter to be read out afore a young lady in
court—and we want to know of you—ez a fair-minded and
impartial man—ef this is the reg'lar kind o' book given to
gals and babies down at the meetin'house."

"The jury will please follow the counsel's speech, without
comment," said the Judge, briefly, fully aware that the defendant's counsel would spring to his feet, as he did
promptly. "The Court will allow us to explain to the gentlemen that the language they seem to object to has been
accepted by the best theologians for the last thousand years
as being purely mystic. As I will explain later, those are
merely symbols of the Church—"

"Of wot?" interrupted the foreman, in deep scorn.

"Of the Church!"

"We ain't askin' any questions *o' you*—and we ain't
takin' any answers," said the foreman, sitting down
promptly.

"I must insist," said the Judge sternly, "that the plaintiff's
counsel be allowed to continue his opening without interruption. You" (to defendant's counsel) "will have your opportunity to reply later."

The counsel sank down in his seat with the bitter conviction that the jury was manifestly against him, and the case
as good as lost. But his face was scarcely as disturbed as his
client's, who, in great agitation, had begun to argue with
him wildly, and was apparently pressing some point against
the lawyer's vehement opposal. The Colonel's murky eyes
brightened as he still stood erect with his hand thrust in
his breast.

"It will be put to you, gentlemen, when the counsel on
the other side refrains from mere interruption and confines
himself to reply, that my unfortunate client has no action—

no remedy at law—because there were no spoken words of endearment. But, gentlemen, it will depend upon *you* to say what are and what are not articulate expressions of love. We all know that among the lower animals, with whom you may possibly be called upon to classify the defendant, there are certain signals more or less harmonious, as the case may be. The ass brays, the horse neighs, the sheep bleats—the feathered denizens of the grove call to their mates in more musical roundelays. These are recognized facts, gentlemen, which you yourselves, as dwellers among nature in this beautiful land, are all cognizant of. They are facts that no one would deny—and we should have a poor opinion of the ass who, at—er—such a supreme moment, would attempt to suggest that his call was unthinking and without significance. But, gentlemen, I shall prove to you that such was the foolish, self-convicting custom of the defendant. With the greatest reluctance, and the—er—greatest pain, I succeeded in wresting from the maidenly modesty of my fair client the innocent confession that the defendant had induced her to correspond with him in these methods. Picture to yourself, gentlemen, the lonely moonlight road beside the widow's humble cottage. It is a beautiful night, sanctified to the affections, and the innocent girl is leaning from her casement. Presently there appears upon the road a slinking, stealthy figure—the defendant, on his way to church. True to the instruction she has received from him, her lips part in the musical utterance" (the Colonel lowered his voice in a faint falsetto, presumably in fond imitation of his fair client), " 'Kerree!' Instantly the night became resonant with the impassioned reply" (the Colonel here lifted his voice in stentorian tones), " 'Kerrow.' Again, as he passes, rises the soft 'Kerree'; again, as his form is lost in the distance, comes back the deep 'Kerrow.' "

A burst of laughter, long, loud, and irrepressible, struck the whole courtroom, and before the Judge could lift his half-composed face and take his handkerchief from his mouth, a faint "Kerree" from some unrecognized obscurity of the courtroom was followed by a loud "Kerrow" from some opposite locality. "The sheriff will clear the court," said the Judge, sternly; but alas, as the embarrassed and choking officials rushed hither and thither, a soft "Kerree" from the spectators at the window, *outside* the courthouse, was answered by a loud chorus of "Kerrows" from the opposite windows, filled with onlookers. Again the laughter arose everywhere—even the fair plaintiff herself sat convulsed behind her handkerchief.

The figure of Colonel Starbottle alone remained erect—white and rigid. And then the Judge, looking up, saw what no one else in the court had seen—that the Colonel was sincere and in earnest; that what he had conceived to be the pleader's most perfect acting, and most elaborate irony, were the deep, serious, mirthless *convictions* of a man without the least sense of humor. There was a touch of this respect in the Judge's voice as he said to him, gently, "You may proceed, Colonel Starbottle."

"I thank Your Honor," said the Colonel, slowly, "for recognizing and doing all in your power to prevent an interruption that, during my thirty years' experience at the bar, I have never yet been subjected to without the privilege of holding the instigators thereof responsible—*personally* responsible. It is possibly my fault that I have failed, oratorically, to convey to the gentlemen of the jury the full force and significance of the defendant's signals. I am aware that my voice is singularly deficient in producing either the dulcet tones of my fair client or the impassioned vehemence of the defendant's response. I will," continued the Colonel, with a fatigued but blind fatuity that ignored the hurriedly knit brows and warning eyes of the Judge, "try again. The note uttered by my client" (lowering his voice to the faintest of falsettos) "was 'Kerree'; the response was 'Kerrow'"— and the Colonel's voice fairly shook the dome above him.

Another uproar of laughter followed this apparently audacious repetition, but was interrupted by an unlooked-for incident. The defendant rose abruptly, and tearing himself away from the withholding hand and pleading protestations of his counsel, absolutely fled from the courtroom, his appearance outside being recognized by a prolonged "Kerrow" from the bystanders, which again and again followed him in the distance. In the momentary silence which followed, the Colonel's voice was heard saying, "We rest here, Your Honor," and he sat down. No less white, but more agitated, was the face of the defendant's counsel, who instantly rose.

"For some unexplained reason, Your Honor, my client desires to suspend further proceedings, with a view to effect a peaceable compromise with the plaintiff. As he is a man of wealth and position, he is able and willing to pay liberally for that privilege. While I, as his counsel, am still convinced of his legal irresponsibility, as he has chosen, however, to publicly abandon his rights here, I can only ask Your Honor's permission to suspend further proceedings until I can confer with Colonel Starbottle."

"As far as I can follow the pleadings," said the Judge, gravely, "the case seems to be hardly one for litigation, and I approve of the defendant's course, while I strongly urge the plaintiff to accept it."

Colonel Starbottle bent over his fair client. Presently he rose, unchanged in look or demeanor. "I yield, Your Honor, to the wishes of my client, and—er—lady. We accept."

Before the court adjourned that day it was known throughout the town that Adoniram K. Hotchkiss had compromised the suit for four thousand dollars and costs.

Colonel Starbottle had so far recovered his equanimity as to strut jauntily towards his office, where he was to meet his fair client. He was surprised, however, to find her already there, and in company with a somewhat sheepish-looking young man—a stranger. If the Colonel had any disappointment in meeting a third party to the interview, his old-fashioned courtesy did not permit him to show it. He bowed graciously, and politely motioned them each to a seat.

"I reckoned I'd bring Hiram round with me," said the young lady, lifting her searching eyes, after a pause, to the Colonel's, "though he *was* awful shy, and allowed that you didn't know him from Adam—or even suspected his existence. But I said, 'That's just where you slip up, Hiram; a pow'ful man like the Colonel knows everything—and I've seen it in his eye.' Lordy!" she continued, with a laugh, leaning forward over her parasol, as her eyes again sought the Colonel's, "don't you remember when you asked me if I loved that old Hotchkiss, and I told you 'That's tellin',' and you looked at me, Lordy! I knew *then* you suspected there was a Hiram *somewhere*—as good as if I'd told you. Now, you, jest get up, Hiram, and give the Colonel a good hand shake. For if it wasn't for *him* and *his* searchin' ways, and *his* awful power of language, I wouldn't hev got that four thousand dollars out o' that flirty fool Hotchkiss—enough to buy a farm, so as you and me could get married! That's what you owe to *him*. Don't stand there like a stuck fool starin' at him. He won't eat you—though he's killed many a better man. Come, have *I* got to do *all* the kissin'!"

It is of record that the Colonel bowed so courteously and so profoundly that he managed not merely to evade the proffered hand of the shy Hiram, but to only lightly touch the franker and more impulsive fingertips of the gentle Zaidee. "I—er—offer my sincerest congratulations—though I think you—er—overestimate—my—er—powers of penetration. Unfortunately, a pressing engagement, which may oblige me also to leave town tonight, forbids my saying more. I have—er—left the—er—business settlement of this —er—case in the hands of the lawyers who do my office-work, and who will show you every attention. And now let me wish you a very good afternoon."

Nevertheless, the Colonel returned to his private room, and it was nearly twilight when the faithful Jim entered, to find him sitting meditatively before his desk. "'Fo' God! Kernel—I hope dey ain't nuffin de matter, but you's lookin' mightly solemn! I ain't seen you look dat way, Kernel, since de day pooh Marse Stryker was fetched home shot froo de head."

"Hand me down the whiskey, Jim," said the Colonel, rising slowly.

The Negro flew to the closet joyfully, and brought out the bottle. The Colonel poured out a glass of the spirit and drank it with his old deliberation.

"You're quite right, Jim," he said, putting down his glass, "but I'm—er—getting old—and—somehow—I am missing poor Stryker damnably!"

A PIECE OF RED CALICO

By Frank R. Stockton

Mr. Editor: If the following true experience shall prove of any advantage to any of your readers, I shall be glad.

I was going into town the other morning, when my wife handed me a little piece of red calico, and asked me if I would have time, during the day, to buy her two yards and a half of calico like that. I assured her that it would be no trouble at all; and putting the piece of calico in my pocket, I took the train for the city.

At lunch-time I stopped in at a large dry-goods store to attend to my wife's commission. I saw a well-dressed man walking the floor between the counters, where long lines of girls were waiting on much longer lines of customers, and asked him where I could see some red calico.

"This way, sir," and he led me up the store. "Miss Stone," said he to a young lady, "show this gentleman some red calico."

"What shade do you want?" asked Miss Stone.

I showed her the little piece of calico that my wife had given me. She looked at it and handed it back to me. Then she took down a great roll of red calico and spread it out on the counter.

"Why, that isn't the shade!" said I.

"No, not exactly," said she; "but it is prettier than your sample."

"That may be," said I; "but, you see, I want to match this piece. There is something already made of this kind of calico, which needs to be made larger, or mended, or something. I want some calico of the same shade."

The girl made no answer, but took down another roll.

"That's the shade," said she.

"Yes," I replied, "but it's striped."

"Stripes are more worn than any thing else in calicoes," said she.

"Yes; but this isn't to be worn. It's for furniture, I think. At any rate, I want perfectly plain stuff, to match something already in use."

"Well, I don't think you can find it perfectly plain, unless you get Turkey red."

"What is Turkey red?" I asked.

"Turkey red is perfectly plain in calicoes," she answered.

"Well, let me see some."

"We haven't any Turkey red calico left," she said, "but we have some very nice plain calicoes in other colors."

"I don't want any other color. I want stuff to match this."

"It's hard to match cheap calico like that," she said, and so I left her.

I next went into a store a few doors farther up Broadway. When I entered I approached the "floor-walker," and handing him my sample, said:

"Have you any calico like this?"

"Yes, sir," said he. "Third counter to the right."

I went to the third counter to the right, and showed my sample to the salesman in attendance there. He looked at it on both sides. Then he said:

"We haven't any of this."

"That gentleman said you had," said I.

"We had it, but we're out of it now. You'll get that goods at an upholsterer's."

I went across the street to an upholsterer's.

"Have you any stuff like this?" I asked.

"No," said the salesman. "We haven't. Is it for furniture?"

"Yes," I replied.

"Then Turkey red is what you want?"

"Is Turkey red just like this?" I asked.

"No," said he; "but it's much better."

"That makes no difference to me," I replied. "I want something just like this."

"But they don't use that for furniture," he said.

"I should think people could use anything they wanted for furniture," I remarked, somewhat sharply.

"They can, but they don't," he said quite calmly. "They don't use red like that. They use Turkey red."

I said no more, but left. The next place I visited was a very large dry-goods store. Of the first salesman I saw I inquired if they kept red calico like my sample.

"You'll find that on the second story," said he.

I went upstairs. There I asked a man:

"Where will I find red calico?"

"In the far room to the left. Right over there." And he pointed to a distant corner.

I walked through the crowds of purchasers and sales-people, and around the counters and tables filled with goods, to the far room to the left. When I got there I asked for red calico.

"The second counter down this side," said the man.

I went there and produced my sample. "Calicoes down-stairs," said the man.

"They told me they were up here," I said.

"Not these plain goods. You'll find 'em downstairs at the back of the store, over on that side."

I went downstairs to the back of the store.

"Where will I find red calico like this?" I asked.

"Next counter but one," said the man addressed, walking with me in the direction pointed out.

"Dunn, show red calicoes."

Mr. Dunn took my sample and looked at it.

"We haven't this shade in that quality of goods," he said.

"Well, have you it in any quality of goods?" I asked.

"Yes; we've got it finer." And he took down a piece of calico, and unrolled a yard or two of it on the counter.

"That's not this shade," I said.

"No," said he. "The goods is finer and the color's better."

"I want it to match this," I said.

"I thought you weren't particular about the match," said the salesman. "You said you didn't care for the quality of the goods, and you know you can't match goods without you take into consideration quality and color both. If you want that quality of goods in red, you ought to get Turkey red."

I did not think it necessary to answer this remark, but said:

"Then you've got nothing to match this?"

"No, sir. But perhaps they may have it in the upholstery department, in the sixth story."

So I got in the elevator and went up to the top of the house.

"Have you any red stuff like this?" I said to a young man.

"Red stuff? Upholstery department,—other end of this floor."

I went to the other end of the floor.

"I want some red calico," I said to a man.

"Furniture goods?" he asked.

"Yes," said I.

"Fourth counter to the left."

I went to the fourth counter to the left, and showed my sample to a salesman. He looked at it, and said:

"You'll get this down on the first floor—calico department."

I turned on my heel, descended in the elevator, and went out on Broadway. I was thoroughly sick of red calico. But I determined to make one more trial. My wife had bought her red calico not long before, and there must be some to be had somewhere. I ought to have asked her where she bought it, but I thought a simple little thing like that could be bought anywhere.

I went into another large dry-goods store. As I entered the door a sudden tremor seized me. I could not bear to take out that piece of red calico. If I had had any other kind of a rag about me—a pen-wiper or any thing of the sort—I think I would have asked them if they could match that.

But I stepped up to a young woman and presented my sample, with the usual question.

"Back room, counter on the left," she said.

I went there.

"Have you any red calico like this?" I asked of the lady behind the counter.

"No, sir," she said, "but we have it in Turkey red."

Turkey red again! I surrendered.

"All right," I said, "give me Turkey red."

"How much sir?" she asked.

"I don't know—say five yards."

The lady looked at me rather strangely, but measured off five yards of Turkey red calico. Then she rapped on the counter and called out "cash!" A little girl, with yellow hair in two long plaits, came slowly up. The lady wrote the number of yards, the name of the goods, her own number, the price, the amount of the bank-note I handed her, and some other matters, probably the color of my eyes, and the direction and velocity of the wind, on a slip of paper. She then copied all this in a little book which she kept by her. Then she handed the slip of paper, the money, and the Turkey red to the yellow-haired girl. This young girl copied the slip in a little book she carried, and then she went away with the calico, the paper slip, and the money.

After a very long time,—during which the little girl probably took the goods, the money, and the slip to some central desk, where the note was received, its amount and number entered in a book, change given to the girl, a copy of the slip made and entered, girl's entry examined and approved, goods wrapped up, girl registered, plaits counted and entered on a slip of paper and copied by the girl in her book, girl taken to a hydrant and washed, number of towel entered on a paper slip and copied by the girl in her book, value of my note and amount of change branded somewhere on the child, and said process noted on a slip of paper and copied in her book,—the girl came to me, bringing my change and the package of Turkey red calico.

I had time for but very little work at the office that afternoon, and when I reached home, I handed the package of calico to my wife. She unrolled it and exclaimed:

"Why, this don't match the piece I gave you!"

"Match it!" I cried. "Oh, no! it don't match it. You didn't want that matched. You were mistaken. What you wanted was Turkey red—third counter to the left. I mean, Turkey red is what they use."

My wife looked at me in amazement, and then I detailed to her my troubles.

"Well," said she, "this Turkey red is a great deal prettier than what I had, and you've got so much of it that I needn't use the other at all. I wish I had thought of Turkey red before."

"I wish from my heart you had," said I.

ANDREW SCOGGIN

MR. DOOLEY ON THE GAME OF FOOTBALL

By Finley Peter Dunne

WHIN I was a young man,' said Mr. Dooley, 'an' that was a long time ago—but not so long ago as manny iv me inimies'd like to believe, if I had anny inimies—I played fut-ball, but 'twas not th' fut-ball I see whin th' Brothers' school an' th' Saint Aloysius Tigers played las' week on th' pee-raries.

'Whin I was a la-ad, iv a Sundah afthernoon we'd get out in th' field where th' oats'd been cut away, an' we'd choose up sides. Wan cap'n'd pick one man, an' th' other another. "I choose Dooley," "I choose O'Connor," "I choose Dimpsey," "I choose Riordan," an' so on till there was twinty-five or thirty on a side. Thin wan cap'n'd kick th' ball, an' all our side'd r-run at it an' kick it back; an' thin wan iv th' other side'd kick it to us, an' afther awhile th' game'd get so timpischous that all th' la-ads iv both sides'd be in wan pile, kickin' away at wan or th' other or at th' ball or at th' impire, who was mos'ly a la-ad that cudden't play an' that come out less able to play thin he was whin he wint in. An', if anny wan laid hands on th' ball, he was kicked be ivry wan else an' be th' impire. We played fr'm noon till dark, an' kicked th' ball all th' way home in the moonlight.

'That was futball, an' I was a great wan to play it. I'd think nawthin' iv histin' th' ball two hundherd feet in th' air, an' wanst I give it such a boost that I stove in th' ribs iv th' Prowtestant minister—bad luck to him, he was a kind man—that was lookin' on fr'm a hedge. I was th' finest player in th' whole country, I was so.

'But this here game that I've been seein' ivry time th' pagan fistival iv Thanksgivin' comes arround, sure it ain't th' game I played. I seen th' Dorgan la-ad comin' up th' sthreet yesterdah in his futball clothes—a pair iv matthresses on his legs, a pillow behind, a mask over his nose, an' a bushel measure iv hair on his head. He was followed be three men with bottles, Dr. Ryan, an' th' Dorgan fam'ly. I jined them. They was a big crowd on th' peerary—a bigger crowd than ye cud get to go f're to see a prize fight. Both sides had their frinds that give th' colledge cries. Says wan crowd: "Take an ax, an ax, an ax to thim. Hooroo, hooroo, hellabaloo. Christyan Bro-others!" an' th' other says, "Hit thim, saw thim, gnaw thim, chaw thim, Saint Aloysius!" Well, afther awhile they got down to wur-ruk. "Sivin, eighteen, two, four," says a la-ad. I've seen people go mad over figures durin' th' free silver campaign, but I niver see figures make a man want f'r to go out an' kill his fellow-men befure. But these here figures had th' same effect on th' la-ads that a mintion iv Lord Castlereagh'd have on their fathers. Wan la-ad hauled off, an' give a la-ad acrost fr'm him a punch in th' stomach. His frind acrost th' way caught him in th' ear. Th' cinter rush iv th' Saint Aloysiuses took a runnin' jump at th' left lung iv wan iv th' Christyan Brothers, an' wint to th' grass with him. Four Christyan Brothers leaped most crooly at four Saint Aloysiuses, an' rolled thim. Th' cap'n iv th' Saint Aloysiuses he took th' cap'n iv th' Christyan Brothers be th' legs, an' he pounded th' pile with him as I've seen a section hand tamp th' thrack. All this time young Dorgan was standin' back, takin' no hand in th' affray. All iv a suddent he give a cry iv rage, an' jumped feet foremost into th' pile. "Down!" says th' impire. "Faith, they are all iv that," says I. "Will iver they get up?" "They will," says ol' man Dorgan. "Ye can't stop thim," says he.

'It took some time f'r to pry thim off. Near ivry man iv th' Saint Aloysiuses was tied in a knot around wan iv th' Christyan Brothers. On'y wan iv them remained on th' field. He was lyin' face down, with his nose in th' mud. "He's kilt," says I. "I think he is," says Dorgan, with a merry smile. " 'Twas my boy Jimmy done it, too," says he. "He'll be arrested f'r murdher," says I. "He will not," says he. "There's on'y wan polisman in town cud take him, an' he's down town doin' th' same f'r somebody," he says. Well, they carried th' corpse to th' side, an' took th' ball out iv' his stomach with a monkey wrinch, an' th' game was ray-shumed. "Sivin, sixteen, eight, eleven," says Saint Aloysius; an' young Dorgan started to run down th' field. They was another young la-ad r-runnin' in fr-front iv Dorgan; an' as fast as wan iv th' Christyan Brothers come up an' got in th' way, this here young Saint Aloysius grabbed him be th' hair iv th' head an' th' sole iv th' fut, an' thrun him over his shoulder. "What's that la-ad doin'?" says I. "Interferin'," says he. "I shud think he was," says I, "an' most impudent," I says. " 'Tis such interference as this," I says, "that breaks up fam'lies"; an' I come away.

' 'Tis a noble sport, an' I'm glad to see us Irish ar-re gettin' into it. Whin we larn it thruly, we'll teach thim colledge joods fr'm th' pie belt a thrick or two.'

'We have already,' said Mr. Hennessy. 'They'se a team up in Wisconsin with a la-ad be th' name iv Jeremiah

Riordan f'r cap'n an' wan named Patsy O'Dea behind him. They come down here, an' bate th' la-ads fr'm th' Chacawgo Colledge down be th' Midway.'

'Iv coorse, they did,' said Mr. Dooley. 'Iv coorse, they did. An' they cud bate anny collection iv Baptists that iver come out iv a tank.'

PIGS IS PIGS

By Ellis Parker Butler

MIKE FLANNERY, the Westcote agent of the Interurban Express Company, leaned over the counter of the express office and shook his fist. Mr. Morehouse, angry and red, stood on the other side of the counter, trembling with rage. The argument had been long and heated, and at last Mr. Morehouse had talked himself speechless. The cause of the trouble stood on the counter between the two men. It was a soap box across the top of which were nailed a number of strips, forming a rough but serviceable cage. In it two spotted guinea-pigs were greedily eating lettuce leaves.

"Do as you loike, then!" shouted Flannery, "pay for thim an' take thim, or don't pay for thim and leave thim be. Rules is rules, Misther Morehouse, an' Mike Flannery's not goin' to be called down fer breakin of thim."

"But, you everlastingly stupid idiot!" shouted Mr. Morehouse, madly shaking a flimsy printed book beneath the agent's nose, "Can't you read it here—in your own plain printed rates? 'Pets, domestic, Franklin to Westcote, if properly boxed, twenty-five cents each.'" He threw the book on the counter in disgust. "What more do you want? Aren't they pets? Aren't they domestic? Aren't they properly boxed? What?"

He turned and walked back and forth rapidly, frowning ferociously.

Suddenly he turned to Flannery, and forcing his voice to an artificial calmness spoke slowly but with intense sarcasm.

"Pets," he said. "P-e-t-s! Twenty-five cents each. There are two of them. One! Two! Two times twenty-five are fifty! Can you understand that? I offer you fifty cents."

Flannery reached for the book. He ran his hand through the pages and stopped at page sixty-four.

"An' I don't take fifty cints," he whispered in mockery. "Here's the rule for ut. 'Whin the agint be in anny doubt regardin' which of two rates applies to a shipment, he shall charge the larger. The consign-ey may file a claim for the overcharge.' In this case, Misther Morehouse, I be in doubt. Pets thim animals may be, an' domestic they be, but pigs I'm blame sure they do be, an' me rules says plain as the nose on yer face, 'Pigs Franklin to Westcote, thirty cints each.' An', Misther Morehouse, by me arithetical knowledge two times thirty comes to sixty cints."

Mr. Morehouse shook his head savagely. "Nonsense!" he shouted, "confounded nonsense, I tell you! Why, you poor ignorant foreigner, that rule means common pigs, domestic pigs, not guinea-pigs!"

Flannery was stubborn.

"Pigs is pigs," he declared firmly. "Guinea-pigs, or dago pigs or Irish pigs is all the same to the Interurban Express Company an' to Mike Flannery. Th' nationality of the pig creates no differentiality in the rate, Misther Morehouse! 'Twould be the same was they Dutch pigs or Rooshun pigs. Mike Flannery," he added, "is here to tind to the expriss business and not to hould conversation wid dago pigs in sivinteen languages fer to discover be they Chinese or Tipperary by birth an' nativity."

Mr. Morehouse hesitated. He bit his lip and then flung out his arms wildly.

"Very well!" he shouted, "you shall hear of this! Your president shall hear of this! It is an outrage! I have offered you fifty cents. You refuse it! Keep the pigs until you are ready to take the fifty cents, but, by George, sir, if one hair of those pigs' heads is harmed I will have the law on you!"

He turned and stalked out, slamming the door. Flannery carefully lifted the soap box from the counter and placed it in a corner. He was not worried. He felt the peace that comes to a faithful servant who has done his duty and done it well.

Mr. Morehouse went home raging. His boy, who had been awaiting the guinea-pigs, knew better than to ask him for them. He was a normal boy and therefore always had a guilty conscience when his father was angry. So the boy slipped quietly around the house. There is nothing so soothing to a guilty conscience as to be out of the path of the avenger.

Mr. Morehouse stormed into the house. "Where's the ink?" he shouted at his wife as soon as his foot was across the doorsill.

Mrs. Morehouse jumped guiltily. She never used ink. She had not seen the ink, nor moved the ink, nor thought of the ink, but her husband's tone convicted her of the guilt of having borne and reared a boy, and she knew that whenever her husband wanted anything in a loud voice the boy had been at it.

"I'll find Sammy," she said meekly.

When the ink was found Mr. Morehouse wrote rapidly, and he read the completed letter and smiled a triumphant smile.

"That will settle that crazy Irishman!" he exclaimed. "When they get that letter he will hunt another job, all right!"

A week later Mr. Morehouse received a long official envelope with the card of the Interurban Express Company in the upper left corner. He tore it open eagerly and drew out a sheet of paper. At the top it bore the number A6754. The letter was short. "Subject—Rate on guinea-pigs," it said. "Dr. Sir—We are in receipt of your letter regarding rate on guinea-pigs between Franklin and Westcote, addressed to the president of this company. All claims for overcharge should be addressed to the Claims Department."

Mr. Morehouse wrote to the Claims Department. He wrote six pages of choice sarcasm, vituperation and argument, and sent them to the Claims Department.

A few weeks later he received a reply from the Claims Department. Attached to it was his last letter.

"Dr. Sir," said the reply. "Your letter of the 16th inst., addressed to this Department, subject rate on guinea-pigs from Franklin to Westcote, rec'd. We have taken up the matter with out agent at Westcote, and his reply is attached herewith. He informs us that you refused to receive the consignment or to pay the charges. You have therefore no claim against this company, and your letter regarding the proper rate on the consignment should be addressed to our Tariff Department."

Mr. Morehouse wrote to the Tariff Department. He stated his case clearly, and gave his arguments in full, quoting a page or two from the encyclopedia to prove that guinea-pigs were not common pigs.

With the care that characterizes corporations when they are systematically conducted, Mr. Morehouse's letter was numbered, O.K.'d, and started through the regular channels. Duplicate copies of the bill of lading, manifest, Flannery's receipt for the package and several other pertinent papers were pinned to the letter, and they were passed to the head of the Tariff Department.

The head of the Tariff Department put his feet on his desk and yawned. He looked through the papers carelessly.

"Miss Kane," he said to his stenographer, "take this letter. 'Agent, Westcote, N. J. Please advise why consignment referred to in attached papers was refused domestic pet rates.'"

Miss Kane made a series of curves and angles on her note book and waited with pencil poised. The head of the department looked at the papers again.

"Huh! guinea-pigs!" he said. "Probably starved to death by this time! Add this to that letter: 'Give condition of consignment at present.'"

He tossed the papers on to the stenographer's desk, took his feet from his own desk and went out to lunch.

When Mike Flannery received the letter he scratched his head.

"Give prisint condition," he repeated thoughtfully. "Now what do thim clerks be wantin' to know, I wonder! 'Prisint condition,' is ut? Thim pigs, praise St. Patrick, do be in good health, so far as I know, but I niver was no veternairy surgeon to dago pigs. Mebby thim clerks wants me to call in the pig docther an' have their pulses took. Wan thing I do know, howiver, which is, they've glorious appytites for pigs of their soize. Ate? They'd ate the brass padlocks off of a barn door! If the paddy pig, by the same token, ate as hearty as these dago pigs do, there'd be a famine in Ireland."

To assure himself that his report would be up to date, Flannery went to the rear of the office and looked into the cage. The pigs had been transferred to a larger box—a dry goods box.

"Wan,—two,—t'ree,—four,—foive,—six,—sivin,—eight!" he counted. "Sivin spotted an' wan all black. All well an' hearty an' all eatin' loike ragin' hippypottymusses." He went back to his desk and wrote.

"Mr. Morgan, Head of Tariff Department," he wrote, "why do I say dago pigs is pigs because they is pigs and will be til you say they ain't which is what the rule book says stop your jollying me you know it as well as I do. As to health they are all well and hoping you are the same. P.S. There are eight now the family increased all good eaters. P.S. I paid out so far two dollars for cabbage which they like shall I put in bill for same what?"

Morgan, head of the Tariff Department, when he received this letter, laughed. He read it again and became serious.

"By George!" he said, "Flannery is right, 'pigs is pigs.' I'll have to get authority on this thing. Meanwhile, Miss Kane, take this letter: 'Agent, Westcote, N. J. Regarding shipment guinea-pigs, File No. A6754. Rule 83, General Instructions to Agents, clearly states that agents shall collect from consignee all costs of provender, etc., etc., required for live stock while in transit or storage. You will proceed to collect same from consignee.'"

Flannery received this letter next morning, and when he read it he grinned.

"Proceed to collect," he said softly. "How thim clerks do loike to be talkin'! *Me* proceed to collect two dollars and twenty-five cints off Misther Morehouse! I wonder do

thim clerks *know* Misther Morehouse? I'll git it! Oh, yes!
'Misther Morehouse, two an' a quarter, plaze.' 'Cert'nly,
me dear frind Flannery. Delighted!' *Not!*"

Flannery drove the express wagon to Mr. Morehouse's
door. Mr. Morehouse answered the bell.

"Ah, ha!" he cried as soon as he saw it was Flannery.
"So you've come to your senses at last, have you? I thought
you would! Bring the box in."

"I hev no box," said Flannery coldly. "I hev a bill agin
Misther John C. Morehouse for two dollars and twenty-five
cints for kebbages aten by his dago pigs. Wud wish to pay
ut?"

"Pay—Cabbages—!" gasped Mr. Morehouse. "Do you
mean to say that two little guinea-pigs——"

"Eight!" said Flannery. "Papa an' mamma an' the six
childer. Eight!"

For answer Mr. Morehouse slammed the door in Flannery's face. Flannery looked at the door reproachfully.

"I take ut the con-*sign*-y don't want to pay for thim kebbages," he said. "If I know signs of refusal, the con-*sign*-y
refuses to pay for wan dang kebbage leaf an' be hanged to
me!"

Mr. Morgan, the head of the Tariff Department, consulted the president of the Interurban Express Company regarding guinea-pigs, as to whether they were pigs or not
pigs. The president was inclined to treat the matter lightly.

"What is the rate on pigs and on pets?" he asked.

"Pigs thirty cents, pets twenty-five," said Morgan.

"Then of course guinea-pigs are pigs," said the president.

"Yes," agreed Morgan. "I look at it that way, too. A thing
that can come under two rates is naturally due to be classed
as the higher. But are guinea-pigs, pigs? Aren't they rabbits?"

"Come to think of it," said the president, "I believe they are more like rabbits. Sort of half-way station between pig and rabbit. I think the question is this—are guinea-pigs of the domestic pig family? I'll ask Professor Gordon. He is an authority on such things. Leave the papers with me."

The president put the papers on his desk and wrote a letter to Professor Gordon. Unfortunately the Professor was in South America collecting zoological specimens, and the letter was forwarded to him by his wife. As the Professor was in the highest Andes, where no white man had ever penetrated, the letter was many months in reaching him. The president forgot the guinea-pigs, Morgan forgot them, Mr. Morehouse forgot them, but Flannery did not. One half of his time he gave to the duties of his agency; the other half was devoted to the guinea-pigs. Long before Professor Gordon received the president's letter Morgan received one from Flannery.

"About them dago pigs," it said, "what shall I do they are great in family life, no race suicide for them, there are thirty-two now shall I sell them do you take this express office for a menagerie, answer quick."

Morgan reached for a telegraph blank and wrote:

"Agent, Westcote. Don't sell pigs."

He then wrote Flannery a letter calling his attention to the fact that the pigs were not the property of the company but were merely being held during a settlement of a dispute ragarding rates. He advised Flannery to take the best possible care of them.

Flannery, letter in hand, looked at the pigs and sighed. The dry goods box cage had become too small. He boarded up twenty feet of the rear of the express office to make a large and airy home for them, and went about his business. He worked with feverish intensity when out on his rounds, for the pigs required attention and took most of his time. Some months later, in desperation, he seized a sheet of paper and wrote "160" across it and mailed it to Morgan. Morgan returned it asking for explanation. Flannery replied:

"There be now one hundred sixty of them dago pigs, for heaven's sake let me sell off some, do you want me to go crazy, what?"

"Sell no pigs," Morgan wired.

Not long after this the president of the express company received a letter from Professor Gordon. It was a long and scholarly letter, but the point was that the guinea-pig was the *Cavia aparoea,* while the common pig was the genus *Sus* of the family *Suidae.* He remarked that they were prolific and multiplied rapidly.

"They are not pigs," said the president, decidedly, to Morgan. "The twenty-five cent rate applies."

Morgan made the proper notation on the papers that had accumulated in File A6754, and turned them over to the Audit Department. The Audit Department took some time to look the matter up, and after the usual delay wrote Flannery that as he had on hand one hundred and sixty guinea-pigs, the property of consignee, he should deliver them and collect charges at the rate of twenty-five cents each.

Flannery spent a day herding his charges through a narrow opening in their cage so that he might count them.

"Audit Dept." he wrote, when he had finished the count, "you are way off there may be was one hundred and sixty dago pigs once, but wake up don't be a back number. I've got even eight hundred now shall I collect for eight hundred or what, how about sixty-four dollars I paid out for cabbages."

It required a great many letters back and forth before the Audit Department was able to understand why the error had been made of billing one hundred and sixty instead of eight hundred, and still more time for it to get the meaning of the "cabbages."

Flannery was crowded into a few feet at the extreme front of the office. The pigs had all the rest of the room and two boys were employed constantly attending to them. The day after Flannery had counted the guinea-pigs there were eight more added to his drove, and by the time the Audit Department gave him authority to collect for eight hundred Flannery had given up all attempts to attend to the receipt or the delivery of goods. He was hastily building galleries around the express office, tier above tier. He had four thousand and sixty-four guinea-pigs to care for. More were arriving daily.

Immediately following its authorization the Audit Department sent another letter, but Flannery was to busy to open it. They wrote another and then they telegraphed:

"Error in guinea-pig bill. Collect for two guinea-pigs, fifty cents. Deliver all to consignee."

Flannery read the telegram and cheered up. He wrote out a bill as rapidly as his pencil could travel over paper and ran all the way to the Morehouse home. At the gate he stopped suddenly. The house stared at him with vacant eyes. The windows were bare of curtains and he could see into the empty rooms. A sign on the porch said, "To Let." Mr. Morehouse had moved! Flannery ran all the way back to the express office. Sixty-nine guinea-pigs had been born during his absence. He ran out again and made feverish inquiries in the village. Mr. Morehouse had not only moved, but he had left Westcote. Flannery returned to the express office and found that two hundred and six guinea-pigs had entered the world since he left it. He wrote a telegram to the Audit Department.

"Can't collect fifty cents for two dago pigs consignee has left town address unknown what shall I do? Flannery."

The telegram was handed to one of the clerks in the Audit Department, and as he read it he laughed.

"Flannery must be crazy. He ought to know that the thing to do is to return the consignment here," said the clerk. He telegraphed Flannery to send the pigs to the main office of the company at Franklin.

When Flannery received the telegram he set to work. The six boys he had engaged to help him also set to work. They worked with the haste of desperate men, making cages out of soap boxes, cracker boxes, and all kinds of boxes, and as fast as the cages were completed they filled them with guinea-pigs and expressed them to Franklin. Day after day the cages of guinea-pigs flowed in a steady stream from Westcote to Franklin, and still Flannery and his six helpers ripped and nailed and packed—relentlessly and feverishly. At the end of the week they had shipped two hundred and eighty cases of guinea-pigs, and there were in the express office seven hundred and four more pigs than when they began packing them.

"Stop sending pigs. Warehouse full," came a telegram to Flannery. He stopped packing only long enough to wire back, "Can't stop," and kept on sending them. On the next train up from Franklin came one of the company's inspectors. He had instructions to stop the stream of guinea-pigs at all hazards. As his train drew up at Westcote station he saw a cattle-car standing on the express company's siding. When he reached the express office he saw the express wagon backed up to the door. Six boys were carrying bushel baskets full of guinea-pigs from the office and dumping them into the wagon. Inside the room Flannery, with his coat and vest off, was shoveling guinea-pigs into bushel baskets with a coal scoop. He was winding up the guinea-pig episode.

He looked up at the inspector with a snort of anger.

"Wan wagonload more an' I'll be quit of thim, an' niver will ye catch Flannery wid no more foreign pigs on his hands. No, sur! They near was the death o' me. Nixt toime I'll know that pigs of whativer nationality is domestic pets—an' go at the lowest rate."

He began shoveling again rapidly, speaking quickly between breaths.

"Rules may be rules, but you can't fool Mike Flannery twice wid the same thrick—whin ut comes to live stock, dang the rules. So long as Flannery runs this expriss office —pigs is pets—an' cows is pets—an' horses is pets—an' lions an' tigers an' Rocky Mountain goats is pets—an' the rate on thim is twinty-foive cints."

He paused long enough to let one of the boys put an empty basket in the place of the one he had just filled. There were only a few guinea-pigs left. As he noted their limited number his natural habit of looking on the bright side returned.

"Well, annyhow," he said cheerfully, " 'tis not so bad as ut might be. What if thim dago pigs had been elephants!"

THE RANSOM OF RED CHIEF

By O. Henry

It looked like a good thing; but wait till I tell you. We were down South, in Alabama—Bill Driscoll and myself—when this kidnapping idea struck us. It was, as Bill afterward expressed it, "during a moment of temporary mental apparition"; but we didn't find that out till later.

There was a town down there, as flat as a flannel-cake, and called Summit, of course. It contained inhabitants of as undeleterious and self-satisfied a class of peasantry as ever clustered around a May-pole.

Bill and me had a joint capital of about six hundred dollars, and we needed just two thousand dollars more to pull off a fraudulent town-lot scheme in Western Illinois with. We talked it over on the front steps of the hotel. Philoprogenitiveness, says we, is strong in semi-rural communities; therefore, and for other reasons, a kidnapping project ought to do better there than in the radius of newspapers that send reporters out in plain clothes to stir up talk about such things. We knew that Summit couldn't get after us with anything stronger than constables, and, maybe, some lackadaisical bloodhounds and a diatribe or two in the *Weekly Farmers' Budget*. So, it looked good.

We selected for our victim the only child of a prominent citizen named Ebenezer Dorset. The father was respectable and tight, a mortgage fancier and a stern, upright collection-plate passer and forecloser. The kid was a boy of ten, with bas-relief freckles, and hair the colour of the cover of the magazine you buy at the news-stand when you want to catch a train. Bill and me figured that Ebenezer would melt down for a ransom of two thousand dollars to a cent. But wait till I tell you.

About two miles from Summit was a little mountain, covered with a dense cedar brake. On the rear elevation of this mountain was a cave. There we stored provisions.

One evening after sundown, we drove in a buggy past old Dorset's house. The kid was in the street, throwing rocks at a kitten on the opposite fence.

"Hey, little boy!" says Bill, "would you like to have a bag of candy and a nice ride?"

The boy catches Bill neatly in the eye with a piece of brick.

"That will cost the old man an extra five hundred dollars," says Bill, climbing over the wheel.

That boy put up a fight like a welter-weight cinnamon bear; but, at last, we got him down in the bottom of the buggy and drove away. We took him up to the cave, and I hitched the horse in the cedar brake. After dark I drove the buggy to the little village, three miles away, where we had hired it, and walked back to the mountain.

Bill was pasting court-plaster over the scratches and bruises on his features. There was a fire burning behind the big rock at the entrance of the cave, and the boy was watching a pot of boiling coffee, with two buzzard tail feathers stuck in his red hair. He points a stick at me when I come up, and says:

"Ha! cursed paleface, do you dare to enter the camp of Red Chief, the terror of the plains?"

"He's all right now," says Bill, rolling up his trousers and examining some bruises on his shins. "We're playing Indian. We're making Buffalo Bill's show look like magic-lantern views of Palestine in the town hall. I'm Old Hank, the Trapper, Red Chief's captive, and I'm to be scalped at daybreak. By Geronimo! that kid can kick hard."

Yes, sir, that boy seemed to be having the time of his life. The fun of camping out in a cave had made him forget that he was a captive himself. He immediately christened me Snake-eye, the Spy, and announced that, when his braves returned from the warpath, I was to be broiled at the stake at the rising of the sun.

Then we had supper; and he filled his mouth full of bacon and bread and gravy, and began to talk. He made a during-dinner speech something like this:

"I like this fine. I never camped out before; but I had a pet 'possum once, and I was nine last birthday. I hate to go to school. Rats ate up sixteen of Jimmy Talbot's aunt's speckled hen's eggs. Are there any real Indians in these woods? I want some more gravy. Does the trees moving make the wind blow? We had five puppies. What makes your nose so red, Hank? My father has lots of money. Are the stars hot? I whipped Ed Walker twice, Saturday. I don't like girls. You dassent catch toads unless with a string. Do oxen make any noise? Why are oranges round? Have you got beds to sleep on in this cave? Amos Murray has got six toes. A parrot can talk, but a monkey or a fish can't. How many does it take to make twelve?"

Every few minutes he would remember that he was a pesky redskin, and pick up his stick rifle and tiptoe to the mouth of the cave to rubber for the scouts of the hated paleface. Now and then he would let out a war-whoop that made Old Hank the Trapper shiver. That boy had Bill terrorized from the start.

"Red Chief," says I to the kid, "would you like to go home?"

"Aw, what for?" says he. "I don't have any fun at home. I hate to go to school. I like to camp out. You won't take me back home again, Snake-eye, will you?"

"Not right away," says I. "We'll stay here in the cave a while."

"All right!" says he. "That'll be fine. I never had such fun in all my life."

We went to bed about eleven o'clock. We spread down some wide blankets and quilts and put Red Chief between us. We weren't afraid he'd run away. He kept us awake for three hours, jumping up and reaching for his rifle and screeching: "Hist! pard," in mine and Bill's ears, as the fancied crackle of a twig or the rustle of a leaf revealed to his young imagination the stealthy approach of the outlaw band. At last, I fell into a troubled sleep, and dreamed that I had been kidnapped and chained to a tree by a ferocious pirate with red hair.

Just at daybreak, I was awakened by a series of awful screams from Bill. They weren't yells, or howls, or shouts, or whoops, or yawps, such as you'd expect from a manly set of vocal organs—they were simply indecent, terrifying, humiliating screams, such as women emit when they see ghosts or caterpillars. It's an awful thing to hear a strong, desperate, fat man scream incontinently in a cave at daybreak.

I jumped up to see what the matter was. Red Chief was sitting on Bill's chest, with one hand twined in Bill's hair. In the other he had the sharp case-knife we used for slicing bacon; and he was industriously and realistically trying to take Bill's scalp, according to the sentence that had been pronounced upon him the evening before.

I got the knife away from the kid and made him lie down again. But, from that moment, Bill's spirit was broken. He laid down on his side of the bed, but he never closed an eye again in sleep as long as that boy was with us. I dozed off for a while, but along toward sun-up I remembered that Red Chief had said I was to be burned at the stake at the rising of the sun. I wasn't nervous or afraid; but I sat up and lit my pipe and leaned against a rock.

"What you getting up so soon for, Sam?" asked Bill.

"Me?" says I. "Oh, I got a kind of a pain in my shoulder. I thought sitting up would rest it."

"You're a liar!" says Bill. "You're afraid. You was to be burned at sunrise, and you was afraid he'd do it. And he would, too, if he could find a match. Ain't it awful, Sam? Do you think anybody will pay out money to get a little imp like that back home?"

"Sure," said I. "A rowdy kid like that is just the kind that parents dote on. Now, you and the Chief get up and cook breakfast, while I go up on the top of this mountain and reconnoitre."

I went up on the peak of the little mountain and ran my eye over the contiguous vicinity. Over toward Summit I expected to see the sturdy yeomanry of the village armed with scythes and pitchforks beating the countryside for the dastardly kidnappers. But what I saw was a peaceful land-scape dotted with one man ploughing with a dun mule. Nobody was dragging the creek; no couriers dashed hither and yon, bringing tidings of no news to the distracted parents. There was a sylvan attitude of somnolent sleepiness pervading that section of the external outward surface of Alabama that lay exposed to my view. "Perhaps," says I to myself, "it has not yet been discovered that the wolves have borne away the tender lambkin from the fold. Heaven help the wolves!" says I, and I went down the mountain to breakfast.

When I got to the cave I found Bill backed up against the side of it, breathing hard, and the boy threatening to smash him with a rock half as big as a cocoanut.

"He put a red-hot boiled potato down my back," explained Bill, "and then mashed it with his foot; and I boxed his ears. Have you got a gun about you, Sam?"

I took the rock away from the boy and kind of patched up the argument. "I'll fix you," says the kid to Bill. "No man ever yet struck the Red Chief but what he got paid for it. You better beware!"

After breakfast the kid takes a piece of leather with strings wrapped around it out of his pocket and goes outside the cave unwinding it.

"What's he up to now?" says Bill anxiously. "You don't think he'll run away, do you, Sam?"

"No fear of it," says I. "He don't seem to be much of a home body. But we've got to fix up some plan about the ransom. There don't seem to be much excitement around Summit on account of his disappearance; but maybe they haven't realized yet that he's gone. His folks may think he's spending the night with Aunt Jane or one of the neighbours. Anyhow, he'll be missed today. Tonight we must get a message to his father demanding the two thousand dollars for his return."

Just then we heard a kind of war-whoop, such as David might have emitted when he knocked out the champion Goliath. It was a sling that Red Chief had pulled out of his pocket, and he was whirling it around his head.

I dodged, and heard a heavy thud and a kind of a sigh from Bill, like a horse gives out when you take his saddle off. A niggerhead rock the size of an egg had caught Bill just behind his left ear. He loosened himself all over and fell in the fire across the frying pan of hot water for washing the dishes. I dragged him out and poured cold water on his head for half an hour.

By and by, Bill sits up and feels behind his ear and says: "Sam, do you know who my favourite Biblical character is?"

"Take it easy," says I. "You'll come to your senses presently."

"King Herod," says he. "You won't go away and leave me here alone, will you, Sam?"

I went out and caught that boy and shook him until his freckles rattled.

"If you don't behave," says I, "I'll take you straight home. Now, are you going to be good, or not?"

"I was only funning," says he sullenly. "I didn't mean to hurt Old Hank. But what did he hit me for? I'll behave, Snake-eye, if you won't send me home, and if you'll let me play the Black Scout today."

"I don't know the game," says I. "That's for you and Mr. Bill to decide. He's your playmate for the day. I'm going away for a while, on business. Now, you come in and make friends with him and say you are sorry for hurting him, or home you go, at once."

I made him and Bill shake hands, and then I took Bill aside and told him I was going to Poplar Cove, a little village three miles from the cave, and find out what I could about how the kidnapping had been regarded in Summit. Also, I thought it best to send a peremptory letter to old man Dorset that day, demanding the ransom and dictating how it should be paid.

"You know, Sam," says Bill, "I've stood by you without batting an eye in earthquakes, fire, and flood—in poker games, dynamite outrages, police raids, train robberies, and cyclones. I never lost my nerve yet till we kidnapped that two-legged skyrocket of a kid. He's got me going. You won't leave me long with him, will you, Sam?"

"I'll be back some time this afternoon," says I. "You must keep the boy amused and quiet till I return. And now we'll write the letter to old Dorset."

Bill and I got paper and pencil and worked on the letter while Red Chief, with a blanket wrapped around him, strutted up and down, guarding the mouth of the cave. Bill begged me tearfully to make the ransom fifteen hundred dollars instead of two thousand. "I ain't attempting," says he, "to decry the celebrated moral aspect of parental affection, but we're dealing with humans, and it ain't human for anybody to give up two thousand dollars for that forty-pound chunk of freckled wildcat. I'm willing to take a chance at fifteen hundred dollars. You can charge the difference up to me."

So, to relieve Bill, I acceded, and we collaborated a letter that ran this way:

Ebenezer Dorset, Esq.:

We have your boy concealed in a place far from Summit. It is useless for you or the most skilled detectives to attempt to find him. Absolutely, the only terms on which you can have him restored to you are these: We demand fifteen hundred dollars in large bills for his return: the money to be left at midnight at the same spot and in the same box as your reply—as hereinafter described. If you agree to these terms, send your answer in writing by a solitary messenger tonight at half-past eight o'clock. After crossing Owl Creek, on the road to Poplar Cove, there are three large trees about a hundred yards apart, close to the fence of the wheat field on the right-hand side. At the bottom of the fence-post

opposite the third tree, will be found a small pasteboard
box.

The messenger will place the answer in this box and return immediately to Summit.

If you attempt any treachery or fail to comply with our
demand as stated, you will never see your boy again.

If you pay the money as demanded, he will be returned
to you safe and well within three hours. These terms are
final, and if you do not accede to them no further com-
munication will be attempted.

TWO DESPERATE MEN.

I addressed this letter to Dorset, and put it in my pocket.
As I was about to start, the kid comes up to me and says:

"Aw, Snake-eye, you said I could play the Black Scout
while you was gone."

"Play it, of course," says I. "Mr. Bill will play with you.
What kind of a game is it?"

"I'm the Black Scout," says the Red Chief, "and I have
to ride to the stockade to warn the settlers that the Indians
are coming. I'm tired of playing Indian myself. I want
to be the Black Scout."

"All right," says I. "It sounds harmless to me. I guess
Mr. Bill will help you foil the pesky savages."

"What am I to do?" asks Bill, looking at the kid suspiciously.

"You are the hoss," says Black Scout. "Get down on your
hands and knees. How can I ride to the stockade without
a hoss?"

"You'd better keep him interested," said I, "till we get
the scheme going. Loosen up."

Bill gets down on his all fours, and a look comes in his
eye like a rabbit's when you catch it in a trap.

"How far is it to the stockade, kid?" he asks, in a husky manner of voice.

"Ninety miles," says the Black Scout. "And you have to hump yourself to get there on time. Whoa, now!"

The Black Scout jumps on Bill's back and digs his heels in his side.

"For Heaven's sake," says Bill, "hurry back, Sam, as soon as you can. I wish we hadn't made the ransom more than a thousand. Say, you quit kicking me or I'll get up and warm you good."

I walked over to Poplar Cove and sat around the post-office and store, talking with the chawbacons that came in to trade. One whiskerando says that he hears Summit is all upset on account of Elder Ebenezer Dorset's boy having been lost or stolen. That was all I wanted to know. I bought some smoking tobacco, referred casually to the price of black-eyed peas, posted my letter surreptitiously and came away. The postmaster said the mail-carrier would come by in an hour to take the mail on to Summit.

When I got back to the cave Bill and the boy were not to be found. I explored the vicinity of the cave, and risked a yodel or two, but there was no response.

So I lighted my pipe and sat down on a mossy bank to await developments.

In about half an hour I heard the bushes rustle, and Bill wobbled out into the little glade in front of the cave. Behind him was the kid, stepping softly like a scout, with a broad grin on his face. Bill stopped, took off his hat and wiped his face with a red handkerchief. The kid stopped about eight feet behind him.

"Sam," says Bill, "I suppose you think I'm a renegade, but I couldn't help it. I'm a grown person with masculine proclivities and habits of self-defense, but there is a time when all systems of egotism and predominance fail. The boy is gone. I have sent him home. All is off. There was martyrs in old times," goes on Bill, "that suffered death rather than give up the particular graft they enjoyed. None of 'em ever was subjugated to such supernatural tortures as I have been. I tried to be faithful to our articles of depredation; but there came a limit."

"What's the trouble, Bill?" I asks him.

"I was rode," says Bill, "the ninety miles to the stockade, not barring an inch. Then, when the settlers was rescued, I was given oats. Sand ain't a palatable substitute. And then, for an hour I had to try to explain to him why there was nothin' in holes, how a road can run both ways and what makes the grass green. I tell you, Sam, a human can only stand so much. I takes him by the neck of his clothes and drags him down the mountain. On the way he kicks my legs black-and-blue from the knees down; and I've got to have two or three bites on my thumb and hand cauterized.

"But he's gone"—continues Bill—"gone home. I showed him the road to Summit and kicked him about eight feet nearer there at one kick. I'm sorry we lose the ransom; but it was either that or Bill Driscoll to the madhouse."

Bill is puffing and blowing, but there is a look of ineffable peace and growing content on his rose-pink features.

"Bill," says I, "there isn't any heart disease in your family, is there?"

"No," says Bill, "nothing chronic except malaria and accidents. Why?"

"Then you might turn around," says I, "and have a look behind you."

Bill turns and sees the boy, and loses his complexion and sits down plump on the ground and begins to pluck aim-

lessly at grass and little sticks. For an hour I was afraid
of his mind. And then I told him that my scheme was to
put the whole job through immediately and that we would
get the ransom and be off with it by midnight if old Dorset
fell in with our proposition. So Bill braced up enough to
give the kid a weak sort of a smile and a promise to play
the Russian in a Japanese war with him as soon as he felt
a little better.

I had a scheme for collecting that ransom without dan‚
ger of being caught by counterplots that ought to commend
itself to professional kidnappers. The tree under which the
answer was to be left—and the money later on—was close
to the road fence with big, bare fields on all sides. If a
gang of constables should be watching for any one to come
for the note they could see him a long way off crossing the
fields or in the road. But no, sirree! At half-past eight I
was up in that tree as well hidden as a tree toad, waiting
for the messenger to arrive.

Exactly on time, a half-grown boy rides up the road
on a bicycle, locates the pasteboard box at the foot of the
fence-post, slips a folded piece of paper into it and pedals
away again back toward Summit.

I waited an hour and then concluded the thing was
square. I slid down the tree, got the note, slipped along
the fence till I struck the woods, and was back at the cave
in another half an hour. I opened the note, got near the
lantern and read it to Bill. It was written with a pen in a
crabbed hand, and the sum and substance of it was this:

Two Desperate Men.

Gentlemen: I received your letter today by post, in re‚
gard to the ransom you ask for the return of my son. I think
you are a little high in your demands, and I hereby make
you a counter-proposition, which I am inclined to believe

you will accept. You bring Johnny home and pay me two hundred and fifty dollars in cash, and I agree to take him off your hands. You had better come at night, for the neighbours believe he is lost, and I couldn't be responsible for what they would do to anybody they saw bringing him back.

Very respectfully,
EBENEZER DORSET.

"Great pirates of Penzance!" says I; "of all the impudent——"

But I glanced at Bill, and hesitated. He had the most appealing look in his eyes I ever saw on the face of a dumb or a talking brute.

"Sam," says he, "what's two hundred and fifty dollars, after all? We've got the money. One more night of this kid will send me to bed in Bedlam. Besides being a thorough gentleman, I think Mr. Dorset is a spendthrift for making us such a liberal offer. You ain't going to let the chance go, are you?"

"Tell you the truth, Bill," says I, "this little he ewe lamb has somewhat got on my nerves, too. We'll take him home, pay the ransom, and make our get-away."

We took him home that night. We got him to go by telling him that his father had bought a silver-mounted rifle and a pair of moccasins for him, and we were going to hunt bears the next day.

It was just twelve o'clock when we knocked at Ebenezer's front door. Just at the moment when I should have been abstracting the fifteen hundred dollars from the box under the tree, according to the original proposition, Bill was counting out two hundred and fifty dollars into Dorset's hand.

When the kid found out we were going to leave him at

home he started up a howl like a calliope and fastened himself as tight as a leech to Bill's leg. His father peeled him
away gradually, like a porous plaster.

"How long can you hold him?" asks Bill.

"I'm not as strong as I used to be," says old Dorset, "but
I think I can promise you ten minutes."

"Enough," says Bill. "In ten minutes I shall cross the
Central, Southern, and Middle Western States, and be
legging it trippingly for the Canadian border."

And, as dark as it was, and as fat as Bill was, and as
good a runner as I am, he was a good mile and a half out
of Summit before I could catch up with him.

LITTLE GENTLEMAN

By Booth Tarkington

THE MIDSUMMER sun was stinging hot outside the little barbershop next to the corner drug store and Penrod, undergoing a toilette preliminary to his very slowly approaching twelfth birthday, was adhesive enough to retain upon his face much hair as it fell from the shears. There is a mystery here: the tonsorial processes are not unagreeable to manhood; in truth, they are soothing; but the hairs detached from a boy's head get into his eyes, his ears, his nose, his mouth, and down his neck, and he does everywhere itch excrutiatingly. Wherefore he blinks, winks, weeps, twitches, condenses his countenance, and squirms; and perchance the barber's scissors clip more than intended—belike an outlying flange of ear.

"Um—muh—*ow*!" said Penrod, this thing having happened.

"D'I touch y' up a little?" inquired the barber, smiling falsely.

"Ooh—*uh*!" The boy in the chair offered inarticulate protest, as the wound was rubbed with alum.

"*That* don't hurt!" said the barber. "You *will* get it, though, if you don't sit stiller," he continued, nipping in the bud any attempt on the part of his patient to think that he already had "it."

"Pfuff!" said Penrod, meaning no disrespect, but en
deavouring to dislodge a temporary moustache from his
lip.

"You ought to see how still that little Georgie Bassett
sits," the barber went on, reprovingly. "I hear everybody
says he's the best boy in town."

"Pfuff! *Phirr!*" There was a touch of intentional con-
tempt in this.

"I haven't heard nobody around the neighbourhood
makin' no such remarks," added the barber, "about nobody
of the name of Penrod Schofield."

"Well," said Penrod, clearing his mouth after a struggle,
"who wants 'em to? Ouch!"

"I hear they call Georgie Bassett the 'little gentleman,'"
ventured the barber, provocatively, meeting with instant
success.

"They better not call *me* that," returned Penrod truc-
ulently. "I'd like to hear anybody try. Just once, that's all!
I bet they'd never try it ag—— *Ouch!*"

"Why? What'd you do to 'em?"

"It's all right what I'd *do*! I bet they wouldn't want to
call me that again long as they lived!"

"What'd you do if it was a little girl? You wouldn't hit
her, would you?"

"Well, I'd—— Ouch!"

"You wouldn't hit a little girl, would you?" the barber
persisted, gathering into his powerful fingers a mop of hair
from the top of Penrod's head and pulling that suffering
head into an unnatural position. "Doesn't the Bible say
it ain't never right to hit the weak sex?"

"Ow! *Say,* look *out!*"

"So you'd go and punch a pore, weak, little girl, would
you?" said the barber, reprovingly.

"Well, who said I'd hit her?" demanded the chivalrous Penrod. "I bet I'd *fix* her though, all right. She'd see!"

"You wouldn't call her names, would you?"

"No, I wouldn't! What hurt is it to call anybody names?"

"Is that *so!*" exclaimed the barber. "Then you was intending what I heard you hollering at Fisher's grocery delivery wagon driver fer a favour, the other day when I was goin' by your house, was you? I reckon I better tell him, because he says to me after*werds* if he ever lays eyes on you when you ain't in your own yard, he's goin' to do a whole lot o' things you ain't goin' to like! Yessir, that's what he says to *me!*"

"He better catch me first, I guess, before he talks so much."

"Well," resumed the barber, "that ain't sayin' what you'd do if a young lady ever walked up and called you a little gentleman. I want to hear what you'd do to her. I guess I know, though—come to think of it."

"What?" demanded Penrod.

"You'd sick that pore ole dog of yours on her cat, if she had one, I expect," guessed the barber derisively.

"No, I would not!"

"Well, what *would* you do?"

"I'd do enough. Don't worry about that!"

"Well, suppose it was a boy, then: what'd you do if a boy come up to you and says, 'Hello, little gentleman'?"

"He'd be lucky," said Penrod, with a sinister frown, "if he got home alive."

"Suppose it was a boy twice your size?"

"Just let him try," said Penrod ominously. "You just let him try. He'd never see daylight again; that's all!"

The barber dug ten active fingers into the helpless scalp before him and did his best to displace it, while the anguished Penrod, becoming instantly a seething crucible of emotion, misdirected his natural resentment into maddened brooding upon what he would do to a boy "twice his size" who should dare to call him "little gentleman." The barber shook him as his father had never shaken him; the barber buffeted him, rocked him frantically to and fro; the barber seemed to be trying to wring his neck; and Penrod saw himself in staggering zigzag pictures, destroying large, screaming, fragmentary boys who had insulted him.

The torture stopped suddenly; and clenched, weeping eyes began to see again, while the barber applied cooling lotions which made Penrod smell like a coloured housemaid's ideal.

"Now what," asked the barber, combing the reeking locks gently, "what would it make you so mad fer, to have somebody call you a little gentleman? It's a kind of compliment, as it were, you might say. What would you want to hit anybody fer *that* fer?"

To the mind of Penrod, this question was without meaning or reasonableness. It was within neither his power nor his desire to analyze the process by which the phrase had become offensive to him, and was now rapidly assuming the proportions of an outrage. He knew only that his gorge rose at the thought of it.

"You just let 'em try it!" he said threateningly, as he slid down from the chair. And as he went out of the door, after further conversation on the same subject, he called back those warning words once more: "Just let 'em try it! Just once—that's all *I* ask 'em to. They'll find out what they *get*!"

The barber chuckled. Then a fly lit on the barber's nose and he slapped at it, and the slap missed the fly but did not miss the nose. The barber was irritated. At this moment his birdlike eye gleamed a gleam as it fell upon customers approaching: the prettiest little girl in the world, leading by the hand her baby brother, Mitchy-Mitch, coming to have Mitchy-Mitch's hair clipped, against the heat.

It was a hot day and idle, with little to feed the mind—and the barber was a mischievous man with an irritated nose. He did his worst.

Meanwhile, the brooding Penrod pursued his homeward way; no great distance, but long enough for several one-sided conflicts with malign insulters made of thin air. "You better *not* call me that!" he muttered. "You just try it, and you'll get what other people got when *they* tried it. You better not ack fresh with *me*! Oh, you *will*, will you?" He delivered a vicious kick full upon the shins of an iron fence-post, which suffered little, though Penrod instantly regretted his indiscretion. "Oof!" he grunted, hopping; and went on after bestowing a look of awful hostility upon the fence-post. "I guess you'll know better next time," he said, in parting, to this antagonist. "You just let me catch you around here again and I'll——" His voice sank to inarticulate but ominous murmurings. He was in a dangerous mood.

Nearing home, however, his belligerent spirit was diverted to happier interests by the discovery that some workmen had left a caldron of tar in the cross-street, close by his father's stable. He tested it, but found it inedible. Also, as a substitute for professional chewing-gum it was unsatisfactory, being insufficiently boiled down and too thin, though of a pleasant, lukewarm temperature. But it had an excess of one quality—it was sticky. It was the stickiest tar Penrod had ever used for any purposes whatsoever, and nothing upon which he wiped his hands served to rid them of it; neither his polka-dotted shirt waist nor his knickerbockers; neither the fence, nor even Duke, who came unthinkingly wagging out to greet him, and retired wiser.

Nevertheless, tar is tar. Much can be done with it, no matter what its condition; so Penrod lingered by the caldron, though from a neighbouring yard could be heard the voices of comrades, including that of Sam Williams. On the ground about the caldron were scattered chips and sticks and bits of wood to the number of a great multitude. Penrod mixed quantities of this refuse into the tar, and interested himself in seeing how much of it he could keep moving in slow swirls upon the ebon surface.

Other surprises were arranged for the absent workmen. The caldron was almost full, and the surface of the tar near the rim. Penrod endeavoured to ascertain how many pebbles and brickbats, dropped in, would cause an overflow. Labouring heartily to this end, he had almost accomplished it, when he received the suggestion for an experiment on a much larger scale. Embedded at the corner of a grass-plot across the street was a white-washed stone, the size of a small watermelon and serving no purpose whatever save the questionable one of decoration. It was easily pried up with a stick; though getting it to the caldron tested the full strength of the ardent labourer. Instructed to perform such a task, he would have sincerely maintained its impossibility; but now, as it was unbidden, and promised rather destructive results, he set about it with unconquerable energy, feeling certain that he would be rewarded with a mighty splash. Perspiring, grunting vehemently, his back aching and all muscles strained, he progressed in short stages until the big stone lay at the base of the caldron. He rested a moment, panting, then

lifted the stone, and was bending his shoulders for the
heave that would lift it over the rim, when a sweet,
taunting voice, close behind him, startled him cruelly.

"How do you do, *little gentleman*!"

Penrod squawked, dropped the stone, and shouted,
"Shut up, you dern fool!" purely from instinct, even before his about-face made him aware who had so spitefully
addressed him.

It was Marjorie Jones. Always dainty, and prettily
dressed, she was in speckless and starchy white today, and
a refreshing picture she made, with the new-shorn and
powerfully scented Mitchy-Mitch clinging to her hand.
They had stolen up behind the toiler, and now stood
laughing together in sweet merriment. Since the passing
of Penrod's Rupe Collins period he had experienced some
severe qualms at the recollection of his last meeting with
Marjorie and his Apache behaviour; in truth, his heart
instantly became as wax at sight of her, and he would have
offered her fair speech; but, alas! in Marjorie's wonderful
eyes there shone a consciousness of new powers for his
undoing, and she denied him opportunity.

"Oh, *oh*!" she cried, mocking his pained outcry. "What
a way for a *little gentleman* to talk! Little gentlemen don't
say wicked——"

"Marjorie!" Penrod, enraged and dismayed, felt himself stung beyond all endurance. Insult from her was bit-
terer to endure than from any other. "Don't you call me
that again!"

"Why not, *little gentleman*?"

He stamped his foot. "You better stop!"

Marjorie sent into his furious face her lovely, spiteful
laughter.

"Little gentleman, little gentleman, little gentleman!"

she said deliberately. "How's the little gentleman, this afternoon? Hello, little gentleman!"

Penrod, quite beside himself, danced eccentrically. "Dry up!" he howled. "Dry up, dry up, dry up, dry *up*!"

Mitchy-Mitch shouted with delight and applied a finger to the side of the caldron—a finger immediately snatched away and wiped upon a handkerchief by his fastidious sister.

" 'Ittle gellamun!" said Mitchy-Mitch.

"You better look out!" Penrod whirled upon this small offender with grim satisfaction. Here was at least something male that could without dishonour be held responsible. "You say that again, and I'll give you the worst——"

"You will *not*!" snapped Marjorie, instantly vitriolic. "He'll say just whatever he wants to, and he'll say it just as *much* as he wants to. Say it again, Mitchy-Mitch!"

" 'Ittle gellamun!" said Mitchy-Mitch promptly.

"Ow-*yah*!" Penrod's tone-production was becoming affected by his mental condition. "You say that again, and I'll——"

"Go on, Mitchy-Mitch," cried Marjorie. "He can't do a thing. He don't *dare*! Say it some more, Mitchy-Mitch— say it a whole lot!"

Mitchy-Mitch, his small, fat face shining with confidence in his immunity, complied.

" 'Ittle gellamun!" he squeaked malevolently. " 'Ittle gellamun! 'Ittle gellamun! 'Ittle gellamun!"

The desperate Penrod bent over the whitewashed rock, lifted it, and then—outdoing Porthos, John Ridd, and Ursus in one miraculous burst of strength—heaved it into the air.

Marjorie screamed.

But it was too late. The big stone descended into the

precise midst of the caldron and Penrod got his mighty splash. It was far, far beyond his expectations.

Spontaneously there were grand and awful effects— volcanic spectacles of nightmare and eruption. A black sheet of eccentric shape rose out of the caldron and descended upon the three children, who had no time to evade it.

After it fell, Mitchy-Mitch, who stood nearest the caldron, was the thickest, though there was enough for all. Bre'r Rabbit would have fled from any of them.

THREE WITHOUT, DOUBLED

By RING W. LARDNER

I

THEY ain't no immediate chance o' you gettin' ast out to our house to dinner—not w'ile round steak and General Motors is sellin' at the same price and common dog biscuit's ten cents a loaf. But you might have nothin' decent to do some evenin' and happen to drop in on the Missus and I for a call; so I feel like I ought to give you a little warnin' in case that comes off.

You know they's lots o' words that's called fightin' words. Some o' them starts a brawl, no matter who they're spoke to. You can't call nobody a liar without expectin' to lose a couple o' milk teeth—that is, if the party addressed has got somethin' besides lemon juice in his veins and ain't had the misfortune to fall asleep on the Panhandle tracks and be separated from his most prominent legs and arms. Then they's terms that don't hit you so much yourself, but reflects on your ancestors and prodigies, and you're supposed to resent 'em for the sake of honor and fix the speaker's map so as when he goes home his wife'll say: 'Oh, kiddies! Come and look at the rainbow!'

Then they's other words and terms that you can call 'em to somebody and not get no rise; but call 'em to somebody else and the insurance companies could hold out on your widow by claimin' it was suicide. For instance, they's young Harold Greiner, one o' the bookkeepers down to the office. I could tell him he was an A.P.A. with a few adjectives, and he'd just smile and say: 'Quit your flirtin'!' But I wouldn't never try that expression on Dan Cahill, the elevator starter, without bein' well out of his earshots. And I don't know what it means, at that.

Well, if you do come out to the house they's a term that you want to lay off of when the Missus is in the room. Don't say: 'San Susie!'

It sounds harmless enough, don't it? They ain't nothin' to it even when its transferred over from the Latin, 'Without no cares.' But just leave her hear it mentioned and watch her grab the two deadliest weapons that's within reach, one to use on you or whoever said it, and the other on me, on general principles.

You think I'm stringin' you, and I admit you got cause —that is, till you've heard the details of our latest plunge in the cesspools o' Society.

II

It was a Friday evenin' about three weeks ago when I come home and found the Wife quaverin' with excitement.

'Who do you think called up?' she ast me.

'I got no idear,' I says.

'Guess!' says she.

So I had to guess.

'Josephus Daniels,' I says. 'Or Henry Ford. Or maybe it was that guy with the scar on his lip that you thought was smilin' at you the other day.'

'You couldn't never guess,' she says. 'It was Mrs. Messenger.'

'Which one?' I ast her. 'You can't mean Mrs. A. D. T. Messenger.'

'If you're so cute I won't tell you nothin' about it,' says she.

'Don't make no rash threats,' I says. 'You're goin' to tell me some time and they's no use makin' yourself sick by tryin' to hold it in.'

'You know very well what Mrs. Messenger I mean,' she says. 'It was Mrs. Robert Messenger that's husband owns this buildin' and the one at the corner, where they live at.'

'Haven't you paid the rent?' I says.

'Do you think a woman like Mrs. Messenger would be buttin' into her husband's business?' says the Missus.

'I don't know what kind of a woman Mrs. Messenger is,' I says. 'But if I owned these here apartments and somebody fell behind in their rent, I wouldn't be surprised to see the owner's wife goin' right over to their flat and takin' it out o' their trousers pocket.'

'Well,' says the Wife, 'we don't owe them no rent and that wasn't what she called up about. It wasn't no business call.'

'Go ahead and spill it,' I says. 'My heart's weak.'

'Well,' she says, 'I was just gettin' through with the lunch dishes and the phone rang.'

'I bet you wondered who it was,' says I.

'I thought it was Mrs. Hatch or somebody,' says the Wife. 'So I run to the phone and it was Mrs. Messenger. So the first thing she says was to explain who she was— just like I didn't know. And the next thing she ast was did I play bridge.'

'And what did you tell her?' says I.

'What do you think I'd tell her?' says the Missus. 'I told her yes.'

'Wasn't you triflin' a little with the truth?' I ast her.

'Certainly not!' she says. 'Haven't I played twice over to Hatches?' So then she ast me if my husband played bridge, too. And I told her yes, he did.'

'What was the idear?' I says. 'You know I didn't never play it in my life.'

'I don't know no such a thing,' she says. 'For all as I know, you may play all day down to the office.'

'No,' I says; 'we spend all our time down there playin' postoffice with the scrubwomen.'

'Well, anyway, I told her you did,' says the Missus. 'Don't you see they wasn't nothin' else I could tell her, because if I told her you didn't that would of ended it.'

'Ended what?' I says.

'We wouldn't of been ast to the party,' says the Missus.

'Who told you they was goin' to be a party?' I says.

'I don't have to be told everything,' says the Missus. 'I got brains enough to know that Mrs. Messenger ain't callin' me up and astin' me do we play bridge just because she's got a headache or feels lonesome or somethin'. But it ain't only one party after all, and that's the best part of it. She ast as if we'd care to join the club.'

'What club?' says I.

'Mrs. Messenger's club, the San Susie Club,' says the Missus. 'You've heard me speak about it a hundred times, and it's been mentioned in the papers once or twice, too— once, anyway, when the members give away them Christmas dinners last year.'

'We can get into the papers,' I says, 'without givin' away no Christmas dinners.'

'Who wants to get into the papers?' says the Wife. 'I don't care nothin' about that.'

'No,' I says; 'I suppose if a reporter come out here and

ast for your pitcher to stick in the society columns, you'd pick up the carvin' knife and run him ragged.'

'I'd be polite to him, at least,' she says.

'Yes,' says I; 'it wouldn't pay to treat him rude; it'd even be justifiable to lock him in w'ile you was lookin' for the pitcher.'

'If you'll kindly leave me talk you may find out what I got to say,' she says. 'I've told you about this club, but I don't suppose you ever paid any attention. It's a club that's made up from people that just lives in this block, twenty o' them altogether; and all but one couple either lives in this buildin' or in the buildin' the Messengers lives in. And they're all nice people, people with real class to them: not no tramps like most o' the ones we been runnin' round with. One o' them's Mr. and Mrs. Arthur Collins that used to live on Sheridan Road and still goes over to parties at some o' the most exclusive homes on the North Side. And they don't have nobody in the club that isn't congenial with each other, but all just a nice crowd o' real people that gets together once a week at one o' the members' houses and have a good time.'

'How did these pillows o' Society happen to light on to us?' I ast her.

'Well,' she says, 'it seems like the Baileys, who belonged to the club, went to California last week to spend the winter. And they had to have a couple to take their place. And Mrs. Messenger says they wouldn't take nobody that didn't live in our block and her and her husband looked over the list and we was the ones they picked out.'

'Probably,' I says, 'that's because we was the only eligibles that can go out nights on account o' not havin' no children.'

'The Pearsons ain't ast,' she says, 'and they ain't got no children.'

'Well,' I says, 'what's the dues?'

'They ain't no dues,' says the Missus. 'But once in a w'ile, instead o' playin' bridge, everybody puts in two dollars apiece and have a theater party. But the regular program is for an evenin' o' bridge every Tuesday night, at different members' houses, somebody different actin' as hosts every week. And each couple puts up two dollars, makin' ten dollars for a gent's prize and ten dollars for a lady's. And the prizes is picked out by the lady that happens to be the hostess.'

'That's a swell proposition for me,' I says. 'In the first place they wouldn't be a chance in the world for me to win a prize, because I don't know nothin' about the game. And, in the second place, suppose I had a whole lot o' luck and did win the prize, and come to find out it was a silver mustache cup that I wouldn't have no more use for than another Adam's apple! If they paid in cash they might be somethin' to it.'

'If you win a prize you can sell it, can't you?' says the Missus. 'Besides, the prizes don't count. It's gettin' in with the right kind o' people that makes the difference.'

'Another thing,' I says: 'when it come our turn to have the party, where would we stick 'em all? We'd have to spread a sheet over the bathtub for one table, and have one couple set on the edges and the other couple toss up for the washbasin and the clothes-hamper. And another two couple'd have to kneel round the bed, and another bunch could stand up round the bureau. That'd leave the dinin'-room table for the fourth set; and for a special treat the remainin' four could play in the parlor.'

'We could hire chairs and tables,' says the Missus. 'We're goin' to have to some time, anyway, when you or I die.'

'You don't need to hire no tables for my funeral,' I says. 'If the pallbearers or the quartet insists on shootin' craps they can use the kitchen floor; or if they want beer and sandwiches you can slip 'em the money to go down to the corner.'

'They's no use worryin' about our end of it yet,' says the Wife. 'We'll be new members and they won't expect us to give no party till everybody else has had their turn.'

'I only got one objection left,' I says. 'How am I goin' to get by at a bridge party when I haven't no idear how many cards to deal?'

'I guess you can learn if I learnt,' she says. 'You're always talkin' about what a swell card player you are. And besides, you've played w'ist, and they ain't hardly any difference.'

'And the next party is next Tuesday night?' I says.

'Yes,' says the Missus, 'at Mrs. Garrett's, the best player in the club, and one o' the smartest women in Chicago, Mrs. Messenger says. She lives in the same buildin' with the Messengers. And they's dinner first and then we play bridge all evenin'.'

'And maybe,' I says, 'before the evenin's over, I'll find out what's trumps.'

'You'll know all about the game before that,' she says. 'Right after supper we'll get out the cards and I'll show you.'

So right after supper she got out the cards and begun to show me. But about all as I learnt was one thing, and that was that if I died without no insurance, the Missus would stand a better show o' supportin' herself by umpirin' baseball in the National League than by teachin' in a bridge-w'ist university. She knew everything except how much the

different suits counted, and how many points was in a
game, and what honors meant, and who done the first
biddin', and how much to bid on what.

After about an hour of it I says:

'I can see you got this thing mastered, but you're like a
whole lot of people that knows somethin' perfect themselves but can't learn it to nobody else.'

'No,' she says; 'I got to admit that I don't know as much
as I thought I did. I didn't have no trouble when I was
playin' with Mrs. Hatch and Mrs. Pearson and Mrs.
Kramer; but it seems like I forgot all they learnt me.'

'It's a crime,' I says, 'that we should have to pass up this
chance to get in right just because we can't play a fool
game o' cards. Why don't you call up Mrs. Messenger and
suggest that the San Susies switches to pedro or five hundred or rummy, or somethin' that you don't need to take
no college course in?'

'You're full o' brilliant idears,' says the Missus. 'They's
only just the one game that Society plays, and that's bridge.
Them other games is jokes.'

'I've noticed you always treated 'em that way,' I says. 'But
they wasn't so funny to me when it come time to settle.'

'I'll tell you what we'll do,' says the Missus: 'we'll call
up Mr. and Mrs. Hatch and tell 'em to come over here
tomorrow night and give us a lesson.'

'That'd be sweet,' I says, 'askin' them to learn us a game
so as we could join a club that's right here in their neighborhood, but they ain't even been ast to join it!'

'Why, you rummy!' she says. 'We don't have to tell 'em
why we want to learn. We'll just say that my two attempts
over to their house has got me interested and I and you
want to master the game so as we can spend many pleasant
evenin's with them; because Mrs. Hatch has told me a

hundred times that her and her husband would rather play bridge than eat.'

So she called up Mrs. Hatch and sprung it on her; but it seemed like the Hatches had an engagement for Saturday night, but would be tickled to death to come over Monday evenin' and give us a work-out. After that was fixed we both felt kind of ashamed of ourselves, deceivin' people that was supposed to be our best friends.

'But, anyway,' the Missus says, 'the Hatches wouldn't never fit in with that crowd. Jim always looks like he'd dressed on the elevated and Mrs. Hatch can't talk about nothin' only shiropody.'

On the Saturday I tried to slip one over by buyin' a book called 'Auction Bridge,' and I read it all the way home from town and then left it on the car. It was a great book for a man that had leant the rudderments and wanted to find out how to play the game right. But for me to try and get somethin' out of it was just like as though some kid'd learn the baseball guide by heart in kindeygarden and then ask Hugh Jennin's for the job in centerfield. I did find out one thing from it though: it says that in every deal one o' the players was a dummy and just laid his cards down and left somebody else play 'em. So when I got home I says:

'We won't need no help from Jim Hatch and his wife. We can just be dummies all the evenin' and they won't nobody know if we're ignorant or not.'

'That's impossible, to be dummy all the time,' says the Missus.

'Not for me,' I says. 'I know it'll be tough for you, but you can chew a lot o' gum and you won't mind it so much.'

'You don't understand,' she says. 'The dummy is the pardner o' the party that gets the bid. Suppose one o' the

people that was playin' against you got the bid; then the
other one'd be dummy and you'd have to play your hand.'

'But I don't need to leave 'em have the bid,' I says. 'I
can take it away from 'em.'

'And if you take it away from 'em,' she says, 'then you
got the bid yourself, and your pardner's dummy, not you.'

Well, the Hatches breezed in Monday night and Mrs.
Hatch remarked how tickled she was that we was goin'
to learn, and what good times we four'd have playin' together. And the Missus and I pretended like we shared her
raptures.

"Ain't you never played at all?' she ast me; and I told
her no.

'The first thing,' she says, 'is how much the different
suits counts; and then they's the bids. And you got to pay
attention to the conventions.'

'I'm through with 'em forever,' I says, 'since they turned
down Roosevelt.'

Well, we started in and Hatch and the Missus played
Mrs. Hatch and I. We kept at it till pretty near midnight,
with three or four intermissions so as Hatch could relieve
the strain on the icebox. My w'ist education kept me from
bein' much of a flivver when it come to playin' the cards;
but, I don't care how bright a guy is, you can't learn everything about biddin' in one evenin', and you can't remember half what you learnt. I don't know what the score was
when we got through, but the Hatches done most o' the
execution and held most o' the cards, which is their regular habit.

'You'll get along all right,' says Mrs. Hatch when they
was ready to go. 'But, o' course, you can't expect to master
a game like bridge in a few hours. You want to keep at it.'

'We're goin' to,' says the Missus.

"Maybe it'd be a good idear,' says Mrs. Hatch, 'to play again soon before you forget what we learnt you. Why don't you come over to our house for another session tomorrow night?'

'Let's see; tomorrow night?' says the Missus, stallin'. 'Why, no, we can't. We got an engagement.'

So Mrs. Hatch stood there like she was expectin' to hear what it was.

'We're goin' to a party,' says the Wife.

'Oh, tell me about it!' says Mrs. Hatch.

'Well,' says the Missus, 'it ain't really a party; it's just a kind of a party; some old friends that's visitin' in town.'

'Maybe they'll play bridge with you,' says Mrs. Hatch.

'Oh, no,' says the Missus, blushin'. 'It'll probably be rummy or pedro; or maybe we'll just go to the pitchers.'

'Why don't you go over to the Acme?' says Mrs. Hatch. 'They got Chaplin in "The Street Sweeper." We're goin', and we could meet you and all go together.'

'N-no,' says the Wife. 'You see, one of our friends has just lost his wife and I know he wouldn't feel like goin' to see something funny.'

'He's already laughed himself sick,' I says.

Well, we wouldn't make no date with 'em and they finally blew with the understandin' that we was to go to their house and play some night soon. When they'd went the Missus says:

'I feel like a criminal, deceivin' 'em like that. But I just couldn't tell 'em the truth. Bertha Hatch is the most jealous thing in the world and it would just about kill her to know that we was in on somethin' good without she and Jim.'

'If you hadn't ast 'em over,' I says, 'we'd of been just as well off and you wouldn't of had to make a perjure out o' yourself.'

'What do you mean, we'd of been just as well off?' she says. 'They done what we expected of 'em, learnt us the game.'

'Yes,' I says; 'and you could take all I remember o' the lesson and feed it to a gnat and he'd say: "Hurry up with the soup course!" '

III

Well, Mrs. Garrett had called up to say that the feed before the game would begin at seven bells; so I and the Missus figured on bein' on hand at half past six, so as to get acquainted with some of our fellow club members and know what to call 'em when we wanted the gravy passed or somethin'. But I had trouble with my studs and it wasn't till pretty near twenty minutes to seven that we rung the Garretts' bell. The hired girl let us in and left us standin' in the hall w'ile she went to tell Mrs. Garrett we was there. Pretty soon the girl come back and says she would take our wraps and that Mrs. Garrett would be with us in a few minutes. So we was showed into the livin'-room.

The apartment was on the second floor and looked about twice as big as our'n.

'What do you suppose this costs 'em?' ast the Missus.

'About fifty-five a month,' I says.

'You're crazy!' says she. 'They got this big livin'-room and two big bedrooms, and a maid's room and a sun parlor, besides their dinin'-room and kitchen and bath. They're lucky if they ain't stuck for seventy.'

'I'll bet you!' I says. 'I'll bet you it's nearer fifty-five than seventy.'

'How much'll you bet?' she says.

'Anything you say,' says I.

'Well,' she says, 'I've got a cinch, and I need a pair o' black silk stockin's. My others has begun to run.'

'All right,' I says. 'A pair o' black silk stockin's to fifty cents cash.'

'You're on,' she says. 'And I'll call up the agent tomorrow and find out.'

Well, it must of been pretty near seven o'clock when Mrs. Garrett finally showed up.

'Good evenin',' she says. 'I suppose this must be our new members. I'm awfully glad you could come and I'm sorry I wasn't quite ready.'

'That's all right,' I says. 'I'm glad to know they's others has trouble gettin' into their evenin' clo'es. I suppose people that does it often enough finally get to be experts.'

'I didn't have no trouble,' says Mrs. Garrett; 'only I didn't expect nobody till seven o'clock. You must of misunderstood me and thought I said half past six.'

Then Mr. Garrett come in and shook hands with us, and then the rest o' the folks begun to arrive and we was introduced to them all. I didn't catch all their names, only Mr. and Mrs. Messenger and Mr. and Mrs. Collins and Mr. and Mrs. Sparks. Mrs. Garrett says dinner was ready and I was glad to hear it.

They set me down between Mrs. Messenger and a lady that I didn't get her name.

'Well,' I says to Mrs. Messenger, 'now we know you personally, we can pay the rent direct without botherin' to go to the real-estate office.'

'I'm afraid that wouldn't do,' she says. 'Our agent's entitled to his commissions. And besides, I wouldn't know how much to take or nothin' about it.'

'We pay thirty-five,' I says, 'and that's all as you could ast for, seein' we only got the four rooms and no sun parlor. Thirty-two and a half would be about the right price.'

'You'll have to argue that out with the agent,' she says.

I was kind of expectin' a cocktail; but nothin' doin'. The hired girl brought in some half sandwiches, made o' toast, with somethin' on 'em that looked like BB shot and tasted like New Year's mornin'.

'Don't we get no liquid refreshments?' I ast Mrs. Messenger.

'No, indeed,' she says. 'The San Susie's a dry club.'

'You should ought to call it the San Sousy, then,' says I.

The Missus was settin' next to Mr. Garrett and I could hear 'em talkin' about what a nice neighborhood it was and how they liked their flats. I thought I and the Missus might as well settle our bet then and there, so I spoke to Mr. Garrett acrost the table.

'Mr. Garrett,' I says, 'w'ile we was waitin' for you and your wife to get dressed, I and the Missus made a little bet, a pair o' silk stockin's against half a buck. I got to pay out two dollars here for the prize and the Missus claims her other stockin's has begun to run; so you might say we're both a little anxious.'

'Is it somethin' I can settle?' he ast.

'Yes, sir,' I says, 'because we was bettin' on the rent you paid for this apartment. The Missus says seventy a month and I says fifty-five.'

'I never decide against a lady,' he says. 'You better buy the stockin's before the others run so far that they can't find their way home.'

'If I lose, I lose,' says I. 'But if you're stuck sixty-five or better, the Missus must of steered me wrong about the number o' rooms you got. I'll pay, though, because I don't never welsh on a bet. So this party's really costin' me two and a half instead o' two.'

'Maybe you'll win the prize,' says Mr. Garrett.

'They ain't much chance,' I says. 'I ain't played this game for a long w'ile.'

'Why, your wife was just tellin' me you played last night,' he says.

'I mean,' says I, 'that I didn't play for a long w'ile before last night; not for thirty-six years,' I says.

Well, when everybody'd got through chokin' down the shot, they brought in some drowned toadstools, and then some little slices o' beef about the size of a checker, and seven Saratoga chips apiece, and half a dozen string beans. Those that was still able to set up under this load finished up on sliced tomatoes that was caught too young and a nickel's worth of ice-cream and an eyedropper full o' coffee.

'Before I forget it,' says Mrs. Collins, w'ile we was staggerin' out o' the dinin'-room, 'you're all comin' to my house next Tuesday night.'

I was walkin' right behind her.

'And I got a suggestion for you,' I says, low enough so as they couldn't nobody else hear: 'Throw some o' the prize money into the dinner; and if they's any skimpin' to be done, do it on the prizes.'

She didn't say nothin' back, because Mrs. Garrett had started to hand us the little cards that showed where we was to play.

'I suppose I better tell you our rules,' she says to me. 'Each table plays four deals. Then the winners moves w'ile the losers sets still, except at the first table, where the winners sets still and the losers moves. You change pardners after every four deals. You count fifty for a game and a hundred and fifty for a rubber.'

'The way I been playin',' I says, 'it was thirty for a game.'

'I never heard o' that,' she says; but I noticed when we got to playin' that everybody that made thirty points called it a game.

'Don't we see the prizes before we start?' I ast her. 'I want to know whether to play my best or not.'

'If you win the prize and don't like it,' she says, 'I guess you can get it exchanged.'

'They tell me you're the shark amongst the women folks,' says I; 'so it's a safe bet that you didn't pick out no lady's prize that isn't O. K.'

I noticed some o' the other men was slippin' her their ante; so I parted with a two-spot. Then I found where I was to set at. It was Table Number Three, Couple Number One. My pardner was a strappin' big woman with a name somethin' like Rowley or Phillips. Our opponents was Mrs. Garrett and Mr. Messenger. Mrs. Garrett looked like she'd been livin' on the kind of a meal she'd gave us, and Mr. Messenger could of set in the back seat of a flivver with two regular people without crowdin' nobody. So I says to my pardner:

'Well, pardner, we got 'em outweighed, anyway.'

They was two decks o' cards on the table. I grabbed one o' them and began to deal 'em face up.

'First jack,' I says.

'If you don't mind, we'll cut for deal,' says Mrs. Garrett.

So we cut the cards and it seemed like the low cut got the deal and that was Mrs. Garrett herself.

'Which deck'll we play with?' I ast.

'Both o' them,' says Mrs. Garrett. 'Mr. Messenger'll make them red ones for you.'

'Make 'em!' I says. 'Well, Messenger, I didn't know you was a card factory.'

Messenger laughed; but the two ladies didn't get it. Mrs. Garrett dealt and it was her turn to bid.

'One without,' she says.

'I'd feel better if I had one within,' says I.

'Are you goin' to bid or not?' she ast me.

'I thought it was the dealer's turn first,' I says.

'I've made my bid,' she says. 'I bid one without.'

'One without lookin', or what?' I says.

'One no trump, if I got to explain it,' she says.

'Oh, that's different,' I says; but I found out that most all o' them said 'One without' when they meant one no trump.

I looked at my hand; but about all as I had was four hearts, with the king and jack high.

'Pardner,' I says, 'I don't see nothin' I can bid, unless it'd be one heart. Does that hit you?'

'No talkin' acrost the boards,' says Mrs. Garrett. 'And besides, one heart ain't over my bid.'

So I passed and Mr. Messenger bid two spades. Then my pardner passed and Mrs. Garrett thought it over a w'ile and then bid two without. So I passed again and the rest o' them passed, and it was my first lead.

Well, I didn't have only one spade—the eight-spot—and I knew it wouldn't do my hand no good as long as I couldn't trump in with it; so I led it out. Messenger was dummy, and he laid his hand down. He had about eight spades, with the ace and queen high.

'I might as well take a chance,' says Mrs. Garrett, and she throwed on Messenger's ten-spot.

Out come my pardner with the king, and it was our trick.

'What kind of a lead was that?' says Mrs. Garrett.

'Pretty good one, I guess,' says I. 'It fooled you, anyway.'

And she acted like she was sore as a boil. Come to find out, she'd thought I was leadin' from the king and was goin' to catch it later on.

Well, her and Messenger took all the rest o' the tricks except my king o' hearts, and they had a game on us, besides forty for their four aces.

'I could of made a little slam as well as not,' she says when it was over. 'But I misunderstood our friend's lead. It's the first time I ever seen a man lead from a sneak in no trump.'

'I'll do a whole lot o' things you never seen before,' I says.

'I don't doubt it,' says she, still actin' like I'd spilled salad dressin' on her skirt.

It was my first bid next time and hearts was my only suit again. I had the ace, queen and three others.

'Pardner,' I says, 'I'm going to bid one heart and if you got somethin' to help me out with, don't let 'em take it away from me.'

'I'll double a heart,' says Messenger.

'Oh, somebody else is gettin' cute!' says I. 'Well, I'll double right back at you.'

'Will you just wait till it comes your turn?' says Mrs. Garrett. 'And besides, you can't redouble.'

'I guess I can,' says I. 'I got five o' them.'

'It's against our rules,' she says.

So my pardner done nothin', as usual, and Mrs. Garrett bid one without again.

'I guess you want to play 'em all,' I says; 'but you'll have to come higher'n that. I'm goin' to bid two hearts.'

'Two no trump,' says Messenger, and my pardner says 'Pass' once more.

'You'll get a sore throat sayin' that,' I told her. 'Don't you never hold nothin'?'

'It don't look like it,' she says.

'Maybe she'd better take a few lessons from you,' says Mrs. Garrett.

'No,' I says, kiddin' her. 'You don't want no more female experts in the club or you might have to buy some cut glass once in a w'ile instead o' winnin' it.'

Well, I bid three hearts; but Mrs. Garrett come up to three no trump and I couldn't go no higher. This time I led out my ace o' hearts, hopin' maybe to catch their king; but I didn't get it. And Mrs. Garrett copped all the rest of 'em for a little slam.

'If your husband ever starts drinkin' hard,' I says, 'you can support yourself by sellin' some o' your horseshoes to the Russian government.'

It wasn't no lie, neither. I never seen such hands as that woman held, and Messenger's was pretty near as good. In the four deals they grabbed two rubbers and a couple o' little slams, and when they left our table they had over nine hundred to our nothin'.

Mr. Collins and another woman was the next ones to set down with us. The rules was to change pardners and Collins took the one I'd been playin' with. And what does she do but get lucky and they give us another trimmin', though nothin' near as bad as the first one. My pardner, this time, was a woman about forty-eight, and she acted like it was way past her bedtime. When it was her turn to say somethin' we always had to wait about five minutes, and all the other tables was through a long w'ile before us. Once she says:

'You'll have to excuse me tonight. I don't somehow seem to be able to keep my mind on the game.'

'No,' I says; 'but I bet you'd perk up if the lady's prize was a mattress. When you're goin' to be up late you should ought to take a nap in the afternoon.'

Well, sir, my next pardner wasn't nobody else but the Missus. She'd started at the fourth table and lost the first time, but win the second. She came along with the husband o' the pardner I'd just had; so here we was family against family, you might say.

'What kind o' luck you been havin'?' the fella ast me.

'No luck at all,' I says. 'But if you're anywheres near as sleepy as your Missus, I and my wife should ought to clean up this time.'

We didn't. They held all the cards except in one hand, and that was one my Missus tried to play. I bid first and made it a no trump, as they was three aces in my hand. Old Slumber began to talk in her sleep and says: 'Two diamonds.' The Missus bid two hearts. Mr. Sleeper passed, and so did I, as I didn't have a single heart in my hand and figured the Missus probably had 'em all. She had six, with the king high and then the nine-spot. Our female opponent had only two, and that left five for her husband, includin' the ace, queen and jack. We was set three.

'Nice work!' I says to the Missus. 'You're the Philadelphia Athletics of auction bridge.'

'What was you biddin' no trump on?' she says. 'I thought, o' course, you'd have one high heart and some suit.'

'You don't want to start thinkin' at your age,' I says. 'You can't learn an old dog new tricks.'

Mrs. Nap's husband cut in.

'O' course,' he says, 'it's a man's privilege to call your wife anything you feel like callin' her. But your Missus don't hardly look old to me.'

'No, not comparatively speakin',' I says, and he shut up.

They moved on and along come Garrett and Mrs. Messenger. I and Mrs. Messenger was pardners and I thought for a w'ile we was goin' to win. But Garrett and the Missus had a bouquet o' fourleaf clovers in the last two deals and licked us. Garrett wasn't supposed to be as smart as his wife, but he was fox enough to keep biddin' over my Missus, so as he'd do the playin' instead o' she.

It wasn't till pretty near the close o' the evenin's entertainment that I got away from that table and moved to Number Two. When I set down there it was I and Mrs. Collins against her husband and Mrs. Sleeper.

'Well, Mrs. Collins,' I says, 'I'll try and hold some good hands for you and maybe I can have two helpin's o' the meat when we come to your house.'

The other lady opened her eyes long enough to ask who was winnin'.

'Oh, Mrs. Garrett's way ahead,' says Mrs. Collins. 'She's got a score o' somethin' like three thousand. And Mr. Messenger is high amongst the men.'

'Who's next to the leadin' lady?' I ast her.

'I guess I am,' she says. 'But I'm three hundred behind Mrs. Garrett.'

Well, the luck I'd just bumped into stayed with me and I and Mrs. Collins won and moved to the head table. Waitin' there for us was our darlin' hostess and Messenger, the two leaders in the pennant race. It was give out that this was to be the last game.

When Mrs. Garrett realized who was goin' to be her pardner I wisht you could of seen her face!

'This is an unexpected pleasure,' she says to me. 'I thought you liked the third table so well you was goin' to stay there all evenin'.'

'I did intend to,' I says; 'but I seen you up here and I heard you was leadin' the league, so I thought I'd like to help you finish in front.'

'I don't need no help,' she says. 'All I ast is for you to not overbid your hands, and I'll do the rest.'

'How many are you, Mrs. Garrett?' ast Mrs. Collins.

'Thirty-two hundred and sixty,' she says.

'Oh, my!' says Mrs. Collins, 'I'm hopeless. I'm only twenty-nine hundred and forty-eight. And how about you, Mr. Messenger?'

'Round thirty-one hundred,' he says.

'Yes,' says Mrs. Garrett, 'and I don't believe any o' the rest o' the men is within five hundred o' that.'

'Well, Messenger,' I says, 'if the men's prize happens to be a case o' beer or a steak smothered in onions, don't forget that I'm payin' you thirty-five a month for a thirty-dollar flat.'

Now, I'd of gave my right eye to see Mrs. Collins beat Mrs. Garrett out. But I was goin' to do my best for Mrs. Garrett just the same, because I don't think it's square for a man to not try and play your hardest all the time in any kind of a game, no matter where your sympathies lays. So when it come my turn to bid on the first hand, and I seen the ace and king and four other hearts in my hand, I raised Mrs. Collins' bid o' two diamonds, and Mrs. Garrett made it two no trump and got away with it. On the next two deals Messenger and Mrs. Collins made a game, and Mrs. Garrett got set a trick once on a bid o' five clubs. The way the score was when it come to the last deal, I figured that if Mrs. Collins and Messenger made another game and rubber, the two women'd be mighty close to even.

Mrs. Garrett dealt 'em, and says:

'One without.'

'Two spades,' says Mrs. Collins.

Well, sir, they wasn't a spade in my hand, and I seen that if Mrs. Collins got it we was ruined on account o' me not havin' a trump. And w'ile I wanted Mrs. Collins to win I was goin' to do my best to not let her. So I says:

'Two without.'

'You know what you're doin', do you?' says Mrs. Garrett.

'What do you mean, know what I'm doin'?' I says.

'No talkin' acrost the boards,' says Messenger.

'All right,' I says; 'but you can depend on me, pardner not to throw you down.'

Well, Messenger passed and so did Mrs. Garrett; but Mrs. Collins wasn't through.

'Three spades,' she says.

'Three without,' says I.

'I hope it's all right,' says Mrs. Garrett.

'I'll tell you one thing,' I says; 'it's a whole lot all-righter than if she played it in spades.'

Messenger passed again and ditto for my pardner.

'I'll double,' says Mrs. Collins, and we let it go at that.

Man, oh, man! You ought to seen our genial hostess when I laid down my cards! And heard her, too! Her face turned all three colors o' Old Glory. She slammed her hand down on the table, face up.

'I won't play it!' she hollers. 'I won't be made a fool of! This poor idiot deliberately told me he had spades stopped, and look at his hand!'

'You're mistaken, Mrs. Garrett,' I says. 'I didn't say nothin' about spades.'

'Shut your month!' she says. 'That's what you ought to done all evenin'.'

'I might as well of,' I says, 'for all the good it done me to keep it open at dinner.'

Everybody in the room quit playin' and rubbered. Finally Garrett got up from where he was settin' and come over.

'What seems to be the trouble?' he says. 'This ain't no barroom.'

'Nobody's ever suspect it o' bein',' I says.

'Look what he done!' says Mrs. Garrett. 'He raised my no-trump bid over three spades without a spade in his hand.'

'Well,' says Mr. Garrett, 'they's no use gettin' all fussed up over a game o' cards. The thing to do is pick up your hand and play it out and take your medicine.'

'I can set her three,' said Mrs. Collins. 'I got seven spades, with the ace, king and queen, and I'll catch her jack on the third lead.'

'And I got the ace o' hearts,' says Messenger. 'Even if it didn't take a trick it'd make aces easy; so our three hundred above the line gives Mrs. Collins a score of about ten more'n Mrs. Garrett.'

'All right, then,' says Garrett. 'Mrs. Collins is entitled to the lady's prize.'

'I don't want to take it,' says Mrs. Collins.

'You got to take it,' says Garrett.

And he gave his wife a look that meant business. Anyway, she got up and went out o' the room, and when she come back she was smilin'. She had two packages in her hand, and she give one to Messenger and one to Mrs. Collins.

'There's the prizes,' she says; 'and I hope you'll like 'em.'

Messenger unwrapped his'n and it was one o' them round

leather cases that you use to carry extra collars in when you're travelin'. Messenger had told me earlier in the evenin' that he hadn't been outside o' Chicago in six years.

Mrs. Collins' prize was a chafin'-dish.

'I don't blame Mrs. Garrett for bein' so crazy to win it,' I says to her when they couldn't nobody hear. 'Her and Garrett both must get hungry along about nine or ten P.M.

'I hate to take it,' says Mrs. Collins.

'I wouldn't feel that way,' I says. 'I guess Mrs. Garrett will chafe enough without it.'

When we was ready to go I shook hands with the host and hostess and says I was sorry if I'd pulled a boner.

'It was to be expected,' says Mrs. Garrett.

'Yes,' I says; 'a man's liable to most anything when he's starvin' to death.'

The Messengers and Collinses was a little ways ahead of us on the stairs and I wanted we should hurry and catch up with 'em.

'You let 'em go!' says the Missus. 'You've spoiled everything now without doin' nothin' more. Every time you talk you insult somebody.'

'I ain't goin' to insult them,' I says. 'I'm just goin' to ask 'em to go down to the corner and have a drink.'

'You are not!' she says.

But she's just as good a prophet as she is a bridge player. They wouldn't go along, though, sayin' it was late and they wanted to get to bed.

'Well, if you won't you won't,' says I. 'We'll see you all a week from tonight. And don't forget, Mrs. Collins, that I'm responsible for you winnin' that chafin'-dish, and I'm fond o' welsh rabbits.'

I was glad that we didn't have to go far to our buildin'. The Missus was pleasant company, just like a bloodhound with the rabies. I left her in the vestibule and went down to help Mike close up. He likes to be amongst friends at a sad hour like that.

At breakfast the next mornin' the Wife was more calm.

'Dearie,' she says, 'they don't neither one of us class as bridge experts. I'll admit I got a lot to learn about the game. What we want to do is play with the Hatches every evenin' this week, and maybe by next Tuesday night we'll know somethin'.'

'I'm willin',' I says.

'I'll call Mrs. Hatch up this forenoon,' she says, 'and see if they want us to come over there this evenin'. But if we do go remember not to mention our club or tell 'em anything about the party.'

Well, she had news for me when I got home.

'The San Susies is busted up,' she says. 'Not forever, but for a few months anyway. Mrs. Messenger called up to tell me.'

'What's the idear?' I says.

'I don't know exactly,' says the Missus. 'Mrs. Messenger says that the Collinses had boxes for the opera every Tuesday night and the rest didn't feel like goin' on without the Collinses, and they couldn't all o' them agree on another night.'

'I don't see why they should bust it up on account o' one couple,' I says. 'Why didn't you tell 'em about the Hatches? They're right here in the neighborhood and can play bridge as good as anybody.'

'I wouldn't think o' doin' it,' says she. 'They may play all right, but think o' how they talk and how they dress!'

'Well,' I says, 'between you and I, I ain't goin' to take cyanide over a piece o' news like this. Somehow it don't appeal to me to vote myself dry every Tuesday night all winter

—to say nothin' o' two dollars a week annual dues to help buy a prize that I got no chance o' winnin' and wouldn't know what to do with it if I had it.'

'It'd of been nice, though,' she says, 'to make friends with them people.'

'Well,' I says, 'I'll feel a little more confident o' doin' that if I see 'em once a year—or not at all.'

IV

I can tell you the rest of it in about a minute. The Missus had became resigned and everything was goin' along smooth till last Tuesday evenin'. They was a new Chaplin show over to the Acme and we was on our way to see it. At the entrance to the buildin' where the Messengers lives we seen Mr. and Mrs. Hatch.

'Hello, there!' says the Wife. 'Better come along with us to the Acme.'

'Not tonight,' says Mrs. Hatch. 'We're tied up every Tuesday evenin'.'

'Some club?' ast the Missus.

'Yes,' says Mrs. Hatch. 'It's a bridge club—the San Susie. The Messengers and Collinses and Garretts and us and some other people's in it. Two weeks ago we was to Collinses', and last week to Beardsleys'; and tonight the Messengers is the hosts.'

The Missus tried to say somethin', and couldn't.

'I been awful lucky,' says Mrs. Hatch. 'I win the prize at Collinses.' It was a silver pitcher—the prettiest you ever seen!'

The Missus found her voice.

'Do you have dinner, too?' she ast.

'I should say we do!' says Mrs. Hatch. 'And simply grand stuff to eat! It was nice last week at Beardsleys'; but you ought to been at Collinses'! First, they was an old-fashioned beefsteak supper; and then, when we was through playin' Mrs. Collins made us welsh rabbits in her chafin'-dish.'

'That don't tempt me,' I says. 'I'd just as soon try and eat a raw mushrat as a welsh rabbit.'

'Well, we got to be goin' in,' says Hatch.

'Good-night,' says Mrs. Hatch; 'and I wisht you was comin' with us.'

The pitcher we seen was called 'The Fly Cop.' Don't never waste a dime on it. They ain't a laugh in the whole show.

MR. AND MRS. FIX-IT

By Ring Lardner

THEY'RE certainly a live bunch in this town. We ain't only been here three days and had calls already from people representin' four different organizations—the Chamber of Commerce, Kiwanis, and I forget who else. They wanted to know if we was comfortable and did we like the town and is they anything they can do for us and what to be sure and see.

And they all asked how we happened to come here instead of goin' somewheres else. I guess they keep a record of everybody's reasons for comin' so as they can get a line on what features tourists is most attracted by. Then they play up them features in next year's booster advertisin'.

Well, I told them we was perfectly comfortable and we like the town fine and they's nothin' nobody can do for us right now and we'll be sure and see all the things we ought to see. But when they asked me how did we happen to come here, I said it was just a kind of a accident, because the real reason makes too long a story.

My wife has been kiddin' me about my friends ever since we was married. She says that judgin' by the ones I've introduced her to, they ain't nobody in the world got a rummier bunch of friends than me. I'll admit that the most of them ain't, well, what you might call hot; they're different some-

159

how than when I first hung around with them. They seem to be lost without a brass rail to rest their dogs on. But of course they're old friends and I can't give 'em the air.

We have 'em to the house for dinner every little w'ile, they and their wives, and what my missus objects to is because they don't none of them play bridge or mah jong or do crossword puzzles or sing or dance or even talk, but just set there and wait for somebody to pour 'em a fresh drink.

As I say, my wife kids me about 'em and they ain't really nothin' I can offer in their defense. That don't mean, though, that the shoe is all on one foot. Because w'ile the majority of her friends may not be quite as dumb as mine, just the same they's a few she's picked out who I'd of had to be under the ether to allow anybody to introduce 'em to me in the first place.

Like the Crandalls, for instance. Mrs. Crandall come from my wife's home town and they didn't hardly know each other there, but they met again in a store in Chi and it went from bad to worse till finally Ada asked the dame and her husband to the house.

Well, the husband turns out to be the fella that win the war, w'ile it seems that Mrs. Crandall was in Atlantic City once and some movin' picture company was makin' a picture there and they took a scene of what was supposed to be society people walkin' up and down the Boardwalk and Mrs. Crandall was in the picture and people that seen it when it come out, they all said that from the way she screened, why if she wanted to go into the business, she could make Gloria Swanson look like Mrs. Gump.

Now it ain't only took me a few words to tell you these things, but when the Crandalls tells their story themselves, they don't hardly get started by midnight and no chance of them goin' home till they're through even when you drop 'em a hint that they're springin' it on you for the hundred and twelfth time.

That's the Crandalls, and another of the wife's friends is the Thayers. Thayer is what you might call a all-around handy man. He can mimic pretty near all the birds and beasts and fishes, he can yodel, he can play a ocarena, or he can recite Kipling or Robert H. Service, or he can do card tricks, and strike a light without no matches, and tie all the different knots.

And besides that, he can make a complete radio outfit and set it up, and take pictures as good as the best professional photographers and a whole lot better. He collects autographs. And he never had a sick day in his life.

Mrs. Thayer gets a headache playin' bridge, so it's mah jong or rhum when she's around. She used to be a teacher of elocution and she still gives readin's if you coax her, or if you don't, and her hair is such a awful nuisance that she would get it cut in a minute only all her friends tells her it would be criminal to spoil that head of hair. And when she talks to her husband, she always talks baby talk, maybe because somebody has told her that she'd be single if he wasn't childish.

And then Ada has got still another pal, a dame named Peggy Flood who is hospital mad and ain't happy unless she is just goin' under the knife or just been there. She's had everything removed that the doctors knew the name of and now they're probin' her for new giblets.

Well, I wouldn't mind if they cut her up into alphabet soup if they'd only do such a good job of it that they couldn't put her together again, but she always comes through O. K. and she spends the intermissions at our place, describin' what all they done or what they're plannin' to do next.

But the cat's nightgown is Tom Stevens and his wife. There's the team that wins the Olympics! And they're Ada's team, not mine.

Ada met Belle Stevens on the elevated. Ada was invited to a party out on the North Side and didn't know exactly where to get off and Mrs. Stevens seen her talkin' to the guard and horned in and asked her what was it she wanted to know and Ada told her, and Mrs. Stevens said she was goin' to get off the same station Ada wanted to get off, so they got off together.

Mrs. Stevens insisted on goin' right along to the address where Ada was goin' because she said Ada was bound to get lost if she wasn't familiar with the neighborhood.

Well, Ada thought it was mighty nice of her to do so much for a stranger. Mrs. Stevens said she was glad to because she didn't know what would happen to her lots of times if strangers hadn't been nice and helped her out.

She asked Ada where she lived and Ada told her on the South Side and Mrs. Stevens said she was sure we'd like it better on the North Side if we'd leave her pick out a place for us, so Ada told her we had a year's lease that we had just signed and couldn't break it, so then Mrs. Stevens said her husband had studied law and he claimed they wasn't no lease that you couldn't break and some evening she would bring him out to call on us and he'd tell us how to break our lease.

Well, Ada had to say sure, come on out, though we was perfectly satisfied with our apartment and didn't no more want to break the lease than each other's jaw. Maybe not as much. Anyway, the very next night, they showed up, Belle and Tom, and when they'd gone, I give 'em the nickname—Mr. and Mrs. Fix-It.

After the introductions, Stevens made some remark about

what a cozy little place we had and then he asked if I would mind tellin' what rent we paid. So I told him a hundred and a quarter a month. So he said, of course, that was too much and no wonder we wanted to break the lease. Then I said we was satisfied and didn't want to break it and he said I must be kiddin' and if I would show him the lease he would see what loopholes they was in it.

Well, the lease was right there in the drawer in the table, but I told him it was in my safety deposit box at the bank. I ain't got no safety deposit box and no more use for one than Judge Landis has for the deef and dumb alphabet.

Stevens said the lease was probably just a regular lease and if it was, they wouldn't be no trouble gettin' out of it, and meanw'ile him and his wife would see if they couldn't find us a place in the same buildin' with them.

And he was pretty sure they could even if the owner had to give some other tenant the air, because he, the owner, would do anything in the world for Stevens.

So I said yes, but suppose we want to stay where we are. So he said I looked like a man with better judgment than that and if I would just leave everything to him he would fix it so's we could move within a month. I kind of laughed and thought that would be the end of it.

He wanted to see the whole apartment so I showed him around and when we come to the bathroom he noticed my safety razor on the shelf. He said, "So you use one of them things," and I said, "Yes," and he asked me how I liked it, and I said I liked it fine and he said that must be because I hadn't never used a regular razor.

He said a regular razor was the only thing to use if a man wanted to look good. So I asked him if he used a regular razor and he said he did, so I said, "Well, if you look good, I don't want to."

But that didn't stop him and he said if I would meet him downtown the next day he would take me to the place where he bought all his razors and help me pick some out for myself. I told him I was goin' to be tied up, so just to give me the name and address of the place and I would drop in there when I had time.

But, no, that wouldn't do; he'd have to go along with me and introduce me to the proprietor because the proprietor was a great pal of his and would do anything in the world for him, and if the proprietor vouched for the razors, I could be sure I was gettin' the best razors money could buy. I told him again that I was goin' to be tied up and I managed to get him on some other subject.

Meanw'ile, Mrs. Stevens wanted to know where Ada had bought the dress she was wearin' and how much had it cost and Ada told her and Mrs. Stevens said it was a crime. She would meet Ada downtown tomorrow morning and take her to the shop where she bought her clothes and help her choose some dresses that really was dresses.

So Ada told her she didn't have no money to spend on dresses right then, and besides, the shop Mrs. Stevens mentioned was too high priced. But it seems the dame that run the shop was just like a sister to Mrs. Stevens and give her and her friends a big reduction and not only that, but they wasn't no hurry about payin'.

Well, Ada thanks her just the same, but didn't need nothin' new just at present; maybe later on she would take advantage of Mrs. Stevens's kind offer. Yes, but right now they was some models in stock that would be just beautiful on Ada and they might be gone later on. They was nothin' for it but Ada had to make a date with her; she wasn't obliged to buy nothin', but it would be silly not to go and look at the stuff that was in the joint and get acquainted with the dame that run it.

Well, Ada kept the date and bought three dresses she didn't want and they's only one of them she's had the nerve to wear. They cost her a hundred dollars a smash and I'd hate to think what the price would of been if Mrs. Stevens and the owner of the shop wasn't so much like sisters.

I was sure I hadn't made no date with Stevens, but just the same he called me up the next night to ask why I hadn't met him. And a couple of days later I got three new razors in the mail along with a bill and a note from the store sayin' that these was three specially fine razors that had been picked out for me by Thomas J. Stevens.

I don't know yet why I paid for the razors and kept 'em. I ain't used 'em and never intended to. Though I've been tempted a few times to test their edge on Stevens's neck.

That same week, Mrs. Stevens called up and asked us to spend Sunday with them and when we got out there, the owner of the buildin' is there, too. And Stevens has told him that I was goin' to give up my apartment on the South Side and wanted him to show me what he had.

I thought this was a little too strong and I said Stevens must of misunderstood me, that I hadn't no fault to find with the place I was in and wasn't plannin' to move, not for a year anyway. You can bet this didn't make no hit with the guy, who was just there on Stevens's say-so that I was a prospective tenant.

Well, it was only about two months ago that this cute little couple come into our life, but I'll bet we seen 'em twenty times at least. They was always invitin' us to their place or invitin' themselves to our place and Ada is one of these here kind of people that just can't say no. Which may be why I and her is married.

Anyway, it begin to seem like us and the Stevenses was livin' together and all one family, with them at the head of it. I never in my life seen anybody as crazy to run other people's business. Honest to heavens, it's a wonder they let us brush our own teeth!

Ada made the remark one night that she wished the ski jumper who was doin' our cookin' would get married and quit so's she wouldn't have to can her. Mrs. Stevens was there and asked Ada if she should try and get her a new cook, but Ada says no, the poor girl might have trouble findin' another job and she felt sorry for her.

Just the same, the next afternoon a Jap come to the apartment and said he was ready to go to work and Mrs. Stevens had sent him. Ada had to tell him the place was already filled.

Another night, Ada complained that her feet was tired. Belle said her feet used to get tired, too, till a friend of hers recommended a chiropodist and she went to him and he done her so much good that she made a regular appointment with him for once every month and paid him a flat sum and no matter how much runnin' around she done, her dogs hadn't fretted her once since this cornhusker started tendin' to 'em.

She wanted to call up the guy at his home right then and there and make a date for Ada and the only way Ada could stop her was by promisin' to go and see him the next time her feet hurt. After that, whenever the two gals met, Belle's first question was "How is your feet?" and the answer was always "Fine, thanks."

Well, I'm quite a football fan and Ada likes to go, too, when it's a big game and lots of excitement. So we decided we'd see the Illinois-Chicago game and have a look at this

"Red" Grange. I warned Ada not to say nothin' about it to Tom and Belle as I felt like we was entitled to a day off.

But it happened that they was goin' to be a game up at Evanston that day and the Stevenses invited us to see that one with them. So we used the other game as a alibi. And when Tom asked me later on if I'd boughten my tickets yet, instead of sayin' yes, I told him the truth and said no.

So then he said:

"I'm glad you ain't, because I and Belle has made up our mind that the Chicago game is the one we ought to see. And we'll all go together. And don't you bother about tickets because I can get better ones than you can as Stagg and I is just like that."

So I left it to him to get the tickets and we might as well of set on the Adams Street bridge. I said to Stevens, I said:

"If these is the seats Mr. Stagg digs up for his old pals, I suppose he leads strangers twenty or thirty miles out in the country and blindfolds 'em and ties 'em to a tree."

Now of course it was the bunk about he and Stagg bein' so close. He may of been introduced to him once, but he ain't the kind of a guy that Stagg would go around holdin' hands with. Just the same, most of the people he bragged about knowin', why it turned out that he really did know 'em; yes, and stood ace high with 'em, too.

Like, for instance, I got pinched for speedin' one night and they give me a ticket to show up in the Speeders' court and I told Stevens about it and he says, "Just forget it! I'll call up the judge and have it wiped off the book. He's a mighty good fella and a personal friend of mine."

Well, I didn't want to take no chances so I phoned Stevens the day before I was supposed to appear in court, and I asked him if he'd talked to the judge. He said he had and I asked him if he was sure. So he said, "If you don't believe me, call up the judge yourself." And he give me the judge's number. Sure enough, Stevens had fixed it and when I thanked the judge for his trouble, he said it was a pleasure to do somethin' for a friend of Tom Stevens's.

Now, I know it's silly to not appreciate favors like that and not warm up to people that's always tryin' to help you along, but still a person don't relish bein' treated like they was half-witted and couldn't button their shirt alone. Tom and Belle meant all right, but I and Ada got kind of tired of havin' fault found with everything that belonged to us and everything we done or tried to do.

Besides our apartment bein' no good and our clothes terrible, we learned that my dentist didn't know a bridge from a mustache cup, and the cigarettes I smoked didn't have no taste to them and the man that bobbed Ada's hair must of been mad at her, and neither of us would ever know what it was to live till we owned a wire-haired fox terrier.

And we found out that the liquor I'd been drinkin' and enjoyin' was a mixture of bath salts and assorted paints, and the car we'd paid seventeen hundred smackers for wasn't nowheres near as much of a car as one that Tom could of got for us for eight hundred on account of knowin' a brother-in-law of a fella that used to go to school with the president of the company's nephew, and that if Ada would take up aesthetic dancin' under a dame Belle knew about, why she'd never have no more trouble with her tonsils.

Nothin' we had or nothin' we talked about gettin' or doin' was worth a damn unless it was recommended or suggested by the Stevenses.

Well, I done a pretty good business this fall and I and

Ada had always planned to spend a winter in the South, so one night we figured it out that this was the year we could spare the money and the time and if we didn't go this year we never would. So the next thing was where should we go, and we finally decided on Miami. And we said we wouldn't mention nothin' about it to Tom and Belle till the day we was goin'. We'd pretend we was doin' it out of a clear sky.

But a secret is just as safe with Ada as a police dog tethered with dental floss. It wasn't more than a day or two after we'd had our talk when Tom and Belle sprang the news that they was leavin' for California right after New Year's. And why didn't we go with them.

Well, I didn't say nothin' and Ada said it sounded grand, but it was impossible. Then Stevens said if it was a question of money, to not let that bother us as he would loan it to me and I could pay it back whenever I felt like it. That was more than Ada could stand, so she says we wasn't as poor as people seemed to think and the reason we couldn't go to California was because we was goin' to Miami.

This was such a surprise that it almost struck 'em dumb at first and all Tom could think of to say was that he'd been to Miami himself and it was too crowded and he'd lay off of it if he was us. But the next time we seen 'em they had our trip all arranged.

First, Tom asked me what road we was goin' on and I told him the Big Four. So he asked if we had our reservations and I told him yes.

"Well," he said, "we'll get rid of 'em and I'll fix you up on the C. & E. I. The general passenger agent is a friend of mine and they ain't nothin' he won't do for my friends. He'll see that you're treated right and that you get there in good shape."

So I said:

"I don't want to put you to all that trouble, and besides I don't know nobody connected with the Big Four well enough for them to resent me travelin' on their lines, and as for gettin' there in good shape, even if I have a secret enemy or two on the Big Four, I don't believe they'd endanger the lives of the other passengers just to see that I didn't get there in good shape."

But Stevens insisted on takin' my tickets and sellin' 'em back to the Big Four and gettin' me fixed on the C. & E. I. The berths we'd had on the Big Four was Lower 9 and Lower 10. The berths Tom got us on the C. & E. I. was Lower 7 and Lower 8, which he said was better. I suppose he figured that the nearer you are to the middle of the car, the less chance there is of bein' woke up if your car gets in another train's way.

He wanted to know, too, if I'd made any reservations at a hotel. I showed him a wire I had from the Royal Palm in reply to a wire I'd sent 'em.

"Yes," he says, "but you don't want to stop at the Royal Palm. You wire and tell 'em to cancel that and I'll make arrangements for you at the Flamingo, over at the Beach. Charley Krom, the manager there, was born and raised in the same town I was. He'll take great care of you if he knows you're a friend of mine."

So I asked him if all the guests at the Flamingo was friends of his, and he said of course not; what did I mean?

"Well," I said, "I was just thinkin' that if they ain't, Mr. Krom probably makes life pretty miserable for 'em. What does he do, have the phone girls ring 'em up at all hours of the night, and hide their mail, and shut off their hot water, and put cracker crumbs in their beds?"

That didn't mean nothin' to Stevens and he went right ahead and switched me from one hotel to the other.

While Tom was reorganizin' my program and tellin' me what to eat in Florida, and what bait to use for barracuda and carp, and what time to go bathin' and which foot to stick in the water first, why Belle was makin' Ada return all the stuff she had boughten to wear down there and buy other stuff that Belle picked out for her at joints where Belle was so well known that they only soaked her twice as much as a stranger. She had Ada almost crazy, but I told her to never mind; in just a few more days we'd be where they couldn't get at us.

I suppose you're wonderin' why didn't we quarrel with 'em and break loose from 'em and tell 'em to leave us alone. You'd know why if you knew them. Nothin' we could do would convince 'em that we didn't want their advice and help. And nothin' we could say was a insult.

Well, the night before we was due to leave Chi, the phone rung and I answered it. It was Tom.

"I've got a surprise for you," he says. "I and Belle has give up the California idear. We're goin' to Miami instead, and on account of me knowin' the boys down at the C. & E. I., I've landed a drawin' room on the same train you're takin'. How is that for news?"

"Great!" I said, and I went back and broke it to Ada. For a minute I thought she was goin' to faint. And all night long she moaned and groaned and had hysterics.

So that's how we happened to come to Biloxi.

DEATH OF RED PERIL

By WALTER D. EDMONDS

I

JOHN brought his off eye to bear on me:

What do them old coots down to the store do? Why, one of 'em will think up a horse that's been dead forty year and then they'll set around remembering this and that about that horse until they've made a resurrection of him. You'd think he was a regular Grattan Bars, the way they talk, telling one thing and another, when a man knows if that horse hadn't had a breeching to keep his tail end off the ground he could hardly have walked from here to Boonville.

A horse race is a handsome thing to watch if a man has his money on a sure proposition. My pa was always a great hand at a horse race. But when he took a boat and my mother he didn't have no more time for it. So he got interested in another sport.

Did you ever hear of racing caterpillars? No? Well, it used to be a great thing on the canawl. My pa used to have a lot of them insects on hand every fall, and the way he could get them to run would make a man have his eyes examined.

The way we raced caterpillars was to set them in a napkin ring on a table, one facing one way and one the other. Outside the napkin ring was drawn a circle in chalk three feet acrost. Then a man lifted the ring and the handlers was allowed one jab with a darning needle to get their caterpillars started. The one that got outside the chalk circle the first was the one that won the race.

I remember my pa tried out a lot of breeds, and he got hold of some pretty fast steppers. But there wasn't one of them could equal Red Peril. To see him you wouldn't believe he could run. He was all red and kind of stubby, and he had a sort of a wart behind that you'd think would get in his way. There wasn't anything fancy in his looks. He'd just set still studying the ground and make you think he was dreaming about last year's oats; but when you set him in the starting ring he'd hitch himself up behind like a man lifting on his galluses, and then he'd light out for glory.

Pa come acrost Red Peril down in Westernville. Ma's relatives resided there, and it being Sunday we'd all gone in to church. We was riding back in a hired rig with a dandy trotter, and Pa was pushing her right along and Ma was talking sermon and clothes, and me and my sister was setting on the back seat playing poke your nose, when all of a sudden Pa hollers, 'Whoa!' and set the horse right down on the breeching. Ma let out a holler and come to rest on the dashboard with her head under the horse. 'My gracious land!' she says. 'What's happened?' Pa was out on the other side of the road right down in the mud in his Sunday pants, a-wropping up something in his yeller handkerchief. Ma begun to get riled. 'What you doing, Pa?' she says. 'What you got there?' Pa was putting his handkerchief back into his inside pocket. Then he come back over the wheel and got him a chew. 'Leeza,' he says, 'I got the fastest caterpillar in seven counties. It's an act of Providence I seen him, the way he jumped the ruts.' 'It's an act of God I ain't laying dead under the back end of that horse,' says Ma. 'I've gone and spoilt my Sunday hat.' 'Never mind,' says Pa; 'Red Peril will earn you a new one.' Just like that he named him. He was the fastest caterpillar in seven counties.

When we got back onto the boat, while Ma was turning up the supper, Pa set him down to the table under the lamp and pulled out the handkerchief. 'You two devils stand there and there,' he says to me and my sister, 'and if you let him get by I'll leather the soap out of you.'

So we stood there and he undid the handkerchief, and out walked one of them red, long-haired caterpillars. He walked right to the middle of the table, and then he took a short turn and put his nose in his tail and went to sleep.

'Who'd think that insect could make such a break for freedom as I seen him make?' says Pa, and he got out a empty Brandreth box and filled it up with some towel and put the caterpillar inside. 'He needs a rest,' says Pa. 'He needs to get used to his stall. When he limbers up I'll commence training him. Now then,' he says, putting the box on the shelf back of the stove, 'don't none of you say a word about him.'

He got out a pipe and set there smoking and figuring, and we could see he was studying out just how he'd make a world-beater out of that bug. 'What you going to feed him?' asks Ma. 'If I wasn't afraid of constipating him,' Pa says, 'I'd try him out with milkweed.'

Next day we hauled up the Lansing Kill Gorge. Ned Kilbourne, Pa's driver, come aboard in the morning, and he took a look at that caterpillar. He took him out of the box and felt his legs and laid him down on the table and went clean over him. 'Well,' he says, 'he don't look like a great lot, but I've knowed some of that red variety could chug along pretty smart.' Then he touched him with a pin. It was a sudden sight.

It looked like the rear end of that caterpillar was racing the front end, but it couldn't never quite get by. Afore either Ned or Pa could bet a move Red Peril had made a turn around the sugar bowl and run solid aground in the butter dish.

Pa let out a loud swear. 'Look out he don't pull a tendon,' he says. 'Butter's a bad thing. A man has to be careful. Jeepers,' he says, picking him up and taking him over to the stove to dry, 'I'll handle him myself. I don't want no rum-soaked bezabors dishing my beans.'

'I didn't mean harm, Will,' says Ned. 'I was just curious.'

There was something extraordinary about that caterpillar. He was intelligent. It seemed he just couldn't abide the feel of sharp iron. It got so that if Pa reached for the lapel of his coat Red Peril would light out. It must have been he was tender. I said he had a sort of a wart behind, and I guess he liked to find it a place of safety.

We was all terrible proud of that bird. Pa took to timing him on the track. He beat all known time holler. He got to know that as soon as he crossed the chalk he would get back safe in his quarters. Only when we tried sprinting him across the supper table, if he saw a piece of butter he'd pull up short and bolt back where he come from. He had a mortal fear of butter.

Well, Pa trained him three nights. It was a sight to see him there at the table, a big man with a needle in his hand, moving the lamp around and studying out the identical spot that caterpillar wanted most to get out of the needle's way. Pretty soon he found it, and then he says to Ned, 'I'll race him agin all comers at all odds.' 'Well, Will,' says Ned, 'I guess it's a safe proposition.'

II

He hauled up the feeder to Forestport and got us a load of potatoes. We raced him there against Charley Mack, the bank-walker's Leopard Pillar, one of them tufted breeds with a row of black buttons down the back. The Leopard was well liked and had won several races that season, and there was quite a few boaters around that fancied him. Pa argued for favorable odds, saying he was racing a maiden caterpillar; and there was a lot of money laid out, and Pa and Ned managed to cover the most of it. As for the race, there wasn't anything to it. While we was putting him in the ring—one of them birchbark and sweet grass Indians make—Red Peril didn't act very good. I guess the smell and the crowd kind of upset him. He was nervous and kept fidgeting with his front feet; but they hadn't more'n lifted the ring than he lit out under the edge as tight as he could make it, and Pa touched him with the needle just as he lepped the line. Me and my sister was supposed to be in bed, but Ma had gone visiting in Forestport and we'd snuck in and was under the table, which had a red cloth onto it, and I can tell you there was some shouting. There was some couldn't believe that insect had been inside the ring at all; and there was some said he must be a cross with a dragon fly or a side-hill gouger; but old Charley Mack, that'd worked in the camps, said he guessed Red Peril must be descended from the caterpillars Paul Bunyan used to race. He • said you could tell by the bump on his tail, which Paul used to put on all his caterpillars, seeing as how the smallest pointed object he could hold in his hand was a peavy.

Well, Pa raced him a couple of more times and he won just as easy, and Pa cleared up close to a hundred dollars in three races. That caterpillar was a mammoth wonder, and word of him got going and people commenced talking him up everywhere, so it was hard to race him around these parts.

But about that time the lock keeper of Number One on the feeder come across a pretty swift article that the people round Rome thought high of. And as our boat was headed down the gorge, word got ahead about Red Peril, and people began to look out for the race.

We come into Number One about four o'clock, and Pa tied up right there and went on shore with his box in his pocket and Red Peril inside the box. There must have been ten men crowded into the shanty, and as many more again outside looking in the windows and door. The lock tender was a skinny bezabor from Stittville, who thought he knew a lot about racing caterpillars; and, come to think of it, maybe he did. His name was Henry Buscerck, and he had a bad tooth in front he used to suck at a lot.

Well, him and Pa set their caterpillars on the table for the crowd to see, and I must say Buscerck's caterpillar was as handsome a brute as you could wish to look it, bright bay with black points and a short fine coat. He had a way of looking right and left, too, that made him handsome. But Pa didn't bother to look at him. Red Peril was a natural marvel, and he knew it.

Buscerck was a sly, twirpish man, and he must've heard about Red Peril—right from the beginning, as it turned out; for he laid out the course in yeller chalk. They used Pa's ring, a big silver one he'd bought second hand just for Red Peril. They laid out a lot of money, and Dennison Smith lifted the ring. The way Red Peril histed himself out from under would raise a man's blood pressure twenty notches. I swear you could see the hair lay down on his back. Why, that black-pointed bay was left nowhere! It didn't seem like he moved. But Red Peril was just gathering himself for a fast finish over the line when he seen it was yeller. He reared right up; he must've thought it was butter, by Jeepers, the way he whirled on his hind legs and went the way he'd come. Pa begun to get scared, and he shook his needle behind Red Peril, but that caterpillar was more scared of butter than he ever was of cold steel. He passed the other insect afore he'd got halfway to the line. By Cripus, you'd ought to've heard the cheering from the Forestport crews. The Rome men was green. But when he got to the line, danged if that caterpillar didn't shy agin and run around the circle twicet, and then it seemed like his heart had gone in on him, and he crept right back to the middle of the circle and lay there hiding his head. It was the pitifullest sight a man ever looked at. You could almost hear him moaning, and he shook all over.

I've never seen a man so riled as Pa was. The water was running right out of his eyes. He picked up Red Peril and he says, 'This here's no race.' He picked up his money and he says, 'The course was illegal, with that yeller chalk.' Then he squashed the other caterpillar, which was just getting ready to cross the line, and he looks at Buscerck and says, 'What're you going to do about that?'

Buscerck says, 'I'm going to collect my money. My caterpillar would have beat.'

'If you want to call that a finish you can,' says Pa, pointing to the squashed bay one, 'but a baby could see he's still got to reach the line. Red Peril got to wire and came back and got to it again afore your hayseed worm got half his feet on the ground. If it was any other man owned him,' Pa says, 'I'd feel sorry I squashed him.'

He stepped out of the house, but Buscerck laid a-hold of his pants and says, 'You got to pay, Hemstreet. A man can't get away with no such excuses in the city of Rome.'

Pa didn't say nothing. He just hauled off and sunk his fist, and Buscerck come to inside the lock, which was at low level right then. He waded out the lower end and he says, 'I'll have you arrested for this.' Pa says, 'All right; but if I ever catch you around this lock again I'll let you have a feel with your other eye.'

Nobody else wanted to collect money from Pa, on account of his build, mostly, so we went back to the boat. Pa put Red Peril to bed for two days. It took him all of that to get over his fright at the yeller circle. Pa even made us go without butter for a spell, thinking Red Peril might know the smell of it. He was such an intelligent, thinking animal, a man couldn't tell nothing about him.

III

But next morning the sheriff comes aboard and arrests Pa with a warrant and takes him afore a justice of the peace. That was old Oscar Snipe. He'd heard all about the race, and I think he was feeling pleasant with Pa, because right off they commenced talking breeds. It would have gone off good only Pa'd been having a round with the sheriff. They come in arm and arm, singing a Hallelujah meeting song; but Pa was polite, and when Oscar says, 'What's this?' he only says, 'Well, well.'

'I hear you've got a good caterpillar,' says the judge.

'Well, well,' says Pa. It was all he could think of to say.

'What breed is he?' says Oscar, taking a chew.

'Well,' says Pa, 'well, well.'

Ned Kilbourne says he was a red one.

'That's a good breed,' says Oscar, folding his hands on his stummick and spitting over his thumbs and between his knees and into the sandbox all in one spit. 'I kind of fancy the yeller ones myself. You're a connesewer,' he says to Pa, 'and so'm I, and between connesewers I'd like to show you one. He's as neat a stepper as there is in this county.'

'Well, well,' says Pa, kind of cold around the eyes and looking at the lithograph of Mrs. Snipe done in a hair frame over the sink.

Oscar slews around and fetches a box out of his back pocket and shows us a sweet little yeller one.

'There she is,' he says, and waits for praise.

'She was a good woman,' Pa said after a while, looking at the picture, "if any woman that's four times a widow can be called such.'

'Not her,' says Oscar. 'It's this yeller caterpillar.'

Pa slung his eyes on the insect which Oscar was holding, and it seemed like he'd just got an idee.

'Fast?' he says, deep down. 'That thing run! Why, a snail with the string-halt could spit in his eye.'

Old Oscar come to a boil quick.

'Evidence. Bring me the evidence.'

He spit, and he was that mad he let his whole chew get away from him without noticing. Buscerck says, 'Here,' and takes his hand off'n his right eye.

Pa never took no notice of nothing after that but the eye. It was the shiniest black onion I ever see on a man. Oscar says, 'Forty dollars!' And Pa pays and says, 'It's worth it.'

But it don't never pay to make an enemy in horse racing or caterpillars, as you will see, after I've got around to telling you.

Well, we raced Red Peril nine times after that, all along the Big Ditch, and you can hear to this day—yes, sir—that there never was a caterpillar alive could run like Red Peril. Pa got rich onto him. He allowed to buy a new team in the spring. If he could only've started a breed from that bug, his

fortune would've been made and Henry Ford would've
looked like a bent nickel alongside of me today. But caterpillars aren't built like Ford cars. We beat all the great
caterpillars of the year, and it being a time for a late winter,
there was some fast running. We raced the Buffalo Big
Blue and Fenwick's Night Mail and Wilson's Joe of Barne-
veld. There wasn't one could touch Red Peril. It was close
into October when a crowd got together and brought up the
Black Arrer of Ava to race us, but Red Peril beat him by
an inch. And after that there wasn't a caterpillar in the state
would race Pa's.

He was mighty chesty them days and had come to be
quite a figger down the canawl. People come aboard to talk
with him and admire Red Peril; and Pa got the idea of
charging five cents a sight, and that made for more money
even if there wasn't no more running for the animile. He
commenced to get fat.

And then come the time that comes to all caterpillars.
And it goes to show that a man ought to be as careful of
his enemies as he is lending money to friends.

IV

We was hauling down the Lansing Kill again and we'd
just crossed the aqueduct over Stringer Brook when the
lock keeper, that minded it and the lock just below, come
out and says there was quite a lot of money being put up on
a caterpillar they'd collected down in Rome.

Well, Pa went in and he got out Red Peril and tried him
out. He was fat and his stifles acted kind of stiff, but you
could see with half an eye he was still fast. His start was a
mite slower, but he made great speed once he got going.

'He's not in the best shape in the world,' Pa says, 'and if
it was any other bug I wouldn't want to run him. But I'll

trust the old brute,' and he commenced brushing him up with a toothbrush he'd bought a-purpose.

'Yeanh,' says Ned. 'It may not be right, but we've got to consider the public.'

By what happened after, we might have known that we'd meet up with that caterpillar at Number One Lock; but there wasn't no sign of Buscerck, and Pa was so excited at racing Red Peril again that I doubt if he noticed where he was at all. He was all rigged out for the occasion. He had on a black hat and a new red boating waistcoat, and when he busted loose with his horn for the lock you'd have thought he wanted to wake up all the deef-and-dumbers in seven counties. We tied by the upper gates and left the team to graze; and there was quite a crowd on hand. About nine morning boats was tied along the towpath, and all the after-noon boats waited. People was hanging around, and when they heard Pa whanging his horn they let out a great cheer. He took off his hat to some of the ladies, and then he took Red Peril out of his pocket and everybody cheered some more.

'Who owns this here caterpillar I've been hearing about?' Pa asks. 'Where is he? Why don't he bring out his pore con-traption?'

A feller says he's in the shanty.

'What's his name?' says Pa.

'Martin Henry's running him. He's called the Horned Demon of Rome.'

'Dinged if I ever thought to see him at my time of life,' says Pa. And he goes in. Inside there was a lot of men talking and smoking and drinking and laying money faster than leghorns can lay eggs, and when Pa comes in they let out a great howdy, and when Pa put down the Bandreth box on the table they crowded round; and you'd

ought to've heard the mammoth shout they give when Red
Peril climbed out of his box. And well they might. Yes, sir!

You can tell that caterpillar's a thoroughbred. He's shining right down to the root of each hair. He's round, but he
ain't too fat. He don't look as supple as he used to, but the
folks can't tell that. He's got the winner's look, and he
prances into the centre of the ring with a kind of delicate
canter that was as near single footing as I ever see a caterpillar get to. By Jeepers Cripus! I felt proud to be in the same
family as him, and I wasn't only a little lad.

Pa waits for the admiration to die down, and he lays out
his money, and he says to Martin Henry, 'Let's see your
ring-boned swivel-hocked imitation of a bug.'

Martin answers, 'Well, he ain't much to look at, maybe,
but you'll be surprised to see how he can push along.'

And he lays down the dangedest lump of worm you ever
set your eyes on. It's the kind of insect a man might expect
to see in France or one of them furrin lands. It's about two
and a half inches long and stands only half a thumbnail at
the shoulder. It's green and as hairless as a newborn egg,
and it crouches down squinting around at Red Peril like a
man with sweat in his eye. It ain't natural nor refined to
look at such a bug, let alone race it.

When Pa seen it, he let out a shout and laughed. He
couldn't talk from laughing.

But the crowd didn't say a lot, having more money on
the race than ever was before or since on a similar occasion.
It was so much that even Pa commenced to be serious. Well,
they put 'em in the ring together and Red Peril kept over on
his side with a sort of intelligent dislike. He was the brain-
iest article in the caterpillar line I ever knowed. The other
one just hunkered down with a mean look in his eye.

Millard Thompson held the ring. He counted, 'One—

two—three—and off.' Some folks said it was the highest he knew how to count, but he always got that far anyhow, even if it took quite a while for him to remember what figger to commence with.

The ring come off and Pa and Martin Henry sunk their needles—at least they almost sunk them, for just then them standing close to the course seen that Horned Demon sink his horns into the back end of Red Peril. He was always a sensitive animal, Red Peril was, and if a needle made him start you can think for yourself what them two horns did for him. He cleared twelve inches in one jump—but then he sot right down on his belly, trembling.

'Foul!' bellers Pa. 'My 'pillars fouled.'

'It ain't in the rule book,' Millard says.

'It's a foul!' yells Pa; and all the Forestport men yell, 'Foul! Foul!'

But it wasn't allowed. The Horned Demon commenced walking to the circle—he couldn't move much faster than a barrel can roll uphill, but he was getting there. We all seen two things, then. Red Peril was dying, and we was losing the race. Pa stood there kind of foamy in his beard, and the water running right out of both eyes. It's an awful thing to see a big man cry in public. But Ned saved us. He seen Red Peril was dying, the way he wiggled, and he figgered, with the money he had on him, he'd make him win if he could.

He leans over and put his nose into Red Peril's ear, and he shouts, 'My Cripus, you've gone and dropped the butter!'

Something got into that caterpillar's brain, dying as he was, and he let out the smallest squeak of a hollering fright I ever listened to a caterpillar make. There was a convulsion got into him. He looked like a three-dollar mule with the wind colic, and then he gave a bound. My holy! How that caterpillar did rise up. When he come down again, he was stone dead, but he lay with his chin across the line. He'd won the race. The Horned Demon was blowing bad and only halfway to the line. . . .

Well, we won. But I think Pa's heart was busted by the squeal he heard Red Peril make when he died. He couldn't abide Ned's face after that, though he knowed Ned had saved the day for him. But he put Red Peril's carcass in his pocket with the money and walks out.

And there he seen Buscerck standing at the sluices. Pa stood looking at him. The sheriff was alongside Buscerck and Oscar Snipe on the other side, and Buscerck guessed he had the law behind him.

'Who owns that Horned Demon?' says Pa.

'Me,' says Buscerck with a sneer. 'He may have lost, but he done a good job doing it.'

Pa walks right up to him.

'I've got another forty dollars in my pocket,' he says, and he connected sizably.

Buscerck's boots showed a minute. Pretty soon they let down the water and pulled him out. They had to roll a couple of gallons out of him afore they got a grunt. It served him right. He'd played foul. But the sheriff was worried, and he says to Oscar, 'Had I ought to arrest Will?' (Meaning Pa.)

Oscar was a sporting man. He couldn't abide low dealing He looks at Buscerck there, shaping his belly over the ... rel, and he says, 'Water never hurt a man. It keeps his hide from crackin'. So they let Pa alone. I guess they didn't think it was safe to have a man in jail that would cry about a caterpillar. But then they hadn't lived alongside of Red Peril like us.

TRAVEL IS SO BROADENING

By Sinclair Lewis

WELL, I want to tell you, Mrs. Babbitt, and I know Mrs. Schmaltz heartily agrees with me, that we've never enjoyed a dinner more—that was some of the finest fried chicken I ever tasted in my life—and it certainly is a mighty great pleasure to be able to just have this quiet evening with you and George. Personally, I'm just as glad the Reverend and his wife couldn't come. I yield to no one in my admiration for Reverend Hickenlooper—as you say, there's probably no greater influence for Christian manhood in Zenith—but it's mighty nice to be able to have a quiet chin with you and George.

Now, George, about this trip to the Yellowstone you were asking about.

I don't know as I can help an old, trained, long-distance motorist like you, with your wealth of experience, though I never did agree with you about not going into low gear in descending steep hills, but I guess you've got me beat on long-distance motoring, and I've often said to Mrs. Schmaltz—haven't I, Mame!—that there sure is one thing I envy George F. Babbitt for, and that's the time he drove three hundred and sixteen miles in one day, between dawn and midnight. But I don't pretend to have that magnificent

186

physical make-up of yours, George, and I've never been able to stand more'n two hundred and ninety-eight miles in one day's tour, and, you might say, really enjoy it and feel I was relaxing.

But same time, any helpful information that I can give you may be of help to you on your trip, if you decide to make it next summer, I'm certainly mighty glad to give you, if you find it helpful.

Now I myself, I didn't quite get to Yellowstone Park. You know, it's a funny thing how many folks in this man's town think I drove clear from Zenith to Yellowstone Park. I've never claimed anything of the kind.

It's true that when I gave my little talk before the West Side Bridge Club about my trip, they billed it—and in a brief way the West Side Tidings column of the *Evening Advocate* spoke of it—as an account of a trip clear to Yellowstone Park.

But it wasn't a trip clear to Yellowstone Park. The fact is, and I've always been the first to acknowledge it, I didn't get clear to Yellowstone Park but only to the Black Hills, in North Dakota.

The fact is, not only did I want to see the scenic and agricultural wonders of Minnesota and Wisconsin and Dakota and all like that, but Mame has a brother-in-law—I'm sure Mrs. Schmaltz will excuse me for speaking of family matters, in the presence of old friends like you two—and she has this brother-in-law that had met with misfortune, and one of the objects of our trip was to stop and see if we couldn't help him straighten out his affairs—why say, the poor devil was in such stresses and difficult straits that he'd actually had to borrow money to help him carry on his business, he's in the drug and stationery business. Why say—

And a mighty fine gentleman he is, and his wife is a

mighty bright cultured little woman; she subscribes to the *Ladies' Home Journal* and reads it right through every month. And poor old Lafayette—that's Mrs. Schmaltz's brother-in-law's name—he was very well educated; he not only went through a pharmacy college and got his degree, but he also studied cost-accountancy by mail. But somehow he just couldn't make a go of it. I guess he was kind of a dreamer. When he started his first drug-store, he also took an agency for the Florida Transplanted Palm and Orange Tree Company, and in Dakota he couldn't hardly sell any palms at all—those Swede farmers may be all right as farmers, but they ain't up to the cultural point of palms yet. And then later in another town he went into partnership with a gentleman that had found oil there, and also wanted to start a radiator factory—

And say, that wasn't such a bad idea as it sounded. Of course this was in town where there wasn't any iron or coal anywheres around, and the railroad connections wasn't very good, but still, it was cold as hell—excuse me, Mrs. Babbitt—it was awful' cold in the winter, and where do you need radiators as much as where it's cold? But still, things didn't work out quite right. Come to find out, there wasn't any oil in the oil field, and somehow the radiator factory couldn't seem to compete with the trust, and so poor old Lafayette lost money almost as fast as he made it.

So when we drove out to see him—

You know how bad luck besets the just with the unjust, and say, by this time, poor old Lafe and his wife were so hard up against it that they didn't even have an automobile!

And their radio was so old and so cheap that they couldn't hardly get Minneapolis on it!

Well, that'll give you an idea about how miserably poor

and pursued by ill fortune they were—they lived in Toma-hawk City, North Dakota.

Well, so, to make a long story short, Mame and I went to see them, and I gave him what advice I could, and then we ran on and gave the Black Hills the once-over, but we didn't have the time to make Yellowstone Park, but still, that was only four, or maybe it might have been six or eight hundred miles farther on, so I can give you practically a detailed description of the road and stopping-places and so on for the whole distance.

And say, I certainly do recommend your making the trip. They can say what they want to. Some people claim that reading books is the greatest cultural influence, and still others maintain that you can get the most in the quickest split-second time by listening to lectures, but what I always say is, "There's nothing more broadening than travel."

Well, now you just take this, just for an example: When I crossed Minnesota, I found—in fact I saw it myself, first-hand—that there were as many Swedes as Germans there. And funny names—say, they certainly had the funniest names! Swanson and Kettleson and Shipstead, and all like that—simply screams. I says to Mame, "Well, Mrs. Schmaltz," I says—I often call her that when we're funning around—"Well, Mrs. Schmaltz," I says, "you wanted to get a kick out of this trip, and here you got it," I says, "in all these funny names."

And all like that.

We get to thinking, here in Zenith, that everybody, I mean every *normal* fellow, lives just like we do, but out there in Minnesota I found a lot of the folks never even heard of our mayor here in Zenith—they just talk about Minneapolis and Saint Paul politics! I tell you, travel like that gives a fellow a whole new set of insights into human character and how big the world is, after all, and as our pastor, Dr. Edwards, often says, the capacity of the Lord for producing new sets of psychological set-ups is practically, you might say, absolutely unlimited.

Well, so I'll give you the main, broad outlines of the trip. Considering that it must be about two thousand miles from here to Yellowstone Park, naturally I can't go into details, but just suggest the big towns that you want to make for, and general cautions about long-distance touring if you're going to do it scientifically.

Yes, thanks, I'll have a cigar, but I'm not drinking anything. Well, make it very mild. Fine, that's fine. After all, as I often tell my boy, Robby, since prohibition *is* a law of the land, we ought to drink nothing at all or only very little. That'll be fine. Whoa-up! Well, since you've poured it, can't waste it, eh? Just a little siphon. Fine! Attaboy!

Well, as I say, I'll make it short. We started out for Dakota, just Mame here and me—the children was busy with their schools and study—

I don't know if I've told you, but Delmerine has found she had more kind of talent for painting than for music, though to me she's got one of the nicest voices I ever heard in so young a girl, but she was informed by some of the best authorities that she'd do even better at art than at music, so she switched to the Art Institute, and Robby had to sort of make up some extra courses this last summer—

But not to go into that, the point is that Mame and I started off just by ourselves.

Now I hope Mame will excuse me—she knows how I like

to kid her now and then—but what I mean is, just about when we were ready to start, she got an idea it'd be a good idea to take along her old Aunt Sarah, that lives out here in Rosedale.

"Let's take Aunt Sarah along, and give her a good time," she says.

"Let's take who along and do what?" I says.

"Why, let's take Aunt Sarah. She hasn't ever been anywhere," she says.

"Fine!" I says. "Say, that'll be just elegant. Let's also and at the same time take along the St. Agatha Orphan Asylum, the Salvation Army, and the convalescents of the Zenith General Hospital," I says, "so we can have a really chummy time."

Well, with Mame here, I can't very well tell you all the remarks we passed, but anyway, we shoved Aunt Sarah into the discard—say, that old girl whistles through her teeth, and the only time she ever was kissed was when Brigham Young passed through here ninety-two years ago—but by golly, I got to admit it, Mame got back at me.

I'd had a kind of a sneaking idea I might work in Jackie, our dog—and a mighty fine useful dog he is, too—but I had to swap Jackie for Aunt Sarah, and so we started off with nobody aboard except Mrs. Schmaltz and me.

Now I know that the first question you'll want to ask me is what kind of an outfit you ought to take along on a trip like this. I don't pretend to be any Ammunsun, and if I've ever found any South Poles, the newspapers forgot to tell me about it. But I'll give you my own experience for what it's worth.

Now about clothes—

There's those that maintain a fellow on as long and you might call it adventurous trip like this had ought to just wear an old suit of regular clothes. And there's those that maintain you ought to wear corduroy. Say, many and many's the hour I've sat in on debates between these two schools. But as for me, say, give me a nice suit of khaki coat and pants, every time. It may get dirtier than hell, but it never shows it's dirty, so what difference does it make?

And Mame the same way. She had specially made up for her a nice khaki jacket and breeches, and while sometimes she used to worry, and ask me if it didn't make her look the least lee-tle bit broad in the hips, I used to say to her, "Hell—" Excuse me, Mrs. Babbitt. "Rats," I said to her, "if you're comfy in 'em and if you find 'em convenient for crawling through barb-wire fences and all like that, whose business is it," I asked her, "whether some folks think it makes you look broad amidships or not!"

Now, Mamie, don't you go giving me those dirty looks, because remember we're right in the bosom of the family, you might say.

And now here's one thing I found mighty important.

Aside from the regular shoes that you wear when driving —and they ought to be a good stout pair of shoes, because who knows when you may want to sneak into an orchard and steal some apples, or even go up on a hill to see a view, or something like that—you ought to take along a pair of easy shoes for the evening—also more elegant; show 'em when you arrive in one of these hick hotels that you may be dressed comfortable for the auto trip, but back home you can dress just as good as the next fellow, and maybe better.

Personally, I was awful' fortunate. I had an old pair of pumps, and I had 'em blacked up and they looked almost practically as good as new.

Funny, I'll never forget buying those pumps.

Here's the way it happened:

I was in Chicago, on a business trip, you understand, and I happened to be wandering along South State Street, in the poorer section, and I come on a bargain sale of shoes and footwear, and I spotted these pumps, and they looked pretty good to me. And the fellow that owned the store, but he was a Kike, you understand, he come out, and he says—of course he spoke practically illiterate—and he says to me, "Hey, mister, I vill sell you dem shoes cheap"—you know how those fellows talk.

Well, I just looked at him in a kind of amused way, and of course I could see that he could see I wasn't the kind of ignorant bird he was accustomed to deal with, and I says to him, "Ah, so, my friend," I says, "so you'll sell them to me cheap, will you!"

"Sure," he says, "you bet; I'll let you have dem at a rock-bottoms price."

"Well, friend," I says to him, "I'm sure that's awful nice of you, but what makes you think—" And I just kind of laughed. "What makes you think," I said, "that I require any such articles of footwear?"

"Vell, I can tell dat you're a gentlemans that puts on a dress-suit frequent, and dese is real dress-suit shoes," he says. "Dey come from the bankrupt sale from the real bon-ton élite store from Chicago," he says, "in fact from Waffleheim and Spoor, and they're too good for my class of custom," he says.

Well sir, just out of idle curiosity, I looked 'em over, and upon my word, if I didn't think he was telling the truth, for once. Say, them pumps, if they was what they looked like they was, wasn't worth one cent less than fifteen bucks, or anyway twelve-fifty. Well, of course I got kind of all excited inside. I knew then just how this Doctor—well, whatever his name is that writes for the *Saturday Evening Post,* I knew just how he feels when he finds a first edition of Harold Bell Wright for a dollar and a quarter and later maybe he's able to sell it for a couple thousand.

Well, I tried not to look excited, and I said, casual, I said to him, "Well, brother, they look like they were about my size, and I'll give you two bucks for 'em."

Well sir, you'd laughed if you could 've seen him go up in the air. Say, he just clawed the air. He hollers and shouts and he claims they're worth five-fifty. You know how these doggone foreigners carry on—and say, if you're a student of philosophy you'll realize that their actions also indicate an inner spiritual something, you might say, that indicates why they can't ever compete with the clear, sure, short-cut mentality of the Nordics. He waves his hands and—

Oh, you know.

But say, I'm afraid I'm drifting away from my subject a little. Fact is, I jewed him down, and I got 'em for three and a half, and say, they fitted like a glove, and I wore 'em at some of them finest parties and soirées in Zenith for five years, and then when we started on the Western tour, they were just the thing to take along to rest your feet in the evening. And be sure and take something like that— stylish but restful.

Now as to your auto equipment, George.

You want to have a Pull-U-Out or some other device for getting you out of a mud-hole if you get stuck in it. It's perfectly true that wherever you go now, motor-touring in the United States, you find perfect cement roads. But sometimes —You know how it is. Here and there there's gaps in the perfect cement highway, and you will get stuck in the mud.

And of course you want chains along, and extra tires. And

what I recommend especially is one of these stoves with solid alcohol. When you're touring, you get a little tired of restaurants where you can't get anything but a small steak and beef stew, but fact is that sometimes you'd like a little *food,* and if you happen to feel inclined that way, of course the only thing you can do is to cook it for yourself.

In 'most all these small towns you go into a place—well, outside it's got a big fine illuminated electric sign with "Eats" or something like that on it, so you think it's going to be a snappy up-to-date joint, but you get in and you find it's run by some retired farmer and his daughter and the old woman.

Pop's principal job is leaning on the cash register and annoying a toothpick. He's too busy thinking about what a civilized city guy he's become to do any work except play cashier—with six customers an hour!—or maybe he's admiring all the art treasures in the place—the snappy picture of two pears and a lobster, and the signs like "Watch Your Hat and Coat," and "No Trust, No Bust," and "Ham and Eggs Country Style, 20c"—country style meaning they throw in a piece of Certain-teed asphalt-treated toast with the relics.

Then out in the kitchen is Ma, doing what she thinks is cooking. The only thing she don't burn is the drinking-water. And Daughter has the idea she's waiting on table. But Daughter ain't interested in anybody but traveling salesmen that she thinks are unmarried—which no traveling salesman is since God made little apples. And all over the place there's a nice pleasing odor of burnt steak and onions.

So you sit up on a nice high stool, that's cleaned regular once a day by wiping it off with the rag that they use to grease the griddle, and you say to Daughter, "Say, could you bring us some cornbeef hash?" And she looks at you like an evangelist looks at a guy that he thinks has put a lead quarter in the plate, and she says, "The hash is out."

And then you think—and you find out you ain't much of a thinker—you'll have a pork chop, or maybe a T-bone steak, or some roast beef, and then finally you says, kind of irritated, "Well what can we get?"

"Say," she says, "don't get fresh! You can have a small steak or you can have ham and eggs—only I think the eggs is all out."

God! I've always held and maintained that America is the one and only nation that knows how to provide elegant chow, but even a patriot like me, sometimes I feel that we got this said elegant chow every place in the country except three: cities, towns, and farmhouses.

So you carry along a little stove.

And then you ought to have a windshield spot-light, and a spade, and—

(Here, by request of the publishers, are omitted thirty-seven other articles recommended by Mr. Schmaltz.— EDITOR.)

Well, the first day, what with one thing and another and packing, we didn't get off till noon, having had a light lunch before starting, and say, I could've killed that Pole hired girl we had at that time—She cooked up some scrambled eggs and never let us know they was ready, and they was all cold, and for a fellow that likes really nice tasty grub, a cold scrambled egg isn't hardly worth eating.

But anyway, we got away at exactly three minutes after twelve—I kind of kept a schedule of our timing on this trip, and mileage, and daily consumption of oil and gas, and say, if I had my figures here, I could show you that we got more mileage on Dainty Daisy gas than on Samson, with all the Samson claims for power-plus, and as I say, we got started kind of late, and so we didn't plan to make much of a run that day, but only to Mittewoc, a hundred and seventy-five miles.

I never like to run more than two hundred and fifty miles a day. I know you don't agree with me, George, but I feel that when you run three hundred or three hundred and fifty, you don't really see all the scenery as thoroughly and study the agriculture and other features of the country as closely as you might if you just jogged along at a nice steady forty-five or fifty miles an hour instead of speeding. But be that as it may. We planned to take it easy and not get in before seven-thirty.

Say, that day was a revelation of progress.

When I first drove that road, it was just a plain dirt road running through a lot of unkempt farms, and now every mile or so you'd find a dandy up-to-date hot-dog stand—some like log-cabins and some like Chinese pagodas or Indian wigwams or little small imitations of Mount Vernon about ten feet high, and all like that, and stocking every known refreshment for the inner man—hot dogs and apple pie and chewing-gum and cigars and so on and so forth—and of course up-to-date billboards all along the road to diversify it, and garages maybe every five miles, and in every town a dandy free auto camp providing free water and wood for the tourists. And so many of the farmers quitting their old toilsome routine and selling apples and cider to the motorists—I asked one of 'em, by the way, how he could keep his supply up, and come to find out, he didn't have an apple tree on the place—he got 'em all from a grocery store in the next town. Oh, motoring certainly has made a great and wonderful change in the country!

We didn't have any special experiences that first day—just one or two little incidents. I remember there was a fellow, he looked like a hobo, he waved his hand and stopped us.

"Well, my friend, what do you want?" I says—he was a shabby-looking cuss.

"Could you give me a lift?" he says.

"A lift?" I says.

"Yuh, I'd like a lift," he says.

"You've got two good feet to walk on, haven't you?" I says.

"Yuh," he says, "but I'm going a long ways."

"Oh you are, are you!" I says. "Look here, my friend, let me give you a piece of advice."

"I ain't asking for advice," he says. "I'm asking for a lift."

Then of course I got a little sore, him sassing me in that uncalled-for fashion, and I says, "Well, I might 've given you a lift," I says, "if you hadn't got so fresh, but now— Well, all I can say is, if you'd buckle down to business and tend to business and earn some money," I says, "you'd maybe have an auto of your own, and you wouldn't have to ask people for a lift. Good *day*!" I says, and I drove on. I guess maybe that taught him a lesson. "You buckle down to work and not waste time asking for a lift," I told him, "and maybe you'll have an auto of your own!"

Then we stopped in a little burg—awful little hick hamlet it was, called, if I remember rightly, New Paris, and we stopped for an ice-cream soda, and when I was parking, I bumped just the least little bit into the car ahead of me. Didn't hurt him one little bit, and just bent my bumper a little, but my God, to hear the other fellow squeal about it, you'd thought I'd smashed his car to pieces and killed his Aunt Jenny. Great big rube he was—fellow with no dignity.

Even though I was born and brought up a city man, I admire the farmer and honor his efforts. What, after all, would we do without wheat and corn and flax and barley and radishes and so on? But same time, a lot of those hicks have no manners or dignity. Like this fellow.

He rushed right across the sidewalk from where he'd been putting in the afternoon holding up the front of the Red Ball Grocery Store, I remember it was—and say, that's one of the best chains of grocery stores in the country—and he bawls:

"Hey, you hit my car!"

"I'm quite aware of the fact," I says, coldly—the big bum! —if he thought he could frighten *me*! And so I got out, and looked things over, and I'd just bumped his spare tire, on the back, the least little bit.

"Well, what are you going to do about it?" he says.

"What am I going to do about it?" I says.

"Yes, what're you going to do about it?"

"Well, inasmuch and considering as I haven't perpetrated the least damage," I informed him, "it strikes me that probably I'm not going to do anything about it."

"We'll see about that!" he says.

"We certainly will!" I says. "You can call the officers of the law," I says, "and we'll see how they'll adjust matters. And I might just call to your attention the fact that you're not parked at the requisite and regulation angle," I says, "and we'll see what the authorities have to say about *that*!"

Well, of course I was pulling an awful bluff. I didn't know what the parking regulations were, at all. But then I figured that probably he didn't, either! And of course I knew that if he did call the constabule, by heck, he'd do a lot of lying and falsifying and all those kind of things that make you so sick when you're dealing with a roughneck. But then, I was all prepared for him—I figured that I'd tell the cop I was a big city lawyer and knew more about motor law than anybody since God was a boy, and bluff him out.

And say, it worked like a charm!

This fellow positively got white.

"Well, you ought to be careful," he grumbles—you'd 'ev died to see him trying to crawl out of it—and say, that ended the whole matter.

And what I didn't tell him, and what I didn't feel called on to tell him, if he couldn't see it himself, was that the way I'd hit his spare tire—something stuck out and I'd smashed hell out of his valve stem, so when Mr. Farmer come to put it on, he'd have one fine awful time, and served him right for the way he'd talked to me—say, many's the time I've laughed when I thought about that poor hick, 'way off seventeen miles from Nowhere, with a puncture, starting to put on this bum tire!

So Mame and I went into the drug-store and I had a strawberry ice-cream soda, and she, if I remember rightly—correct me, Mame, if I'm wrong—she had a lemon phosphate, and then we drove to the nearest garage, and I had my bumper straightened.

That was a nice garage, too, for such a tiny little burg.

I drove up and tooted my horn, and out come a young fellow in overalls, and I said, "Say, Cap'n, I hit a mosquito up the road a piece, and I wonder if you could straighten my bumper."

"Sure," he says.

"Could you do it right away?" I says. "I've got a date up the road to meet Gertrude Ederle and swim across the Channel with her."

"Sure," he says. You could see (my God, think of what it must mean to live in a hog-wallow like that and not hardly ever meet any educated people except when they stopped like I did!)—you could see he appreciated a little real Kiwanis Club kidding.

And so he got busy, and say, with a jack he had that bumper straightened in about ten seconds, and so we drove on.

And those were about all the interesting incidents, and considering I want to get on and outline the whole itinerary for you—

Oh, there was one little thing.

We stopped at a farmhouse for a drink of water—not water for the radiator, you understand; isn't it one of the wonders of modern science the way the radiator of a really fine car don't hardly need refilling at all?—I mean just for some water to drink. Well, I went up to the front door, and some old hag of a farm-wife came to the door, and I took off my hat, just as polite as if she was an important customer in my store, and I says to her, "Madam, I wonder if my wife and I can trouble you for a drink of water."

Well, she stands there and looks at me—by golly, I got kind of irritated, discourtesy like that to a wayfarer—and she looks at me and she says, "You're the sixteenth autoist today that's stopped and asked for a drink of water. And every time I've gone 'way down by the barn, to the pump, and brought it. And the last person, and she called herself a lady, kicked like all get out because she didn't think the glass I brought her was clean enough. And all I have to do is to cook and bake and sweep and mend and do for four men, and tend the chickens, and hoe the garden, and help milk the cows. And I'm getting tired of being a free waitress for city autoists on top of that!"

Well, there may have been a certain modicum of reason to what she said.

I tell you, George, I'm always the first to open his heart and purse-strings to the call of the poor and needy. Why say, here just a couple of months ago, we took up a collection at the Kiwanis Club to buy a newsboy a suit of clothes. But same *time*—

Why do these hicks insist on giving themselves away? Why can't they try to learn nice manners, like you and I do?

What I'd 've liked to do was to give her one quick wallop on the jaw, but I just raised my hat again, like I was the Beau of Brummell, and I says, "I am very sorry to have bothered you, madam! Good *afternoon*!"

And I marched off and never looked back once! I'll bet she felt ashamed, and I hope to God she did!

Along about five we stopped to get some hot dogs and sauerkraut and coffee at a mighty nice little burg, right up to date, all brick pavement and snappy little bungalows and a lovely movie palace and a new brick armory and one of the highest water-towers we saw on the whole trip and a dandy cigar-store called "The Hang-out," and important industrially, too—big cheese factory and a rubber factory—place I'd always wanted to see and had heard a lot about—is was called Carcassonne.

And then we hiked on, and we got to Mittewoc at 7:13 on the dot.

And then, if I can just get Mame to admit it, we had the father and mother of a row about where we were going to stay that night.

There was a nice hotel there—the Ishpeming Arms—nice big clean lobby with elegant deep leather rocking-chairs, and

the brass spittoons shined up like they were table ware—
and Mame thought we ought to go there.

But I says to her, "It isn't a question of money," I says. "I
guess I can afford the best hotels about as well as the next
fellow. But it never *hurts* to save a little money; and besides," I says, "it's half the fun, as well as information, of a
trip like this to get right down among the common, ordinary folks that ride in flivvers," I said, "and I've heard
they've got a dandy tourist auto camp here, camping and
parking space free, and with cottages with bedclothes at a
dollar a night," I says, "and I vote we try it once, and brush
up against the common people, and if we don't like it tonight," I says, "we don't need to try it again."

Well, we argued a lot, but Mame is a mighty good little
sport, if she'll let me say so in her presence, and make a long
story short, we drove over to the tourist park.

Well sir, it was as pretty a place and fixed up as swell as
you'd want to see anywhere. It was right on the bank of
the Appleseed River, and there was several nice willow trees
scattered through the grounds, and even, if I remember
rightly—correct me if I'm wrong, Mame—there was a nice
big oak tree. Of course the grounds were just the least little
bit dirty, but what could you expect, with forty to sixty people camping there every night?

They had a dandy little store, painted in an art yellow
with a mighty artistic sign, "Ye Old Autoists' General
Store," that, say, that place had every want and necessity for
a touring party, even with kids along. They carried tires
and canvas water buckets and gas and canned goods and
diapers and lolly pops and cotton gloves and maps and
magazines and near-beer and everything you could think of.

Then there was a lot of marked-out spaces for cars and for

tents, for those that had tents, and a nice line of outdoor ovens with plenty of wood provided free, and dandy shower baths in tents, and finally about half a dozen cottages for them that didn't carry tents, and we got one. And for a dollar, say, it wasn't so bad—it had a double bed with nice clean linen, and a chair.

So we settled down, and I says to Mame, "Let's make out like we're just tourists, without a bean to our names," and she entered right into the spirit of the thing, and we bought a frying-pan and a stew-pan at the store, and some canned stuff, and we had a dandy little supper, cooked by Mame's own fair hands—canned vegetable soup, and canned wienies (say, did you ever know that wienies are named after Ween, a German city?) and fried potatoes, and to top it off, some chocolate-almond bars.

Well, some of the folks had started a big camp-fire and we all sat around it, just like one big family, and we sang a lot of old-time songs—and what I always say is, these modern songs haven't got the melody and sentiment like those old ancient songs have—we sang "After the Ball," and "Daisy, Daisy, Gimme Your Answer True," and "Onward, Christian Soldiers," and "Toy Land," and "Two Little Girls in Blue," and all like that.

And I got to talking with a lot of different folks, and say, hardly more'n 40 per cent. were up to the Chevrolet class, and yet they were as fine a bunch of folks as you'd want to meet—I mean, just to idle a few hours away with. And I learned a lot of different facts that *I* hadn't known before—say, there's certainly nothing that broadens a fellow like traveling.

Just for an example, I learned that Chattanooga, Tennessee —or it might 've been Nashville—but anyway it's right on a fine river, and you can see the mountains from there. And

I learned that the largest Presbyterian church in the country was in Seattle, Washington. And I learned that Zion City, Illinois—or is it Wisconsin?—this old hangout of Dowie[1]— has not only a very large lace factory, which of course everybody knows, but also one of the largest biscuit factories in the country. And I learned from a gentleman who was a veterinarian that one of the best foods for dogs was corn-meal mush cooked up with slivers of meat, thus making what they call a balanced ration—for dogs, I mean.

And say, that was a mighty funny thing. This veterinarian, Dr. Lepewski, his name was, but he explained he was really of German extraction and not one of these Lithuanians or some foreign stock like that, he happened to mention that about a year ago, or it might have been longer than that—this Dr. Lepewski, I may say, wasn't any of your tin-can flivver tourists, in fact he was driving an Oakland, and a high-class gentleman in every way, and I guess he was just staying at the tourist camp for the fun of the adventure, like Mame and me—and he said he was in Chicago, here about a year or so ago, in a hotel—I think it was the LaSalle, but it may have been some other hotel—and he ran into—I'd just happened to mention that I came from Zenith, and he said that in this hotel he happened to run into a gentleman from Zenith.

Well, naturally, I was interested right away, and I said to him, "What was this gentleman's name?"

"Well, if I remember rightly," he said to me, "his name was Claude Bundy—in the sash and blind business. Do you happen to know him?"

---

[1] The patron saint and model for such organizations as the Anti-Saloon League and the Lord's Day Alliance. Like Mrs. Mary Baker Eddy, he preached Divine Healing of all ills until his unfortunate death.

"Well sir," I says to the doctor, "can you beat that? Say, it's a pretty doggone small world after all, isn't it! No, I don't happen to know Claude himself, but several times I've met his cousin, Victor Bundy, the lawyer," I said, "and I imagine I must know several people who've known Claude!"

So that's how it went—a mighty profitable as well as pleasant evening, and Mame and I turned in and hit the hay sometime along about a quarter of eleven, and we slept pretty good, and next morning we rolled out about seven and got some breakfast at a little lunch-counter near there—

Eh?

My Lord, you're right, Mame!

It's eleven-fifteen, and we'll have to be trotting along home, and I haven't even completed my account of the trip as far as the Black Hills. Well, I'll tell you, George; we'll get together again soon, and I can tell you the rest in half an hour.

I've enjoyed the evening a whole lot, and I hope what I've told you may be helpful—

And oh, there is one thing I *must* say before we skip. Be sure and carry along a drinking-cup. Now there's various kinds. You can get a small glass in a metal case, or one of these folding metal cups, or just a plain enamel-ware cup. Now let me tell you in just a brief word my experience with each of these—

THE CRAZY FOOL

By DONALD OGDEN STEWART

––––––––

THE twelve-forty-five left at twelve-forty-five.

'We're off!' cried Charlie, with all the eager, excited assurance of eternal Youth in the face of the Great Adventure. The old gentleman only smiled—the wise smile of Age—Age mellowed and saddened by Experience.

Five minutes later, Charlie again looked out of the window.

'If I'm not too inquisitive,' he said, 'may I ask a question?'

'My name is King,' said the old gentleman, 'Horace King. You may ask me anything.'

'Well, in the first place,' said Charlie, 'isn't that the same man out there we saw back at the station?'

Mr. King looked out.

'Yes,' he said, 'I believe it is.'

Charlie took out an envelope and did some figuring on the back.

'Well, then,' he said, at last, 'either he is moving—or we're not.'

'I'll ask him,' said the old gentleman affably, and he tried to raise the window.

'Here, I'll help you,' said Charlie, and together they succeeded in getting their hands very dirty.

'It won't raise,' said Charlie.

'Ah, my boy,' said the old man patiently, 'maybe it's *us* who won't *lower.* Did you ever stop to think of that?'

'No,' replied Charlie, so he and the old man lowered.

'Maybe if I had a diamond,' said Mr. King, 'I could cut a hole in the glass and get out.'

Just then an employee in overalls walked through the car, carrying a pail and a mop.

'I beg your pardon,' said Mr. King, 'but have you a diamond?'

The man stared dumbly.

'*Pardonnez-moi,*' said Charlie quickly, '*mais est-ce que vous avez une diamant . . .*'

'It's masculine, I think,' said Mr. King.

'Isn't he, though!' said Charlie. 'And what a mustache!'

'I meant the word,' explained Mr. King; '*diamant*—it's "*un diamant,*" if I'm not too mistaken.'

'*Un diamant,*' repeated Charlie to the man, but with no better result.

'*Bitte,*' began Mr. King. '*Haben Sie vielleicht . . .*'

The man turned and left the car.

'In my time,' said Mr. King, 'employees were taught courtesy.'

'And French and dancing,' said Charlie. 'And ladies were ladies and did the gavotte,' and he pretended to execute a few quaint steps in the aisle. 'Will you join me?'

'Ah, me,' sighed Mr. King. 'The good old days.'

'Maybe,' said Charlie, 'if we don't let the window know we are trying to open it, we can catch it unawares.'

'All right,' said Mr. King, and they sat down and pretended to go to sleep. Suddenly Charlie leaped up and grabbed the window and after a tremendous struggle forced it open.

'See!' he said triumphantly, 'I told you.'

Mr. King, however, still had his eyes closed and did not answer.

'That's a wonderful piece of acting,' said Charlie, and he held a mirror in front of Mr. King's mouth to see if by any chance he were dead.

Mr. King soon opened his eyes and looked out the window.

'That's that same man,' he said, somewhat petulantly. 'I wish he would go away'—and he called to the man.

'I beg your pardon,' he said, 'but can you tell me what station this is?'

'New York,' replied the man.

'New York,' repeated Mr. King, with a puzzled look. 'I see. Thank you.'

He turned to Charlie. 'We left New York at twelve-forty-five,' he said.

'I know it,' said Charlie. 'I was there,' and he turned to the man. 'We left New York at twelve-forty-five,' he said.

'Did you?' replied the man.

'Yes, we "did you,"' said Charlie, somewhat irritated.

'Careful,' said Mr. King. 'Let me talk to him. Are you sure,' he said presently, 'that this is New York? Are you acquainted here?'

The man put his fingers to his mouth and whistled shrilly. 'Hey, Bill!' he called.

Bill came, wiping his hands on a piece of waste.

'Here's a couple of guys,' said the man, 'want to know if this is New York.'

Bill looked at Charlie and Mr. King, then tossed the waste onto the next track.

'Come on, Eddie,' he said. 'We've got to finish that truck on thirteen.'

Bill and Eddie left to finish the truck on thirteen. Charlie looked at Mr. King. Then they picked up their baggage and walked out of the car by the front end.

'I guess they didn't take this car,' said Charlie, somewhat crestfallen.

'You'll learn, my boy,' said Mr. King wisely, 'not to count on anything.'

Charlie was looking through a time-table.

'That's not the right railroad,' said Mr. King.

'I know it,' said Charlie, 'but it's the only time-table I've ever had. We were Southerners,' he added, 'and proud.'

'Time-tables are like women,' said Mr. King. 'The more you something or other them, the more they—I forget the exact words.'

'How's the tune go?' asked Charlie. 'Maybe I can help you out.'

'There used to be a two-thirteen,' said Mr. King, 'but I can't remember where it was a two-thirteen from. My memory is getting worse every day.'

'New York?' suggested Charles. 'Chicago?'

'Maybe,' replied Mr. King. 'Anyway, we can ask. It never does any harm to ask, my boy.'

So they picked up their bags and walked back through the gate to the Information Bureau.

'Is there a two-thirteen?' asked Mr. King politely, but the information man was talking on the telephone and did not answer.

'It's your turn to ask a question now,' said Mr. King to Charlie when the man had finished. So Charlie asked a question.

The man reached under the counter, handed Charlie a purple time-table and answered a call on another telephone.

'Now I'll ask one,' said Mr. King, so the next time the man seemed to be free, Mr. King asked one.

'What great English statesman,' he began, 'is sometimes referred to as——'

Mr. King was handed a time-table—a red-and-black one.

'Dear, dear,' he said. 'We don't seem to be getting anywhere. And it gets dark early around here, too.'

'It's the fault of our colleges,' said Charlie. 'College graduates don't know anything.'

'When I was at college,' said Mr. King, 'a young man had to work,' and he glared at the smooth-faced youngster behind the counter.

'I tell you what,' suggested Charlie. 'Let's get all the time-tables and go over in a corner and look for a two-thirteen—and the first one who finds it can sit next the window all the way.

So, with a little patience, they collected a large assortment of time-tables and retired to a cold marble bench on which Mr. King had spread out a newspaper before he sat down.

'You'll understand,' he explained to Charlie, 'when you're older.'

'Oh, go on, tell me now,' said Charlie, but Mr. King wisely refused.

'Here's a two-thirteen!' he cried, 'I get the seat.'

'Let's see,' said Charlie. 'The only trouble is,' he said, 'that that train goes to St. Louis.'

'I've been to St. Louis,' said Mr. King. 'I was there in '84—no, '85—I can remember just as well. We got there about two in the afternoon—phew, wasn't it hot—and I kept saying——'

'Here's a train,' interrupted Charlie, 'which might do.'

'You mustn't hesitate to interrupt me,' said Mr. King, 'any time. I'm old and I get to talking and I know it doesn't interest anyone, so don't you hesitate to cut right in. So that afternoon in St. Louis, I kept saying, "My, but I wish it would rain," and the man I was with, John Bradshaw——'

'Do you think this is our train?' asked Charlie, holding up the time-table.

'That's right—you just interrupt whenever you want,' said Mr. King. 'Well, John Bradshaw—he was from Cleveland, then, although he came originally from Albany and I had known him for several years—oh, ever since he and I were youngsters——'

'All I want to know is,' asked Charlie, 'if you think this is our train,' and he pointed to a column on the forty-second page.

'That's what I like to see,' said Mr. King, taking out his spectacles, 'a young man who isn't afraid to ask questions. So John Bradshaw said, "I bet it doesn't rain before night," and I said, "I bet it does"—and along about five-thirty, it began to look as if it might rain and, sure enough, just about six o'clock, it began to rain and it rained all night. Now isn't that about as dull a story as you ever heard?'

'It's pretty dull,' said Charlie. 'And yet it's probably true.'

'Well, as a matter of fact,' said Mr. King, 'it isn't true. I never knew any John Bradshaw.'

'Do you mean to say,' asked Charlie, 'that you made that all up out of your own head?'

Mr. King smiled. 'Most of it,' he said. 'The part about the rain I got from watching rain.'

'With an imagination like that,' said Charlie, 'you ought to write books.'

'I wrote a book,' said Mr. King.

'I bet you did,' said Charlie, 'and I bet I've read it a hundred times without knowing it.'

'The book's not so bad,' said Mr. King. 'It's got more of a plot.'

'More of a plot than what?' asked Charlie.

'Than the story that I just told,' replied Mr. King.

'About John Bradshaw?' asked Charlie.

'Yes,' replied the old man, 'I told that story more or less just for the dialogue—and the character study.'

'The dialogue was a knockout,' said Charlie, 'and that reminds me—I'm going over and find out the truth about our train.'

'The truth never hurt anyone,' said Mr. King.

'Now you sit right here,' said Charlie, 'and be quiet, and Charlie will be back as quick as you can say Jack Robinson.'

'Jack Robinson,' said Mr. King.

'You've got to shut your eyes,' said Charlie, 'and count up to a hundred.'

'But when I shut my eyes,' protested Mr. King, 'I go to sleep.'

'Not if you drink coffee,' said Charlie. 'I'll bring you some.'

'And a cheese sandwich,' added the old man, but Charlie had gone. So Mr. King shut his eyes and when Charlie came back, he was asleep.

'This is very discouraging,' said Charlie. 'I'll never make good and marry Judith if this nice old gentleman is going to go to sleep all the time,' and he woke Mr. King up by laying him flat on the bench, loosening his collar and working his arms up and down and backward and forward until artificial respiration began.

'Where am I?' asked Mr. King, opening his eyes.

'In St. Louis,' replied Charlie, 'and it is just beginning to rain and we'll have to hurry if we want to catch the two-thirteen. My name's Bradshaw.'

'Where's my cheese sandwich?' asked Mr. King.

'We haven't time,' replied Charlie.

'Time and tide——' began Mr. King, but Charlie picked up the bags and started for the gate.

'You promised me a cheese sandwich,' said Mr. King reproachfully, as he hurried along beside the young man.

'Later,' said Charlie.

'But I want it *now*,' said Mr. King.

'Later—Charlie said "*later*." '

'But——'

'Do you want Charlie to give you a good sock in the eye?'

Mr. King was silent, and they reached the gates.

'Have you got the tickets?' asked Charlie.

Mr. King began fumbling through his pockets.

'Maybe you swallowed them,' suggested the gatekeeper, sarcastically.

Mr. King stopped and considered.

'No,' he said at last, 'I don't think I did. That was a hat-check I swallowed.'

'He puts everything in his mouth,' explained Charlie.

'I was only kidding,' said the gateman. 'Hurry up.'

'Maybe they dropped down inside your trousers,' said Charlie. 'You might take them off and look.'

'You can't do that here,' warned the gatekeeper, instantly.

'Why not?' asked Charlie, looking around for a 'No-Taking-Off-of-Trousers' sign.

'Say are you two trying to kid me?' asked the gateman.

'Dear me, no,' exclaimed Charlie. 'Not *you*.'

'Here they are,' said Mr. King. 'They were on my fore-

head all the time.' And after the tickets had been indignantly punched, they passed through the gates and on to
the train.

'Are you sure this train stops at our station?' asked Charlie nervously, after the bags had been swung up into the
rack. 'I can't afford to make any mistakes at the start.'

'There's only one way to be sure,' replied Mr. King,
'and that's the right way,' and so together they walked
through the coach, out onto the platform, and up to where
the engine was standing.

'That's quite an engine you've got there,' remarked Mr.
King, looking up pleasantly at the engineer and resting
one hand on the cab.

'Mustn't touch!' cautioned Charlie.

The engineer regarded Mr. King in silence.

'Yes, sir,' went on the old gentleman, 'that's certainly
quite an engine.'

'Yeh?' said the engineer.

'Tell me,' said Mr. King—'and I don't want to seem inquisitive—but are you connected with this road?'

'I'm the engineer,' replied the other.

'Ah,' said Mr. King. 'I thought so. The engineer—well,
well,' and he turned to Charlie with a smile. 'He says he's
the engineer.'

Charlie raised his hat, deferentially.

'And this is certainly quite an engine,' went on Mr. King.
'Yes, sir—quite an engine. I suppose these engines go in
and out of the station pretty regularly?'

There was no answer.

'I should imagine they did,' said Mr. King. 'Yes, sir—
pretty regularly. On schedules, probably—or am I pre-
suming too much?'

'They have regular schedules, if that's what you mean,' said the engineer.

'Well, now, that's very interesting,' said Mr. King, and he turned once more to Charlie. 'They have regular schedules, he says.'

'And I suppose,' went on Mr. King, 'that you have a perfectly definite list of places where you are expected to stop—of course, I'm not a railroad man in any sense of the word—but that is what I would suppose.'

There was no response from the cab.

'They tell me,' continued Mr. King, 'that one of these trains used to stop at a place called Lodge Junction—I think that was the name——'

'This train stops at Lodge Junction, if that's what *you* want to know,' said the engineer.

'Thank you,' said Mr. King. 'That's just what I wanted to know. Come, Charles,' and they walked triumphantly back to their seats.

'Yes, sir,' explained Mr. King. 'You can get anything you wish if you only go about it in the right way.'

'Well, I wish this train would start,' said Charlie, looking at his watch.

'It will,' said Mr. King, 'with time and patience,' and at that, the train gave a couple of tugs and started.

'See?' said Mr. King, smiling wisely at the impatient youth. 'When you're as old as I am——' But just then the train stopped suddenly with a jerk and Charlie's golf bag crashed down from the rack onto Mr. King's straw hat.

'I didn't need to have brought my extra putter,' said Charlie apologetically.

'That's perfectly all right,' said Mr. King, rubbing his head. 'That's what I get for being selfish. I should have given *you* that seat.'

For the first hour or so, Charlie and Mr. King gazed out of the window, more or less in silence.

'It's sort of an unusual place you're going to,' said Mr. King at last. 'The people may strike you as a little—well, different—but I think you'll learn to enjoy them.'

'If they're at all like you,' replied Charlie, 'I will.'

'Well, they're like me,' said Mr. King, pleased, 'and they're not—that's quite a paradox, isn't it?' he said. 'I'll have to remember that.'

Charlie leaned back in his seat and began to think about Judith.

'It must be great to be married,' he murmured, but Mr. King did not answer, so Charlie turned to the lady sitting alone across the aisle.

'It must be great to be married,' he said.

She was reading, but looked up with a smile. There was something unusual about her, too—and something quite interesting. Beautiful, well-dressed, veiled, and with a curious birdlike voice.

'It's terrible to be married,' she said, with a faint shrug of one small shoulder.

'Why, you're crazy,' replied Charlie. 'And, besides, you don't know Judith.'

'There are lots of people I don't know,' she said. 'I don't know you, for example.'

'I'm just old Charlie Hatch,' he explained. 'I was born in a log cabin and then I became a surveyor, and many stories are told about my honesty and my marksmanship, until one day I came across a copy of Shakespeare in the pocket of an old Indian chief and that made me want to go to college. So I walked twenty-one miles to the little old schoolhouse, but it wasn't there, and just then a kind old gentleman, driving by in his automobile, saw me splitting rails in my coonskin cap and asked me if this was the road to New York and I said, "No." "A bright lad," he said, turning to his wife, who was driving. "How would you like to go to college?" "Fine." I replied, so they laughed and drove on, and sometimes, as I sit around the fire with my wife and kiddies I think I am the happier, don't you?'

'I think you are very nice,' said the lady. 'And now I will tell you who I am. I was a poor little girl born in a tenement and my mother and father used to be drunk all the time and beat me so I grew up to be sweet and pure and beautiful and one day when the Prince of Wales knocked a polo ball into our alley he saw me and fell in love with me and married me and we lived happily ever after and now I think I shall return to my book,' and with another intriguing smile, she began to read and Charlie noticed that it was a French book written in French.

Suddenly, as though a thought had just come to her, she wrote something on a piece of paper, got up and walked past Charlie to the front of the car and out, and when Charlie looked down he saw that the slip of paper was in his lap.

'There is a man in the third seat back of you,' he read, 'who has been annoying me. If he follows me out of the car, and you are an American gentleman, you will take care of him for me.'

'Say, listen——' said Charlie, but she had disappeared, so he slowly and cautiously turned around to look.

The gentleman in the third seat back of him was one of the largest men Charlie had ever seen. And as he looked, the fellow slowly got up out of his seat and started forward.

When he was opposite Charlie, Charlie stood up.

'Take that, you cad,' he said, and he aimed a blow at the man's jaw, but missed.

'Down where ah come from,' said Charlie, 'they string 'em up for less than that,' and he swung, and missed again.

'Say, listen,' said Charlie. 'How can I knock you down if you don't hold still?'

'All right,' said the man, and he stood still and Charlie knocked him down.

'Now *you* hold still,' said the stranger, getting up, 'and I'll knock *you* down.'

'What for?' asked Charlie.

'I don't know,' said the man. 'I've never been down South,' and with that he knocked Charlie down.

'Now what do we do?' he asked, picking Charlie up.

'I don't know,' confessed Charlie. 'How do you feel?'

'My jaw hurts a little,' said the man.

'So does mine,' said Charlie. 'I tell you what—if you apologize to the lady, my honor will be satisfied.'

'All right,' said the man. 'I'm sort of shy with ladies, though. Who is she?'

'Why, don't you know?' and Charlie looked at the big man angrily.

'No. I was just going up to get a drink of water,' explained the man.

'Well,' said Charlie, 'you want to be careful about that in the future.'

'Yes, sir,' said the man.

Charlie relented, held out his hand, and smiled. 'No hard feelings, stranger,' he said, and the two men shook hands.

'Now can I get my drink of water?' asked the man.

'You sure can,' said Charlie heartily, and so the stranger passed forward out of his life and so, apparently, had the interesting lady.

After the second hour, the train seemed to become considerable of a local—at least, it made a great many unnecessary stops for such a nice train, and Charlie impatiently woke Mr. King up and suggested that they go forward again and ask the engineer if there was anything they could do about it.

'He's probably just lonely,' said Charlie, as the train once more came to a halt. 'Or maybe it's his wind. Too many cigarettes are very harmful in excess.'

'Perhaps he ate something which didn't agree with him,' said Mr. King. 'I wonder what it could have been?'

'Egg plant,' suggested Charlie. 'That doesn't go with some things at all.'

'I've got some bicarbonate of soda in my bag,' said Mr. King, and Charlie took down the suitcase and opened it.

'The only drawback,' said Charlie, 'is that it might offend him to have us comparative strangers climb up into his cab with some bicarbonate, especially if he is just renting the cab for the afternoon.'

'Not if you do it in the right way,' said Mr. King. 'Leave it to me.'

So Mr. King dug around in his bag until he found some notepaper and then he sat down and began to write.

'Would you say, "Dear Engineer"?' he asked, 'or, "Dear Mr. Engineer"?'

' "Dear Mr. Engineer," ' replied Charlie, 'unless it is a relative, or a very dear friend.'

'I don't think he's a relative,' said Mr. King, 'most of our family were professional men,' so he wrote, 'Dear Mr. Engineer,' and stopped.

'Unless,' he added thoughtfully, 'it is Cousin Lemuel. Cousin Lemuel was sort of the black sheep of the family—he eloped with an actress his sophomore year at Columbia. It might just possibly be Cousin Lemuel and he was always very sensitive,' so he crossed out the 'Mr.' and wrote 'Dear Engineer,' and then added, apologetically '(If I may call you so).'

'There,' he said, and waited for an inspiration.

' "In reply to yours of even date," ' suggested Charlie. Mr. King shook his head.

'Too formal,' he said, 'and, besides, there wasn't any "yours of even date." '

'It's just a business form,' said Charlie. 'I learned it in the bank.'

The two men were silent in the face of what seemed an insurmountable difficulty. Charlie at last took out a pencil and wrote something on the back of an envelope. 'Here,' and he read: ' "I suppose you are bothered with letters like this all the time, but I have always been a great admirer of your work and I just couldn't refrain from writing to tell you how much I enjoy the way you handle that engine and if you ever need any bicarbonate of soda, I hope you will let me be the first to know about it." '

Mr. King shook his head.

'You forgot to ask him for a photograph,' he said, 'and, besides, those letters are always answered by the engineer's mother or his secretary.'

Charlie chewed the pencil disconsolately.

'No,' said Mr. King, 'I think it would probably be better to start with something a little less stereotyped—a little more personal,' and after a long interval, he began to write.

' "It is very pleasant here now," ' he read, as he went along, ' "with just the right amount of tang in the air, and I often think of you up there in that hot cab and wish you were here." '

The train came to a stop.

' "Although quite warm at noon," ' continued Mr. King, ' "the nights are always cool and Thursday we actually slept between blankets. Think of that!" '

'Now for the body of the letter,' said Mr. King.

' "As I sit at my window and look out, I see——" ' The train started and Mr. King looked out.

'Oh, good Heavens!' he cried. 'This is our station!' and he slammed the bag shut and jumped up. Charlie grabbed everything in sight and they fled down the aisle and off the moving train.

MR. AND MRS. HADDOCK ABROAD

By Donald Ogden Stewart

———

Is THIS the boat for Europe?' asked Mr. Haddock of the uniformed attendant at the gangplank.

'No, sir,' replied he. 'The boat for Europe has left.'

'Oh, dear!' said Mrs. Haddock.

Mr. Haddock's lips tightened and he grabbed his four suitcases and gave Mildred to the porter and strode over to another man in uniform.

'Is this the boat for Europe?' he asked.

'Yes, sir,' replied he.

'This seems a little foolish,' said Mr. Haddock, wiping the perspiration from his forehead. 'That man over there told me the boat for Europe had left.'

'Aw, he doesn't know what he's talking about,' said the man. 'He's new on the job.'

'Oh!' said Mr. Haddock, and so he and Mrs. Haddock and little Mildred showed their tickets and their passports and walked over the gangplank into the floating palace that was to transport them to the land of their dreams.

'When does the bar open?' asked Mr. Haddock of the steward who was carrying their bags to their stateroom.

'When we drop the pilot,' replied the steward.

'Why, is he a prohibition agent?' asked Mrs. Haddock, but the steward had already entered their stateroom.

'Here you are, sir,' he said in English.

'Ah, yes,' said Mr. Haddock, and then he added, 'Ah, yes.'

'Electric lights,' said the steward, snapping a switch and flooding the stateroom with artificial light. 'Modern plumbing,' and he pointed to what looked like a folding desk, 'Hot and cold running water,' and he pulled open the desk and revealed a wash basin with faucets.

'It would be a bit small to give very large parties in,' said Mr. Haddock. 'What do you think, dear?'

'Ah, but the location,' said the steward, 'right on the sea. Sea breezes every night. And the view!'

'That's something,' said Mr. Haddock.

'You can see Mount Monadnock on a clear day,' said the steward.

'Really!' said Mrs. Haddock.

'A beautiful neighborhood,' said the steward. 'How many children have you?'

'One,' said Mr. Haddock, pointing to Mildred. 'And one married son. He's living with his wife, though,' he added.

'I tell you what,' said the steward confidentially. 'You'd be making a great mistake not to take this.'

'If we had any more children,' said Mr. Haddock to Mrs. Haddock, 'we could build.'

'Exactly,' said the steward. 'Every man ought to own his own home.'

'How about transportation?' asked Mr. Haddock shrewdly.

The steward shrugged his shoulders. 'The very best,' he replied.

'What do you think, dear?' asked Mr. Haddock.

'Well,' said Mrs. Haddock, 'we could move that bunk over there—and put that wash-stand under the window.'

'I'm sorry,' said the steward, 'but that wash-stand can't be moved.'

'What direction is that?' asked Mrs. Haddock, pointing out of the port hole.

'South,' replied the steward.

'Hmmm—sun in the afternoon,' said Mrs. Haddock.

'I'll guarantee it,' said the steward, 'except under unfavorable weather conditions.'

'Such as, for instance, clouds,' said Mr. Haddock.

'How about mosquitoes?' asked Mrs. Haddock.

'You can look at me,' said the steward, starting to remove his white coat. 'I haven't been bitten all year.'

'Well!' said Mrs. Haddock, 'we might try it, Will. After all, it *is* near the sea.'

'The best thing in the world,' said the steward to Mr. Haddock, 'for hay fever.'

'But I haven't got hay fever,' said Mr. Haddock.

'Are you sure?' asked the steward, and Mr. Haddock felt very uncomfortable.

'How do you like it, Mildred?' said Mrs. Haddock.

'I'm sure the little girl will like it,' said the steward quickly, giving Mildred a nice smile. 'All children do.'

'Oh, they do, do they?' said Mildred.

'Yes, they do, do they,' said the steward, and he added, 'What a disagreeable child!'

'Isn't she,' agreed Mr. Haddock. 'And we have tried so hard, too.'

Just then a loud blast of a whistle sounded from above.

'Oh, dear!' said Mrs. Haddock, 'we're near a factory. That means a lot of smoke and soot, Will.'

'Not at all, madam,' said the steward, 'that's just the boat signaling. We'll be leaving in ten minutes now.'

'Let's go upstairs,' said Mr. Haddock, 'and see us leave.

And, steward, just put those bags under the bunk.'

'Yes, sir,' said the steward, and as they were leaving he aimed a sly kick at Mildred but missed.

Upstairs, on the main deck, all was bustle and confusion. 'Everybody off!' yelled a tall man in a blue uniform, blowing a shrill whistle. 'Everybody off!'

'That doesn't mean us,' said Mr. Haddock, clutching his wife's arm. 'I'm sure it doesn't, dear.'

So they stayed on, and after a while people began running down gangplanks blowing whistles, and running up gangplanks, with baskets of fruit and flowers, and on the shore people began waving handkerchiefs and American flags, and calling 'Good-bye,' and on the boat people began throwing kisses and flowers, and Ganna Walska began to be photographed for the Sunday supplements, and tugs began whistling in the river, and an airplane flew past overhead and the man next to Mr. Haddock began trying to tell somebody on shore that he had forgot to telephone Mrs. McDonald about the something fixtures, and the man on shore wasn't getting it very well, and 'I guess we're off,' said Mr. Haddock, and it was so exciting that his voice broke a little and Mrs. Haddock began to cry.

And half an hour later he looked at his watch and said, 'I wonder why we don't start.'

And an hour later the people on the dock began to feel a little foolish, and the people on the boat began to feel a little irritated, and some of them went below to their staterooms, and some of the people on the dock went home, and then finally the ship's whistle blew another big long blast, and they let down the gangplank, and on walked Mayor Hylan's son-in-law, and they started.

'Well, I guess we're off,' said Mr. Haddock with just

the shadow of a doubt in his voice, but as the boat swung around into the river and moved down past the Woolworth building and the Battery, his doubts gradually became a little dissipated.

'There's the Statue of Liberty,' whispered Mrs. Haddock, who was really very excited.

'Look, Mildred!' said Mr. Haddock, 'there's the Statue of Liberty.'

'I'm hungry,' said Mildred, and so he knew they were really off for Europe.

When they went down to their stateroom to wash for lunch they were surprised and delighted to find seven baskets and eleven boxes, containing among other things 103 oranges, 67 bunches of hot-house grapes, 241 fresh figs, 119 cured figs, and 141 prunes.

'This one is from Mrs. Gueminder,' said Mrs. Haddock, reading a card.

'I wonder how she knew I was so constipated,' mused Mr. Haddock, but delighted, just the same, with the timely gift.

Mrs. Haddock began folding up the tissue paper and string in order to save them for some occasion in their travels when they might be terribly in need of tissue paper and string, while Mr. Haddock took out a pencil and began figuring on the back of an envelope.

'Dear,' he said at last, 'I may be a fraction of a decimal off, either plus or minus, but in round numbers I figure that if we concentrate all our efforts and cut out theaters and sleep we can just finish the last of this fruit before we get to France.'

'Oh, dear!' said Mrs. Haddock, 'what *will* we do with it all?'

'Eat it!' said Mr. Haddock. 'Now, for the first three days I have allotted to you 165 grapes, 68 figs, 54 prunes, and 49 oranges.'

'But I don't like oranges,' said Mrs. Haddock.

'That doesn't matter,' said Mr. Haddock severely. 'In a crisis like this we must forget our petty individual likes or dislikes and work only for the good of the whole.'

'Our forefathers'—and Mr. Haddock pointed to the large American flag above him—'who wisely forged this country out of the melting pot of European chaos—our forefathers who beat their swords into plough-shares in order that our children might today enjoy the advantages of this beautiful new free public school—the man whom we meet today to honor and who gave his acres and his name to this beautiful amusement park—would not permit it. No, my friends,' said Mr. Haddock, and the vast stateroom became strangely hushed and quiet. 'No, my friends, the monument which we consecrate today may be to some a mere drinking fountain in the center of our beautiful city, where horses may quench their thirst with water from our proud Muscatawney and pass on, with, perhaps, a prayer of gratitude to the brave little lady whose name it bears, but my friends'—and Mr. Haddock's voice fell impressively 'to others, "something more." There is another thirst, my friends—a higher thirst—a more divine thirst. And in presenting to this convention this afternoon the name of Alexander P. Sturgis I can only say that he combines in one man all those qualities which have so endeared him to rich and poor alike and I point with pride—I point with pride, my friends—to the fact that he stands in a larger sense—in a larger sense——'

Mr. Haddock stopped and wiped his brow nervously. 'In a larger sense,' he repeated.

'Oh, dear!' whispered Mrs. Haddock to Mildred. 'That's just the place where he got stuck this morning.'

'In a larger sense,' said Mr. Haddock, and someone tittered audibly. 'In a larger sense,' and then to everyone's intense relief he went on. 'In a larger sense we cannot consecrate, we cannot dedicate, we cannot hallow this ground. The brave men living and dead who fought here have done so far beyond our petty power to add or detract. It is for us the living rather to consecrate our lives to the end that the ideals for which they fought shall not be forgotten and that government of the people, by the people, and for the people shall not perish from the earth. My friends, I thank you,' and he put on his silk hat and sat down beside Mrs. Haddock.

'You did awfully well, dear,' she whispered behind her white gloved hand, but Mr. Haddock was standing up and bowing and waving his hands to friends and suddenly he picked little Mildred up in his arms and let the crowd see her and the cheering grew louder than ever and then he made Mrs. Haddock stand up and the crowd went wild and there was no doubt that if a vote had been taken then he would have been elected by a large plurality over Jones (Dem.) who had, however, made heavy gains upstate, especially among a certain discontented element in the cities and among the farmers in the rural districts where the new tariff hit hardest.

But just then a knock came on the door and a pink, chubby face appeared and said, 'I'm the bath steward—and I'm afraid I'm awfully late.'

'Not at all,' said Mr. Haddock. 'Do come in. You know Mrs. Haddock, of course—and this is Mildred, our youngest.'

'Don't tell me this is Mildred,' said the bath steward,

patting the child's head. 'Why, the last time I saw this little girl she was no bigger than a minute. Well, they do grow up, don't they.'

'Don't they,' said Mildred, drawing away from under his hand and quitting the stateroom with an ill-concealed oath.

'I got caught in the traffic,' explained the bath steward, 'and I'm on my way to the Hemingways and I can just stay a minute.'

'Awfully good of you to drop in,' said Mrs. Haddock. 'Won't you have some fruit?'

'Oh, don't bother, please,' said the bath steward, taking a banana.

'It will just take a minute,' said Mrs. Haddock.

'Let her fix you some,' said Mr. Haddock. 'She likes to do it, really.'

'Oh, no, I couldn't think of it,' said the bath steward, putting two oranges in his pocket. 'I've really just finished lunch. At the Osbornes', you know—and what a lunch. Everybody was there. I'm surprised you weren't asked.'

'The Osbornes don't seem to know us,' said Mrs. Haddock. 'I guess we don't move high enough for them. I met them once when he and Will were on that Booster committee together—you remember, Will, that afternoon at the Elks Club, and I will say that I never saw three such ill-behaved children in my life.'

'Perfectly frightful!' said the bath steward, smiling sympathetically.

'They do say she has a lovely house,' said Mrs. Haddock. 'But I certainly will not be the first to call, would you?'

'No, indeed!' murmured the bath steward.

'And I hear,' went on Mrs. Haddock, beginning to rock

the boat back and forth with her chair, 'that he and she have been on the verge of a divorce several times.'

'I could tell you a lot worse than that,' said the bath steward.

'Please sit down,' said Mrs. Haddock; 'I don't think you find that bunk very comfortable. Will, you get up and give him that place and Mildred you run out again for a while, will you, dear?'

'No, really,' said the bath steward. 'I can't stay. I only dropped in to ask you what hour you wanted to take your bath.'

'Awfully good of you,' murmured Mr. Haddock. 'Please take some more fruit.'

'What hours have you?' asked Mrs. Haddock in a sudden business-like manner.

'Well,' said the bath steward, 'of course, there has been quite a demand for hours this year.'

'Of course,' said Mr. Haddock sympathetically.

'But I saved something very special for you and Mrs. Haddock—one of our finest hours. Oh, I'm sure you'll be crazy about it.'

'I'm sure we will,' said Mr. Haddock. 'Can we take it with us now?'

'I think we had better see it first,' said Mrs. Haddock, practically.

'Why Hattie,' said Mr. Haddock, 'do you think that's necessary? The gentleman has been so nice as to save it for us.'

'I think we had better see it first,' repeated Mrs. Haddock, with dignity.

'Of course, madam,' said the bath steward, and smiling understandingly at Mr. Haddock, who felt quite a little embarrassed, he bowed his way out of the stateroom in order to get his bath book.

'You're such a fool, Will,' said Mrs. Haddock after he had gone, but before Mr. Haddock had time to reply they were interrupted by the loud blast of a bugle blown just outside their door.

'Come in,' said Mr. Haddock, and he added reassuringly to his wife, 'It's probably only a few soldiers. Don't bother to change your clothes.'

But the bugle blew again and no one entered, so Mr. and Mrs. Haddock began reading the instructions regarding life belts.

'It's a little confusing,' said Mr. Haddock. 'In the first place, that man in the picture has got a mustache——'

'You silly,' said Mrs. Haddock for the second time that day, 'you don't have to have a mustache to wear a life belt properly.'

'Are you sure?' asked Mr. Haddock, but just at that moment little Mildred burst into the cabin.

'That's the bugle for lunch,' she announced, so with a few reassuring prunes and a cheery 'Good luck' all around they went out into the corridor and down into the main dining saloon where they partook of luncheon in company with three other people who seemed to Mrs. Haddock, as the meal progressed, to be a little strange.

'I think they are a little strange,' she said to Mr. Haddock after lunch, as they were sitting in their stateroom.

'What do you mean?' asked Mr. Haddock.

'Well—that lady with the beard, for instance,' said Mrs. Haddock.

'What's wrong about that?' asked Mr. Haddock, indignantly.

'Well, nothing,' said Mrs. Haddock baffled, 'except that

it is sort of funny to see her sitting there with a beard.'

'My dear Harriet,' said Mr. Haddock, 'you must remember that we are, after all, strangers here—practically guests of this boat. And, furthermore, we are from the middle West and have had practically no contact with European life. So please, my dear Harriet,' he said patiently, 'let's try and not be too provincial.'

'All right,' said Mrs. Haddock. 'But I don't see why you have to make a fool of yourself over the first young chippet who comes along with a beard.'

'I wasn't making a fool of myself,' said Mr. Haddock, somewhat exasperated. 'I was just being nice to a young girl who seemed to be traveling alone.'

'Alone!' said Mrs. Haddock. 'I'll bet she's alone! Who were those other two men?'

'I'm sure I don't know,' said Mr. Haddock. 'Probably two international crooks.'

'She spoke to them,' said Mrs. Haddock.

'On a boat like this,' said Mr. Haddock, 'we are just one big family.'

'There never was a bearded lady in our family,' said Mrs. Haddock, 'and you know it.'

'I assure you,' said Mr. Haddock, jesting, 'that my interests were purely tonsorial.'

'Fiddlesticks,' said Mrs. Haddock. 'Have some fruit?'

'No, thank you,' said Mr. Haddock, putting his hands quickly in his pockets. 'I'm not eating fruit. I think I shall go up on deck and walk.'

'I shall lie here,' said Mrs. Haddock, 'and eat fruit.'

'One of you,' said little Mildred, 'is going to be very seasick before long and then I shall know which to do. I wish you would hurry, though, for I feel rather strange.'

'Come with me, Mildred,' said her father, but just then

a knock came on the door and the steward appeared with some telegrams and letters.

'Haddock?' he asked.

'Haddock,' replied Mr. Haddock, for it was he.

'How do you spell it?' asked the steward, looking at the telegrams.

'"H" as in "Haddock,"' began Mr. Haddock. '"A" as in "Arthur"——'

'Arthur who?' asked the steward.

'I don't know,' said Mr. Haddock.

'Nothing here for Arthur Haddock,' said the steward.

'But that isn't my name,' said Mr. Haddock.

'What is your name?' asked the steward.

'Haddock,' replied Mr. Haddock, becoming a little exasperated. 'William P. Haddock—and this is my wife——'

'Your wife?' asked the steward.

'My wife—my wife,' screamed Mr. Haddock. 'Wife as in "Wife taking my fun where I found it"'

'Oh,' said the steward. 'Mrs. Haddock.'

'Practically,' said Mr. Haddock, 'and that is my daughter Mildred. I'm sorry I lost my temper.'

'I guess there's nothing for you,' said the steward. 'No—nothing for Mildred Haddock. Sorry.'

'Well, is there anything for me?' asked Mr. Haddock.

'I'll look,' said the steward, and he looked.

'Is that you?' he said, and handed Mr. Haddock a telegram.

'Yes,' said Mr. Haddock.

'That's all,' said the steward, and he left, only to reappear almost immediately.

'Say, do you know a Mr.—a Mr.,' and he looked at the letter, 'a Mr. Blumenstein—Mr. Sol Blumenstein—I think that's it.'

'No,' replied Mr. Haddock. 'Sorry.'

'Do you?' the steward then asked Mrs. Haddock.

'No, I do not,' she replied.

'Maybe you do?' he said, turning to Mildred.

'No,' replied Mildred with a sneer. 'I have not had the pleasure of Mr. Blumenstein's acquaintance.'

'He's a peach of a fellow,' said the steward. 'Well, good day.'

'Good day,' they called, cheerfully, and Mr. Haddock opened the telegram.

'It's from Frank and Edith,' he said.

'What does it say?' asked Mrs. Haddock excitedly.

'Bon voyage,' replied Mr. Haddock.

'That means "a good voyage" in French,' said Mildred.

'How I envy you your knowledge of the language,' said her father, but just then another knock came on the door and a passenger appeared.

'Mr. Haddock?' he asked.

'I think so,' said Mr. Haddock.

'Here are some letters and telegrams for you,' the stranger said. 'The steward just left them in my cabin. I opened them by mistake.'

'Anything interesting?' asked Mr. Haddock.

'No,' said the stranger. 'Not much. They all send much love and say "have a good time." Your Uncle George's teeth are worse—but then,' and he smiled, 'you know how Uncle George is.'

'I'm surprised he's hung on this long,' said Mr. Haddock.

'Why doesn't he go to a good dentist?' asked the stranger.

'You've got me there,' said Mr. Haddock. 'He's a bit "near," you know.'

'Anything else?' asked Mrs. Haddock. 'How were the twins?'

'Bully,' said the stranger. 'And oh yes—Alice Kent is going to have a baby in September.'

'You don't say so,' exclaimed Mr. Haddock. 'Well, well. What do you think of that, Hattie?'

'We'll be back by September,' said Mrs. Haddock. 'Won't we now, Will?'

'Oh sure,' replied her husband. 'Anything else?'

'Well,' said the stranger, 'your Aunt Flora got into trouble with the gas company again the day you left and they've threatened to sue her—but I think it will be all right.'

'Oh sure,' said Mr. Haddock. 'Don't you worry yourself about that. Well, it's mighty nice of you to bring these letters to us.'

'Not at all,' said the stranger. 'Maybe you can do the same for me sometime.'

'I'd be glad to,' said Mr. Haddock, and they shook hands and the stranger left.

'Here's a telegram he didn't open,' said Mrs. Haddock. 'It's from Mame.'

'What does she say?' asked Mr. Haddock.

' "Bon voyage," ' replied Mrs. Haddock.

'That means "a good voyage" in French,' said Mr. Haddock, chucking his daughter under the chin. 'Come on, Mildred—let's go on deck.'

On deck they found a number of people seated in steamer chairs.

'I wonder how one goes about getting a steamer chair,' said Mr. Haddock half to himself, half aloud, and there was a flash of smoke, a smell of sulphur, and a gentleman appeared, on whose face was a curiously sinister smile.

'I am the deck steward,' he said.

'Oh yes,' said Mr. Haddock, a little nervously. 'I want three chairs, about the center——'

The deck steward's smile became somewhat patronizing.

'The center has been sold out for the next eight weeks,' he said wearily.

'Well—the side then,' said Mr. Haddock.

Just then a rather stout woman pushed her way between Mr. Haddock and the deck steward and demanded, 'Have you got something for Smithers?'

'But madam,' protested Mr. Haddock, and she turned and glared at him.

'What name?' asked the deck steward.

'Smithers—Mrs. Pearl Smithers,' she replied.

The deck steward consulted his book.

'Nothing here for Smithers,' he said.

'Are you sure?' she demanded.

'Nothing for Smithers,' said the deck steward. 'Next.'

'I want three chairs——' began Mr. Haddock.

'But Mr. Henderson said they would be left here in my name,' continued Mrs. Smithers.

'Nothing for Smithers, madam,' said the deck steward.

'That's very funny,' said Mrs. Smithers.

'Next,' said the deck steward.

'I'm sure Mr. Henderson wouldn't have made a mistake,' said the lady, turning to Mr. Haddock.

'I'm sure he wouldn't,' agreed Mr. Haddock.

'Next,' called the deck steward.

'Look under Talcott, then,' said the woman. 'H. A. Talcott.'

'Nothing under Talcott, madam,' said the deck steward.

'Firestone?' she suggested. 'Mr. or Mrs. Firestone?'

'Nothing under Firestone,' said the deck steward. 'Please, madam—*next*!'

'I would like three chairs——' began Mr. Haddock automatically, but curiously enough he now found that he was third in line, two very large women having in some way gotten in ahead of him.

'What have you got in medium priced chairs?' asked the first lady.

'What night?' asked the deck steward.

The lady turned to the lady behind her.

'What night, Alice?' she asked.

'I don't know,' said Alice. 'How would Wednesday do?'

'Wednesday?' said the lady. 'No—Wednesday the Freemans are coming to dinner.'

'Please, madam,' said the deck steward, 'what night?'

'Thursday I can't get off,' said Alice, 'how about Tuesday?'

'All right,' said the lady. 'Tuesday,' and she turned to the deck steward, 'What have you got in medium priced chairs for Tuesday?'

'How many, madam?' he asked.

She turned to Alice.

'How many, Alice?' she asked.

'I don't know,' said Alice. 'Do you think Frank can come?'

'Oh, I wouldn't ask Frank,' said the lady.

'Who would you ask?' asked Alice. 'George?'

'How many, how many, how many?' said the deck steward.

By this time a rather long line had formed behind Mr. Haddock, and signs of no small impatience were beginning to be manifested by the crowd.

'Well,' said the lady, 'we could get four and then if George couldn't come we could ask Frank.'

'Or we could turn in the seat,' suggested Alice.

'Can you turn in seats you don't use?' asked the lady of the deck steward.

'No, madam,' he replied.

'Why not?' she asked.

'It's a rule of the management,' said the deck steward. 'How many seats do you want?'

'Well—four then,' she replied.

'Four for Tuesday,' he said. 'Four on the side—second row.'

'How much?' she asked.

'Two twenty apiece with tax,' he replied.

'How much?' she asked.

'Two twenty apiece,' he repeated. 'Please hurry, madam.'

The lady turned to Alice.

'They're two twenty apiece,' she said. 'What do you think?'

Alice shook her head.

'Haven't you anything cheaper?' the lady asked.

'Not for Tuesday night,' he replied.

Alice nudged her friend. 'Ask about matinées,' she said.

'When are matinées?' she asked.

'All sold out,' he said.

'What?' asked the lady.

'All sold out,' he repeated.

'Matinées? No more seats?' she asked.

'Matinées,' he said, 'all sold out.'

'Oh shoot,' said the lady. 'What will we do, Alice?'

'I don't know,' said Alice.

By this time the line behind Mr. Haddock and the two ladies had extended half way around the boat and out into the street and included men and women from all walks of life, for it did not seem that Alice and her friend were ever going to be able to decide what to do.

'It looks like rain,' said Mr. Haddock, stroking his long

white beard and speaking not as one of them but as a prophet.

And it grew dark and in the distance could be heard rumblings of distant thunder.

'If there is a God,' said Mr. Haddock, who had been reading H. G. Wells only that morning, 'and I strongly suspect that there is one—He will give us a sign.'

And it grew darker and darker, and over the sea advanced the pattering rain, and storm clouds gathered over the plunging ship, and the wind whistled through the rigging, and then suddenly there was a terrific flash of lightning and a deafening peal of thunder, and then, out on the water, floated a large white object, too large to be a swan.

'A whale!' cried Mr. Haddock, joyously.

'A miracle!' they all cried. 'A miracle.'

So they took Alice and her friend and threw them into the ocean, and the whale swallowed them, and a choir of 300 mixed voices from the South Bethlehem Tonkunst and Liederkranz Society burst into the final chorus, 'Gott ist ewig,' and the whale was slowly lifted out of the ocean and gradually but jerkily ascended into heaven with a slight creaking of ropes, and the afternoon was over.

'How did you like it?' asked Mr. Haddock of an elderly gentleman as they slowly filed out.

The old gentleman shook his head sadly. 'There aren't any good whales any more,' he said. 'Did you ever go to Bayreuth?'

'No,' replied Mr. Haddock.

'Ah me,' sighed the old gentleman. 'There were whales in those days.'

'I bet there were,' said Mr. Haddock, who, under the broadening influence of this trip, was gradually becoming quite a bit of a philosopher. 'I bet there were.'

BENNY AND THE BIRD-DOGS

By Marjorie Kinnan Rawlings

You can't change a man, no-ways. By the time his mammy turns him loose and he takes up with some innocent woman and marries her, he's what he is. If it's his nature to set by the hearthfire and scratch hisself, you just as good to let him set and scratch. If it's his nature, like Will Dover, my man, to go to the garage in his Sunday clothes and lay down under some backwoods Cracker's old greasy Ford and tinker with it, you just as good to let him lay and tinker. And if it's his nature, like Uncle Benny, to prowl; if it's his nature to cut the fool; why, it's interfering in the ways of Providence even to stop to quarrel with him about it. Some women is born knowing that. Sometimes a woman, like the Old Hen (Uncle Benny's wife, poor soul!), has to quarrel a lifetime before she learns it. Then when it does come to her, she's like a cow has tried to jump a high fence and has got hung up on it—she's horn-swoggled.

The Old Hen's a mighty fine woman—one of the finest I know. She looks just the way she did when she married Uncle Benny Mathers thirty years ago, except her hair has turned gray, like the feathers on an Irish Gray game hen. She's plump and pretty and kind of pale from thirty years' fretting about Uncle Benny. She has a disposition, by nature, as sweet as new cane syrup. When she settled down for a lifetime's quarrelling at him, it was for the same reason syrup sours—the heat had just been put to her too long.

I can't remember a time when the Old Hen wasn't quarrelling at Uncle Benny. It begun a week after they was married. He went off prowling by hisself, to a frolic or such as that, and didn't come home until four o'clock in the morning. She was setting up waiting for him. When she crawled him about it, he said, "Bless Katy, wife, let's sleep now and quarrel in the morning." So she quarrelled in the morning and just kept it up. For thirty years. Not for meanness—she just kept hoping she could change him.

Change him? When he takened notice of the way she was fussing and clucking and ruffling her feathers, he quit calling her by her given name and began calling her the Old Hen. That's all I could ever see she changed him.

Uncle Benny's a sight. He's been constable here at Oak Bluff, Florida, for twenty years. We figure it keeps him out of worse trouble to let him be constable. He's the quickest shot in three counties and the colored folks is all as superstitious of him as if he was the devil hisself. He's a comical-appearing somebody. He's small and quick and he don't move—he prances. He has a little bald sun-tanned head with a rim of white hair around the back of it. Where the hair ends at the sides of his head, it sticks straight up over his ears in two little white tufts like goat-horns. He's got bright blue eyes that look at you quick and wicked, the way a goat looks. That's exactly what he looks and acts like—a mischievous little old billy-goat. And he's been popping up under folks' noses and playing tricks on them as long as Oak Bluff has knowed him. Doc in particular. He loved to torment Doc.

And stay home? Uncle Benny don't know what it is to stay home. The Old Hen'll cook hot dinner for him and he won't come. She'll start another fire in the range and warm it up for him about dusk-dark and he won't come. She'll set up till midnight, times till daybreak, and maybe just about the time the east lightens and the birds gets to whistling good, he'll come home. Where's he been? He's been with somebody 'gatoring, or with somebody catching crabs to Salt Springs; he's been to a square-dance twenty miles away in the flat-woods; he's been on the highway in that Ford car, just rambling as long as his gas held out—and them seven pieded bird-dogs setting up in the back keeping him company.

It was seven years ago, during the Boom, that he bought the Model-T and begun collecting bird-dogs. Everybody in Florida was rich for a whiles, selling gopher holes to the Yankees. Now putting an automobile under Uncle Benny was like putting wings on a wild-cat—it just opened up new territory. Instead of rambling over one county, he could ramble over ten. And the way he drove—like a bat out of Torment. He's one of them men just loves to cover the ground. And that car and all them bird-dogs worked on the Old Hen like a quart of gasoline on a camp-fire. She really went to raring. I tried to tell her then 'twasn't no use to pay him no mind, but she wouldn't listen.

I said, "It's just his nature. You can't do a thing about it but take it for your share and go on. You and Uncle Benny is just made different. You want him home and he don't want to be home. You're a barnyard fowl and he's a wild fowl."

"Mis' Dover," she said, "it's easy for you to talk. Your man runs a garage and comes home nights. You don't know how terrible it is to have a man that prowls."

I said, "Leave him prowl."

She said, "Yes, but when he's on the prowl, I don't no

more know where to look for him than somebody's tom-cat."

I said, "If 'twas me, I wouldn't look for him."

She said, "Moonlight nights he's the worst. Just like the varmints."

I said, "Don't that tell you nothing?"

She said, "If he'd content hisself with prowling— But he ain't content until he cuts the fool. He takes that Ford car and them seven bird-dogs and maybe a pint of moonshine, and maybe picks up Doc to prowl with him, and he don't rest until he's done something crazy. What I keep figuring is, he'll kill hisself in that Ford car, cutting the fool."

I said, "You don't need to fret about him and that Ford. What's unnatural for one man is plumb natural for another. And cutting the fool is so natural for Uncle Benny, it's like a bird in the air or a fish in water—there won't no harm come to him from it."

She said, "Mis' Dover, what the devil throws over his back has got to come down under his belly."

I said, "Uncle Benny Mathers is beyond rules and sayings. I know men-folks, and if you'll listen to me, you'll settle down and quit quarrelling and leave him go his way in quiet."

I happened to be in on it this spring, the last time the Old Hen ever quarrelled at Uncle Benny. Me and Doc was both in on it. It was the day of old lady Weller's burying. Doc carried me in his car to the cemetery. My Will couldn't leave the garage, because the trucks hauling the Florida oranges north was bringing in pretty good business. Doc felt obliged to go to the burying. He's a patent-medicine sales-man—a big fat fellow with a red face and yellow hair. He sells the Little Giant line of remedies. Old lady Weller had been one of his best customers. She'd taken no nourishment the last week of her life except them remedies, and Doc figured he ought to pay her the proper respect and show everybody he was a man was always grateful to his customers.

Uncle Benny and the Old Hen went to the burying in the Model-T. And the seven bird-dogs went, setting up in the back seat. They always went to the buryings.

Uncle Benny said, "Walls nor chains won't hold 'em. Better to have 'em go along riding decent and quiet, than to bust loose and foller the Model-T like a daggone pack of bloodhounds."

That was true enough. Those bird-dogs could hear that old Ford crank up and go off in low gear, clear across the town. They'd always hope it was time to go bird-hunting again, and here they'd come, trailing it. So there were the bird-dogs riding along to old lady Weller's burying, with their ears flopping and their noses in the air for quail. As constable, Uncle Benny sort of represented the town, and he was right in behind the hearse. I mean, that car was a pain, to be part of a funeral procession. In the seven years he'd had it, he'd all but drove it to pieces, and it looked like a rusty, mangy razor-back hog. The hood was thin and narrow, like a shoat's nose—you remember the way all Model-T Fords were built. It had no top to it, nor no doors to the front seat, and the back seat rose up in a hump where the bird-dogs had squeezed the excelsior chitlin's out of it.

The Old Hen sat up stiff and proud, not letting on she minded. Doc and I figured she's been quarrelling at Uncle Benny about the bird-dogs, because when one of them put his paws on her shoulders and begun licking around her ears, she turned and smacked the breath out of him.

The funeral procession had just left the Oak Bluff dirt

road and turned onto No. 9 Highway, when the garage keeper at the bend ran out.

He hollered, "I just got a 'phone call for Uncle Benny Mathers from the high sheriff!"

So Uncle Benny cut out of the procession and drove over to the pay station by the kerosene tank to take the message. He caught up again in a minute and called to Doc, "A drunken nigger is headed this way in a Chevrolet and the sheriff wants I should stop him."

About that time here comes the Chevrolet and started to pass the procession, wobbling back and forth as if it had the blind staggers. You may well know the nigger was drunk or he wouldn't have passed a funeral. Uncle Benny cut out of line and took out after him. When he saw who was chasing him, the nigger turned around and headed back the way he'd come from. Uncle Benny was gaining on him when they passed the hearse. The bird-dogs begun to take an interest and rared up, barking. What does Uncle Benny do but go to the side of the Chevrolet so the nigger turns around— and then Uncle Benny crowded him so all he could do was to shoot into line in the funeral procession. Uncle Benny cut right in after him and the nigger shot out of line and Uncle Benny crowded him in again.

I'll declare, I was glad old lady Weller wasn't alive to see it. She'd had no use for Uncle Benny, she'd hated a nigger, and she'd despised dogs so to where she kept a shotgun by her door to shoot at them if one so much as crossed her cornfield. And here on the way to her burying, where you'd figure she was entitled to have things the way she liked them, here was Uncle Benny chasing a nigger in and out of line, and seven bird-dogs were going Ki-yippity-yi! Ki-yippity-yi! Ki-yippity-yi! I was mighty proud the corpse was no kin to me.

The Old Hen was plumb mortified. She put her hands over her face and when the Ford would swerve by or cut in ahead of us, Doc and me could see her swaying back and forth and suffering. I don't scarcely need to say Uncle Benny was enjoying hisself. If he'd looked sorrowful-like, as if he was just doing his duty, you could of forgive him. Near a filling-station the Chevrolet shot ahead and stopped and the nigger jumped out and started to run. Uncle Benny stopped and climbed out of the Ford and drew his pistol and called "Stop!" The nigger kept on going.

Now Uncle Benny claims that shooting at niggers in the line of duty is what keeps him in practice for bird-shooting. He dropped a ball to the right of the nigger's heel and he dropped a ball to the left of it. He called "Stop!" and the nigger kept on going. Then Uncle Benny took his pistol in both hands and took a slow aim and he laid the third ball against the nigger's shin-bone. He dropped like a string-haltered mule.

Uncle Benny said to the man that ran the filling-station, "Get your gun. That there nigger is under arrest and I deputize you to keep him that-a-way. The sheriff'll be along to pick him up direckly."

He cut back into the funeral procession between us and the hearse, and we could tell by them wicked blue eyes he didn't know when he'd enjoyed a burying like old lady Weller's. When we got back from the burying, he stopped by Will's garage. The Old Hen was giving him down-the-country.

She said, "That was the most scandalous thing I've ever knowed you to do, chasing that nigger in and out of Mis' Weller's funeral."

Uncle Benny's eyes begun to dance and he said, "I know

it, wife, but I couldn't help it. 'Twasn't me done the chasing—it was the Model-T."

Doc got in to it then and sided with the Old Hen. He gets excited, the way fat men do, and he swelled up like a spreading adder.

"Benny," he said, "you shock my modesty. This ain't no occasion for laughing or lying."

Uncle Benny said, "I know it, Doc. I wouldn't think of laughing nor lying. You didn't know I've got that Ford trained? I've got it trained to where it'll do two things. It's helped me chase so many niggers, I've got it to where it just naturally takes out after 'em by itself."

Doc got red in the face and asked, real sarcastic, "And what's the other piece of training?"

Uncle Benny said, "Doc, that Ford has carried me home drunk so many times, I've got it trained to where it'll take care of me and carry me home safe when I ain't fitten."

Doc spit halfway across the road and he said, "You lying old jaybird."

Uncle Benny said, "Doc, I've got a pint of moonshine and if you'll come go camping with me to Salt Springs this evening, I'll prove it."

The Old Hen spoke up and she said, "Benny, Heaven forgive you for I won't, if you go on the prowl again before you've cleared the weeds out of my old pindar field. I'm a month late now, getting it planted."

Doc loves Salt Springs crab and mullet as good as Uncle Benny does, and I could see he was tempted.

But he said, "Benny, you go along home and do what your wife wants, and when you're done—when she says you're done—then we'll go to Salt Springs."

So Uncle Benny and the Old Hen drove off. Doc watched after them.

He said, "Anyways, cutting the fool at a burying had ought to last Benny quite a while."

I said, "You don't know him. Cutting the fool don't last him no time at all."

I was right. I ain't so special wise a woman, but if I once know a man, I can come right close to telling you what he'll do. Uncle Benny hadn't been gone hardly no time, when somebody come by the garage hollering that he'd done set the Old Hen's pindar field on fire.

I said to Doc, "What did I tell you? The last thing in the world was safe for that woman to do, was to turn him loose on them weeds. He figured firing was the quickest way to get shut of them."

Doc said, "Let's go see."

We got in his car and drove out to Uncle Benny's place. Here was smoke rolling up back of the house, and the big live oak in the yard was black with soldier blackbirds the grass fire had drove out of the pindar field. The field hadn't had peanuts in it since fall, but bless Katy, it was full of something else. Uncle Benny's wife had it plumb full of setting guinea-hens. She hadn't told him, because he didn't like guineas.

Far off to the west corner of the field was the Old Hen, trying to run the guineas into a coop. They were flying every which-a-way and hollering *Pod-rac!* *Pod-rac!* the way guineas holler. All the young uns in the neighborhood were in the middle of the field, beating out the grass fire with palmettos. And setting up on top of the east gate, just as unconcerned, was Uncle Benny, with them two little horns of white hair curling in the heat. Now what do you reckon he was doing? He had all seven of them bird-dogs running back and forth retrieving guinea eggs. He'd say now and again, "Dead—fetch!" and they'd wag their tails and go hunt up another nest and here they'd come, with guinea eggs carried gentle in their mouths. He was putting the eggs in a basket.

When the commotion was over, and the fire out, and everybody gone on but Doc and me, we went to the front porch to set down and rest. The Old Hen was wore out. She admitted it was her fault not letting Uncle Benny know about the setting guinea-hens. She was about to forgive him setting the field a-fire, because him and the bird-dogs had saved the guinea eggs. But when we got to the porch, here lay the bird-dogs in the rocking chairs. There was one to every chair, rocking away and cutting their eyes at her. Their coats and paws were smuttied from the burnt grass—and the Old Hen had put clean sugar-sacking covers on every blessed chair that morning. That settled it. She was stirred up anyway about the way he'd cut the fool at the burying, and she really set in to quarrel at Uncle Benny. And like I say, it turned out to be the last piece of quarrelling she ever done.

She said to him, "You taught them bird-dogs to rock in a rocking chair just to torment me. Ever' beast or varmint you've brought home, you've learned to cut the fool as bad as you do."

"Now wife, what beast or varmint did I ever learn to cut the fool?"

"You learned the 'coon to screw the tops off my syrup cans. You learned the 'possum to hang upside down in my cupboards, and I'd go for a jar of maybe pepper relish and put my hand on him. . . . There's been plenty of such as that. I've raised ever'thing in the world for you but a stallion horse."

Doc said, "Give him time, he'll have one of them stabled in the kitchen."

"Bird-dogs is natural to have around," she said. "I was raised to bird-dogs. But it ain't natural for 'em to rock in a rocking-chair. There's so terrible many of them, and when they put in the night on the porch laying in the rocking-chairs and rocking, I don't close my eyes for the fuss."

Uncle Benny said, "You see, Doc? You see, Mis' Dover? She's always quarrelling that me and the dogs ain't never home at night. Then when we do come in, she ain't willing we should all be comf'table.

"We just as good to go on to Salt Springs, Doc. Wait while I go in the house and get my camping outfit and we'll set out."

He went in the house and came out with his camping stuff. She knowed he was gone for nobody knew how long.

We walked on down to the gate and the Old Hen followed, sniffling a little and twisting the corner of her apron.

"Benny," she said, "please don't go to Salt Springs. You always lose your teeth in the Boil."

"I ain't lost e'm but three times," he said, and he cranked up the Model-T and climbed in. "I couldn't help losing 'em the first time. That was when I was laughing at the Yankee casting for bass, and his plug caught me in the open mouth and lifted my teeth out. Nor I couldn't help it the second time, when Doc and me was rassling in the rowboat and he pushed me in."

"Yes," she said, "an how'd you lose 'em the third time?"

His eyes twinkled and he shoved the Ford in low. "Cuttin' the fool," he said.

"That's just it," she said, and the tears begun to roll out of her eyes. "Anybody with false teeth hadn't ought to cut the fool!"

Now I always thought it was right cute, the way Uncle Benny fooled Doc about the trained Ford. You know how the old-timey Fords get the gas—it feeds from the hand-throttle on the wheel. Well, Uncle Benny had spent the day before old lady Weller's funeral at Will's garage, putting in a foot accelerator. He didn't say a word to anybody, and Will and me was the only ones knowed he had it. Doc and Uncle Benny stayed three-four days camping at Salt Springs. Now the night they decided to come home, they'd both had something to drink, but Uncle Benny let on like he was in worse shape than he was.

Doc said, "Benny, you better leave me drive."

Uncle Benny pretended to rock on his feet and roll his head and he said, "I've got that Model-T trained to carry me home, drunk or sober."

Doc said, "Never mind that lie again. You get up there in the seat and whistle in the dogs. I'm fixing to drive us home."

Well, I'd of give a pretty to of been in the back seat with them bird-dogs that night when Doc drove the Ford back to Oak Bluff. It's a treat, any ways, to see a fat man get excited. The first thing Doc knowed, the Ford was running away with him. The Ford lights were none too good, and Doc just did clear a stump by the roadside, and he run clean over a blackjack sapling. He looked at the hand-throttle on the wheel and here it was where the car had ought to be going about twenty miles an hour and it was going forty-five. That rascal of an Uncle Benny had his foot on the foot accelerator.

Doc shut off the gas altogether and the Ford kept right on going.

He said, "Something's the matter."

Uncle Benny seemed to be dozing and didn't pay no mind. The Ford whipped back and forth in the sand road like a 'gator's tail. Directly they got on to the hard road and the Model-T put on speed. They begun to get near a curve. It was a dark night and the carlights wobbling, but Doc could see it coming. He took a tight holt of the wheel and begun to sweat. He felt for the brakes, but Uncle Benny never did have any.

He said, "We'll all be kilt."

When they started to take the curve, the Model-T was going nearly fifty-five—and then just as they got there, all of a sudden it slowed down as if it knowed what it was doing, and went around the curve as gentle as a day-old kitten. Uncle Benny had eased his foot off the accelerator. Doc drawed a breath again.

It's a wonder to me that trip didn't make Doc a nervous wreck. On every straightaway the Ford would rare back on its haunches and stretch out like a greyhound. Every curve they come to, it would go to it like a jack-rabbit. Then just as the sweat would pour down Doc's face and the drops would splash on the wheel, and he'd gather hisself together ready to jump, the Ford would slow down. It was a hot spring night, but Uncle Benny says Doc's teeth were chattering. The Model-T made the last mile lickety-brindle with the gas at the hand-throttle shut off entirely—and it coasted down in front of Will's garage and of its own free will come to a dead stop.

It was nine o'clock at night. Will was just closing up and I had locked the candy and cigarette counter and was waiting for him. There was a whole bunch of men and boys around, like always, because the garage is the last place in Oak Bluff to put the lights out. Doc climbed out of the Ford trembling like a dish of custard. Uncle Benny eased out after him and I looked at him and right away I knowed he'd been up to mischief.

Doc said, "I don't know how he done it—but dogged if

he wasn't telling the truth when he said he had that blank-
ety-blank Model-T trained to carry him home when he
ain't fitten."

Will asked, "How come?" and Doc told us. Will looked
at me and begun to chuckle and we knowed what Uncle
Benny had done to him. I think maybe I would of let Uncle
Benny get away with it, but Will couldn't keep it.

"Come here, Doc," he said. "Here's your training."

I thought the bunch would laugh Doc out of town. He
swelled up like a toadfish and he got in his car without a
word and drove away.

It's a wonderful thing just to set down and figure out
how many different ways there are to be crazy. We never
thought of Uncle Benny as being really crazy. We'd say,
"Uncle Benny's cutting the fool again," and we'd mean he
was just messing around some sort of foolishness like a daggone young un. We figured his was what you might call
the bottom kind of craziness. The next would be the half-
witted. The next would be the senseless. The next would be
what the colored folks call "mindless." And clear up at the
top would be what you'd call cold-out crazy. With all his
foolishness, we never figured Uncle Benny was cold-out
crazy.

Well, we missed Uncle Benny from Oak Buffs a day or
two. When I came to ask questions, I found he'd gone on a
long prowl and was over the Withlacoochie River camping
with some oyster fishermen. I didn't think much of it, because he was liable to stay off that-a-way. But time rocked
on and he didn't show up. I dropped by his house to ask the
Old Hen about him. She didn't know a blessed thing.

She said, "Ain't it God's mercy we've got no young uns?
The pore things would be as good as fatherless."

And then a few days later Doc came driving up to the garage. He got out and blew his nose and we could see his eyes were red.

He said, "Ain't it awful! I can't hardly bear to think about it."

Will said, "Doc, if you know bad news, you must be carrying it. Ain't nothing sorrowful I know of, except the prohi's have found Philbin's still."

Doc said, "Don't talk about such little accidents at a time like this. You don't mean you ain't heerd about Benny?"

The bunch was there and they all perked up, interested. They knowed if it was Uncle Benny, they could expect 'most any news.

I said, "We ain't heerd a word since he went off to the west coast."

"You ain't heerd about him going crazy?"

I said, "Doc, you mean being crazy. He's always been that-a-way."

"I mean being crazy and going crazy, pore ol' Benny Mathers has gone really cold-out crazy."

Well, we all just looked at him and we looked at one another. And it came over the whole bunch of us that we weren't surprised. A nigger setting by the free air hose said, "Do, Jesus!" and eased away to tell the others.

Doc blew his nose and wiped his eyes and he said, "I'm sure we all forgive the pore ol' feller all the things he done. He wasn't responsible. I feel mighty bad, to think the hard way I've often spoke to him."

Will asked, "How come it to finally happen?"

Doc said, "He'd been up to some foolishness all night, raring through some of them Gulf coast flat-woods. Him and the fellers he was camping with was setting on the steps of the camp-house after breakfast. All of a sudden Uncle

Benny goes to whistling, loud and shrill like a jay-bird. Then he says, 'I'm Sampson,' and he begun to tear down the camp-house."

Will asked, "What'd they do with him?"

Doc said, "You really ain't heerd? I declare, I can't believe the news has come so slow. They had a terrible time holding him and tying him. They got in the doctors and the sheriff and they takened pore ol' Uncle Benny to the lunatic asylum at Chattahoochie."

Doc wiped his eyes and we all begun to sniffle and our eyes to burn. I declare, it was just as if Uncle Benny Mathers had died on us.

I said, "Oh, his poor wife—"

Will said, "We'll have to be good to him and go see him and take him cigarettes and maybe slip him a pint of 'shine now and again."

I said, "The way he loved his freedom—shutting him up in the crazy-house will be like putting a wild-cat in a crocus sack."

Doc said, "Oh, he ain't in the asylum right now. He's broke loose. That's what makes me feel so bad. He's headed this way, and no telling the harm he'll do before he's ketched again."

Everybody jumped up and begun feeling in their hip pockets for their guns.

Doc said, "No use to try to put no guns on him. He's got his'n and they say he's shooting just as accurate as ever."

That was enough for me. I ran back of the counter at the garage and begun locking up.

I said, "Doc, you're a sight. 'Tain't no time to go to feeling sorry for Uncle Benny and our lives and property in danger."

Doc said, "I know, but I knowed him so long and I knowed him so good. I can't help feeling bad about it."

I said, "Do something about it. Don't just set there, and him liable to come shooting his way in any minute."

Doc said, "I know, but what can anybody do to stop him? Pore man, with all them deputies after him."

Will said, "Deputies?"

Doc said, "Why, yes. The sheriff at Ocala asked me would I stop along the road and leave word for all the deputies to try and ketch him. Pore ol' Benny, I'll swear. I hated doing it the worst way."

I scooped the money out of the cash register and I told them, "Now, men, I'm leaving. I've put up with Uncle Benny Mathers when he was drunk and I've put up with him when he was cutting the fool. But the reckless way he drives that Ford and the way he shoots a pistol, I ain't studying on messing up around him and him gone cold-out crazy."

Doc said, "Ain't a thing in the world would stop him when he goes by, and all them deputies after him, but a barricade across the road."

I said, "Then for goodness' sake, you sorry, low-down, no-account, varminty white men, tear down the wire fence around my chicken yard and fix Uncle Benny a barricade."

Doc said, "I just hated to suggest it."

Will said, "He'd slow down for the barricade and we could come in from behind and hem him in."

Doc said, "It'll be an awful thing to hem him in and have to see him sent back to Chattahoochie."

Will said, "I'll commence pulling out the posts and you-all can wind up the fencing."

They worked fast and I went out and looked up the road

now and again to see if Uncle Benny was coming. Doc had stopped at the Standard filling-station on his way, to leave the news, and we could see the people there stirring around and going out to look, the same as we were doing. When we dragged the roll of wire fencing out into the road we hollered to them so they could see what we were doing and they all cheered and waved their hats. The word had spread, and the young uns begun traipsing barefooted down to the road, until some of their mammies ran down and cuffed them and hurried them back home out of the way of Uncle Benny. The men strung the fencing tight across the road between the garage on one side and our smokehouse on the other. They nailed it firm at both ends.

Doc said, "Leave me drive the last nail, men—it may be the last thing I can do for Benny this side of Chattahoochie."

I talked the men into unloading their guns.

"He'll have to stop when he sees the barricade," I said, "and then you can all go in on him with your guns drawed and capture him. I just can't hear to a loaded gun being drawed on him, for fear of somebody getting excited and shooting him."

Doc wiped the sweat off his forehead and he said, "Men, this is a mighty serious occasion. I'd be mighty proud if you'd all have a little snort on me," and he passed the bottle.

"Here's to Uncle Benny, the way we all knowed him before he went cold-out crazy," he said.

And then we heerd a shouting up the dirt road and young uns whistling and women and girls screaming and chickens scattering.

"Yonder comes Uncle Benny!"

And yonder he came.

The Model-T was swooping down like a bull-bat after a nosquito. The water was boiling up out of the radiator in a foot-high stream. The seven pieded bird-dogs were hanging out of the back seat and trembling as if they craved to tell the things they'd seen. And behind Uncle Benny was a string of deputy sheriffs in Fords and Chevrolets and motorcycles that had gathered together from every town between Oak Bluff and Ocala. And Uncle Benny was hunched over the steering wheel with them two tufts of goat-horn hair sticking up in the breeze—and the minute I laid eyes on him I knowed he wasn't one mite crazier than he ever had been. I knowed right then Doc had laid out to get even with him and had lied on him all the way down the road.

It was too late then. I knowed, whatever happened, there'd be people to the end of his life would always believe it. I knowed there'd be young uns running from him and niggers hiding. And I knowed there wasn't a thing in the world now could keep him out of Chattahoochie for the time being. I know'd he'd fight when he was taken, and all them mad and hot and dusty deputies would get him to the lunatic asylum quicker than a black snake can cross hot ashes. And once a man that has cut the fool all his life, like Uncle Benny, is in the crazy-house, there'll be plenty of folks to say to keep him there.

It was too late. Uncle Benny was bearing down toward the garage and right in front of him was the barricade.

Doc hollered, "Be ready to jump on him when he stops!"

Stop? Uncle Benny stop? He kept right on coming. The sight of that chicken-wire barricade was no more to him than an aggravation. Uncle Benny and the Model-T dived into the barricade like a water-turkey into a pool. The barricade held. And the next thing we knowed, the Ford had somersaulted over the fencing and crumpled up like a paper shoe-box and scattered bird-dogs over ten acres and laid Uncle Benny in a heap over against the wall of the smokehouse. I was raised to use the language of a lady, but I could hold in.

"Doc," I said, "you low-down son of a ——"

He said, "Mis' Dover, the name's too good. I've killed my friend."

Killed him? Killed Uncle Benny? It can't be done until the Almighty Hisself hollers "Sooey!" Uncle Benny was messed up considerable, but him nor none of the bird-dogs was dead.

The doctor took a few stitches in him at the garage before he come to, and tied up his head right pretty in a white bandage. We left Will to quiet the deputies and we put Uncle Benny in Doc's car and carried him home to the Old Hen. Naturally, I figured it would set her to quarrelling. Instead, it just brought out all her sweetness. I can guess a man, but I can't guess another woman.

"The pore ol' feller," she said. "I knowed he had it coming to him. What the devil throws over his back—. I knowed he'd kill hisself in that Ford car, cutting the fool and prowling. The biggest load is off my mind. Now," she said, "now, by God's mercy, when it did come to him, he got out alive."

She begun fanning him with a palmetto fan where he lay on the bed, and Doc poured out a drink of 'shine to have ready for him when he come to. Doc's hand was trembling. Uncle Benny opened his eyes. He eased one hand up to the bandage across his head and he groaned and grunted. He looked at Doc as if he couldn't make up his mind whether or not to reach for his pistol. Doc put the 'shine to his mouth and Uncle Benny swallowed. Them wicked blue eyes begun to dance.

"Doc," he said, "how will I get home when I'm drunk, now you've tore up my trained Ford?"

Doc broke down and cried like a little baby.

"I ain't got the money to replace it," he said, "but I'll give you my car. I'll carry the Little Giant line of remedies on foot."

Uncle Benny said, "I don't want your car. It ain't trained."

Doc said, "Then I'll tote you on my back, anywheres you say."

The Old Hen let in the bird-dogs, some of them limping a little, and they climbed on the bed and beat their tails on the counterpane and licked Uncle Benny. We felt mighty relieved things had come out that way.

Uncle Benny was up and around in a few days, with his head bandaged, and him as pert as a woodpecker. He just about owned Oak Bluff—all except the people that did like I figured, never did get over the idea he'd gone really crazy. Most people figured he'd had a mighty good lesson and it would learn him not to cut the fool. The Old Hen was as happy as a bride. She was so proud to have the Ford torn up, and no money to get another, that she'd even now and again pet one of the bird-dogs. She waited on Uncle Benny hand and foot and couldn't do enough to please him.

She said to me, "The pore ol' feller sure stays home nights now."

Stay home? Uncle Benny stay home? Two weeks after the accident the wreck of the Model-T disappeared from behind the garage where Will had dragged it. The next day the seven bird-dogs disappeared. The day after that Doc and Uncle Benny went to Ocala in Doc's car. Will wouldn't answer me when I asked him questions. The Old Hen stopped by the garage and got a Coca-Cola and she didn't know any more than I did. Then Will pointed down the road.

He said, "Yonder he comes."

And yonder he came. You could tell him way off by the white bandage with the tufts of hair sticking up over it. He was scrooched down behind the wheel of what looked like a brand-new automobile. Doc was following behind him. They swooped into the garage.

Will said, "It's a new second-hand body put on the chassis and around the engine of the old Ford."

Uncle Benny got out and he greeted us.

He said, "Will, it's just possible it was the motor of the Model-T that had takened the training. The motor ain't hurt, and me and Doc are real hopeful."

The Old Hen said, "Benny, where'd you get the money to pay for it?"

He said, "Why, a daggone bootlegger in a truck going from Miami to New York bought the bird-dogs for twenty-five dollars apiece. The low-down rascal knowed good and well they was worth seventy-five."

She brightened some. Getting shut of the bird-dogs was a little progress. She walked over to the car and begun looking around it.

"Benny," she said, and her voice come kind of faintified, "if you sold the bird-dogs, what's this place back here looks like it was fixed for 'em?"

We all looked, and here was a open compartment-like in the back, fixed up with seven crocus sacks stuffed with corn shucks. About that time here come a cloud of dust down the road. It was the seven bird-dogs. They were about give out. Their tongues were hanging out and their feet looked blistered.

Uncle Benny said, "I knowed they'd jump out of that bootlegger's truck. I told him so."

I tell you, what's in a man's nature you can't change. It takened the Old Hen thirty years and all them goings-on to learn it. She went and climbed in the front seat of the car and just sat there waiting for Uncle Benny to drive home for his dinner. He lifted the bird-dogs up and set them down to rest on the corn-shucks cushions, and he brought them a pan of water.

He said, "I figure they busted loose just about Lawtey."

The Old Hen never opened her mouth. She hasn't quarrelled at him from that day to this. She was hornswoggled

THE LEGISLATURE

By James M. Cain

The third room on your left as you enter the south wing of the State Capitol. It is an afternoon in mid-winter, and three gentlemen, MESSRS. HAYES, LOMAN *and* FRIEND, *are sitting at one end of the table. They constitute a quorum of the Committee on Education of the House of Representatives, and before them is a large pile of bills, resolutions, and memoranda.*

MR. HAYES

Well, looking at them don't do no good.

MR. LOMAN

It sure don't.

MR. HAYES

Might as well get busy.

MR. LOMAN

A hell of a fine time them other guys on this committee picked to get the flu!

MR. HAYES

How you say we do? Take up them schoolhouses, or leave them wait till we got a couple other things out of the way first?

MR. LOMAN

Leave them schoolhouses till last. That was referred jointly anyhow, and it ain't no use of us wasting no sweat on them till Ways and Means has said what they're goin' to do.

MR. HAYES

All right, then. Authorizing constable of town of Gale's Island to act as truant officer. Authorizing commissioners of town of Shawville to close certain streets to motor traffic during hours when public schools are in session. Them things don't amount to nothing and here's about forty more just like them. Shoot them right through, hey? Report them favorable and be done with it?

MR. LOMAN

Hell, yes.

MR. HAYES

All set on them, then.

MR. LOMAN

Pitch them over to one side. That's a start anyways.

MR. HAYES

All right, then. Le's get on this here Evolution Bill. Bill prohibiting the teaching of certain doctrines in educational institutions supported in whole or in part by public funds. What do you say on that?

MR. LOMAN

I say that bill ought to been passed about ten year ago.

MR. HAYES

That bill hits me pretty good too. Still, it's pretty important, so I guess we better consider it some.

MR. LOMAN

What's the use of considering? I don't need no considering to know how I'm going to vote.

MR. HAYES

How do you feel about that, Mr. Friend?

MR. FRIEND

Hunh?

MR. HAYES

This here Evolution Bill. We're getting ready to report
on it now and we kind of want to make sure we got the
right idea about it.

MR. FRIEND

Hunh.

MR. HAYES

So if you got anything to say about it, now is the time to
say it.

MR. FRIEND

They hadn't ought to kill no cows thouten they pay for
them.

MR. LOMAN

Now, what in the hell has the Committee on Education
got to do with cows?

MR. HAYES

No, this ain't the Tubercular Cattle Bill. This is the Evolution Bill. Or Anti-evolution Bill, some of them calls it.

MR. LOMAN

Evolution!

MR. FRIEND

I ain't deef.

MR. HAYES

You read it?

MR. FRIEND

Maybe I read it.

MR. LOMAN

He ain't asked you *maybe* did you read it. He asked you did you *read* it. Come on. If you ain't deef, then act like you was awake.

MR. FRIEND

What's reading got to do with it?

MR. HAYES

Well, we're kind of busy this afternoon, Mr. Friend, and it would kind of save time if you had read the bill.

MR. FRIEND

I reckon I can read it if I have to. Where's it at?

MR. LOMAN

You mean to say you been a member of this Legislature a whole month and attended all the hearings this committee has held and ain't read that bill yet?

MR. HAYES

Now, Loman, it don't do no good to get sore.

MR. LOMAN

No, but what does the taxpayers pay a bum like that for?

MR. FRIEND

All right. Where's it at?

MR. HAYES

Well, Mr. Friend, it's pretty late in the day to start reading the bill now. I reckon the best way is for us to kind of explain to you what's in it. Then you can tell us how you feel about it.

MR. FRIEND

I can read. But I ain't all the time bragging on it.

MR. LOMAN

I bet you ain't.

MR. HAYES

Well, le's see. Le's see now. Le's see how I can put it.

MR. FRIEND

I never seen such a place in my life. They can't never do nothing thouten some man stands up and starts reading something. All the time showing off how good they can read. Up my way the people ain't got time for all this here reading.

MR. LOMAN

They can read them pain-killer ads though.

MR. HAYES

Well, first off, Mr. Friend, you know what this here evolution is, don't you?

MR. FRIEND

Maybe.

MR. LOMAN

You say maybe oncet more and maybe you stay where you're sitting and maybe you take a dive in that spittoon.

MR. FRIEND

Yeah, I hear tell of it. I hear the preachers talk about it plenty of times.

MR. HAYES

And you know what it is?

MR. FRIEND

Mister, go ahead and do your talking. Don't worry about me. I'll git the hang of it time you git done.

MR. HAYES

The main idea, the way I get it, is that men is descended from monkeys.

MR. FRIEND

Hunh?

MR. LOMAN

Dam, it does break my heart to think of the people of this State paying out their money for this.

MR. HAYES

That men is descended from monkeys.

MR. FRIEND

De—?

MR. LOMAN

Aw hell!

MR. HAYES

Descended. You got a father, ain't you?

MR. FRIEND

Doggone it, come on and say what you're gitting at. I'm tired of all this here funny talk. All the time using big words. All the time talking and nobody can't tell what it means. Sure I got a father. How you think I got here if I didn't have no father? What you ask me that for, anyway?

MR. LOMAN

Just to be o'n'ry.

MR. HAYES

Keep out of this, will you, Loman? It's hard enough without no help.

MR. LOMAN

Why don't you go out there and talk to that tree?

MR. HAYES

Because the tree ain't on the committee.

MR. LOMAN

That's a dam shame.

MR. HAYES

Mr. Friend, we ain't giving you no funny talk. We're explaining this here evolution as good as we can, and we'd get along better if you would listen at what we're trying to tell you and quit all the time putting up a bum argument about how we're doing it.

MR. FRIEND

I ain't ask you to explain me nothing. Go on and do your talking. I already told you I'll git the hang of it time you git done. I ain't never seen nothing yet I couldn't git the hang of.

MR. LOMAN

If you was to get the hang of a manila rope, that would be a fine thing for the people of this State.

MR. HAYES

All right, you got a father. And you got a grandfather, ain't you? Or maybe had one?

MR. FRIEND

All right. All right. Just keep on with your funny talk. All right, mister, now I'll ask *you* something. If I didn't have no grandfather, how would I have a father? How would my father of got here, hunh? Tell me that!

MR. LOMAN

That's a tough one, all right.

MR. HAYES

Loman, just as a favor to me, will you stay out of this and quit balling it up? All right. You want to get in it, you take him awhile. See what you can do.

MR. LOMAN

No, thanks. I pass.

MR. FRIEND

You can read so good, tell me that.

MR. HAYES

All right, Mr. Friend, you got a father and you got a grandfather. Now you're *descended* from your *father* and your *grandfather*, you got *that*? And your *father* and your *grandfather*, they're *descended* from *their father* and *their grandfather*, you got *that*? And so are *you* descended from their father and their grandfather, and *so* on and *so* on, you got *that*?

MR. FRIEND

I already told you I ain't deef.

MR. HAYES

And then *evolutionists* says *men* is *descended* from *monkeys*.

MR. FRIEND

You quit hollering at me.

MR. HAYES

Hollering at you! Goddam it, I'll crown you with a brick in a minute!

MR. LOMAN

Who's balling it up now?

MR. HAYES

Well anyway, I ain't balling it up on purpose.

MR. FRIEND

All the time hollering at me. I ain't going to take no more of it.

MR. HAYES

Mr. Friend, did you hear what I just now told you about how them evolutionists says men is descended from monkeys?

MR. FRIEND

That's better, mister. That's a whole lot better. You talk to me right, I'll talk to you right.

MR. LOMAN

You hear that, don't you, Hayes? Now you know where you get off.

MR. HAYES

Mr. Friend.

MR. FRIEND

Hunh?

MR. HAYES

Are we talking to suit you this way? Is this all right, the way I'm talking now?

MR. FRIEND

But that ain't how you was talking just now. You was hollering at me.

MR. HAYES

Never mind how I was talking just now. Am I talking to suit you now?

MR. FRIEND

And another thing, mister. I'll thank you to quit cussing at me. I ain't no mule.

MR. HAYES

All right, then.

MR. FRIEND

I don't allow nobody to cuss at me. You just as well understand that right now.

MR. HAYES

Where was I at?

MR. LOMAN

Where you was at was about them monkeys, but was you going or coming I wouldn't like to say.

MR. HAYES

Oh yeah. Them monkeys. Now, Mr. Friend, have you got it straight about that? About how them evolutionists says men is descended from monkeys?

MR. FRIEND

Who says so?

MR. HAYES

Them evolutionists.

MR. FRIEND

Ev—?

MR. LOMAN

I swear this is the worst crime I ever seen.

MR. HAYES

—olutionists.

MR. FRIEND

All right, mister, keep it up. Just keep it up. Some day the people is going to find out how things is run in this place. All the time showing off how good they can read. All the time showing off how many big words they know. All the time making speeches and using big words. I sit in that place over there every night for to help pass the laws, and then what? I can't never git the meaning of nothing. I can't never git the meaning on account of all them big words.

MR. HAYES

Well, it ain't no other word for these people we're talking about, Mr. Friend, so you just as well learn this one.

MR. LOMAN

That's it. Just take a week off and learn it.

MR. FRIEND

Why don't they talk so's somebody can understand them?

MR. HAYES

All right, Mr. Friend, we won't argue about it. We'll just forget that word and go on with what we're doing.

MR. LOMAN

What in the hell are we doing anyway?

MR. HAYES

We'll just say there's some people that says this here, and not bother about no name for them at all. Have you got it straight what they say now? That men is descended from monkeys?

MR. FRIEND

But I don't never git the right meaning of nothing.

MR. LOMAN

Well, that's tough, but don't let it worry you none. You got plenty of company. If them delegates ever found out what they was voting for 'stead of getting descended from monkeys they would get ascended up into heaven. 'Cause God is the only one knows, and even He ain't so dam sure.

MR. FRIEND

Monkeys!

MR. HAYES

That's what we're talking about, Mr. Friend. Monkeys.

MR. LOMAN

Monkey-demonk!

MR. FRIEND

Ain't these people in this place got nothing better to do, mister, than think up a whole lot of devilment about monkeys? Don't they never do no work?

MR. HAYES

Never mind about whether they work or not, Mr. Friend. Have you got it straight about how men is descended from monkeys? Or supposed to be, anyhow?

MR. FRIEND

All the time thinking up some new kind of devilment. All the time showing off how good they can read. All the time showing off how many big words they know. Mister, what we talking about monkeys for, anyhow? Why ain't we talking about something that is some good? Why ain't we talking about is Flint Neck going to git their new schoolhouse?

MR. HAYES

We've been all over that, Mr. Friend. The bills on them schoolhouses was referred jointly to the Committee on Education and the Ways and Means Committee and we're postponing action on them until the Ways and Means takes up the money part, and then we'll consider the Flint Neck schoolhouse on its merits same as all the rest. What we're considering now is the Evolution Bill and I'll appreciate it if you'll get your mind on that so we'll maybe have something to show for our time.

MR. FRIEND

Let me tell you something, mister. I got elected for to git Flint Neck their new schoolhouse and I ain't got no time to set around talking about monkeys.

MR. HAYES

Loman, what in the hell am I going to do about this?

MR. LOMAN

I don't know. I never seen nothing like it in my life.

MR. FRIEND

Them people needs that schoolhouse, mister. They got hard times, and if some of them don't git some money working on the new schoolhouse I don't see how they're going to eat.

MR. HAYES

Because look here, Loman, if we don't get three to vote on it I ain't so sure we can report the bill out at all. Anyway not without a whole lot of jockeying around on the floor.

MR. LOMAN

That's the hell of it.

MR. HAYES

But how I'm going to keep this up I don't know. I ain't even got past the monkeys yet.

MR. LOMAN

If he ain't even got it straight about the monkeys he's going to have a hell of a time with the Bible.

MR. FRIEND

Hunh?

MR. HAYES

Nothing at all, Mr. Friend. We was just talking about how we could explain it to you a little better.

MR. FRIEND

You was mumbling about that Bible.

MR. LOMAN

That Bible! It ain't only one Bible.

MR. FRIEND

It weren't my Bible! My Bible was in the house all the time!

MR. HAYES

Oh my God!

MR. FRIEND

And it weren't my still! I already told them it weren't my still! It was on my place but I never knowed nothing about it. It was 'way down by the creek!

MR. LOMAN

Anh-hanh. Anh-hanh.

MR. FRIEND

Lemme alone! Quit putting on me about that Bible!

MR. LOMAN

Anh-hanh. So you're the guy the Flint Neck Ku Klux was talking about last month, hey? Using a Bible to prop up the pipe with, where it run down from the still to the coil? Anh-hanh. Well, a fine delegate to the Legislature you turned out to be!

MR. FRIEND

Lemme alone! It weren't my Bible!

MR. HAYES

Loman, I swear to God I don't know which is the dumbest, you or this guy or the monkeys. Now look what you done. How the hell am I *ever* going to get this thing through his nut if you go on like this, scaring the hell out of him about his still? What do we care if he was running a still?

MR. LOMAN

No, but what gets me is a bum like that that gets elected to the Legislature and then they find a still on his place. And propped up with a Bible.

MR. HAYES

I don't care if it was propped up with a couple of Bibles and a hymn-book. I'm trying to get something done here and if you'll just kindly keep your mouth the hell! out of it, maybe we'll get done by corn-planting time.

MR. LOMAN

All right.

MR. HAYES

You got a spare handkerchief? Thanks. I ain't sweat so much since I used to pitch hay.

MR. FRIEND

Lemme alone! I'm going out of this place! I'm going home!

MR. LOMAN

Set down! Set down and quit that blubbering and listen at what Mr. Hayes is telling you or I'll take a poke at you. You hear me?

MR. HAYES

Now, Mr. Friend, I already told you about how them people says men is *descended from monkeys!*

MR. LOMAN

Monkeys—you get it?

MR. HAYES

And that there monkey stuff is *all crossed up with the Bible!*

MR. LOMAN

Bible—what you prop up your still with!

MR. HAYES

The Adam and Eve part, 'cause men couldn't be descended from *monkeys and Adam and Eve both!*

MR. LOMAN

Couldn't be descended from both—you get it?

MR. HAYES

So this here bill says they can't teach that stuff no more and then we throw out all the monkey books and buy new books in their place and *that's all there is to it!*

MR. LOMAN

That's all. Just buy new books and *that's all there is to it!*

MR. HAYES

So that's the bill *and now what do you say on it?*

MR. FRIEND

Lemme alone! I don't know nothing about no bill!

MR. HAYES

Mr. Friend, listen. It don't make no difference which way you vote, yes or no. 'Cause even if you're in favor of this here monkey stuff it'll be two to one the other way and all we want you to do is say yes or no for the record. Now will you please say *one way or the other, yes or no?*

MR. FRIEND

Lemme alone!

MR. LOMAN

Well, Hayes, there you are!

MR. HAYES

Loman, I'm going to report this guy to the Speaker. I don't know if anything can be done about it, but I'm going to find out. I'm going to report him at the night session. You're right. This here is a right down swindle on the taxpayers. Just think of it! A great moral measure like this here Evolution Bill being held up by a bum like that!

MR. LOMAN

They ought to send him back to Flint Neck. That's where he wants to go and they ought to let him.

MR. FRIEND

I'm agin it.

MR. HAYES, MR. LOMAN

What was that?

MR. FRIEND

I'm agin this here bill. Paying out a whole lot of money for new books and—

MR. LOMAN

Whoops!

MR. HAYES

By gosh we're done! He's voted, and he's agin it, and we're done!

MR. FRIEND

All the time paying out money for books. . . . Reading. . . . Big words. . . . Monkeys. . . .

THE LITTLE HOURS

By DOROTHY PARKER

Now WHAT's this? What's the object of all this darkness all over me? They haven't gone and buried me alive while my back was turned, have they? Ah, now would you think they'd do a thing like that! Oh, no, I know what it is. I'm awake. That's it. I've waked up in the middle of the night. Well, isn't that nice. Isn't that simply ideal. Twenty minutes past four, sharp, and here's Baby wide-eyed as a marigold. Look at this, will you? At the time when all decent people are just going to bed, I must wake up. There's no way things can ever come out even, under this system. This is as rank as injustice is ever likely to get. This is what brings about hatred and bloodshed, that's what *this* does.

Yes, and you want to know what got me into this mess? Going to bed at ten o'clock, that's what. That spells ruin. T-e-n-space-o-apostrophe-c-l-o-c-k: ruin. Early to bed, and you'll wish you were dead. Bed before eleven, nuts before seven. Bed before morning, sailors give warning. Ten o'clock, after a quiet evening of reading. Reading—there's an institution for you. Why, I'd turn on the light and read, right this minute, if reading weren't what contributed toward driving me here. I'll show it. God, the bitter misery that reading works in this world! Everybody knows that—everybody who *is* everybody. All the best minds have been off reading for years. Look at the swing La Rochefoucauld

284

took at it. He said that if nobody had ever learned to read, very few people would be in love. There was a man for you, and that's what *he* thought of it. Good for you, La Rochefoucauld; nice going, boy. I wish I'd never learned to read. I wish I'd never learned to take off my clothes. Then I wouldn't have been caught in this jam at half-past four in the morning. If nobody had ever learned to undress, very few people would be in love. No, his is better. Oh, well, it's a man's world.

La Rochefoucauld, indeed, lying quiet as a mouse, and me tossing and turning here! This is no time to be getting all steamed up about La Rochefoucauld. It's only a question of minutes before I'm going to be pretty darned good and sick of La Rochefoucauld, once and for all. La Rochefoucauld this and La Rochefoucauld that. Yes, well, let me tell you that if nobody had ever learned to quote, very few people would be in love with La Rochefoucauld. I bet you I don't know ten souls who read him without a middleman. People pick up those scholarly little essays that start off "Was it not that lovable old cynic, La Rochefoucauld, who said . . ." and then they go around claiming to know the master backwards. Pack of illiterates, that's all they are. All right, let them keep their La Rochefoucauld, and see if I care. I'll stick to La Fontaine. Only I'd be better company if I could quit thinking that La Fontaine married Alfred Lunt.

I don't know what I'm doing mucking about with a lot of French authors at this hour, anyway. First thing you know, I'll be reciting *Fleurs du Mal* to myself, and then I'll be little more good to anybody. And I'll stay off Verlaine too; he was always chasing Rimbauds. A person would be better off with La Rochefoucauld, even. Oh, damn La Rochefoucauld. The big Frog. I'll thank him to keep out of my head. What's he doing there, anyhow? What's La Rochefoucauld to me, or he to Hecuba? Why, I don't even know the man's first name, that's how close I ever was to *him*. What am I supposed to be, a hostess to La Rochefoucauld? That's what *he* thinks. Sez he. Well, he's only wasting his time, hanging around here. I can't help him. The only other thing I can remember his saying is that there is always something a little pleasing to us in the misfortunes of even our dearest friends. That cleans me all up with Monsieur La Rochefoucauld. *Maintenant c'est fini, ça.*

Dearest friends. A sweet lot of dearest friends *I've* got. All of them lying in swinish stupors, while I'm practically up and about. All of them stretched sodden through these, the fairest hours of the day, when man should be at his most productive. Produce, produce, produce, for I tell you the night is coming. Carlyle said that. Yes, and a fine one *he* was, to go shooting off his face on production. *Oh,* Thomas Car*li*-yill, what *I* know about *you*-oo! No, that will be enough of that. I'm not going to start fretting about Carlyle, at this stage of the game. What did he ever do that was so great, besides founding a college for Indians? (That one ought to make him spin.) Let him keep his face out of this, if he knows what's good for him. I've got enough trouble with that lovable old cynic, La Rochefoucauld—him and the misfortunes of his dearest friends!

The first thing I've got to do is get out and whip me up a complete new set of dearest friends; that's the first thing. Everything else can wait. And will somebody please kindly be so good as to inform me how I am ever going to meet up with any new people when my entire scheme of living is out of joint—when I'm the only living being awake while the rest of the world lies sleeping? I've got to get this thing adjusted. I must try to get back to sleep right now. I've got to conform to the rotten little standards of this sluggard civilization. People needn't feel that they have to change their ruinous habits and come my way. Oh, no, no; no, indeed. Not at all. I'll go theirs. If that isn't the woman of it for you! Always having to do what somebody else wants, like it or not. Never able to murmur a suggestion of her own.

And what suggestion has anyone to murmur as to how I am going to drift lightly back to slumber? Here I am, awake as high noon what with all this milling and pitching around with La Rochefoucauld. I really can't be expected to drop everything and start counting sheep, at my age. I hate sheep. Untender it may be in me, but all my life I've hated sheep. It amounts to a phobia, the way I hate them. I can tell the minute there's one in the room. They needn't think that I am going to lie here in the dark and count their unpleasant little faces for them; I wouldn't do it if I didn't fall asleep again until the middle of next August. Suppose they never get counted—what's the worst that can happen? If the number of imaginary sheep in this world remains a matter of guesswork, who is richer or poorer for it? No, sir; *I'm* not their scorekeeper. Let them count themselves, if they're so crazy mad after mathematics. Let them do their own dirty work. Coming around here, at this time of day, and asking me to count them! And not even *real* sheep, at that. Why, it's the most preposterous thing I ever heard in my life.

But there must be *something* I could count. Let's see. No, I already know by heart how many fingers I have. I could count my bills, I suppose. I could count the things I didn't do yesterday that I should have done. I could count the things I should do today that I'm not going to do. I'm never going to accomplish anything; that's perfectly clear to me. I'm never going to be famous. My name will never be writ large on the roster of Those Who Do Things. I don't do anything. Not one single thing. I used to bite my nails, but I don't even do that any more. I don't amount to the powder to blow me to hell. I've turned out to be nothing but a bit of flotsam. Flotsam and leave 'em— that's me from now on. Oh, it's all terrible.

Well. This way lies galloping melancholia. Maybe it's because this is the zero hour. This is the time the swooning soul hangs pendant and vertiginous between the new day and the old, nor dares confront the one or summon back the other. This is the time when all things, known and hidden, are iron to weight the spirit; when all ways, traveled or virgin, fall away from the stumbling feet, when all before the straining eyes is black. Blackness now, everywhere is blackness. This is the time of abomination, the dreadful hour of the victorious dark. For it is always darkest— Was it not that lovable old cynic, La Rochefoucauld, who said that it is always darkest before the deluge?

There. Now you see, don't you? Here we are again, practically back where we started. La Rochefoucauld, we are here. Ah, come on, son—how about your going your way and letting me go mine? I've got my work cut out for me right here; I've got all this sleeping to do. Think how I am going to look by daylight if this keeps up. I'll be a seamy sight for all those rested, clear-eyed, fresh-faced dearest friends of mine—the rats! My *dear,* whatever have you been doing; I thought you were so good lately. Oh, I was helling around with La Rochefoucauld till all hours; we couldn't stop laughing about your misfortunes. No, this is getting too thick, really. It isn't right to have this happen to a person, just because she went to bed at ten o'clock once in her life. Honest, I won't ever do it again. I'll go straight, after this. I'll never go to bed again, if I can only sleep now. If I can tear my mind away from a certain French cynic, *circa* 1650, and slip into lovely oblivion. 1650. I bet I look as if I'd been awake since then.

How do people go to sleep? I'm afraid I've lost the knack. I might try busting myself smartly over the temple with the night-light. I might repeat to myself, slowly and soothingly, a list of quotations beautiful from minds profound; if I can remember any of the damn things. That might do it. And it ought effectually to bar that visiting foreigner that's been hanging around ever since twenty minutes past four. Yes, that's what I'll do. Only wait till I turn the pillow; it feels as if La Rochefoucauld had crawled inside the slip.

Now let's see—where shall we start? Why—er—let's see. Oh, yes, I know one. This above all, to thine own self be true and it must follow, as the night the day, thou canst not then be false to any man. Now they're off. And once they get started, they ought to come like hot cakes. Let's see. Ah, what avail the sceptered race and what the form divine, when every virtue, every grace, Rose Aylmer, all were thine. Let's see. They also serve who only stand and wait. If Winter comes, can Spring be far behind? Lilies that fester smell far worse than weeds. Silent upon a peak in Darien. Mrs. Porter and her daughter wash their feet in soda-water. And Agatha's Arth is a hug-the-hearth, but my true love is false. Why did you die when lambs were cropping, you should have died when apples were dropping. Shall be together, breathe and ride, so one day more am I deified, who knows but the world will end tonight. And he shall hear the stroke of eight and not the stroke of nine. They are not long, the weeping and the laughter; love and desire and hate I think will have no portion in us after we pass the gate. But none, I think, do there embrace. I think that I shall never see a poem lovely as a tree. I think I will not hang myself today. Ay tank Ay go home now.

Let's see. Solitude is the safeguard of mediocrity and the stern companion of genius. Consistency is the hobgoblin of little minds. Something is emotion remembered in tranquillity. A cynic is one who knows the price of everything and the value of nothing. That lovable old cynic is one who—oops, there's King Charles's head again. I've got to watch myself. Let's see. Circumstantial evidence is a trout in the milk. Any stigma will do to beat a dogma. If you would learn what God thinks about money, you have only to look at those to whom He has given it. If nobody had ever learned to read, very few people——

All right. That fixes it. I throw in the towel right now. I know when I'm licked. There'll be no more of this nonsense; I'm going to turn on the light and read my head off. Till the next ten o'clock, if I feel like it. And what does La Rochefoucauld want to make of that? Oh, he *will*, eh? Yes, he will! He and who else? La Rochefoucauld and *what* very few people?

BUT THE ONE ON THE RIGHT

By DOROTHY PARKER

I KNEW IT. I knew if I came to this dinner, I'd draw something like this baby on my left. They've been saving him up for me for weeks. Now, we've simply got to have him—his sister was so sweet to us in London; we can stick him next to Mrs. Parker—she talks enough for two. Oh, I should never have come, never. I'm here against my better judgment, to a decision. That would be a good thing for them to cut on my tombstone: Wherever she went, including here, it was against her better judgment. This is a fine time of the evening to be thinking about tombstones. That's the effect he's had on me, already, and the soup hardly cold yet. I should have stayed at home for dinner. I could have had something on a tray. The head of John the Baptist, or something. Oh, I should not have come.

Well, the soup's over, anyway. I'm that much nearer to my Eternal Home. Now the soup belongs to the ages, and I have said precisely four words to the gentleman on my left. I said, 'Isn't this soup delicious?'; that's four words. And he said, 'Yes, isn't it?'; that's three. He's one up on me.

At any rate, we're in perfect accord. We agree like lambs. We've been all through the soup together, and never a cross word between us. It seems rather a pity to let the subject drop, now we've found something on which we harmonize so admirably. I believe I'll bring it up again;

I'll ask him if that wasn't delicious soup. He says, 'Yes, wasn't it?' Look at that, will you; perfect command of his tenses.

Here comes the fish. Goody, goody, goody, we got fish. I wonder if he likes fish. Yes, he does; he says he likes fish. Ah, that's nice. I love that in a man. Look, he's talking! He's chattering away like a veritable magpie! He's asking me if I like fish. Now does he really want to know, or is it only a line? I'd better play it cagey. I'll tell him, 'Oh, pretty well.' Oh, I like fish pretty well; there's a fascinating bit of autobiography for him to study over. Maybe he would rather wrestle with it alone. I'd better steal softly away, and leave him to his thoughts.

I might try my luck with what's on my right. No, not a chance there. The woman on his other side has him cold. All I can see is his shoulder. It's a nice shoulder, too; oh, it's a nice, *nice* shoulder. All my life, I've been a fool for a nice shoulder. Very well, lady; you saw him first. Keep your Greek god, and I'll go back to my Trojan horse.

Let's see, where were we? Oh, we'd got to where he had confessed his liking for fish. I wonder what else he likes. Does he like cucumbers? Yes, he does; he likes cucumbers. And potatoes? Yes, he likes potatoes, too. Why, he's a regular old Nature-lover, that's what he is. I would have to come out to dinner, and sit next to the Boy Thoreau. Wait, he's saying something! Words are simply pouring out of him. He's asking me if I'm fond of potatoes. No, I don't like potatoes. There, I've done it! I've differed from him. It's our first quarrel. He's fallen into a moody silence. Silly boy, have I pricked your bubble? Do you think I am nothing but a painted doll with sawdust for a heart? Ah, don't take it like that. Look, I have something to tell you that will bring back your faith. I do like cucumbers. Why, he's better already. He speaks again. He says, yes, he likes them, too. Now we've got that all straightened out, thank heaven. We both like cucumbers. Only he likes them twice.

I'd better let him alone now, so he can get some food. He ought to try to get his strength back. He's talked himself groggy.

I wish I had something to do. I hate to be a mere drone. People ought to let you know when they're going to sit you next to a thing like this, so you could bring along some means of occupation. Dear Mrs. Parker, do come to us for dinner on Friday next, and don't forget your drawnwork. I could have brought my top bureau drawer and tidied it up, here on my lap. I could have made great strides towards getting those photographs of the groups on the beach pasted up in the album. I wonder if my hostess would think it strange if I asked for a pack of cards. I wonder if there are any old copies of *St. Nicholas* lying about. I wonder if they wouldn't like a little help out in tne kitchen. I wonder if anybody would want me to run up to the corner and get a late paper.

I could do a little drinking, of course, all by myself. There's always that. Oh, dear, oh, dear, oh, dear, there's always that. But I don't want to drink. I'll get *vin triste*. I'm melancholy before I even start. I wonder what this stiff on my left would say, if I told him I was in a fair way to get *vin triste*. Oh, look at him, hoeing into his fish! What does he care whether I get *vin triste* or not? His soul can't rise above food. Purely physical, that's all he is. Digging his grave with his teeth, that's what he's doing. Yah, yah, ya-ah! Digging your grave with your tee-eeth! Making a god of your stommick! Yah, yah, ya-ah!

He doesn't care if I get *vin triste*. Nobody cares. Nobody gives a damn. And me so nice. All right, you baskets,

I'll drink myself to death, right in front of your eyes, and
see how you'll feel. Here I go. . . . Oh, my God, it's
Chablis. And of a year when the grapes failed, and they
used Summer squash, instead. Fifteen dollars for all you
can carry home on your shoulder. Oh, now, listen, where
I come from, we feed this to the pigs. I think I'll ask old
Chatterbox on my left if this isn't rotten wine. That ought
to open up a new school of dialectics for us. Oh, he says he
really wouldn't know—he never touches wine. Well, that
fairly well ends that. I wonder how he'd like to step to
hell, anyway. Yah, yah, ya-ah! Never touches wi-yine! Don't
know what you're miss-sing! Yah, yah, ya-ah!

I'm not going to talk to him any more. I'm not going to
spend the best years of my life thinking up pearls to scat-
ter before him. I'm going to stick to my Chablis, rotten
though it be. From now on, he can go his way, and I'll go
mine. I'm better than anybody at this table. Ah, but am I
really? Have I, after all, half of what they have? Here I
am lonely, unwanted, silent, and me with all my new clothes
on. Oh, what would Louiseboulanger say if she saw her
gold lamé going unnoticed like this? It's life, I suppose.
Poor little things, we dress, and we plan, and we hope—
and for what? What is life, anyway? A death sentence.
The longest distance between two points. The bunch of
hay that's tied to the nose of the tired mule. The——

Well, well, well, here we are at the *entrecôte*. Button up
your *entrecôte*, when the wind is free—no, I guess not.
Now I'll be damned if I ask old Loquacity if he likes meat.
In the first place, his likes and dislikes are nothing to me,
and in the second—well, look at him go after it! He must
have been playing hard all afternoon; he's Mother's Hungry
Boy, tonight. All right, let him worry it all he wants. As
for me, I'm on a higher plane. I do not stoop to him. He's

less than the dust beneath my chariot wheel. Yah, yah, ya-
ah! Less than the du-ust! Before I'd be that way. Yah, yah,
ya-ah!

I'm glad there's red wine now. Even if it isn't good, I'm
glad. Red wine gives me courage. The Red Badge of Courage. I need courage. I'm in a thin way, here. Nobody knows
what a filthy time I'm having. My precious evening, that
can never come again, ruined, ruined, ruined, and all because of this Somewhat Different Monologist on my left.
But he can't lick me. The night is not yet dead, no, nor
dying. You know, this really isn't bad wine.

Now what do you suppose is going on with the Greek
God on my right? Ah, no use. There's still only the shoulder—the nice, *nice* shoulder. I wonder what the woman's
like, that's got him. I can't see her at all. I wonder if she's
beautiful. I wonder if she's Greek, too. When Greek meets
immovable body—you might be able to do something with
that, if you only had the time. I'm not going to be spine-
less any longer. Don't think for a minute, lady, that I've
given up. He's still using his knife and fork. While there's
hands above the table, there's hope.

Really, I suppose out of obligation to my hostess, I ought
to do something about saying a few words to this macaw
on my left. What shall I try? Have you been reading anything good lately, do you go much to the play, have you
ever been to the Riviera? I wonder if he would like to hear
about my Summer on the Riviera; hell, no, that's no good
without lantern slides. I bet, though, if I started telling
him about That One Night, he'd listen. I won't tell him
—it's too good for him. Anybody that never touches wine
can't hear that. But the one on the right—he'd like that.
He touches wine. Touches it, indeed! He just threw it for
a formidable loss.

Oh, look, old Silver Tongue is off again! Why, he's mad
with his own perfume! He's rattling away like lightning.
He's asking me if I like salad. Yes, I do; what does he want
to make of that? He's telling me about salad through the
ages. He says it's so good for people. So help me God, if
he gives me a talk on roughage, I'll slap his face. Isn't that
my life, to sit here, all dressed up in my best, and listen
to this thing talk about romaine? And all the time, right
on my right——

*Well, I thought you were never going to turn around.
. . . You haven't? . . . You have? Oh, Lord, I've been
having an awful time, too. . . . Was she? . . . Well, you
should have seen what I drew. . . . Oh, I don't see how
we could. . . . Yes, I know it's terrible, but how can we
get out of it? . . . Well. . . . Well, yes, that's true. . . .
Look, right after dinner, I'll say I have this horrible headache, and you say you're going to take me home in your
car, and——*

THE SNATCHING OF BOOKIE BOB

By Damon Runyon

Now it comes on the spring of 1931, after a long hard winter, and times are very tough indeed, what with the stock market going all to pieces, and banks busting right and left, and the law getting very nasty about this and that, and one thing and another, and many citizens of this town are compelled to do the best they can.

There is very little scratch anywhere and along Broadway many citizens are wearing their last year's clothes and have practically nothing to bet on the races or anything else, and it is a condition that will touch anybody's heart.

So I am not surprised to hear rumors that the snatching of certain parties is going on in spots, because while snatching is by no means a high-class business, and is even considered somewhat illegal, it is something to tide over the hard times.

Furthermore, I am not surprised to hear that this snatching is being done by a character by the name of Harry the Horse, who comes from Brooklyn, and who is a character who does not care much what sort of business he is in, and who is mobbed up with other characters from Brooklyn such as Spanish John and Little Isadore, who do not care what sort of business they are in, either.

In fact, Harry the Horse and Spanish John and Little
Isadore are very hard characters in every respect, and
there is considerable indignation expressed around and
about when they move over from Brooklyn into Manhattan
and start snatching, because the citizens of Manhattan feel
that if there is any snatching done in their territory, they
are entitled to do it themselves.

But Harry the Horse and Spanish John and Little Isadore
pay no attention whatever to local sentiment and go on the
snatch on a pretty fair scale, and by and by I am hearing
rumors of some very nice scores. These scores are not extra
large scores, to be sure, but they are enough to keep the
wolf from the door, and in fact from three different doors,
and before long Harry the Horse and Spanish John and
Little Isadore are around the race-tracks betting on the
horses, because if there is one thing they are all very fond of,
it is betting on the horses.

Now many citizens have the wrong idea entirely of the
snatching business. Many citizens think that all there is
to snatching is to round up the party who is to be snatched
and then just snatch him, putting him away somewhere
until his family or friends dig up enough scratch to pay
whatever price the snatchers are asking. Very few citizens
understand that the snatching business must be well organ-
ized and very systematic.

In the first place, if you are going to do any snatching,
you cannot snatch just anybody. You must know who you
are snatching, because naturally it is no good snatching
somebody who does not have any scratch to settle with.
And you cannot tell by the way a party looks or how he
lives in this town if he has any scratch, because many a
party who is around in automobiles, and wearing good

clothes, and chucking quite a swell is nothing but the phonus bolonus and does not have any real scratch whatever.

So of course such a party is no good for snatching, and of course guys who are on the snatch cannot go around inquiring into bank accounts, or asking how much this and that party has in a safe-deposit vault, because such questions are apt to make citizens wonder why, and it is very dangerous to get citizens to wondering why about anything. So the only way guys who are on the snatch can find out about parties worth snatching is to make a connection with some guy who can put the finger on the right party.

The finger guy must know the party he fingers has plenty of ready scratch to begin with, and he must also know that this party is such a party as is not apt to make too much disturbance about being snatched, such as telling the gendarmes. The party may be a legitimate party, such as a business guy, but he will have reasons why he does not wish it to get out that he is snatched, and the finger must know these reasons. Maybe the party is not leading the right sort of life, such as running around with blondes when he has an ever-loving wife and seven children in Mamaroneck, but does not care to have his habits known, as is apt to happen if he is snatched, especially if he is snatched when he is with a blonde.

And sometimes the party is such a party as does not care to have matches run up and down the bottom of his feet, which often happens to parties who are snatched and who do not seem to wish to settle their bill promptly, because many parties are very ticklish on the bottom of the feet, especially if the matches are lit. On the other hand, maybe the party is not a legitimate guy, such as a party who is running a crap game or a swell speakeasy, or who has some other dodge he does not care to have come out, and who also does not care about having his feet tickled.

Such a party is very good indeed for the snatching business, because he is pretty apt to settle without any argument. And after a party settles one snatching, it will be considered very unethical for anybody else to snatch him again very soon, so he is not likely to make any fuss about the matter. The finger guy gets a commission of twenty-five per cent of the settlement, and one and all are satisfied and much fresh scratch comes into circulation which is very good for the merchants. And while the party who is snatched may know who snatches him, one thing he never knows is who puts the finger on him, this being considered a trade secret.

I am talking to Waldo Winchester, the newspaper scribe, one night and something about the snatching business comes up, and Waldo Winchester is trying to tell me that it is one of the oldest dodges in the world, only Waldo calls it kidnaping, which is a title that will be very repulsive to guys who are on the snatch nowadays. Waldo Winchester claims that hundreds of years ago guys are around snatching parties, male and female, and holding them for ransom, and furthermore Waldo Winchester says they even snatch very little children and Waldo states that it is all a very, very wicked proposition.

Well, I can see where Waldo is right about it being wicked to snatch dolls and little children, but of course no guys who are on the snatch nowadays will ever think of such a thing, because who is going to settle for a doll in these times when you can scarcely even give them away? As for little children, they are apt to be a great nuisance, because their mamas are sure to go around hollering bloody murder about them, and furthermore little children are very dangerous, indeed, what with being apt to break out with measles and mumps and one thing and another any minute and give it to everybody in the neighborhood.

Well, anyway, knowing that Harry the Horse and Spanish John and Little Isadore are now on the snatch, I am by no means pleased to see them come along one Tuesday evening when I am standing at the corner of Fiftieth and Broadway, although of course I give them a very jolly hello, and say I hope and trust they are feeling nicely.

They stand there talking to me a few minutes, and I am very glad indeed that Johnny Brannigan, the strong-arm cop, does not happen along and see us, because it will give Johnny a very bad impression of me to see me in such company, even though I am not responsible for the company. But naturally I cannot haul off and walk away from this company at once, because Harry the Horse and Spanish John and Little Isadore may get the idea that I am playing the chill for them, and will feel hurt.

"Well," I say to Harry the Horse, "how are things going, Harry?"

"They are going no good," Harry says. "We do not beat a race in four days. In fact," he says, "we go overboard today. We are washed out. We owe every bookmaker at the track that will trust us, and now we are out trying to raise some scratch to pay off. A guy must pay his bookmaker no matter what."

Well, of course this is very true, indeed, because if a guy does not pay his bookmaker it will lower his business standing quite some, as the bookmaker is sure to go around putting the blast on him, so I am pleased to hear Harry the Horse mention such honorable principles.

"By the way," Harry says, "do you know a guy by the name of Bookie Bob?"

Now I do not know Bookie Bob personally, but of course I know who Bookie Bob is, and so does everybody else in this town that ever goes to a race-track, because Bookie Bob is the biggest bookmaker around and about, and has plenty of scratch. Furthermore, it is the opinion of one and all that Bookie Bob will die with this scratch, because he is considered a very close guy with his scratch. In fact, Bookie Bob is considered closer than a dead heat.

He is a short fat guy with a bald head, and his head is always shaking a little from side to side, which some say is a touch of palsy, but which most citizens believe comes of Bookie Bob shaking his head "No" to guys asking for credit in betting on the races. He has an ever-loving wife, who is a very quiet little old doll with gray hair and a very sad look in her eyes, but nobody can blame her for this when they figure that she lives with Bookie Bob for many years.

I often see Bookie Bob and his ever-loving wife eating in different joints along in the Forties, because they seem to have no home except a hotel, and many a time I hear Bookie Bob giving her a going-over about something or other, and generally it is about the price of something she orders to eat, so I judge Bookie Bob is as tough with his ever-loving wife about scratch as he is with everybody . else. In fact, I hear him bawling her out one night because she has on a new hat which she says costs her six bucks, and Bookie Bob wishes to know if she is trying to ruin him with her extravagances.

But of course I am not criticizing Bookie Bob for squawking about the hat, because for all I know six bucks may be too much for a doll to pay for a hat, at that. And furthermore, maybe Bookie Bob has the right idea about keeping down his ever-loving wife's appetite, because I know many a guy in this town who is practically ruined by dolls eating too much on him.

"Well," I say to Harry the Horse, "if Bookie Bob is one of the bookmakers you owe, I am greatly surprised to see that you seem to have both eyes in your head, because I never before hear of Bookie Bob letting anybody owe him without giving him at least one of their eyes for security. In fact," I say, "Bookie Bob is such a guy as will not give you the right time if he has two watches."

"No," Harry the Horse says, "we do not owe Bookie Bob. But," he says, "he will be owing us before long. We are going to put the snatch on Bookie Bob."

Well, this is most disquieting news to me, not because I care if they snatch Bookie Bob or not, but because somebody may see me talking to them who will remember about it when Bookie Bob is snatched. But of course it will not be good policy for me to show Harry the Horse and Spanish John and Little Isadore that I am nervous, so I only speak as follows:

"Harry," I say, "every man knows his own business best, and I judge you know what you are doing. But," I say, "you are snatching a hard guy when you snatch Bookie Bob. A very hard guy, indeed. In fact," I say, "I hear the softest thing about him is his front teeth, so it may be very difficult for you to get him to settle after you snatch him."

"No," Harry the Horse says, "we will have no trouble about it. Our finger gives us Bookie Bob's hole card, and it is a most surprising thing, indeed. But," Harry the Horse says, "you come upon many surprising things in human nature when you are on the snatch. Bookie Bob's hole card is his ever-loving wife's opinion of him.

"You see," Harry the Horse says, "Bookie Bob has been putting himself away with his ever-loving wife for years as a very important guy in this town, with much power and influence, although of course Bookie Bob knows very well he stands about as good as a broken leg. In fact," Harry the Horse says, "Bookie Bob figures that his ever-loving wife is the only one in the world who looks on him as a big guy, and he will sacrifice even his scratch, or anyway some of it, rather than let her know that guys have such little respect for him as to put the snatch on him. It is what you call psychology," Harry the Horse says.

Well, this does not make good sense to me, and I am thinking to myself that the psychology that Harry the Horse really figures to work out nice on Bookie Bob is tickling his feet with matches, but I am not anxious to stand there arguing about it, and pretty soon I bid them all good evening, very polite, and take the wind, and I do not see Harry the Horse or Spanish John or Little Isadore again for a month.

In the meantime, I hear gossip here and there that Bookie Bob is missing for several days, and when he finally shows up again he gives it out that he is very sick during his absence, but I can put two and two together as well as anybody in this town and I figure that Bookie Bob is snatched by Harry the Horse and Spanish John and Little Isadore, and the chances are it costs him plenty.

So I am looking for Harry the Horse and Spanish John and Little Isadore to be around the race-track with plenty of scratch and betting them higher than a cat's back, but they never show up, and what is more I hear they leave Manhattan and are back in Brooklyn working every day handling beer. Naturally this is very surprising to me, because the way things are running beer is a tough dodge just now, and there is very little profit in same, and I figure that with the scratch they must make off Bookie Bob, Harry the Horse and Spanish John and Little Isadore have a right to be taking things easy.

Now one night I am in Good Time Charley Bernstein's little speak in Forty-eight Street, talking of this and that with Charley, when in comes Harry the Horse, looking very weary and by no means prosperous. Naturally I gave him a large hello, and by and by we get to gabbing together and I ask him whatever becomes of the Bookie Bob matter, and Harry the Horse tells me as follows:

Yes [Harry the Horse says], we snatch Bookie Bob all right. In fact, we snatch him the very next night after we are talking to you, or on a Wednesday night. Our finger tells us Bookie Bob is going to a wake over in his old neighborhood on Tenth Avenue, near Thirty-eighth Street, and this is where we pick him up.

He is leaving the place in his car along about midnight, and of course Bookie Bob is alone as he seldom lets anybody ride with him because of the wear and tear on his car cushions, and Little Isadore swings our flivver in front of him and makes him stop. Naturally Bookie Bob is greatly surprised when I poke my head into his car and tell him I wish the pleasure of his company for a short time, and at first he is inclined to argue the matter, saying I must make a mistake, but I put the old convincer on him by letting him peek down the snozzle of my John Roscoe.

We lock his car and throw the keys away, and then we take Bookie Bob in our car and go to a certain spot on Eighth Avenue where we have a nice little apartment all ready. When we get there I tell Bookie Bob that he can call up anybody he wishes and state that the snatch is on him and that it will require twenty-five G's, cash money, to take it off, but of course I also tell Bookie Bob that he is not to mention where he is or something may happen to him.

Well, I will say one thing for Bookie Bob, although everybody is always weighing in the sacks on him and saying he is no good—he takes it like a gentleman, and very calm and businesslike.

Furthermore, he does not seem alarmed, as many citizens are when they find themselves in such a situation. He recognizes the justice of our claim at once, saying as follows:

"I will telephone my partner, Sam Salt," he says. "He is the only one I can think of who is apt to have such a sum as twenty-five G's cash money. But," he says, "if you gentlemen will pardon the question, because this is a new experience to me, how do I know everything will be okay for me after you get the scratch?"

"Why," I say to Bookie Bob, somewhat indignant, "it is well known to one and all in this town that my word is my bond. There are two things I am bound to do," I say, "and one is to keep my word in such a situation as this, and the other is to pay anything I owe a bookmaker, no matter what, for these are obligations of honor with me."

"Well," Bookie Bob says, "of course I do not know you gentlemen, and, in fact, I do not remember ever seeing any of you, although your face is somewhat familiar, but if you pay your bookmaker you are an honest guy, and one in a million. In fact," Bookie Bob says, "if I have all the scratch that is owing to me around this town, I will not be telephoning anybody for such a sum as twenty-five G's. I will have such a sum in my pants pocket for change."

Now Bookie Bob calls a certain number and talks to somebody there but he does not get Sam Salt, and he seems much disappointed when he hangs up the receiver again.

"This is a very tough break for me," he says. "Sam Salt goes to Atlantic City an hour ago on very important business and will not be back until tomorrow evening, and they do not know where he is to stay in Atlantic City. And," Bookie Bob says, "I cannot think of anybody else to call to get this scratch, especially anybody I will care to have know I am in this situation."

"Why not call your ever-loving wife?" I say. "Maybe she can dig up this kind of scratch."

"Say," Bookie Bob says, "you do not suppose I am chump enough to give my ever-loving wife twenty-five G's, belonging to me, do you? I give my ever-loving wife ten bucks per week for spending money," Bookie Bob says, "and this is enough scratch for any doll, especially when you figure I pay for her meals."

Well, there seems to be nothing we can do except wait until Sam Salt gets back, but we let Bookie Bob call his ever-loving wife, as Bookie Bob says he does not wish to have her worrying about his absence, and tells her a big lie about having to go to Jersey City to sit up with a sick Brother Elk.

Well, it is now nearly four o'clock in the morning, so we put Bookie Bob in a room with Little Isadore to sleep, although, personally, I consider making a guy sleep with Little Isadore very cruel treatment, and Spanish John and I take turns keeping awake and watching out that Bookie Bob does not take the air on us before paying us off. To tell the truth, Little Isadore and Spanish John are somewhat disappointed that Bookie Bob agrees to settle so promptly, because they are looking forward to tickling his feet with great relish.

Now Bookie Bob turns out to be very good company

when he wakes up the next morning, because he knows
a lot of race-track stories and plenty of scandal, and he
keeps us much interested at breakfast. He talks along with
us as if he knows us all his life, and he seems very non-
chalant indeed, but the chances are he will not be so non-
chalant if I tell him about Spanish John's thought.

Well, about noon Spanish John goes out of the apartment and comes back with a racing sheet, because he
knows Little Isadore and I will be wishing to know what
is running in different spots although we do not have anything to bet on these races, or any way of betting on them,
because we are overboard with every bookmaker we know.

Now Bookie Bob is also much interested in the matter
of what is running, especially at Belmont, and he is bending over the table with me and Spanish John and Little
Isadore, looking at the sheet, when Spanish John speaks
as follows:

"My goodness," Spanish John says, "a spot such as this
fifth race with Questionnaire at four to five is like finding money in the street. I only wish I have a few bobs to
bet on him at such a price," Spanish John says.

"Why," Bookie Bob says, very polite, "if you gentlemen
wish to bet on these races I will gladly book to you. It is
a good way to pass away the time while we are waiting
for Sam Salt, unless you will rather play pinochle?"

"But," I say, "we have no scratch to play the races, at
least not much."

"Well," Bookie Bob says, "I will take your markers, because I hear what you say about always paying your bookmaker, and you put yourself away with me as an honest
guy, and these other gentlemen also impress me as honest
guys."

Now what happens but we begin betting Bookie Bob

on the different races, not only at Belmont, but at all the other tracks in the country, for Little Isadore and Spanish John and I are guys who like plenty of action when we start betting on the horses. We write out markers for whatever we wish to bet and hand them to Bookie Bob, and Bookie Bob sticks these markers in an inside pocket, and along in the late afternoon it looks as if he has a tumor on his chest.

We get the race results by 'phone off a poolroom downtown as fast as they come off, and also the prices, and it is a lot of fun, and Little Isadore and Spanish John and Bookie Bob and I are all little pals together until all the races are over and Bookie Bob takes out the markers and starts counting himself up.

It comes out then that I owe Bookie Bob ten G's, and Spanish John owes him six G's, and Little Isadore owes him four G's, as Little Isadore beats him a couple of races out west.

Well, about this time, Bookie Bob manages to get Sam Salt on the 'phone, and explains to Sam that he is to go to a certain safe-deposit box and get out twenty-five G's, and then wait until midnight and hire himself a taxicab and start riding around the block between Fifty-first and Fifty-second, from Eight to Ninth Avenues, and to keep riding until somebody flags the cab and takes the scratch off him.

Naturally Sam Salt understands right away that the snatch is on Bookie Bob, and he agrees to do as he is told, but he says he cannot do it until the following night because he knows there is not twenty-five G's in the box and he will have to get the difference at the track the next day. So there we are with another day in the apartment and Spanish John and Little Isadore and I are just as well pleased because Bookie Bob has us hooked and we naturally wish to wiggle off.

But the next day is worse than ever. In all the years I am playing the horses I never have such a tough day, and Spanish John and Little Isadore are just as bad. In fact, we are all going so bad that Bookie Bob seems to feel sorry for us and often lays us a couple of points above the track prices, but it does no good. At the end of the day, I am in a total of twenty G's, while Spanish John owes fifteen, and Little Isadore fifteen, a total of fifty G's among the three of us. But we are never any hands to hold post-mortems on bad days, so Little Isadore goes out to a delicatessen store and lugs in a lot of nice things to eat, and we have a fine dinner, and then we sit around with Bookie Bob telling stories, and even singing songs together until time to meet Sam Salt.

When it comes on midnight Spanish John goes off and lays for Sam, and gets a little valise off Sam Salt. Then Spanish John comes back to the apartment and we open the valise and the twenty-five G's are there okay, and we cut this scratch three ways.

Then I tell Bookie Bob he is free to go about his business, and good luck to him, at that, but Bookie Bob looks at me as if he is very much surprised, and hurt, and says to me like this:

"Well, gentlemen, thank you for your courtesy, but what about the scratch you owe me? What about these markers? Surely, gentlemen, you will pay your bookmaker?"

Well, of course we owe Bookie these markers, all right, and of course a man must pay his bookmaker, no matter what, so I hand over my bit and Bookie Bob put down something in a little notebook that he takes out of his kick.

Then Spanish John and Little Isadore hand over their dough, too, and Bookie Bob puts down something more in the little note-book.

"Now," Bookie Bob says, "I credit each of your accounts with these payments, but you gentlemen still owe me a matter of twenty-five G's over and above the twenty-five I credit you with, and I hope and trust you will make arrangements to settle this at once because," he says, "I do not care to extend such accommodations over any considerable period."

"But," I say, "we do not have any more scratch after paying you the twenty-five G's on account."

"Listen," Bookie Bob says, dropping his voice down to a whisper, "What about putting the snatch on my partner, Sam Salt, and I will wait over a couple of days with you and keep booking to you, and maybe you can pull yourselves out. But of course," Bookie Bob whispers, "I will be entitled to twenty-five per cent of the snatch for putting the finger on Sam for you."

But Spanish John and Little Isadore are sick and tired of Bookie Bob and will not listen to staying in the apartment any longer, because they say he is a jinx to them and they cannot beat him in any manner, shape or form. Furthermore, I am personally anxious to get away because something Bookie Bob says reminds me of something.

It reminds me that besides the scratch we owe him, we forget to take out six G's two-fifty for the party who puts the finger on Bookie Bob for us, and this is a very serious matter indeed, because everybody will tell you that failing to pay a finger is considered a very dirty trick. Furthermore, if it gets around that you fail to pay a finger, nobody else will ever finger for you.

So [Harry the Horse says] we quit the snatching business

because there is no use continuing while this obligation is outstanding against us, and we go back to Brooklyn to earn enough scratch to pay our just debts.

We are paying off Bookie Bob's IOU a little at a time, because we do not wish to ever have anybody say we welsh on a bookmaker, and furthermore we are paying off the six G's two-fifty commission we owe our finger.

And while it is tough going, I am glad to say our honest effort is doing somebody a little good, because I see Bookie Bob's ever-loving wife the other night all dressed up in new clothes, very happy indeed.

And while a guy is telling me she is looking so happy because she gets a large legacy from an uncle who dies in Switzerland, and is now independent of Bookie Bob, I only hope and trust [Harry the Horse says] that it never gets out that our finger in this case is nobody but Bookie Bob's ever-loving wife.

AN INTERESTING CURE

By Frank Sullivan

Coming down on the subway last Tuesday, as I sometimes do on alternate Tuesdays, I noticed a man sitting on the seat opposite who appeared to be in a high state of nervous excitement. He was staring wide-eyed at one of the advertising cards in the car. I took my stethoscope and rushed over to him.

He was about five feet ten inches in height and just a bit bald. I said he was bald and I still maintain he was bald, but a Mrs. Maria M. Sturgeon, sixty-seven, of No. 2 Grand Concourse, who sat nearby, said he was not bald.

'I know baldness when I see it,' said Mrs. Sturgeon. 'All our family is bald. Early piety, Grandma Finch used to say it was. My Fred was bald when he was twenty-two, but Uncle Homer always likes sugar on his tomatoes. Now this gentleman is not bald. He just has a high forehead.'

I said that it was not a case of high forehead in my twenty years of practice, and I know a high forehead when I see one. This was a clear case of baldness. I said so, and I didn't care who heard me.

The patient, whom we shall call Mr. X., was forty-four, and one of ten or fifteen children. His maternal grandfather had fought in the Civil War and after going through two battles developed a pronounced case of ennui and left the

313

army. The patient's mother had suffered from Hodgkin's disease, Potts's disease, Alexander F. Detwiller's disease, and had been tapped for Riggs's disease, but did not join.

The patient's retina reacted favorably to light. He had had the usual children's diseases: measles when he was thirty-seven, scarlatina when he was thirty-eight and whooping-cough when he was forty, but he had never had chicken pox, although his son, Alvah, now going on thirteen and smart as a whip, had had chicken pox when he was five and once again, for good measure, when he was eight.

'You ought to see that kid,' said Mr. X. 'He's into everything. He has a radio and gets Davenport, Ia., on it every night. He got a hundred in geography seven months running last year. He's about four feet ten inches in height, light brown, curly hair, freckles, all his front teeth out, and when last seen wore a blue cotton shirt, patched brown pants and no shoes or stockings.'

'Well, I wouldn't be too much alarmed about my condition, if I were you,' I told the patient. 'I can tell you definitely, without even a detailed examination, that your condition is not serious. You are a trifle neurasthenic, perhaps. You know, America is getting to be a land of neurasthenics. It's the pace we set ourselves—jazz, money-madness, modern hooch, and that sort of thing. Americans, too, are prone to worry. Now, you think that the morbid sensations you experience are peculiar to yourself. My dear man,' I told him, adjusting my glasses, 'there are many like you. Many come to me who are in far greater difficulty than you,' I told him, adjusting his necktie. 'That man you saw just leaving the train at 14th Street is a tugboat captain, and do you know the phobia I am treating him for? He's afraid of sharp instruments. In the medical world we have a term for that phobia. We call it being afraid of sharp instruments.

'I am treating another man who is mortally afraid of

closed places, such as the subway, the tubes or a crowded theater. We call that claustrophobia, for lack of a better name. Isn't it remarkable how far medical science has progressed? Now, another very common fear is the fear of insanity. What makes you think you are going crazy?'

He pointed a shaking hand at a car advertisement telling about the virtues of a certain collar.

'It will not wilt, shrink, crack or wrinkle,' proclaimed the ad.

'Yes,' I said, sympathetically, adjusting my suspenders, 'what about it?'

'It's got me,' he moaned. 'I can't say it. Oh, my God, I can't say it! Take me away.'

'Tut, my dear man,' I assured him. 'You can say it, of course you can. You simply have a psychoneurosis. You have panic hysteria. You must have regular exercise, plenty of good, plain food, and eight hours' sleep at night. Now try and say it.'

'It—it will not wilt, crink, wack or shrinkle,' he said, and with a cry of despair flung his head into his arms.

'Come now, again,' I urged.

'It's no use,' he cried, 'I've been trying to do it all the way down from Dyckman Street and I can't.'

'Oh, now, be yourself!' I encouraged him. 'Ready now. One for the money, two for the show, three to get ready and four to—GO!'

'It will not wilt, kink, shack or winkle,' he cried, and burst into a flood of tears.

It was a rather strange case. I asked him what dreams he had dreamed the preceding night. He said he hadn't slept. I saw that he had a marked Œdipus fixation. I thought I saw a way to help him. I would set an example for him, and leave the rest to suggestion. Suggestion is very powerful.

'Listen to me,' I told him, 'and learn how perfectly simple

the whole thing is, when you have rid yourself of your in-
hibitions.'

I continued in a firm tone: 'It will not wink, shink, wack
or crinkle.'

Odd, I thought, but due, of course, to the power of suggestion. He had actually communicated a bit of his hysteria
to me.

'Pardon me, my error,' I told him, 'I'll try again. It will
not wilt, kink, wack or shinkle.'

Damn!

A faint smile played about Mr. X.'s mouth. His pulse
was much better, his respiration was normal, and his hu-
midity had sunk to three-thirty. He was able to partake of
a little custard, a glass of sherry and egg, and a planked
steak or two.

'Now I'm going to try again,' I told him, briskly, 'and
this time watch me get it."

But I didn't.

Mr. X. was laughing heartily now, and appeared to be
in a greatly improved frame of mind. His disorientation
ceased and he remembered being in Washington at Harding's inauguration.

'Why, it's a cinch,' he told me. 'All you have to do is to
get rid of your psychoneurosis, and just read plain English.
Listen: It will not wilt, shrink, crack or wrinkle.'

I was delighted. The man was cured. The passengers
crowded about me, shaking my hand. Several lifted me to
their shoulders and began singing 'For He's a Jolly Good
Fellow!' but my head got caught in one of the fans, and
when I came to it was midnight, and we were at 242d Street
and Van Cortlandt Park. Somebody had lifted my watch-
chain, Sunday school medals and my $1.40 pin money for
the week. I consider the cure of Mr. X. one of the great
triumphs of my career.

GENDARMES AND THE MAN

By Donald Moffat

Rosy was a second-hand Renault of eleven horsepower, a nice friendly machine, partly covered with second-hand paint and adorned with a high tonneau or bustle, like the poop of a galleon. Although really quite fond of Rosy, Mr. Mott, a sensitive man, didn't quite like to leave her hanging round outside the Hotel Crillon, as he felt that the contrast between her out-moded raiment and that of her smartly dressed sisters might cause her (and him) mental anguish. She was perfectly at home in front of Mr. Mott's own hôtel, however, and was undeniably an object of pride to Pierre, the combined valet, concierge, and chasseur, who loved to stand outside in his striped apron and felt slippers, with one hand resting affectionately on the fender, and open the door for the Motts and smile them out of sight.

Mr. Mott's first act after taking Rosy over from an Englishman named Wrightstoneham, her most recent protector, was to drive her the two blocks from her little *rez-de-chaussée,* or garage, to the hôtel, proudly honking the squeaky little horn all the way like a real Parisian. There he left her by the sidewalk, and went upstairs for as long as it takes a man to recite 'The Wreck of the Hesperus,' and came down again with a song on his lips and a bright smile for Célie, known in the hotel as the maid-of-all-work because she did all the work. *'Monsieur va faire un petit tour?'*

Ah-ha! Wasn't he just—and monsieur skipped out the door.

And immediately ceased being Monsieur.

A sinister figure in blue and red was leaning over Rosy. In his hand was a notebook, and he was moistening a pencil at his lips. Rosy looked furtive. as if this sort of thing had happened to her before, *en faisant le trottoir*.

Mr. Mott murmured: 'What is it that it has, Mr. the Agent? She is to me, the carriage.'

He turned his attention from Rosy. 'Ha!' he stated. 'She is to you, the carriage. Then!' Mr. Mott thought he had seldom seen a more unpleasant face.

'One has, maybe, committed a fault of which one is ignorant?'

'Evidently!'

'May one be permitted to inquire the nature of this fault?'

'Ha!' stated the gendarme again. 'One has placed the carriage at the bad side of the street; see you, how can other carriages circulate in these old ways so contracted? Thus, if all the world pleases but himself without consideration of no matter what other voyagers, what *tohubohu* does not then arrive, by example?'

Mr. Mott brightened. 'But yesterday,' he said, 'I observed the carriage of the merchant of wine and carbon at the same side, here.' A mistake.

'Yesterday! But yesterday is not today, figure to yourself.'

Mr. Mott bowed, with dignity.

'Show me then the gray card,' the gendarme demanded sternly.

Mr. Mott unbuckled his portfolio of licenses and dealt a hand from the top of the deck. The gendarme sorted them skillfully and discarded onto the front seat, keeping only the gray registration card and the pink driving license. He read them attentively, then looked at the nickel plaque on Rosy's instrument board, which the law requires to be inscribed with the owner's name and address, and gave a sudden start.

'Then!' he thundered, pointing dramatically to the plaque. 'The name on the gray card is not in rapport with the one on the plaque, evidently! That is your name engraved on the dashboard.' And so it came about that Mr. Mott was known as Monsieur Vrrigstonhonh throughout the subse‑ quent proceedings.

Mr. Mott tried to deny it, with some confidence at first. 'But no, monsieur. That is the name of the old proprietor. I am the proprietor since fifteen days, and was even now on road to the graver for my proper plaque, already com‑ manded.'

'Make no histories,' the gendarme ordered darkly. 'I can read, I.'

At this point the investigating committee was swelled by the arrival of a bicycle bearing another and more potent gendarme, and on his heels a little group consisting of a stubby patriarch with a long yellow beard, part of a bowler hat, and one half of a pair of suspenders; an old and re‑ spectable female in black, with a figure, who had been wash‑ ing out a bit of flannel in the fresh current of the gutter; and a man-child with long bare legs, a downy beard, and serious tonsil trouble.

The committee rose long enough for the ranking gen‑ darme to suggest politely to this trio that possibly it had, then, other affairs to claim its attention than breathing on the foreign sir, a suggestion for which the prisoner was grateful. They drifted on a few yards, and the committee took up the minutes.

Mr. Mott's man said: 'The carriage of this sir rests, evi‑ dently, at the bad side of the street. He pretends, too, that

the carriage is to him, when see you, my sergeant, the name
of another, a Monsieur Mott, is inscribed on the gray card.'

The true owner of the name opened his mouth to take
exception to this use of the word 'pretend,' but was interrupted by the sergeant, a tall, lean man with an apoplectic
face who, like all his rank, believed in action: 'Get the hell
over there on the other side of the street where you belong,
then we'll take up the paper work,' and Mr. Mott, glad
of something to do besides being talked at, sprang in,
started the motor, and in order to turn round as quickly as
possible, backed Rosy up.

Instantly he heard a gentle crashing, crumpling sound
from behind, then two bellows, or screams, one hoarse and
low, the other shrill and vibrant, which Mr. Mott traced
quickly to the two gendarmes. He stopped and looked over
the side, more in curiosity than apprehension . . .

A bicycle had been left leaning against the curb behind
Rosy.

One had backed Rosy over the bicycle.

To whom was the bicycle?

The bicycle was to the tall gendarme with the hoarse
voice.

What says the tall gendarme?

The words of the tall gendarme would have no meaning
except to another Frenchman.

The tall gendarme angers himself of it, *hein*?

Yes, he angers himself of it formidably.

And the companion of the tall one, he, too, has choler
not badly.

For the bicycle of the tall gendarme lies by the ground,
riven by the foreign sir.

Eventually the filibuster, with gestures, began to simmer

down, and Mr. Mott began to get his first tips on Paris traffic regulations; he learned, for instance, about the crime of backing up, with or without destruction of police bicycles. And there was something mysterious and obviously childish said about parking on the odd and even sides of the street, to the undisguised interest of the little group of assorted bystanders who had, it was apparent, nothing better to do that day after all than to breathe upon the foreign sir.

The gendarmes collared all Mr. Mott's documents, told him to follow in the car, and started to walk away, carrying the injured bicycle. This brought up what Mr. Mott considered a nice point of behavior.

He bleated: 'How, then, is one to follow, since it is forbidden to recoil and the way is too narrow to make a turn?'

'Drive round the block,' they snarled over their shoulders, as who should say: Go take a running dive off the Eiffel Tower. 'One awaits your return here.'

Rosy and Mr. Mott obediently scuttled off down the street, took their first left, and instantly heard a whistle. They stopped, shuddering with emotion. A stout gendarme with a red beard and pince-nez was approaching with deliberate tread. He leaned affectionately over Rosy's shoulder.

'Attend, my little,' he said indulgently. 'Is it that one knows not how to read?' He pointed to a red disk high up on the corner building: *'Sens interdit.'*—One-way Street.

'My God!' thought Mr. Mott.

The gendarme said: 'Let me see your gray card.'

'Mr. the Agent,' Mr. Mott replied, 'I come from being arrested by two other agents of high rank who have taken all my papers and even now await my return from this voyage round the block. I now find that it is forbidden to advance further; nor can I retreat, as that, too, is forbidden. Must one then rest here forever, a mute inglorious warning to all other foreign conductors?'

The gendarme roared with dignified laughter. 'Recoil, then, my old,' adding to himself, Mr. Mott felt sure, 'and may Heaven protect thee.'

Mr. Mott backed up, or recoiled, while the gendarme held up three swiftly converging streams of taxis whose drivers honked their horns and bellowed personal remarks, and drove slowly back to his original captors. They were looking suggestively at their watches.

Mr. Mott followed them round the corner to the police station and left Rosy behind a taxi which Heaven had sent to be his guide in the still mysterious matter of parking. He entered the building and, closely attended by his guards, approached the desk. A squat man with one evil eye and a face slashed with old scars examined his papers and listened to the sergeant's story of his crimes. When the commissioner asked him his true name, then, he rashly reached across the desk to point it out on the gray card which the commissioner held in his hand. This proved to be an error. The commissioner shouted 'Halte!' snatched the card away, and glared. The gendarmes each seized one of Mr. Mott's arms, and glared; a huge black cat that had been sleeping quietly on the desk sprang to its feet, humped its back, glared, *and* spat at him. Mr. Mott waited, in terror, to be searched for arms.

Finally, after a prolonged discussion in which he took no part, as his French had utterly deserted him in the stress of emotion, Mr. Mott's true identity was established with the help of his passport, it was decided that he had an honest face, that very likely he had not actually stolen the car, and that he might be treated with indulgence on account of his ignorance of the ways of a civilized country. The parking mystery was not further explained. Nor was any mention made of the smashed bicycle. Mr. Mott learned why in the corridor outside, when the owner whispered that he had not mentioned it to the commissioner because he counted on Mr. Mott to make private reparation, and that fifty francs would be just about the right amount.

Mr. Mott paid the fifty francs, and after shaking hands all round they parted, the gendarmes on their wheels—the damage to the bicycle had apparently been exaggerated—and Mr. Mott to return Rosy temporarily to her garage, draw a deep breath or two, and hasten for something to restore his injured nerve tissues at the nearest café—a rather pleasant feature of Paris life which I won't go into just now because I think something has already been written on the subject.

CARNIVAL WEEK IN SUNNY LAS LOS

By Robert Benchley

You have all doubtless wanted to know, at one time or another, a few of the quaint customs which residents of the continent of Europe seem to feel called upon to perpetuate from one century to another. You may know about a few of them already, such as childbearing (which has been taken up on this continent to such an alarming extent) and others of the more common variety of folk mannerisms, but I am very proud and happy to be able to tell you today of some of the less generally known customs of the inhabitants of that medieval Spanish province Las Los (or Los Las, as it was formerly called, either way meaning 'The The' *pl.*) where I have had the extremely bad fortune to be spending the summer.

Las Los, nestling, as it does, in the intercostal nooks of the Pyrenees, makes up into one of the nicest little plague-spots on the continent of Europe. Europe has often claimed that Las Los was *not* a part of it, and in 1356 Spain began a long and costly war with France, the loser to take Los Las and two outfielders. France won and Spain built an extension onto the Pyrenees in which to hide Los Las. They succeeded in hiding it from view, but there was one thing about Los Las that they forgot; so you always know that it is there.

It was in this little out-of-the-way corner of the world,

then, that I set up my easel and began painting my fingers and wrists. I soon made friends with the natives (all of whom were named Pedro) and it was not long before they were bringing me their best Sunday knives and sticking them in my back for me to try to tell which was which. And such laughter would go up when I guessed the wrong one! All Latins, after all, are just children at heart.

But I am not here to tell you of the many merry days I myself spent in Las Los, but of some of the native customs which I was privileged to see, and, once in a while, take part in. They rather resent an outsider taking part in most of them, however, for there is an old saying in Las Los that 'when an outsider takes part, rain will surely dart' (meaning 'dart' from the clouds, you see) and above all things rain is abhorred in that section of the country, as rain has a tendency to cleanse whatever it touches, and, as another old proverb has it, 'clean things, dead things'—which isn't exactly accurate, but appeals to these simple, childish people, to whom cleanliness is next to a broken hip.

First of all, then, let us tiptoe up on the natives of Las Los during their carnival time. The carnival week comes during the last week in July, just when it is hottest. This makes it really ideal for the Los Lasians, for extreme heat, added to everything else, renders their charming little town practically unbearable. This week was chosen many hundreds of years ago and is supposed to mark the anniversary of the marriage of old Don Pedro's daughter to a thunderbolt, a union which was so unsatisfactory to the young lady that she left her husband in two days and married a boy named Carlos, who sold tortillas. This so enraged the thunderbolt that he swore never to come to Los Las again, and, from that day to this (so the saying goes, I know not whether it be true or not) that region has never had any locusts. (This would almost make it seem that the repulsed bridegroom had been a locust, but the natives, on being questioned, explain that the *patois* for 'thunderbolt' [*enjuejoz*] is very much like the *patois* for 'locust' [*enjuejoz*] and that the thunder god, in giving his order for the future of Los Las, put the accent on the wrong syllable and cut them off from locusts instead of thunder storms). This may, or may not, be the truth, but, as I said to the old man who told me, 'Who the hell cares?'

The first day of the Carnival of the Absence of Locusts (just why they should be so cocky about having no locusts is not clear. Locusts would be a god-send compared to some of the things they *have* got) is spent in bed, storing up strength for the festival. On this day all the shops, except those selling wine, are closed. This means that a little shop down by the river which sells sieves is closed. People lie in bed and send out to the wine-shops for the native drink, which is known as *wheero*. All that is necessary to do with this drink is to place it in an open saucer on the window sill and inhale deeply from across the room. In about eight seconds the top of the inhaler's head rises slowly and in a dignified manner until it reaches the ceiling where it floats, bumping gently up and down. The teeth then drop out and arrange themselves on the floor to spell 'Portage High School, 1930,' the eyes roll upward and backward, and a strange odor of burning rubber fills the room. This is followed by an unaccountable feeling of intense lassitude.

Thus we may expect nothing from the natives for the first two days of the carnival, for the second day is spent in looking for bits of head and teeth, and in general moaning. (A sorry carnival, you will say—and *I* will say, too.) But later on, things will brighten up.

On the third day the inhabitants emerge, walking very

carefully in order not to jar off their ears, and get into a lot of decorated ox carts. They are not very crazy about getting into these ox carts, but it is more or less expected of them at carnival time. Pictures are taken of them riding about and are sent to the London illustrated papers, and if they were to pass up one year without riding in decorated ox carts, it wouldn't seem like carnival week to the readers of the London illustrated papers. You can hardly blame a man with a *wheero* hangover, however, for not wanting to bump around over cobblestones in an old two-wheeled cart, even if it has got paper flowers strung all over it. One of the saddest sights in the world is to see a native, all dressed up in red and yellow, with a garland of orange roses around his neck, jolting and jouncing along over hard stone bumps with a girl on his knee, and trying to simulate that famous Spanish smile and gay abandon, all the time feeling that one more bump and away goes that meal he ate several days ago, along with his legs and arms and portions of his lower jaw. No wonder Spaniards look worried.

However, there is a great deal of shouting and cawing among those who can open their mouths, and occasionally someone hits a tambourine. This is usually frowned upon by the person standing next to the tambourine-hitter and a remark, in Spanish, is made which could roughly be translated as: 'For the love of God, shut up that incessant banging!'

The carnival, which is known as *Romeria*, is supposed to be a festival of the picnic type combined with a religious pilgrimage to some sort of shrine. This shrine, however, is never reached, as along about noon of the third day some desperate guy, with a hangover no longer to be borne, evolves a cure on the 'hair of the dog that bit you' theory, and the *wheero* is brought out again. The village watering trough is filled with it and a sort of native dance is held around the trough, everyone inhaling deeply. Those who are still unable to inhale are carried to the edge of the trough and a little *wheero* is rubbed on their upper-lips, just under the nose. Then it is 'good-night all, and a merry, merry trip to Blanket Bay,' for the festive villagers, and the carnival is shot to hell. A week later business is quietly resumed.

On the fifth day of the carnival there is supposed to be a bull chase through the streets. The principle of the thing is that a bull is let loose and everyone chases it, or vice versa. As, however, there was nobody fit to chase a butterfly, much less a bull, on the fifth day of this carnival, I had to take care of the bull myself. The two of us sat all alone in the public square among the cadavers drinking a sort of lemon squash together.

'A dash of *wheero*?' I asked the bull.

Well, you should have heard him laugh! After that, I got up on his back and rode all around the town, visiting the points of interest and climbing several of the better looking mountains. Pretty soon we were in Turkey, where we saw many interesting sights and then, swinging around through the Balkans, I got back just in time for me to scramble into bed. I must have hit my head on the footboard while pulling up the sheet, for the next morning (or whenever it was) when I awoke, I had quite a bad headache. Thank heaven I knew enough to lay off that *wheero*, however. I'm no fool.

THE GUEST[1]

By Marc Connelly

_____

*The scene is Room 1257 in the North American Hotel.
Mr. Kenneth Mercer is sitting on the edge of his bed, in
his nightshirt, using the telephone.*

Mr. Mercer—Hello, Aussel, Aussel, Coyne, and Mehoff?
. . . Mr. Watson, please. . . . No, ma'am, I haven't an
appointment. I *did* have one at nine-thirty but they didn't
waken me at the hotel. . . . Yes, ma'am, I know it's ten
o'clock. . . . But I've been traveling three days just to see
him before he left for Europe. Will you connect me with
him? (*While he waits for Mr. Watson, Mr. Mercer reads
the card under the glass top of his bed-table. It tells all
about the Service Plus which one receives in North American Hotels. It seems the North American Chain has gone
the limit in making every patron feel he is 'not merely a
guest but a friend.' Mr. Mercer finally gets tired reading
and jiggles the hook of the telephone.*) Hello. . . . Is this
Aussel, Aussel, Coyne, and Mehoff? . . . Oh, the hotel
operator. . . . No, ma'am, I wasn't through. . . . Will you
please get them back for me? . . . Barker 2348. . . . And in
the meantime I'd like to have a little breakfast. . . . Which
button? . . . All right. Get that number, please.

[1] Copyrighted by Marc Connelly. No performance may be given
without the permission of the author.

(Mr. Mercer goes to an idiotic instrument near the door. It has a mouthpiece and several buttons. Beside it is a neat card reading:

MEALDICATOR

Just another example of North American Hotels, Inc., Service Plus. Merely press the button and state what you wish from our kitchens. 'Waiting for the waiter' never bothers a North American Hotel guest.

Mr. Mercer faces the mouthpiece and pushes the button. Nothing happens.)

MR. MERCER—A cup of coffee, please. *(Nobody seems to care.)* A cup of coffee, please. *(Mr. Mercer waits a moment, hopes somebody heard him, and looks around the room for the suit of clothes which he'd ordered to be pressed and delivered at eight-thirty sharp this morning. He goes to the telephone again.)* Hello, operator. . . . What? . . . *(Excitedly)* Aussel, Aussel, Coyne, and Mehoff? . . . Operator, did you have them back on there? . . . Yes, I *did* want them. . . . Please get them back and . . . Look, operator, last night I gave a bellboy a gray suit I wanted pressed and . . . Which button?

(He goes to a panel near the door with a few more buttons about it and a small sign reading:

THE QUIET VALET

Just another example of North American Service Plus. Merely press the top button and the clothing you wished cleaned or pressed will be returned to you moth-free and fresh in this Byer-Schlaffing All-Cedar Suit Protector.

Mr. Mercer presses the button, the panel swings open and there is somebody's full-dress suit. Mr. Mercer goes to the telephone again.)

Mr. Mercer—Look, operator, that isn't my suit. . . . I say, that isn't my suit. . . . Well, it's just somebody else's suit. . . . What number? . . . Certainly, I want that number. . . . All right, keep working on that number . . . . Never mind the suit. *(Mr. Mercer goes into the bathroom to shave. Just as his face is nicely lathered he hears a voice in his bedroom.)*

The Voice—Good morning! Good morning! You wished to be called at eight-thirty. Well, eight-thirty it is. Eight-thirty of a beautiful morning. *(Mr. Mercer has now run back into the bedroom and is looking frantically for the speaker.)*

Mr. Mercer—You lie! It's after ten o'clock. Don't tell me it's any eight-thirty, because I happen to have a watch that . . . *(Mr. Mercer observes that the voice is coming from the Time Announcer, just another example of North American Service plus, over his bed.)*

The Voice—And now for a tip-top breakfast, eh? Merely instruct the Mealdicator what you wish and it will be served piping hot in jig time. *(The Time Announcer stops announcing and Mr. Mercer, a little selfconsciously, goes to the Mealdicator again. He presses a button.)*

Mr. Mercer—Don't forget the coffee.

(Mr. Mercer sees several other buttons about the Mealdicator and presses them all, one at a time. The last one turns on a beautiful waltz from the room radio, which he hadn't noticed before. Mr. Mercer does not want to hear the radio, so he presses the button again to make it stop. It doesn't. About a foot away is a loud speaker and under

it is another inviting button which Mr. Mercer presses.
This makes the waltz become louder. Mr. Mercer decides
he might as well go back to the bathroom and finish shav-
ing. As he picks up his razor there is a knock on the door.)

MR. MERCER—Come in. *(A bellboy enters with a plate*
of dog meat.) Well?

BELLBOY—For the dog, sir.

MR. MERCER—For the dog?

BELLBOY—Yes, sir.

MR. MERCER—Do they give you a dog here too? *(The*
bellboy laughs pleasantly.)

BELLBOY—It's just the way you ordered it, sir.

MR. MERCER—I ordered a cup of coffee.

BELLBOY—One should never give coffee to a dog.

MR. MERCER—The coffee is for me.

BELLBOY—Well, this is for the dog. *(The bellboy puts the*
plate on the floor and looks around for the dog. Mr. Mercer
wishes he had an old-fashioned instead of a safety razor.)

MR. MERCER—Would you mind fixing that radio? *(He*
goes back into the bathroom. The bellboy does something
to the radio which makes it louder.)

BELLBOY—Better, sir?

MR. MERCER—Ideal. *(Mr. Mercer freshens the lather on*
his face and the telephone rings.)

BELLBOY—I'll answer it, sir. *(The bellboy hears some-*
thing over the phone which makes him laugh.) What? *(He*
laughs again.) No, this isn't Ausser, Ausser, Coyle, and
Mehaugh . . . *(Mr. Mercer runs out of the bathroom and*
has seized the telephone.)

MR. MERCER—Hello. . . . Operator. . . . Did you have
them back on there? . . . Yes, I do want them. . . . Well,
that was a mistake. . . . I'll hold the line. *(The door from*

the hall opens. An assistant manager and two electricians enter.)

ASSISTANT MANAGER—I beg your pardon, sir, we thought this room was vacant. I'm afraid the Time Announcer over your bed is out of order.

MR. MERCER *(at the phone)*—Look, operator, I'm in a sort of a hurry . . .

ASSISTANT MANAGER—So with your permission we will fix it. All right, boys. *(The two electricians climb over Mr. Mercer and begin hammering at the Time Announcer. There is another knock at the door.)* Come in. *(A head waiter and two other waiters enter with a table set for four. Two busboys follow them bearing a large nickel food-warmer. Mr. Mercer, who has been trying to talk over the telephone from under a pillow, comes up for air and sees them.)*

MR. MERCER—Is that the coffee?

HEAD WAITER—Did you want the coffee now, sir? *(This disturbs Mr. Mercer's patience and he speaks sternly into the telephone.)*

MR. MERCER—Operator, I wish to make a complaint! *(The others are aghast.)*

HEAD WAITER—They distinctly said they wanted the coffee afterwards.

MR. MERCER *(to the assemblage)*—Excuse my being in this nightshirt with soap on my face, gentlemen, but I am a little upset. I can't get called in time, I can't get a suit of clothes I ordered, I can't get a cup of coffee, I can't get a telephone call through, and that young man over there brings me dog meat. I've been in hotels all over this country, but . . . *(The air is suddenly charged with electricity. All the others begin to murmur, 'Mr. Pitcairn!' because T.*

Francis Pitcairn, general Eastern manager of the North American Hotels Chain, has entered the room too.)

MR. PITCAIRN—What is this about a complaint? *(His manner is very benign.)*

MR. MERCER *(witheringly)*—Oh, nothing, nothing.

MR. PITCAIRN—We are not used to complaints in the North American Chain. We of the Chain pride ourselves and rightly so on the fact that there is no comfort, no luxury which we do not provide in more than full measure to our guests. However, we do not like having our guests take advantage of our good nature. In fact we are resolute in insisting that our hotels be not turned into bedlams. Turn off that radio. *(One of the electricians turns it off.)* That's better. Now what is our guest's name?

ASSISTANT MANAGER—Kenneth Mercer, Columbus, Ohio.

MR. PITCAIRN—Ah, I have many friends in Columbus.

MR. MERCER—I've only been trying to get a little service.

MR. PITCAIRN—You have been getting plenty of service. Probably more than you have ever enjoyed in your own home. Fortunately, the hotel man of today knows how to protect himself from persons of your stripe, Mr. Mercer, and has taken legal measures to do so. *(There is now a deathlike hush.)*

MR. MERCER—You mean you're going to sue?

MR. PITCAIRN—If our attorneys so advise us. Just pack up his things. He will now leave the hotel. *(Everybody but Mr. Mercer begins to pack his things. The assistant manager offers Mr. Mercer his hat and overcoat.)*

MR. MERCER—But I have a nightgown on.

MR. PITCAIRN—You will notice, gentlemen, he is refusing to go.

MR. MERCER—No, I'm not.

BELLBOY—May I carry your bag, sir?

MR. MERCER—Thank you. I have no change; I'll have to break a bill downstairs.

BELLBOY—That's quite all right, sir. (*Mr. Mercer starts to leave the room.*)

MR. PITCAIRN—By the bye, who are your attorneys?

MR. MERCER—Aussel, Aussel, Coyne, and Mehoff. (*Mr. Mercer stops at the Mealdicator, just as he goes out. He presses a button and steps to the mouthpiece.*) Never mind the coffee.

PRIMROSE PATH

By Sally Benson

———

Judy Graves opened the pale-blue envelope addressed to her in Mary Caswell's handwriting. She was prepared for the invitation it contained, but she was not prepared for the formal and elegant wording. To the left of the page, on the upper corner, was a butterfly printed in a darker shade of blue, and underneath it was Mary's name, also printed. The invitation, which was written in longhand, read:

Miss Mary Caswell
Requests the pleasure of
Miss Judy Graves' company
At a dance to be given at her home,
Twenty East Seventy-eighth Street,
New York City,
on
Friday, February Twenty-first,
Nineteen Hundred and Forty-One.
R. S. V. P.

Judy stared at it, impressed. "Well," she said. "What do you know about that!"

Her sister, Lois, who was rubbing vaseline into her eyebrows in front of the dressing-table mirror, turned around. "What is it?" she asked.

"It's the invite to Mary's dance," Judy said. "And it's formal."

Lois took the sheet of paper. "How too silly! If she was trying to be ritzy, why didn't she have them engraved? And a dance for a lot of kids. You'll trample one another to death. Thank heavens, I don't have to go."

"You're too old," Judy said. "I wonder if Mrs. Caswell will stay in her room the whole time the way Mrs. Adams did when Fuffy had her party."

"Well, if she does, there won't be much dancing," Lois said. "The boys will go into a huddle and the whole thing will end in a brawl. Besides, what are you going to dance *to*? Victrola records or the radio or something?"

"To records," Judy told her. "Mary wanted a band, but there wasn't room. Mr. Caswell is going to change the records. They're going to move the victrola out into the hall so he won't be in the way."

She took the invitation from Lois and read it again. "I don't get it," she said. "Mrs. Caswell wrote one out for a sample and Mary brought it to school. It wasn't like this one at all. It just said that Mary was going to have a party. Jean Drummond told Mary it was too babyish, and she loaned Mary an etiquette book. I guess Mary copied this one out of the book."

"I wouldn't know."

"Well," Judy said, "I better get going. I have to be at Fuffy's this morning to meet a friend of her brother's. If it's all right, he's going to take me to the dance."

"If what's all right?" Lois asked.

"Oh, you know." Judy's eyelids fluttered nervously. "If

it's O.K. If he says he won't, Mrs. Adams told Barlow he'd have to take both Fuffy and me."

Lois's laugh was scornful. "Before I'd go and be looked over like a prize horse or something!"

"I don't mind," Judy said mildly. She went to her closet and took out her coat and hat. "Barlow says he doesn't like girls."

"Who?"

"This boy. His name is Haskell Cummings. He's going to Exeter next year." Judy smoothed her hair carefully before she put on her hat. "Barlow says he really doesn't mind girls so much if they're good sports. Well, I'll be seeing you."

"Mmm," Lois murmured. She turned back to the mirror and again massaged her eyebrows gently.

When Judy rang the bell at the Adamses' apartment, Fuffy opened the door. "They're in Barlow's room," she whispered. "They're throwing darts."

"Oh," Judy said. She followed Fuffy into the living room and took off her coat and hat and laid them across the arm of the couch. "How tall is he?" she asked.

"As tall as you are. Maybe a little bit taller," Fuffy said. "If they don't come out pretty soon, I'll call them."

"You'd better not," Judy said. "They'll have to come out sometime."

Fuffy sat down on the couch. "Maybe you're right," she said. "Mom asked them if they didn't want to stay for lunch with us, but they said they'd rather eat at the Automat."

"The Automat is nice."

The two girls were silent. They could hear the sound of the darts as they hit the target, which was nailed to the door of Barlow's room, and they could hear Barlow's voice as he called "Bull's-eye!"

"Let's play cards or something," Judy said. "It will look funny if they find us just sitting here waiting."

"O.K.," Fuffy said. She went to the hall closet and got out the card table. "Beat you at double Canfield!" Her voice was loud and enthusiastic. She set the table up and, taking two packs of cards from the desk drawer, held them out to Judy. "Which'll you have? The reds or the greens?"

"The reds." Judy drew a straight chair up to the table and began to shuffle. "Have you answered your invitation yet?"

"What did you think of it?" Fuffy asked. "Did you ever?"

"Well," Judy said, "I suppose she wanted it formal."

"Formal!" Fuffy laughed. "I thought it looked lousy."

"It did look funny," Judy agreed. "But that's on account of Mary's handwriting. I think it was all right, though. I mean the way it was put."

"It slayed Daddy. And Mom says she doesn't think Mrs. Caswell *knew*. She thinks Mary did it on her own."

"Oh, I don't doubt *that*," Judy said. "I don't doubt that at all." She put a two and a three of hearts on Fuffy's ace.

The door of Barlow's room opened, and at the sound the two girls began to laugh shrilly. "Oh!" Fuffy screamed. "You rat! That was my ace!"

They started to play furiously, slapping the cards down on the table and knocking them to the floor in their excitement. They appeared to be too engrossed in their game to look up as the boys entered the room.

"And a nine, and a ten, and a jack!" Judy cried. "I can't move until you get something. Get a hump on! You're too slow!"

Fuffy went through the remaining cards in her hand once more. "I'm bust, too," she said. She glanced at the boys carelessly. "Hello. Oh, that's right, Haskell. You don't know Judy Graves, do you? Judy, this is Haskell Cummings."

Judy stopped sorting the cards long enough to look up and smile. "Hello," she said. "Hello, Barlow."

The two boys moved nearer the table, and Fuffy counted the score. "Thirty-nine for you, Judy. And only *twenty* for me!"

Judy threw herself back heavily in the chair. "Wow! I'm bushed!" she said. "Well, I'm nineteen ahead anyway. Of course, it doesn't matter as long as we're not playing for money."

Haskell Cummings took a dime from his pocket, tossed it into the air, and caught it expertly. "I took this away from Adams," he said.

The girls looked at him in admiration. He was a slender boy with straight, light hair that fell over his forehead. He wore a belted tweed jacket and long, pale-gray trousers. His nose was slightly hooked and his chin receded only slightly, thanks to the family dentist, who had been working on it for five years.

"I wish," Fuffy said, "that Mary would have games. Not silly games, you know, but real ones with cards."

"Me too," Judy said. "I've known how to play poker for years."

"Even if she doesn't," Fuffy went on, "there's no good reason why we four can't play something if we want to. After all, what's the good of *dancing* all evening?"

"Well, I said I'd go, but I didn't say I'd dance." Barlow kicked at the leg of the bridge table.

"I tell you what we could do," Judy said. "We could do exactly what we *want*. I mean what's the sense of sitting around like sticks? As long as we *have* to go, we might as well have some fun. We had loads of fun at your party, Fuffy."

"What happened?" Haskell Cummings asked.

"Oh, that's right, you weren't there," Judy said. "It was last year and I guess you didn't know Barlow then. Well, for one thing, we threw water out the window."

"Judy hit a man on the street." Fuffy laughed and shook her head at the happy memory. "For a while we thought he was going to come up and complain or something. But he didn't. Not that we'd of cared."

"If he had come," Judy said, "I'd of told him to go sell his papers."

"Judy's *crazy*," Fuffy said loyally. "She'll do anything."

Haskell Cummings looked at Judy speculatively, and she stared back at him unflinching. "I'll do anything when I happen to feel like it," she said.

"She's the best basketball player at school," Fuffy said.

"Oh, for heaven's sake!" Judy protested modestly.

"Where do you go in the summer?" Haskell Cummings asked her.

"South Dorset, Vermont," Judy said. "We've been going there for years. Where do you go?"

"Madison, Connecticut," he answered.

"I've been there. I visited my Aunt Julia there one summer."

"Do you know Jane Garside?" Haskell Cummings asked.

Judy held her breath and took the plunge. "That drip," she said.

Haskell's face lighted up. "Drip is right!" he said. "Where

did you swim? At the Yacht Club or at the Country Club?"

"At the Country Club," Judy answered. She waited for Haskell Cummings' decision.

"That's where I swim," he said.

"Well, isn't that the funniest thing!" Judy said, and began to laugh. There was relief and excitement in her laughter.

"Hey, look out!" Fuffy warned her. "You'll get the hiccoughs!"

"Oh, don't!" Judy gasped. "Every time you say that, I *do* get them. And"—she drew in her breath—"I *have* got them!"

"Grab her arms! Grab her arms, and hold them over her head, and I'll get the vinegar!" Fuffy cried, and ran to the kitchen.

Haskell Cummings sprang into action and, taking Judy's arms, he yanked them in the air. "Somebody scare her!" he called. He let her go and, grabbing the back of her chair, tipped it over until it almost reached the floor. She shrieked wildly as he tilted the chair down and brought it swiftly up again. Her hair fell over her face and she giggled weakly.

"Well," Fuffy asked, as she came back into the room carrying the vinegar bottle, "how are they?"

Judy waited, scarcely breathing. "They're gone," she said. "Haskell cured them."

"That's the first time I've ever known Judy to have the hiccoughs and get over them like that," Fuffy said.

"When they get hiccoughs, the best thing to do is to scare them," Haskell said.

"It certainly worked, all right," Judy said. "Thanks a lot."

"Well," Barlow said, "we'd better get going."

"Thanks an *awful* lot," Judy said.

Haskell pulled down his tweed jacket and straightened his tie. "I can almost always cure hiccoughs," he said.

The two boys went out in the hall to get their hats and coats, and Fuffy followed them. Judy could hear them as they whispered together. Fuffy came back into the room as the front door closed.

"It's all right," she said. "He's going to take you. He says you are a darned good sport and not a *bit* affected."

They looked at one another and smiled. "I think he's nice," Judy said. "And we can have some fun now. I mean, we can stir up something and not poke around dancing."

"Oh, dancing!" Fuffy said. "Phooey to that stuff."

In the week that followed, Judy called Fluffy up every night to talk about the party, and by the time Friday arrived she was weak with excitement. She bathed before dinner, which was served at half past six on her account. And when she had finished her dessert, Mrs. Graves offered to help her get into her dress.

"No, thanks just the same," Judy said. "Just keep Lois out of the way. She makes me nervous picking on me."

"Well, don't yank at your dress too hard when you pull it down or the net will tear," her mother said.

Judy laughed. "It'll probably be a *wreck* before the night's over! Fuffy and Haskell and Barlow and I aren't going to bother much about *dancing*. *We're* going to play games and stuff."

"Don't be too rough," Mrs. Graves said.

The lamp on the bureau was lighted when Judy went into the room she shared with Lois. She closed the door and took off her flannel bathrobe, standing in front of her mirror in a white slip that reached to the floor. Earlier in the day she had rolled up the ends of her hair in curlers, and now she began to unfasten them slowly. Her dark-brown hair, which usually fell straight to her shoulders, lay in soft curls around her head. She fluffed it out and, going to the closet, took out her new white net dress. Although she had bought it early in January with the money her Aunt Julia had sent her for Christmas, there had been no occasion to wear it before. It had a long, full skirt, caught up in places by tiny blue bows, and there was another, larger bow on the right shoulder. She slipped it over her head. As she walked back to the mirror, the skirt swirled and rustled about her feet.

Leaning closer to the mirror, she rested her elbows on the top of the bureau, her chin in the palms of her hands. The light from the lamp cast oblique shadows across her face. Her eyes looked bright and dark, and her hair was a dusky contrast against the whiteness of her throat. She tilted her head up, lowered her eyes, and studied herself through her lashes. The round fullness of her face seemed to fade, and she could see the outlines of her cheekbones. She looked older and slimmer. "I look as pretty as Lois," she thought.

For a long while she stood there, her eyes half closed. Then she turned and, walking briskly across the room, opened the top bureau drawer of Lois's bureau. She found a small bottle of pale-pink nail polish and, sitting on the edge of the bed, she carefully applied it to her nails. When the polish was dry, she put the bottle back in the drawer and rummaged around until she found a small white enamel compact and a rose-colored Roger & Gallet lipstick. She brushed the powder on her face and neck and applied the lipstick. In her own handkerchief case she found a large white chiffon handkerchief embroidered with pink roses, and she carefully wrapped the compact and lipstick in it.

Once more she leaned close to the mirror, and fell in love with what she saw reflected there. Her blue satin slippers were soft on her feet, and her dress, billowing out below the waist, gave her a sense of lightness and well-being. She heard the doorbell ring and knew that Haskell Cummings had arrived to take her to the dance.

There was a rap on the door, and her mother's voice called "Judy!"

"In a minute," she answered.

She picked up the handkerchief, opened the door, and walked across the hall to the living room. Haskell Cummings was talking to her mother and father and Lois. He stood with his back to Judy as she entered the room. He wore a dark-blue suit and his hair was brushed slickly back.

Mr. Graves looked up at Judy. "Well," he said. "Well."

Haskell Cummings turned around. He started to say, "Hiyah there, Judy," but the words died in his throat.

"Good evening," Judy said, and held out her hand. "Aren't you nice to be so prompt!"

Something about the tone of her voice made him feel that he had been more than prompt, that he had been too early.

"We don't have to go yet if you don't want to," he said. "We can wait a while."

"Oh, goodness, it doesn't matter. As long as you're here we might as well go," Judy said.

Mr. Graves got up from his chair. "I'll get your cape," he said. He went to the hall closet and brought Judy's cape to her.

"Here, Haskell," she said, handing him the compact and lipstick wrapped in her chiffon handkerchief. "Keep these in your pocket for me. I'm simply terrible. I lose everything."

He tucked them into the pocket of his coat and stared at Judy, not saying a word. She turned to her father and, raising her face, kissed him tenderly on the cheek.

"Well, good night, Daddy," she said. She walked across the room, her skirts swaying and her soft hair moving gently across the collar of her cape. Bending down, she kissed her mother lightly. "Good night," she said again.

"Have a nice time, darling."

Judy shrugged her shoulders and smiled. Her eyes drooped wearily. "Well, you know parties," she said. She nodded brightly to Lois and swept from the room, followed by Haskell Cummings, who had managed to mutter something that sounded like "Good night."

Judy stood to one side, waiting for Haskell to open the front door for her. "I do love to dance, though," she said. "Don't you?" She went out and Haskell followed her, closing the door behind him.

Mr. and Mrs. Graves looked at one another. "She had lipstick on," Lois said. "And powder. And nail polish. And that Haskell Cummings acted like a dope."

Mr. Graves jingled the coins in his pocket. "Can you beat it!" he said. "She sold him down the river. Sold him down the river, by God!" His voice was rich with pride and satisfaction. "By God, if she didn't!"

THE SECRET LIFE OF WALTER MITTY

By James Thurber

We're going through!" The Commander's voice was like thin ice breaking. He wore his full-dress uniform, with the heavily braided white cap pulled down rakishly over one cold gray eye. "We can't made it, sir. It's spoiling for a hurricane, if you ask me." "I'm not asking you, Lieutenant Berg," said the Commander. "Throw on the power lights! Rev her up to 8,500! We're going through!" The pounding of the cylinders increased: ta-poketa-pocketa-pocketa-*pocketa-pocketa*. The Commander stared at the ice forming on the pilot window. He walked over and twisted a row of complicated dials. "Switch on No. 8 auxiliary!" he shouted. "Switch on No. 8 auxiliary!" repeated Lieutenant Berg. "Full strength in No. 3 turret!" shouted the Commander. "Full strength in No. 3 turret!" The crew, bending to their various tasks in the huge, hurtling eight-engined Navy hydroplane, looked at each other and grinned. "The Old Man'll get us through," they said to one another. "The Old Man ain't afraid of Hell!" . . .

"Not so fast! You're driving too fast!" said Mrs. Mitty. "What are you driving so fast for?"

"Hmm?" said Walter Mitty. He looked at his wife in the seat beside him, with shocked astonishment. She seemed grossly unfamiliar, like a strange woman who had yelled at him in a crowd. "You were up to fifty-five," she said.

"You know I don't like to go more than forty. You were up to fifty-five." Walter Mitty drove on toward Waterbury in silence, the roaring of the SN202 through the worst storm in twenty years of Navy flying fading in the remote, intimate airways of his mind. "You're tensed up again," said Mrs. Mitty. "It's one of your days. I wish you'd let Dr. Renshaw look you over."

Walter Mitty stopped the car in front of the building where his wife went to have her hair done. "Remember to get those overshoes while I'm having my hair done," she said. "I don't need overshoes," said Mitty. She put her mirror back into her bag. "We've been all through that," she said, getting out of the car. "You're not a young man any longer." He raced the engine a little. "Why don't you wear your gloves? Have you lost your gloves?" Walter Mitty reached in a pocket and brought out the gloves. He put them on, but after she had turned and gone into the building and he had driven on to a red light, he took them off again. "Pick it up, brother!" snapped a cop as the light changed, and Mitty hastily pulled on his gloves and lurched ahead. He drove around the streets aimlessly for a time, and then he drove past the hospital on his way to the parking lot.

. . . "It's the millionaire banker, Wellington McMillan," said the pretty nurse. "Yes?" said Walter Mitty, removing his gloves slowly. "Who has the case?" "Dr. Renshaw and Dr. Benbow, but there are two specialists here, Dr. Remington from New York and Mr. Pritchard-Mitford from London. He flew over." A door opened down a long, cool corridor and Dr. Renshaw came out. He looked distraught and haggard. "Hello, Mitty," he said. "We're having the devil's own time with McMillan, the millionaire banker and close personal friend of Roosevelt. Obstreosis of the

ductal tract. Tertiary. Wish you'd take a look at him."
"Glad to," said Mitty.

In the operating room there were whispered introductions: "Dr. Remington, Dr. Mitty. Mr. Pritchard-Mitford, Dr. Mitty." "I've read your book on streptothricosis," said Pritchard-Mitford, shaking hands. "A brilliant performance, sir." "Thank you," said Walter Mitty. "Didn't know you were in the States, Mitty," grumbled Remington. "Coals to Newcastle, bringing Mitford and me up here for a tertiary." "You are very kind," said Mitty. A huge, complicated machine, connected to the operating table, with many tubes and wires, began at this moment to go pocketa-pocketa-pocketa. "The new anesthetizer is giving way!" shouted an interne. "There is no one in the East who knows how to fix it!" "Quiet, man!" said Mitty, in a low, cool voice. He sprang to the machine, which was now going pocketa-pocketa-queep-pocketa-queep. He began fingering delicately a row of glistening dials. "Give me a fountain pen!" he snapped. Someone handed him a fountain pen. He pulled a faulty piston out of the machine and inserted the pen in its place. "That will hold for ten minutes," he said. "Get on with the operation." A nurse hurried over and whispered to Renshaw, and Mitty saw the man turn pale. "Coreopsis has set in," said Renshaw nervously. "If you would take over, Mitty?" Mitty looked at him and at the craven figure of Benbow, who drank, and at the grave, uncertain faces of the two great specialists. "If you wish," he said. They slipped a white gown on him; he adjusted a mask and drew on thin gloves; nurses handed him shining . . .

"Back it up, Mac! Look out for that Buick!" Walter Mitty jammed on the brakes. "Wrong lane, Mac," said the parking-lot attendant, looking at Mitty closely. "Gee. Yeh," muttered Mitty. He began cautiously to back out of the lane marked "Exit Only." "Leave her sit there," said the attendant. "I'll put her away." Mitty got out of the car. "Hey, better leave the key." "Oh," said Mitty, handing the man the ignition key. The attendant vaulted into the car, backed it up with insolent skill, and put it where it belonged.

They're so damn cocky, thought Walter Mitty, walking along Main Street; they think they know everything. Once he had tried to take his chains off, outside New Milford, and he had got them wound around the axles. A man had had to come out in a wrecking car and unwind them, a young, grinning garageman. Since then Mrs. Mitty always made him drive to a garage to have the chains taken off. The next time, he thought, I'll wear my right arm in a sling; they won't grin at me then. I'll have my right arm in a sling and they'll see I couldn't possibly take the chains off myself. He kicked at the slush on the sidewalk. "Overshoes," he said to himself, and he began looking for a shoe store.

When he came out into the street again, with the overshoes in a box under his arm, Walter Mitty began to wonder what the other thing was his wife had told him to get. She had told him, twice, before they set out from their house for Waterbury. In a way he hated these weekly trips to town—he was always getting something wrong. Kleenex, he thought, Squibb's, razor blades? No. Toothpaste, toothbrush, bicarbonate, carborundum, initiative and referendum? He gave it up. But she would remember it. "Where's the what's-its-name?" she would ask. "Don't tell me you forgot the what's-its-name." A newsboy went by shouting something about the Waterbury trial.

. . . "Perhaps this will refresh your memory." The District Attorney suddenly thrust a heavy automatic at the quiet figure on the witness stand. "Have you ever seen this before?" Walter Mitty took the gun and examined it expertly. "This is my Webley-Vickers 50.80," he said calmly. An excited buzz ran around the courtroom. The Judge rapped for order. "You are a crack shot with any sort of firearms, I believe?" said the District Attorney, insinuatingly. "Objection!" shouted Mitty's attorney. "We have shown that the defendant could not have fired the shot. We have shown that he wore his right arm in a sling on the night of the fourteenth of July." Walter Mitty raised his hand briefly and the bickering attorneys were stilled. "With any known make of gun," he said evenly, "I could have killed Gregory Fitzhurst at three hundred feet *with my left hand*." Pandemonium broke loose in the courtroom. A woman's scream rose above the bedlam and suddenly a lovely, dark-haired girl was in Walter Mitty's arms. The District Attorney struck at her savagely. Without rising from his chair, Mitty let the man have it on the point of the chin. "You miserable cur!" . . .

"Puppy biscuit," said Walter Mitty. He stopped walking and the buildings of Waterbury rose up out of the misty courtroom and surrounded him again. A woman who was passing laughed. "He said 'Puppy biscuit,'" she said to her companion. "That man said 'Puppy biscuit' to himself." Walter Mitty hurried on. He went into an A. & P., not the first one he came to but a smaller one farther up the street "I want some biscuit for small, young dogs," he said to the clerk. "Any special brand, sir?" The greatest pistol shot in the world thought a moment. "It says 'Puppies Bark for It' on the box," said Walter Mitty.

His wife would be through at the hairdresser's in fifteen minutes, Mitty saw in looking at his watch, unless they had trouble drying it; sometimes they had trouble drying it. She didn't like to get to the hotel first; she would want him to be there waiting for her as usual. He found a big leather chair in the lobby, facing a window, and he put the overshoes and the puppy biscuit on the floor beside it. He picked up an old copy of *Liberty* and sank down into the chair. "Can Germany Conquer the World Through the Air?" Walter Mitty looked at the pictures of bombing planes and of ruined streets.

. . . "The cannonading has got the wind up in young Raleigh, sir," said the sergeant. Captain Mitty looked up at him through touseled hair. "Get him to bed," he said wearily. "With the others. I'll fly alone." "But you can't, sir," said the sergeant anxiously. "It takes two men to handle that bomber and the Archies are pounding hell out of the air. Von Richtman's circus is between here and Saulier." "Somebody's got to get that ammunition dump," said Mitty. "I'm going over. Spot of brandy?" He poured a drink for the sergeant and one for himself. War thundered and whined around the dugout and battered at the door. There was a rending of wood and splinters flew through the room. "A bit of a near thing," said Captain Mitty carelessly. "The box barrage is closing in," said the sergeant. "We only live once, Sergeant," said Mitty, with his faint, fleeting smile. "Or do we?" He poured another brandy and tossed it off. "I never see a man could hold his brandy like you, sir," said the sergeant. "Begging your pardon, sir." Captain Mitty stood up and strapped on his huge Webley-Vickers automatic. "It's forty kilometers through hell, sir," said the sergeant. Mitty finished one last brandy. "After all," he said softly, "what isn't?" The pounding of the cannon increased; there was the rat-tat-tatting of machine guns, and from somewhere came the menacing pocketa-pocketa-pocketa of the new flame-throwers. Walter Mitty walked to the door of the dugout humming "Auprès de Ma Blonde." He turned and waved to the sergeant. "Cheerio!" he said. . . .

Something struck his shoulder. "I've been looking all over this hotel for you," said Mrs. Mitty. "Why do you have to hide in this old chair? How did you expect me to find you?" "Things close in," said Walter Mitty vaguely. "What?" Mrs. Mitty said. "Did you get the what's-its-name? The puppy biscuit? What's in that box?" "Overshoes," said Mitty. "Couldn't you have put them on in the store?" "I was thinking," said Walter Mitty. "Does it ever occur to you that I am sometimes thinking?" She looked at him. "I'm going to take your temperature when I get you home," she said.

They went out through the revolving doors that made a faintly derisive whistling sound when you pushed them. It was two blocks to the parking lot. At the drugstore on the corner she said, "Wait here for me. I forgot something. I won't be a minute." She was more than a minute. Walter Mitty lighted a cigarette. It began to rain, rain with sleet in it. He stood up against the wall of the drugstore, smoking. . . . He put his shoulders back and his heels together. "To hell with the handkerchief," said Walter Mitty scornfully. He took one last drag on his cigarette and snapped it away. Then, with that faint, fleeting smile playing about his lips, he faced the firing squad; erect and motionless, proud and disdainful, Walter Mitty the Undefeated, inscrutable to the last.

THE NIGHT THE BED FELL

By James Thurber

I suppose that the high-water mark of my youth in Columbus, Ohio, was the night the bed fell on my father. It makes a better recitation (unless, as some friends of mine have said, one has heard it five or six times) than it does a piece of writing, for it is almost necessary to throw furniture around, shake doors, and bark like a dog, to lend the proper atmosphere and verisimilitude to what is admittedly a somewhat incredible tale. Still, it did take place.

It happened, then, that my father had decided to sleep in the attic one night, to be away where he could think. My mother opposed the notion strongly because, she said, the old wooden bed up there was unsafe: it was wobbly and the heavy headboard would crash down on my father's head in case the bed fell, and kill him. There was no dissuading him, however, and at a quarter past ten he closed the attic door behind him and went up the narrow twisting stairs. We later heard ominous creakings as he crawled into bed. Grandfather, who usually slept in the attic bed when he was with us, had disappeared some days before. (On these occasions he was usually gone six or eight days and returned growling and out of temper, with the news that the federal Union was run by a passel of blockheads and that the Army of the Potomac didn't have any more chance than a fiddler's bitch.)

We had visiting us at this time a nervous first cousin of mine named Briggs Beall, who believed that he was likely to cease breathing when he was asleep. It was his feeling that if he were not awakened every hour during the night, he might die of suffocation. He had been accustomed to setting an alarm clock to ring at intervals until morning, but I persuaded him to abandon this. He slept in my room and I told him that I was such a light sleeper that if any-body quit breathing in the same room with me, I would wake instantly. He tested me the first night—which I had suspected he would—by holding his breath after my regular breathing had convinced him I was asleep. I was not asleep, however, and called to him. This seemed to allay his fears a little, but he took the precaution of putting a glass of spirits of camphor on a little table at the head of his bed. In case I didn't arouse him until he was almost gone, he said, he would sniff the camphor, a powerful reviver. Briggs was not the only member of his family who had his crotchets. Old Aunt Melissa Beall (who could whistle like a man, with two fingers in her mouth) suffered under the premonition that she was destined to die on South High Street, because she had been born on South High Street and married on South High Street. Then there was Aunt Sarah Shoaf, who never went to bed at night without the fear that a burglar was going to get in and blow chloroform under her door through a tube. To avert this calamity—for she was in greater dread of anesthetics than of losing her household goods—she always piled her money, silverware, and other valuables in a neat stack just outside her bedroom, with a note reading: "This is all I have. Please take it and do not use your chloroform, as this is all I have." Aunt Gracie Shoaf also had a burglar phobia, but she met it with more fortitude. She was confident that burglars had been getting into her house every night for forty years. The fact that she never missed anything was to her no proof to the contrary. She always claimed that she scared them off before they could take anything, by throwing shoes down the hallway. When she went to bed she piled, where she could get at them handily, all the shoes there were about her house. Five minutes after she had turned off the light, she would sit up in bed and say "Hark!" Her husband, who had learned to ignore the whole situation as long ago as 1903, would either be sound asleep or pretend to be sound asleep. In either case he would not respond to her tugging and pulling, so that presently she would arise, tiptoe to the door, open it slightly and heave a shoe down the hall in one direction, and its mate down the hall in the other direction. Some nights she threw them all, some nights only a couple of pair.

But I am straying from the remarkable incidents that took place during the night that the bed fell on father. By midnight we were all in bed. The layout of the rooms and the disposition of their occupants is important to an understanding of what later occurred. In the front room upstairs (just under father's attic bedroom) were my mother and my brother Herman, who sometimes sang in his sleep, usually "Marching Through Georgia" or "Onward Christian Soldiers." Briggs Beall and myself were in a room adjoining this one. My brother Roy was in a room across the hall from ours. Our bull terrier, Rex, slept in the hall.

My bed was an army cot, one of those affairs which are made wide enough to sleep on comfortably only by putting up, flat with the middle section, the two sides which ordinarily hang down like the sideboards of a drop-leaf table. When these sides are up, it is perilous to roll too far toward the edge, for then the cot is likely to tip completely over, bringing the whole bed down on top of one, with a tremendous banging crash. This, in fact, is precisely what happened, about two o'clock in the morning. (It was my mother who, in recalling the scene later, first referred to it as "the night the bed fell on your father.")

Always a deep sleeper, slow to arouse (I had lied to Briggs), I was at first unconscious of what had happened when the iron cot rolled me onto the floor and toppled over on me. It left me still warmly bundled up and unhurt, for the bed rested above me like a canopy. Hence I did not wake up, only reached the edge of consciousness and went back. The racket, however, instantly awakened my mother, in the next room, who came to the immediate conclusion that her worst dread was realized: the big wooden bed upstairs had fallen on father. She therefore screamed, "Let's go to your poor father!" It was this shout, rather than the noise of my cot falling, that awakened Herman, in the same room with her. He thought that mother had become, for no apparent reason, hysterical. "You're all right, Mamma!" he shouted, trying to calm her. They exchanged shout for shout for perhaps ten seconds: "Let's go to your poor father!" and "You're all right!" That woke up Briggs. By this time I was conscious of what was going on, in a vague way, but did not yet realize that I was under my bed instead of on it. Briggs, awakening in the midst of loud shouts of fear and apprehension, came to the quick conclusion that he was suffocating and that we were all trying to "bring him out." With a low moan, he grasped the glass of camphor at the head of his bed and instead of sniffing it poured it over himself. The room reeked of camphor. "Ugf, ahfg," choked Briggs, like a drowning man, for he had almost suceeded in stopping his breath under the deluge of pungent spirits. He leaped out of bed and groped toward the open window, but he came up against one that was closed. With his hand, he beat out the glass, and I could hear it crash and tinkle on the alleyway below. It was at this juncture that I, in trying to get up, had the uncanny sensation of feeling my bed above me! Foggy with sleep, I now suspected, in my turn, that the whole uproar was being made in a frantic endeavor to extricate me from what must be an unheard-of and perilous situation. "Get me out of this!" I bawled. "Get me out!" I think I had the nightmarish belief that I was entombed in a mine. "Gugh," gasped Briggs, floundering in his camphor.

By this time my mother, still shouting, pursued by Herman, still shouting, was trying to open the door to the attic, in order to go up and get my father's body out of the wreckage. The door was stuck, however, and wouldn't yield. Her frantic pulls on it only added to the general banging and confusion. Roy and the dog were now up, the one shouting questions, the other barking.

Father, farthest away and soundest sleeper of all, had by this time been awakened by the battering on the attic door. He decided that the house was on fire. "I'm coming, I'm coming!" he wailed in a slow, sleepy voice—it took him many minutes to regain full consciousness. My mother, still believing he was caught under the bed, detected in his "I'm coming!" the mournful, resigned note of one who is preparing to meet his Maker. "He's dying!" she shouted.

"I'm all right!" Briggs yelled to reassure her. "I'm all right!" He still believed that it was his own closeness to death that was worrying mother. I found at last the light switch in my room, unlocked the door, and Briggs and I joined the others at the attic door. The dog, who never did like Briggs, jumped for him—assuming that he was the culprit in whatever was going on—and Roy had to throw Rex and hold him. We could hear father crawling out of bed upstairs. Roy pulled the attic door open, with a mighty jerk and father came down the stairs, sleepy and irritable but safe and sound. My mother began to weep when she saw him. Rex began to howl. "What in the name of God is going on here?" asked father.

The situation was finally put together like a gigantic jigsaw puzzle. Father caught a cold from prowling around in his bare feet but there were no other bad results. "I'm glad," said mother, who always looked on the bright side of things, "that your grandfather wasn't here."

THE NIGHT THE GHOST GOT IN

By James Thurber

The ghost that got into our house on the night of November 17, 1915, raised such a hullabaloo of misunderstandings that I am sorry I didn't just let it keep on walking, and go to bed. Its advent caused my mother to throw a shoe through a window of the house next door and ended up with my grandfather shooting a patrolman. I am sorry, therefore, as I have said, that I ever paid any attention to the footsteps.

They began about a quarter past one o'clock in the morning, a rhythmic, quick-cadenced walking around the dining-room table. My mother was asleep in one room upstairs, my brother Herman in another; grandfather was in the attic, in the old walnut bed which, as you will remember, once fell on my father. I had just stepped out of the bathtub and was busily rubbing myself with a towel when I heard the steps. They were the steps of a man walking rapidly around the dining-room table downstairs. The light from the bathroom shone down the back steps, which dropped directly into the dining-room; I could see the faint shine of plates on the plate-rail; I couldn't see the table. The steps kept going round and round the table; at regular intervals a board creaked, when it was trod upon. I supposed at first that it was my father or my brother Roy, who had gone to Indianapolis but were expected home at any time. I suspected next that it was a burglar. It did not enter my mind until later that it was a ghost.

After the walking had gone on for perhaps three minutes, I tiptoed to Herman's room. "Psst!" I hissed, in the dark, shaking him. "Awp," he said, in the low, hopeless tone of a despondent beagle—he always half suspected that something would "get him" in the night. I told him who I was. "There's something downstairs!" I said. He got up and followed me to the head of the back staircase. We listened together. There was no sound. The steps had ceased. Herman looked at me in some alarm: I had only the bath towel around my waist. He wanted to go back to bed, but I gripped his arm. "There's something down there!" I said. Instantly the steps began again, circled the dining-room table like a man running, and started up the stairs toward us, heavily, two at a time. The light still shone palely down the stairs; we saw nothing coming; we only heard the steps. Herman rushed to his room and slammed the door. I slammed shut the door at the stairs top and held my knee against it. After a long minute, I slowly opened it again. There was nothing there. There was no sound. None of us ever heard the ghost again.

The slamming of the doors had aroused mother: she peered out of her room. "What on earth are you boys doing?" she demanded. Herman ventured out of his room. "Nothing," he said, gruffly, but he was, in color, a light green. "What was all that running around downstairs?" said mother. So she had heard the steps, too! We just looked at her. "Burglars!" she shouted, intuitively. I tried to quiet her by starting lightly downstairs.

"Come on, Herman," I said.

"I'll stay with mother," he said. "She's all excited."

I stepped back onto the landing.

"Don't either of you go a step," said mother. "We'll

call the police." Since the phone was downstairs, I didn't
see how we were going to call the police—nor did I want
the police—but mother made one of her quick, incompa-
rable decisions. She flung up a window of her bedroom
which faced the bedroom windows of the house of a neigh-
bor, picked up a shoe, and whammed it through a pane of
glass across the narrow space that separated the two houses.
Glass tinkled into the bedroom occupied by a retired en-
graver named Bodwell and his wife. Bodwell had been
for some years in rather a bad way and was subject to
mild "attacks." Most everybody we knew or lived near had
some kind of attacks.

It was now about two o'clock of a moonless night; clouds
hung black and low. Bodwell was at the window in a minute, shouting, frothing a little, shaking his fist. "We'll sell
the house and go back to Peoria," we could hear Mrs. Bodwell saying. It was some time before Mother "got through"
to Bodwell. "Burglars!" she shouted. "Burglars in the
house!" Herman and I hadn't dared to tell her that it was
not burglars but ghosts, for she was even more afraid of
ghosts than of burglars. Bodwell at first thought that she
meant there were burglars in his house, but finally he
quieted down and called the police for us over an extension phone by his bed. After he had disappeared from the
window, mother suddenly made as if to throw another
shoe, not because there was further need of it but, as she
later explained, because the thrill of heaving a shoe through
a window glass had enormously taken her fancy. I pre-
vented her.

The police were on hand in a commendably short time:
a Ford sedan full of them, two on motorcycles, and a patrol
wagon with about eight in it and a few reporters. They
began banging at our front door. Flashlights shot streaks
of gleam up and down the walls, across the yard, down

the walk between our house and Bodwell's. "Open up!" cried a hoarse voice. "We're men from Headquarters!" I wanted to go down and let them in, since there they were, but mother wouldn't hear of it. "You haven't a stitch on," she pointed out. "You'd catch your death." I wound the towel around me again. Finally the cops put their shoulders to our big heavy front door with its thick beveled glass and broke it in: I could hear a rending of wood and a splash of glass on the floor of the hall. Their lights played all over the living-room and crisscrossed nervously in the dining-room, stabbed into hallways, shot up the front stairs and finally up the back. They caught me standing in my towel at the top. A heavy policeman bounded up the steps. "Who are you?" he demanded. "I live here," I said. "Well, whattsa matta, ya hot?" he asked. It was, as a matter of fact, cold; I went to my room and pulled on some trousers. On my way out, a cop stuck a gun into my ribs. "Whatta you doin' here?" he demanded. "I live here," I said.

The officer in charge reported to mother. "No sign of nobody, lady," he said. "Musta got away—whatt'd he look like?" "There were two or three of them," mother said, "whooping and carrying on and slamming doors." "Funny," said the cop. "All ya windows and doors was locked on the inside tight as a tick."

Downstairs, we could hear the tramping of the other police. Police were all over the place; doors were yanked open, drawers were yanked open, windows were shot up and pulled down, furniture fell with dull thumps. A half-dozen policemen emerged out of the darkness of the front hallway upstairs. They began to ransack the floor: pulled beds away from walls, tore clothes off hooks in the closets, pulled suitcases and boxes off shelves. One of them found an old zither that Roy had won in a pool tournament. "Looky here, Joe," he said, strumming it with a big paw.

The cop named Joe took it and turned it over. "What is it?" he asked me. "It's an old zither our guinea pig used to sleep on," I said. It was true that a pet guinea pig we once had would never sleep anywhere except on the zither, but I should never have said so. Joe and the other cop looked at me a long time. They put the zither back on a shelf.

"No sign o' nuthin'," said the cop who had first spoken to mother. "This guy," he explained to the others, jerking a thumb at me, "was nekked. The lady seems historical." They all nodded, but said nothing; just looked at me. In the small silence we all heard a creaking in the attic. Grandfather was turning over in bed. "What's 'at?" snapped Joe. Five or six cops sprang for the attic door before I could intervene or explain. I realized that it would be bad if they burst in on grandfather unannounced, or even announced. He was going through a phase in which he believed that General Meade's men, under steady hammering by Stonewall Jackson, were beginning to retreat and even desert.

When I got to the attic, things were pretty confused. Grandfather had evidently jumped to the conclusion that the police were deserters from Meade's army, trying to hide away in his attic. He bounded out of bed wearing a long flannel nightgown over long woolen underwear, a nightcap, and a leather jacket around his chest. The cops must have realized at once that the indignant white-haired old man belonged in the house, but they had no chance to say so. "Back, ye cowardly dogs!" roared grandfather. "Back t' the lines, ye goddam lily-livered cattle!" With that, he fetched the officer who found the zither a flat-handed smack alongside his head that sent him sprawling. The others beat a retreat, but not fast enough; grandfather grabbed Zither's gun from its holster and let fly. The report seemed to crack the rafters; smoke filled the attic. A cop cursed and shot his hand to his shoulder. Somehow, we all finally got down-

stairs again and locked the door against the old gentleman. He fired once or twice more in the darkness and then
went back to bed. "That was grandfather," I explained to
Joe, out of breath. "He thinks you're deserters." "I'll say he
does," said Joe.

The cops were reluctant to leave without getting their
hands on somebody besides grandfather; the night had been
distinctly a defeat for them. Furthermore, they obviously
didn't like the "layout"; something looked—and I can see
their viewpoint—phony. They began to poke into things
again. A reporter, a thin-faced, wispy man, came up to me
I had put on one of mother's blouses, not being able to find
anything else. The reporter looked at me with mingled sus-
picion and interest. "Just what the hell is the real lowdown
here, Bud?" he asked. I decided to be frank with him. "We
had ghosts," I said. He gazed at me a long time as if I were
a slot machine into which he had, without results, dropped
a nickel. Then he walked away. The cops followed him, the
one grandfather shot holding his now-bandaged arm,
cursing and blaspheming. "I'm gonna get my gun back
from that old bird," said the zither-cop. "Yeh," said Joe.
"You—and who else?" I told them I would bring it to the
station house the next day.

"What was the matter with that one policeman?" mother
asked, after they had gone. "Grandfather shot him," I said.
"What for?" she demanded. I told her he was a deserter. "Of
all things!" said mother. "He was such a nice-looking young
man."

Grandfather was fresh as a daisy and full of jokes at
breakfast next morning. We thought at first he had forgotten
all about what had happened, but he hadn't. Over his third
cup of coffee, he glared at Herman and me. "What was the
idee of all them cops tarryhootin' round the house last
night?" he demanded. He had us there.

UNIVERSITY DAYS

By James Thurber

I passed all the other courses that I took at my University, but I could never pass botany. This was because all botany students had to spend several hours a week in a laboratory looking through a microscope at plant cells, and I could never see through a microscope. I never once saw a cell through a microscope. This used to enrage my instructor. He would wander around the laboratory pleased with the progress all the students were making in drawing the involved and, so I am told, interesting structure of flower cells, until he came to me. I would just be standing there. "I can't see anything," I would say. He would begin patiently enough, explaining how anybody can see through a microscope, but he would always end up in a fury, claiming that I could *too* see through a microscope but just pretended that I couldn't. "It takes away from the beauty of flowers anyway," I used to tell him. "We are not concerned with beauty in this course," he would say. "We are concerned solely with what I may call the *mechanics* of flars." "Well," I'd say, "I can't see anything." "Try it just once again," he'd say, and I would put my eye to the microscope and see nothing at all, except now and again a nebulous milky substance—a phenomenon of maladjustment. You were supposed to see a vivid, restless clockwork of sharply defined plant cells. "I see what looks like a lot of milk," I would tell him. This, he claimed, was the result of my not having adjusted the microscope properly, so he would readjust it for me, or rather, for himself. And I would look again and see milk.

I finally took a deferred pass, as they called it, and waited a year and tried again. (You had to pass one of the biological sciences or you couldn't graduate.) The professor had come back from vacation brown as a berry, bright-eyed, and eager to explain cell-structure again to his classes. "Well," he said to me, cheerily when we met in the first laboratory hour of the semester, "we're going to see cells this time, aren't we?" "Yes, sir," I said. Students to right of me and to left of me and in front of me were seeing cells; what's more, they were quietly drawing pictures of them in their notebooks. Of course, I didn't see anything.

"We'll try it," the professor said to me, grimly, "with every adjustment of the microscope known to man. As God is my witness, I'll arrange this glass so that you see cells through it or I'll give up teaching. In twenty-two years of botany, I—" He cut off abruptly for he was beginning to quiver all over, like Lionel Barrymore, and he genuinely wished to hold onto his temper; his scenes with me had taken a great deal out of him.

So we tried it with every adjustment of the microscope known to man. With only one of them did I see anything but blackness or the familiar lacteal opacity, and that time I saw, to my pleasure and amazement, a variegated constellation of flecks, specks, and dots. These I hastily drew. The instructor, noting my activity, came back from an adjoining desk, a smile on his lips and his eyebrows high in hope. He looked at my cell drawing. "What's that?" he demanded, with a hint of squeal in his voice. "That's what I saw," I said. "You didn't, you didn't, you *did*n't!" he screamed, losing control of his temper instantly, and he bent over and squinted into the microscope. His head snapped up. "That's your eye!" he shouted. "You've fixed the lens so that it reflects! You've drawn your eye!"

Another course that I didn't like, but somehow managed to pass, was economics. I went to that class straight from the botany class, which didn't help me any in understanding either subject. I used to get them mixed up. But not as mixed up as another student in my economics class who came there direct from a physics laboratory. He was a tackle on the football team, named Bolenciecwcz. At that time Ohio State University had one of the best football teams in the country, and Bolenciecwcz was one of its outstanding stars. In order to be eligible to play it was necessary for him to keep up in his studies, a very difficult matter, for while he was not dumber than an ox he was not any smarter. Most of his professors were lenient and helped him along. None gave him more hints, in answering questions, or asked him simpler ones than the economics professor, a thin, timid man named Bassum. One day when we were on the subject of transportation and distribution, it came Bolenciecwcz's turn to answer a question. "Name one means of transportation," the professor said to him. No light came into the big tackle's eyes. "Just any means of transportation," said the professor. Bolenciecwcz sat staring at him. "That is," pursued the professor, "any medium, agency, or method of going from one place to another." Bolenciecwcz had the look of a man who is being led into a trap. "You may choose among steam, horse-drawn, or electrically propelled vehicles," said the instructor. "I might suggest the one which we commonly take in making long journeys across land." There was a profound silence in which everybody stirred uneasily, including Bolenciecwcz and Mr. Bassum. Mr. Bassum abruptly broke this silence in an amazing manner. "Choo-choo-choo," he said, in a low voice, and turned instantly scarlet. He glanced appealingly around the room. All of us, of course, shared Mr. Bassum's desire that Bolenciecwcz should stay abreast of the class in economics, for the Illinois game, one of the hardest and most important of the season, was only a week off. "Toot, toot, too-toooooot!" some student with a deep voice moaned, and we all looked encouragingly at Bolenciecwcz. Somebody else gave a fine imitation of a locomotive letting off steam. Mr. Bassum himself rounded off the little show. "Ding, dong, ding, dong," he said, hopefully. Bolenciecwcz was staring at the floor now, trying to think, his great brow furrowed, his huge hands rubbing together, his face red.

"How did you come to college this year, Mr. Bolenciecwcz?" asked the professor. "*Chuf*fa chuffa, *chuf*fa chuffa."

"M'father sent me," said the football player.

"What on?" asked Bassum.

"I git an 'lowance," said the tackle, in a low, husky voice, obviously embarrassed.

"No, no," said Bassum. "Name a means of transportation. What did you *ride* here on?"

"Train," said Bolenciecwcz.

"Quite right," said the professor. "Now, Mr. Nugent, will you tell us——"

If I went through anguish in botany and economics—for different reasons—gymnasium work was even worse. I don't even like to think about it. They wouldn't let you play games or join in the exercises with your glasses on and I couldn't see with mine off. I bumped into professors, horizontal bars, agricultural students, and swinging iron rings. Not being able to see, I could take it but I couldn't dish it out. Also, in order to pass gymnasium (and you had to pass it to graduate) you had to learn to swim if you didn't know how. I didn't like the swimming pool, I didn't like swimming, and I didn't like the swimming instructor, and after all these years I still don't. I never swam but I passed my gym work anyway, by having another student give my gymnasium number (978) and swim across the pool in my place. He was a quiet, amiable blonde youth, number 473, and he would have seen through a microscope for me if we could have got away with it, but we couldn't get away with it. Another thing I didn't like about gymnasium work was that they made you strip the day you registered. It is impossible for me to be happy when I am stripped and being asked a lot of questions. Still, I did better than a lanky agricultural student who was cross-examined just before I was. They asked each student what college he was in—that is, whether Arts, Engineering, Commerce, or Agriculture. "What college are you in?" the instructor snapped at the youth in front of me. "Ohio State University," he said promptly.

It wasn't that agricultural student but it was another a whole lot like him who decided to take up journalism, possibly on the ground that when farming went to hell he could fall back on newspaper work. He didn't realize, of course, that that would be very much like falling back full-length on a kit of carpenter's tols. Haskins didn't seem cut out for journalism, being too embarrassed to talk to anybody and unable to use a typewriter, but the editor of the college paper assigned him to the cow barns, the sheep house, the horse pavilion, and the animal husbandry department generally. This was a genuinely big "beat," for it took up five times as much ground and got ten times as great a legislative appropriation as the College of Liberal Arts. The agricultural student knew animals, but nevertheless his stories were dull and colorlessly written. He took all afternoon on each of them, on account of having to hunt for each letter on the typewriter. Once in a while he had to ask somebody to help him hunt. "C" and "L," in particular, were hard letters for him to find. His editor finally got pretty much annoyed at the farmer-journalist because his pieces were so uninteresting. "See here, Haskins," he snapped at him one day, "Why is it we never have anything hot from you on the horse pavilion? Here we have two hundred head of horses on this campus—more than any other university in the Western Conference except Purdue—and yet you never get any real lowdown on them. Now shoot over to the horse barns and dig up something lively." Haskins shambled out and came back in about an hour; he said he had something. "Well, start it off snappily," said the editor. "Something people will read." Haskins set to work and in a couple of hours brought a sheet of typewritten paper to the desk; it was a two-hundred word story about some disease that had broken out among the horses. Its opening sentence was simple but arresting. It read: "Who has noticed the sores on the tops of the horses in the animal husbandry building?"

Ohio State was a land grant university and therefore two years of military drill was compulsory. We drilled with old Springfield rifles and studied the tactics of the Civil War even though the World War was going on at the time. At 11 o'clock each morning thousands of freshmen and sophomores used to deploy over the campus, moodily creeping up on the old chemistry building. It was good training for the kind of warfare that was waged at Shiloh but it had no connection with what was going on in Europe. Some people used to think there was German money behind it, but they didn't dare say so or they would have been thrown in jail as German spies. It was a period of muddy thought and marked, I believe, the decline of higher education in the middle West.

As a soldier I was never any good at all. Most of the cadets were glumly indifferent soldiers, but I was no good at all. Once General Littlefield, who was commandant of the cadet corps, popped up in front of me during regimental drill and snapped, "You are the main trouble with this university!" I think he meant that my type was the main trouble with the university but he may have meant me individually. I was mediocre at drill, certainly—that is, until my senior year. By that time I had drilled longer than anybody else in the Western Conference, having failed at military at the end of each preceding year so that I had to do it all over again. I was the only senior still in uniform. The uniform which, when new, had made me look like an interurban railway conductor, now that it had become faded and too tight made me look like Bert Williams in his bell-boy act. This had a definitely bad effect on my morale. Even so, I had become by sheer practise little short of wonderful at squad manoeuvres.

One day General Littlefield picked our company out of the whole regiment and tried to get it mixed up by putting it through one movement after another as fast as we could execute them: squads right, squads left, squads on right into line, squads right about, squads left front into line, etc. In about three minutes one hundred and nine men were marching in one direction and I was marching away from them at an angle of forty degrees, all alone. "Company, halt!" shouted General Littlefield, "That man is the only man who has it right!" I was made a corporal for my achievement.

The next day General Littlefield summoned me to his office. He was swatting flies when I went in. I was silent and he was silent too, for a long time. I don't think he remembered me or why he had sent for me, but he didn't want to admit it. He swatted some more flies, keeping his eyes on them narrowly before he let go with the swatter. "Button up your coat!" he snapped. Looking back on it now I can see that he meant me although he was looking at a fly, but I just stood there. Another fly came to rest on a paper in front of the general and began rubbing its hind legs together. The general lifted the swatter cautiously. I moved restlessly and the fly flew away. "You startled him!" barked General Littlefield, looking at me severely. I said I was sorry. "That won't help the situation!" snapped the General, with cold military logic. I didn't see what I could do except offer to chase some more flies toward his desk, but I didn't say anything. He stared out the window at the faraway figures of co-eds crossing the campus toward the library. Finally, he told me I could go. So I went. He either didn't know which cadet I was or else he forgot what he wanted to see me about. It may have been that he wished to apologize for having called me the main trouble with the university; or maybe he had decided to compliment me on my brilliant drilling of the day before and then at the last minute decided not to. I don't know. I don't think about it much any more.

THE MAN WHO HATED MOONBAUM

By James Thurber

After they had passed through the high, grilled gate they walked for almost a quarter of a mile, or so it seemed to Tallman. It was very dark; the air smelled sweet; now and then leaves brushed against his cheek or forehead. The little, stout man he was following had stopped talking, but Tallman could hear him breathing. They walked on for another minute. "How we doing?" Tallman asked, finally. "Don't ask me questions!" snapped the other man. "Nobody asks me questions! You'll learn." The hell I will, thought Tallman, pushing through the darkness and the fragrance and the mysterious leaves; the hell I will, baby; this is the last time you'll ever see me. The knowledge that he was leaving Hollywood within twenty-four hours gave him a sense of comfort.

There was no longer turf or gravel under his feet; there was something that rang flatly: tile, or flagstones. The little man began to walk more slowly and Tallman almost bumped into him. "Can't we have a light?" said Tallman. "There you go!" shouted his guide. "Don't get me screaming! What are you trying to do to me?" "I'm not trying to do anything to you," said Tallman. "I'm trying to find out where we're going."

The other man had come to a stop and seemed to be

groping around. "First it's wrong uniforms," he said, "then it's red fire—red fire in Scotland, red fire three hundred years ago! I don't know why I ain't crazy!" Tallman could make out the other man dimly, a black, gesturing blob. "You're doing all right," said Tallman. Why did I ever leave the Brown Derby with this guy? he asked himself. Why did I ever let him bring me to his house—if he has a house? Who the hell does he think he is?

Tallman looked at his wristwatch; the dial glowed wanly in the immense darkness. He was a little drunk, but he could see that it was half past three in the morning. "Not trying to do anything to me, he says!" screamed the little man. "Wasn't his fault! It's never anybody's fault! They give me ten thousand dollars' worth of Sam Browne belts for Scotch Highlanders and it's nobody's fault!" Tallman was beginning to get his hangover headache. "I want a light!" he said. "I want a drink! I want to know where the hell I am!" "That's it! Speak out!" said the other. "Say what you think! I like a man who knows where he is. We'll get along." "Contact!" said Tallman. "Camera! Lights! Get out that hundred-year-old brandy you were talking about."

The response to this was a soft flood of rose-colored radiance; the little man had somehow found a light switch in the dark. God knows where, thought Tallman; probably on a tree. They were in a courtyard paved with enormous flagstones which fitted together with mosaic perfection. The light revealed the dark stones of a building which looked like the Place de la Concorde side of the Crillon. "Come on, you people!" said the little man. Tallman looked behind him, half expecting to see the shadowy forms of Scottish Highlanders, but there was nothing but the shadows of trees and of oddly shaped plants closing in on the courtyard. With a key as small as a dime, the little man opened a door that was fifteen feet high and made of wood six inches thick.

Marble stairs tumbled down like Niagara into a grand canyon of a living room. The steps of the two men sounded sharp and clear on the stairs, died in the soft depths of an immensity of carpet in the living room. The ceiling towered above them. There were highlights on dark wood medallions, on burnished shields, on silver curves and edges. On one wall a forty-foot tapestry hung from the ceiling to within a few feet of the floor. Tallman was looking at this when his companion grasped his arm. "The second rose!" he said. "The second rose from the right!" Tallman pulled away. "One of us has got to snap out of this, baby," he said. "How about that brandy?" "Don't interrupt me!" shouted his host. "That's what Whozis whispers to What's-His-Name —greatest love story in the world, if I do say so myself— king's wife mixed up in it—knights riding around with spears—Whozis writes her a message made out of twigs bent together to make words: 'I love you'—sends it floating down a stream past her window—they got her locked in— goddamnedest thing in the history of pictures. Where was I? Oh—'Second rose from the right,' she says. Why? Because she seen it twitch, she seen it move. What's-His-Name is bending over her, kissing her maybe. He whirls around and shoots an arrow at the rose—second from the right, way up high there—down comes the whole tapestry, weighs eleven hundred pounds, and out rolls this spy, shot through the heart. What's-His-Name sent him to watch the lovers." The little man began to pace up and down the deep carpet. Tallman lighted a fresh cigarette from his glowing stub and sat down in an enormous chair. His host came to a stop in front of the chair and shook his finger at its occupant.

"Look," said the little man. "I don't know who you are and I'm telling you this. You could ruin me, but I got to tell you. I get Moonbaum here—I get Moonbaum himself here—you can ask Manny or Sol—I get the best arrow shot in the world here to fire that arrow for What's-His-Name—"

"Tristram," said Tallman. "Don't prompt me!" bellowed the little man. "For Tristram. What happens? Do I know he's got arrows you shoot bears with? Do I know he ain't got caps on 'em? If I got to know that, why do I have Mitnik? Moonbaum is sitting right there—the tapestry comes down and out rolls this guy, shot through the heart—only the arrow is in his stomach. So what happens? So Moonbaum laughs! That makes Moonbaum laugh! The greatest love story in the history of pictures, and Moonbaum laughs!" The little man raced over to a large chest, opened it, took out a cigar, stuck it in his mouth, and resumed his pacing. "How do you like it?" he shouted. "I love it," said Tallman. "I love every part of it. I always have." The little man raised his hands above his head. "He loves it! He hears one—maybe two—scenes, and he loves every part of it! Even Moonbaum don't know how it comes out, and you love every part of it!" The little man was standing before Tallman's chair again, shaking his cigar at him. "The story got around," said Tallman. "These things leak out. Maybe you talk when you're drinking. What about that brandy?"

The little man walked over and took hold of a bell rope on the wall, next to the tapestry. "Moonbaum laughs like he's dying," he said. "Moonbaum laughs like he's seen Chaplin." He dropped the bell rope. "I hope you really got that hundred-year-old brandy," said Tallman. "Don't keep telling me what you hope!" howled the little man. "Keep listening to what I hope!" He pulled the bell rope savagely. "Now we're getting somewhere," said Tallman. For the first time the little man went to a chair and sat down; he chewed on his unlighted cigar. "Do you know what Moonbaum wants her called?" he demanded, lowering his heavy lids. "I can guess," said Tallman. "Isolde." "Birds of a feather!" shouted his host. "Horses of the same color! Isolde! Name of God, man, you can't call a woman Isolde! What do I want her called?" "You have me there," said Tallman. "I want her called Dawn," said the little man, getting up out of his chair. "It's short, ain't it? It's sweet, ain't it? You can say it, can't you?" "To get back to that brandy," said Tallman, "who is supposed to answer that bell?" "Nobody is supposed to answer it," said the little man. "That don't ring, that's a fake bell rope; it don't ring anywhere. I got it to remind me of an idea Moonbaum ruined. Listen: Louisiana mansion—guy with seven daughters—old-Southern-colonel stuff—Lionel Barrymore could play it—we open on a room that looks like a million dollars—Barrymore crosses and pulls the bell rope. What happens?" "Nothing," said Tallman. "You're crazy!" bellowed the little man. "Part of the wall falls in! Out flies a crow—in walks a goat, maybe —the place has gone to seed, see? It's just a hulk of its former self, it's a shallows!" He turned and walked out of the room. It took him quite a while.

When he came back, he was carrying a bottle of brandy and two huge brandy glasses. He poured a great deal of brandy into each glass and handed one to Tallman. "You and Mitnik!" he said, scornfully. "Pulling walls out of Southern mansions. Crows you give me, goats you give me! What the hell kind of effect is that?" "I could have a bad idea," said Tallman, raising his glass. "Here's to Moonbaum. May he maul things over in his mind all night and never get any spontanuity into 'em." "I drink nothing to Moonbaum," said the little man. "I hate Moonbaum. You know where they catch that crook—that guy has a little finger off one hand and wears a glove to cover it up? What does Moonbaum want? Moonbaum wants the little finger to *flap*! What do I want? I want it stuffed. What do I want it stuffed with? Sand. Why?" "I know," said Tallman. "So that when he closes his hand over the head of his cane, the little finger sticks out stiffly, giving him away." The little man seemed to leap into the air; his brandy splashed out of his glass. "Suitcase!" he screamed. "Not cane! Suitcase! He grabs hold of a suitcase!" Tallman didn't say anything; he closed his eyes and sipped his brandy; it was wonderful brandy. He looked up presently to find his host staring at him with a resigned expression in his eyes. "All right, then, suitcase," the little man said. "Have it suitcase. We won't fight about details. I'm trying to tell you my story. I don't tell my stories to everybody." "Richard Harding Davis stole that finger gag—used it in 'Gallegher,'" said Tallman. "You could sue him." The little man walked over to his chair and flopped into it. "He's beneath me," he said. "He's beneath me like the dirt. I ignore him."

Tallman finished his brandy slowly. His host's chin sank upon his chest; his heavy eyelids began to close. Tallman waited several minutes and then tiptoed over to the marble stairs. He took off his shoes and walked up the stairs, carefully. He had the heavy door open when the little man shouted at him. "Birds of a feather, all of you!" he shouted. "You can tell Moonbaum I said so! Shooting guys out of tapestries!" "I'll tell him," said Tallman. "Good night. The brandy was wonderful." The little man was not listening. He was pacing the floor again, gesturing with an empty brandy glass in one hand and the unlighted cigar in the other. Tallman stepped out into the cool air of the court-yard and put on one shoe and laced it. The heavy door swung shut behind him with a terrific crash. He picked up the other shoe and ran wildly toward the trees and the oddly shaped plants. It was daylight now. He could see where he was going.

FATHER AND HIS HARD-ROCKING SHIP

By Clarence Day

FATHER said that one great mystery about the monthly household expenses was what made them jump up and down so. "Anyone would suppose that there would be some regularity after a while which would let a man try to make plans, but I never know from one month to another what to expect."

Mother said she didn't, either. Things just seemed to go that way.

"But they have no business to go that way, Vinnie," Father declared. "And what's more I won't allow it."

Mother said she didn't see what she could do about it. All she knew was that when the bills mounted up, it didn't mean that she had been extravagant.

"Well, it certainly means that you've spent a devil of a lot of money," said Father.

Mother looked at him obstinately. She couldn't exactly deny this, but she said that it wasn't fair.

Appearances were often hopelessly against Mother but that never daunted her. She wasn't afraid of Father or anybody. She was a woman of great spirit who would have flown at and pecked any tyrant. It was only when she had a bad conscience that she had no heart to fight. Father had the best of her there because he never had a bad conscience.

And he didn't know that he was a tyrant. He regarded himself as a long-suffering man who asked little of anybody, and who showed only the greatest moderation in his encounters with unreasonable beings like Mother. Mother's one advantage over him was that she was quicker. She was particularly elusive when Father was trying to hammer her into shape.

When the household expenses shot up very high, Father got frightened. He would then, as Mother put it, yell his head off. He always did some yelling anyhow, merely on general principles, but when his alarm was genuine he roared in real anguish.

Usually this brought the total down again, at least for a while. But there were times when no amount of noise seemed to do any good, and when every month for one reason or another the total went up and up. And then, just as Father had almost resigned himself to this awful outgo, and just as he had eased up on his yelling and had begun to feel grim, the expenses, to his utter amazement, would take a sharp drop.

Mother didn't keep track of these totals, she was too busy watching small details, and Father never knew whether to tell her the good news or not. He always did tell her, because he couldn't keep things to himself. But he always had cause to regret it.

When he told her, he did it in as disciplinary a manner as possible. He didn't congratulate her on the expenses having come down. He appeared at her door, waving the bills at her with a threatening scowl, and said, "I've told you again and again that you could keep the expenses down if you tried, and this shows I was right."

Mother was always startled at such attacks, but she didn't lose her presence of mind. She asked how much less the amount was and said it was all due to her good management, of course, and Father ought to give her the difference.

At this point Father suddenly found himself on the defensive and the entire moral lecture that he had intended to deliver was wrecked. The more they talked, the clearer it seemed to Mother that he owed her that money. Only when he was lucky could he get out of her room without paying it.

He said that this was one of the things about her that was enough to drive a man mad.

The other thing was her lack of system, which was always cropping up in new ways. He sometimes looked at Mother as though he had never seen her before. "Upon my soul," he said, "I almost believe you don't know what system is. You don't even want to know, either."

He had at last invented what seemed a perfect method of recording expenses. Whenever he gave any money to Mother, he asked her what it was for and made a note of it in his pocket notebook. His idea was that these items, added to those in the itemized bills, would show him exactly where every dollar had gone.

But they didn't.

He consulted his notebook. "I gave you six dollars in cash on the twenty-fifth of last month," he said, "to buy a new coffeepot."

"Yes," Mother said, "because you broke your old one. You threw it right on the floor."

Father frowned. "I'm not talking about that," he answered. "I am simply endeavoring to find out from you, if I can—"

"But it's so silly to break a nice coffeepot, Clare, and that was the last of those French ones, and there was nothing the matter with the coffee that morning; it was made just the same as it always is."

"It wasn't," said Father. "It was made in a damned barbaric manner."

"And I couldn't get another French one," Mother continued, "because that little shop the Auffmordts told us about has stopped selling them. They said the tariff wouldn't let them any more, and I told Monsieur Duval he ought to be ashamed of himself to stand there and say so. I said that if I had a shop, I'd like to see the tariff keep me from selling things."

"But I gave you six dollars to buy a new pot," Father firmly repeated, "and now I find that you apparently got one at Lewis & Conger's and charged it. Here's their bill: 'one brown earthenware drip coffeepot, five dollars.'"

"So I saved you a dollar," Mother triumphantly said, "and you can hand it right over to me."

"Bah! What nonsense you talk!" Father cried. "Is there no way to get this thing straightened out? What did you do with the six dollars?"

"Why, Clare! I can't tell you now, dear. Why didn't you ask at the time?"

"Oh, my God!" Father groaned.

"Wait a moment," said Mother. "I spent four dollars and a half for that new umbrella I told you I wanted, and you said I didn't need a new one, but I did, very much."

Father got out his pencil and wrote "New Umbrella for V." in his notebook.

"And that must have been the week," Mother went on, "that I paid Mrs. Tobin for two extra days' washing, so that was two dollars more out of it, which makes it six-fifty. There's another fifty cents that you owe me."

"I don't owe you anything," Father said. "You have managed to turn a coffeepot for me into a new umbrella for you. No matter what I give you money for, you buy something else with it, and if this is to keep on, I might as well not keep account books at all."

"I'd like to see you run this house without having any money on hand for things," Mother said.

"I am not made of money," Father replied. "You seem to think I only have to put my hand in my pocket to get some."

Mother not only thought this, she knew it. His wallet always was full. That was the provoking part of it—she knew he had the money right there, but he tried to keep from giving it to her. She had to argue it out of him.

"Well, you can put your hand in your pocket and give me that dollar-fifty this minute," she said. "You owe me that, anyhow."

Father said he didn't have a dollar-fifty to spare and tried to get back to his desk, but Mother wouldn't let him go till he paid her. She said she wouldn't put up with injustice.

Mother said it hampered her dreadfully never to have any cash. She was always having to pay out small amounts for demands that she had forgot to provide for, and in such emergencies the only way to do was to juggle things around. One result, however, of all these more or less innocent shifts was that in this way she usually took care of all her follies herself. All the small ones, at any rate. They never got entered on Father's books, except when they were monstrous.

She came home one late afternoon in a terrible state. "Has it come yet?" she asked the waitress.

The waitress said nothing had come that she knew of.

Mother ran upstairs with a hunted expression and flung herself down on her bed. When we looked in, she was sobbing.

It turned out that she had gone to an auction, and she had become so excited that she had bought but not paid for a grandfather's clock.

Mother knew in her heart that she had no business going to auctions. She was too suggestible, and if an hypnotic auctioneer once got her eye, she was lost. Besides, an auction aroused all her worst instincts—her combativeness, her recklessness, and her avaricious love of a bargain. And the worst of it was that this time it wasn't a bargain at all. At least she didn't think it was now. The awful old thing was about eight feet tall, and it wasn't the one she had wanted. It wasn't half as nice as the clock that old Miss Van Derwent had bought. And inside the hood over the dial, she said, there was a little ship which at first she hadn't noticed, a horrid ship that rocked up and down every time the clock ticked. It made her ill just to look at it. And she didn't have the money, and the man said he'd have to send it this evening, and what would Father say?

She came down to dinner, and left half-way through. Couldn't stand it. But an hour or two later, when the door-bell rang, she bravely went to tell Father.

She could hardly believe it, but she found that luck was with her, for once. If the clock had come earlier, there might have been a major catastrophe, but Father was in a good mood and he had had a good dinner. And though he never admitted it or spoke of it, he had a weakness for clocks. There were clocks all over the house, which he would allow no one to wind but himself. Every Sunday between break-fast and church he made the rounds, setting them at the right time by his infallible watch, regulating their speed, and telling us about every clock's little idiosyncrasies. When he happened to be coming downstairs on the hour, he cocked his ear, watch in hand, to listen to as many of them as he could, in the hope that they would all strike at once. He would reprove the impulsive pink clock in the spare room for striking too soon, and the big solemn clock in the dining-room for being a minute too late.

So when Mother led him out in the hall to confess to him and show him what she had bought, and he saw it was a clock, he fell in love with it, and made almost no fuss at all.

The let-down was too much for Mother. She tottered off to her room without another word and went straight to bed, leaving Father and the auctioneer's man setting up the new clock alongside the hatrack. Father was especially fascinated by the hard-rocking ship.

THE PRINCE

By Ruth McKenney

ONE OF my earliest beaux was a Georgian prince who came from the same general neighborhood as the Mdivanis. He was, however, a simple fellow with annoying habits. His first name was Gregory. He was studying dairy science at Ohio State University when I met him, and if his stock of stolen diamonds is holding out, he probably still is. He was simply fascinated by dairy science and talked about it constantly. In fact, we parted over that issue.

One night I said firmly, "Say, listen, if you can't talk about anything but cows, you may as well go home."

He went, looking hurt. He was a big eater, too, and my grandmother used to complain bitterly. He dropped in for dinner so often we took to ordering three chops instead of two as a regular practice. He used to demolish a whole batch of butter cookies in one evening, carrying on a steady flow of small talk about breeding cows, in between bites.

He was handsome enough, if you like that dark, beady type. Personally, one Georgian prince was enough for me. Every time I now see a pair of what Grandmother used, scornfully, to call "snake" eyes, I shudder. I met Gregory at an Engineers' Frolic. He never explained what he, an earnest dairy-science student, was doing at an engineers' dance, but at the time I didn't ask. I foolishly thought he was quite a catch—handsome, and with a title, too, even if slightly shopworn. After all, Georgian princes were distinctly *comme il faut* in 1930, and even Eileen, the belle of the Midwest, hadn't been able to gather in, during her heart-smashing career, so much as a Belgian count.

Gregory, however, was disappointing from the first. He didn't talk much about Georgia, for instance; he said the subject bored him. He settled down on the sofa, that first evening he called, and began firmly, "Since I have been a leetle boy, people have been asking me about how I escape, how I get to this country, what happen to Papa, and all the rest of it. Well, I tell you wance and then we shut oop about the subject, yes?"

I said, "Yes," slightly dazed, and he recited rapidly, in a bored tone, the more salient points in his explosive career. He had been a lad of tender years, ten or eleven, when the revolution broke out. For many years his canny father had been expecting the worst. All the family wealth was in loose diamonds, except for a few scattered sheep. But alas for Papa and Gregory when they went to look for the diamonds! It turned out the Georgian equivalent of the butler had stolen them all. This left the fledgling prince and his father and other relatives, very numerous, in something of a hole. But Father was a quick thinker. He went over to the next castle and stole the neighbors' supply of diamonds.

"All it ees fair," Gregory remarked at this point in his recital, "in luff and war." This gave me food for reflection. If Gregory conducted his love affairs in the same spirit in which his family conducted wars, obviously he was a man who would bear close watching.

As it turned out, however, the neighbors didn't need their diamonds, anyway. They were killed, the whole lot of them.

"They were very what you call mean to the poor people," Gregory said simply, "so they all get killed."

Gregory paused at this point in his recital, perhaps for effect, perhaps for a moment's painful reflection. Then he said, "All our family got killed too, except me. I hide in a big drawer."

I said "My!"

He replied, "Yes, our family was also mean to what you call the poor people. They kick tham around, no?"

I said I supposed he was pretty down on the Communists.

"I was," he agreed, nodding, "but I am not any more, cause they have got the only gud onderstanding of dairy science of any government in the whole wurld, yes. They have got posi-tive *mir*-acles of dairy farms. Such people that onderstand dairy science, they cannot be wrong, no? But just the same," Gregory added, chuckling, "if I should ever meet any of those paysants who murdered my papa, I would keel them right off. But I stay out of their way, no?" He laughed uproariously, slapping his knee.

"So then what happened to you?" I said, bringing him back to his story.

"Oh," he said, the interest dying out of his heavy voice, "oh, then I escape, with the diamonds, and, believe me, it was pretty hard work for a leetle fellow like I was. But soon I met some fellow from my home town. He was also ronning away, and I went with him, only he stole all my diamonds— he was a no-good, believe me."

"How did you live?" I cried in anxiety.

"I stole tham back, and all of his, too," Gregory said simply.

Finders keepers was a game with prestige in Georgia, I gathered. Poor little Gregory had a bad time escaping from his native land. He hid in a camel's pack, stowed away on a

Soviet vessel, rode across the Arabian desert, was captured by the Turkish equivalent of the juvenile court, and spent two years in a Moslem orphanage. Finally he ended up, triumphant, in Berlin, still with most of his diamonds.

"Although I was only feevteen then," Gregory said sadly, "already I was a man of the wurld, so much it had happened to me."

I understood, I said. "So then I traveled," Gregory continued. "I go to Eetaly, to Paris, to London, to Holland. I see much, but I don' like. I get older, but nawthing suit me, nawthing please me."

It was a pathetic picture, a poor little homesick Georgian princeling, living on the neighbors' diamonds, traveling from one world capital to another, always bored, always sad. It brought a tear to my sympathetic eye.

"Weemin!" Gregory intoned in his gutteral bass. "Wine! Sung! All it ees vanity."

I sighed and he sighed.

"I was twenty-two," Gregory said, finally, coming to what he thought was the climax of his story, "when I discover dairy science. Since then I have been happy, almost."

I was so shocked by this dairy-science revelation that it took me some time to ask him, "Almost?"

"Two things," Gregory said promptly, "keep me from being happy. One, I cannot go to the Soviet Union to see the dairy farms, the best in the whole wurld; and two, I have not got a wife."

At this point he looked firmly at me with what I considered an evil gleam in those black eyes of his. There was something fearfully direct about Gregory; it gave you quite a turn. "That's tough about Russia," I said hastily. "What's the matter? Won't they let you in?"

"I have not ask," he said, "but of course they could not.

I might see some of those paysants who cut up my papa, and then I would have to keel tham."

"Russia is a big country," I said helpfully. "Besides, how would they know you were going to kill anybody?"

"I would have to tell tham," Gregory said sorrowfully.

He paused, thinking, no doubt, of the horrid scene: a famous dairy scientist, full of Communist honors, caught red-handed in the murder of a fellow-worker, and a political murder, at that.

"Yess," he said heavily, "if I keel tham, it would set back dairy science in the Soviet Union tan years, easy."

His remark fell into a nervous silence.

"Well," Gregory added, after several minutes had ticked by uncomfortably, "well, wife."

I looked up at him, startled. It was a mistake. "Now how about the sweedhard, the wife?" he cried, with heavy humor.

I had some difficulty getting rid of Gregory that first night he called, and if I had had any sense I would never again have let him in the quiet apartment my grandmother and I occupied together. But there was a touch, to put it mildly, of the exotic about Gregory, and I was nineteen. Exotics appealed to me then. They did not, however, appeal to my grandmother, especially Gregory.

"You remide me," Gregory said to her one night, "of an old Armenian lady I knew wance, log ago."

"Indeed?" said my grandmother, who looks extremely young for her age, and who has her hair and nails done every week.

"Yes," Gregory said, a merry twinkle in his eye. "The Turks, they smawthered her to death. Like this." He rose, seized a soft pillow, and energetically ground it into the carpet with his knee.

My grandmother paled, but her perfect manners did not fail her. "How interesting," she murmured. It was a mistake, a bad one.

"You thank so?" Gregory chuckled, pleased. "That's nawthing. You should see what they do to the young ones." He took out a knife, whipped it open, and was apparently prepared to slice up the sofa pillow when my grandmother, gulping hard, diverted his interest.

From the first night on, Gregory kept pressing me on the question of the wife, and I kept making coy excuses until one night, in desperation, I told him a fearful lie. "Alas," I said earnestly, "I am already engaged."

"Yes?" Gregory asked, his beady black eyes fixed firmly on my face. So, having told one whopper, I went on, as is my unhappy custom, and told several more. Gregory sat in what I thought was saddened silence while I recited a pathetic tale of woe. My father was making me marry this youth, in whom I had only the slightest interest, so that Eileen could have a college education.

When I finished this sorry story, Gregory rose energetically. "It ees easy," he said, shrugging his shoulders. "I keel him, yes?"

"I should say not," I said hastily, stunned by this unusual turn of affairs. "My!"

Gregory ignored my protests. He was an overbearing type, anyway. "You tell me his name, his address," he said gruffly, "and after this term final examination, and after Elizabeth she is calved, I keel him."

I was stung. To think he would put Elizabeth, his experimental Jersey, ahead of killing his rival! Chivalry, I felt, was dead, even among Georgian princes. Elizabeth's time was some weeks off, however, and I felt fairly easy in my mind.

Unfortunately, my tranquillity was soon shattered, because, shortly after, Robbin showed up. Robbin played a brief but dramatic role in my relations with Gregory, and I fear that I will have to explain him, disagreeable as that task is. Even now, looking back on Robbin, I can't think why I ever liked him, even for a moment. Youth does not explain everything.

Robbin was pale, blond, and pimply. He was a graduate of Georgia Tech, and he never let you forget it for a moment. He was constantly singing a vile song that begins, "I'm a ramblin' wreck from Georgia Tech." Also, Robbin had written across the back of his very yellow raincoat—a garment he wore constantly, rain or no rain—the legend "Georgia Tech 27, Alabama 0." I'm not sure of the exact figures, but that was the general idea. Everywhere I went with Robbin, this sign printed on his back caused the most unpleasant kind of remarks from taxicab drivers, soda jerkers, and the like.

Robbin lived in Cleveland, and I had met him a few days before I left for Columbus to go back to college. Thus our romance was brief. I forgot all about him until the awful Saturday night when he appeared at our Columbus apartment, smiling toothily. It seems he wanted to surprise me. He certainly did. The moment I saw him, I thought of Gregory, my tiger prince, and the fearful lie I had told him. Gregory had a habit of just dropping in. Suppose he found Robbin sitting on the davenport with me?

Robbin had dinner with us that terrible night, and I couldn't eat, I was so panic-stricken. Grandmother, who was a model of tact, then announced she was going to the movies with the lady who lived downstairs, and she supposed we would be going out, later in the evening. Robbin all but clapped hands. Apparently this suited his plans perfectly.

"No," I said, my hand shaking on my coffee cup. "No, you stay home, Grandma. Don't you go anywhere. Please don't!" I felt that if anybody could stay Gregory's murderous hand, it would be Grandma.

Grandma blinked in surprise, but she stayed home. It turned out afterward that she had drawn the wrong conclusions. She thought I was afraid of Robbin, who was actually the most harmless of men, and she stayed firmly in the living room all evening, keeping a stern eye on the man she thought I thought was a beast.

Robbin was pretty dashed. He kept suggesting all through the early part of the evening that we should go dancing or walking or go to the movies. Grandmother, however, said firmly that I wasn't to put a foot outside the house *that* night.

The whole situation was so hopelessly confused I didn't think that even if I took Grandma out in the kitchen and explained everything to her, I could make it clear. So I just sat miserably on the sofa with Robbin and waited for the inevitable. About ten o'clock, Gregory came thumping up the stairs.

I opened the door. I smiled weakly. "Hello," I said faintly.

He stalked in, looking neither to the right nor left. "Such a day!" he said, breathing hard. "I can only stay a minute. I came to tell you that Elizabeth, she ees sick." With that he sank down dramatically on the sofa, right beside Robbin, who jumped slightly.

"This is Mr. Wilkins," I said, breathlessly. "Robbin, this is Prince Gregory."

"Prince, eh?" Robbin said brightly.

Gregory ignored the introduction. "She ees very sick. I think it ees the weather. She ees so delicad."

"That's too bad," my grandmother murmured politely.

"You feel bad, eh?" Gregory said, brightening up. "I also feel bad. It hurts me in the heart to see Elizabeth so sick like she ees." He turned to me, and said accusingly, "She ees in pain, but you don' care, eh?"

I said I did too care; I felt very sad about Elizabeth. Gregory turned to Robbin. "You care for cows?" he asked heavily.

"Sure," Robbin, who was a weakling and afraid to cross anybody, replied.

There was a pause. Nobody felt like starting a new and happier theme of conversation. Suddenly Gregory turned on Robbin. He looked him right in the eye. "Who are *you*?" he roared. My heart nearly stopped. "Ha!" he said, leaping to his feet. "You are *heem*!"

"I am *not*," Robbin said hastily, to be on the safe side, and added, "What's the big idea, anyway?"

"No, no," I shouted desperately, "he isn't! Really he isn't!" My grandmother and Robbin goggled.

"Yes," Gregory said with sinister emphasis, "yes, I can see who you are now." Robbin turned much paler than his usual pasty white. He shook his head in terrified denial, too frightened to speak. He certainly didn't make a very good showing in the whole affair.

My grandmother, however, rose to the occasion. "Gregory," she said calmly, although she thought she was addressing a madman, "don't you think you ought to stay with Elizabeth if she is so ill?"

"I am thinging of Elizabeth," Gregory said slowly. "I am trying to figure out if I got time to feex heem before I go back to Elizabeth."

I kept moaning, "He isn't the one, he isn't the one," but Gregory, as usual, paid no attention to me. He just stood there, a mighty figure of a man, thinking, while Robbin turned piteous eyes to me for an explanation of this awful situation.

"No," Gregory said finally, "I have not the time. I must go." He seized his hat, bowed, and went to the door. "I find you," he said to Robbin, who huddled, shaking with fear, in the sofa pillows, "lader on." We all heard him thumping down the stairs.

Robbin left Columbus on the milk train, absolutely unimpressed by my sincere explanations. He said, frankly, that he thought I was perfectly terrible for letting him in for an experience like that.

"You better look out," he said darkly, as he left. "I'm going to write a letter as soon as I get home and give it to my lawyer, in case anything happens to me. You'll be an accomplice, under the law."

That was just like Robbin, a worm of the first water, selfish to the last. Elizabeth recovered, unfortunately, and that was really why my Georgian prince and I parted. I felt that he thought more of Elizabeth than he did of me.

"Yes," Gregory said heavily, just before the end, "I guess I am wadded to my science."

It was a curious choice of bride, for a Georgian prince.

CHOCOLATE FOR THE WOODWORK

By Arthur Kober

THE DOORBELL rang, but no one in the Gross household made
the slightest move to answer it. It rang again, clearly and
demandingly.

"Nu?" yelled Mrs. Gross from the kitchen, where she was
washing the breakfast dishes. "So just because is here Sunday, is a vacation fa evvebody, ha? Listen the way it rings
the bell—like a regelleh fecktree fomm lomm clocks. So
open op the door, somebody!"

From the bathroom, Bella shouted, "What'sa matter
with evveybody arounn here? Are they deef or something?
Fa heaven's sakes, can'tcha hear the bell?"

The task of opening the door clearly devolved upon Pa
Gross. He angrily threw his newspaper to the floor and got
up from his rocker. "Evvey time a persin sits donn to ridd a
couple woids in the paper is alluva sumn a big busy here in
house. So who is here the soiving goil? Me! . . . Aw right
awready!" The last remark was addressed to the clamoring
bell. "You can't see I'm coming?"

The man Mr. Gross ushered into the dining room was a
study in sartorial splendor. His Panama hat, which he didn't
bother to remove, had a band resplendent in many colors.
The Palm Beach suit he wore contrasted vividly with his
blue shirt, which, together with a blue tie and a carefully
folded blue kerchief which peeped from his breast pocket,

gave an ensemble effect. Black-and-white sports shoes and purple socks with red vertical stripes completed a dazzling costume. For a moment, Pa stared in wide-eyed wonder at the magnificent stranger, then he sniffed. There was a pervasive odor about the visitor which he quickly identified as turpentine. This, then, must be the long-awaited painter whose magic was going to transform the dingy Gross apartment into a thing of beauty.

"Good munning, good munning!" Pa twinkled at the fashion plate who stood before him. "So you is the paintner the lendludd is sending, no?"

"No! The paintner is woiking fa me." There was implied rebuke in the man's tone. "I'm the *boss* paintner. Wait, I'll give you mine cott." He reached into his inside pocket, whipped out a stained wallet, and from one of its many folds extracted several cards. By this time Mrs. Gross and Bella were standing beside Pa, and the visitor solemnly presented each of them with a card.

The three Grosses studied the slips of pasteboard in their hands. A good portion of them was taken up by a design of an open can with the name "Eagle" on it. Above this was the phrase "Old Dutch Process" and below it the legend "Employ a Good Painter. Good Painters Use White Lead. White Lead Lasts." There was barely enough room left for the name, Philip Rudnick, and an address and telephone number.

While the Grosses examined his card, Mr. Rudnick's attention was devoted to their apartment. With his fingers he dug at a flaky wall, peeling huge hunks from it and leaving a white, gaping wound in a vast field of yellow. "Tchk, tchk, tchk!" Phillip Rudnick's oscillating head tacitly rebuked Mr. and Mrs. Gross. "How people can live in such a place! Lookit how is falling donn the wall in liddle pieces."

He continued scraping with his fingers. "Some place you got it here! Comes the Boarder Felt and right away you is gung to get a summints!"

"I begya podden!" Bella's voice was hard and chilly. "We happen not to be inarrested in what the Board of Health is gonna do to us. What we happen to be inarrested in is having this here apartment fixed up so that evvey individual or person who comes along won't stick in their two cents' worth of what's wrong with this place. What we wanna know is just what you intend to do regarding the fixing up of this here apartment."

Mr. Rudnick stared at Bella as if seeing her for the first time. Then, turning to Mr. Gross, he said, "The dutter?" Pa nodded. Mr. Rudnick scraped his purple chin with his nails and eyed Bella reflectively. "She is esking what is Rudnick gung to do with this apottment. Listen, lady." He clasped his hands behind his back and rocked on his heels. "You know hommany yirrs is Rudnick in the paintning business? Plenty! You know hommany apottments is Rudnick fixing op? Plenty, believe me!" His voice suddenly became conversational. "I want you should enswer me a question. You a woiking goil?"

"Uf cuss!" sang out Pa Gross.

"So what is your line?" Mr. Rudnick asked.

"I happen to be the privitt seckatary fa a very important pardy who is inclined along financial matters," said Bella.

"Aha, a seckatary! So how you would like if your boss say to you, 'How you gung to write the letter you putting donn by you in the shuthend book? You gung to put the paper in the machine with the left hend under the right hend? You gung to use by you the liddle pinkie undder the whole hend?' 'What's the diffrince?' you is gung to give the boss an enswer. 'Mine job is to write it fa you the lettis.

If you like mine job, so is O.K. If you don't like it, then you give me the seck. But how I'm doing the job, that's strickly mine business.'" He waved a finger at Bella. "So the same is with Rudnick. How I'm gung to fix by you the apottment, that's strickly mine business."

"He's positiffly got it right!" declared Pa Gross, placing a hand on the visitor's shoulder. "Mr. Rudnick is foist gung to do the paintning job, then we'll complain when he is finndished."

Mrs. Gross felt it her duty to come to her daughter's defense. "Say, what is here—Europe, maybe, a persin dassent tukk a couple woids? She says something, Bella, and right away is evveybody yelling on her 'Sharrop!'" She glowered at the two men. "Cossacks!"

Mr. Rudnick, busy blotting the back of his neck with his handkerchief, ignored this attack. "Oooh," he complained, "is very hot here in house. Look," he said, "why you so stingy with the winda opening when is here like a regelleh stove?" He walked to the window and raised it. He looked down at the street and then, wildly waving his fist, he cried out, "Hey, you little bestidds, kipp away from mine machine, you hear? In two seconds I'll come downstairs and I'll fix you good, you tramps, you!" He turned away from the window and scowled at the Grosses. "A fine neighborhood you got it here! Some foist-cless gengsters is gung to be the kits in the stritt. I'm leaving mine uttemobill donnstairs—mine machine is a Chevvy," he added parenthetically—"and right away they scretching op by me the machine, the no-good bummers! Where I am living, on the Concuss, is O.K. to leave mine machine a whole day on the stritt and will come no kits to scretch by me the car. But here in this neighborhood—" A shrug of his shoulders completed his comment.

"A lotta people I know," said Bella icily, "they ride with the subway, where they got no worries who scratches up the cars."

"Excuse me!" Mr. Rudnick's tone was laden with disdain. "Evveything I say is with her no good. Now is a sin to have a machine, ha? Today is a paint job in this neighborhood, temorreh is a paint job in that neighborhood, next day is a paint job maybe in the Heights. So the boss paintner shouldn't have a machine? Listen, you think I get maybe pleasure from mine Chevvy? Nah! Is expenses fa ges, is expenses fa tires, is all the time expenses. You know hommuch it custs me, mine expenses? Plenty! And that's with you a sin, ha?"

"Parm me," said Bella, somewhat chastened, "but I 1appen not to be criticizing whether you have a car or you don't have one. I happen to be criticizing that just because some little kids are playing arounn on the street and your car happens to be in the way, that is no excuse you should indulge in vulgarity or to criticize this neighborhood, which we happen to be living in at the present time."

Mr. Rudnick seemed about to say something sharp and cutting, but thought better of it. "Listen," he said, forcing a smile, "in mine house if mine dutter tukked so fresh to a guest, you know what I would give her? Plenty! But what can a persin speck from this neighborhood?" Before Bella could find a fitting rejoinder he had whipped out a notebook and pencil. "Nu, Rudnick is not here to make spitches. Rudnick is here to see with the paint job." He abandoned the Grosses to inspect the walls. "Paint with stipple finish the whole thing complete," he mumbled as he made notes. "Wash op the cilling, take away the crecks, fix it the loose plester, and don't fegget you should do kelsomine job. With the flurr—scrape, uf cuss, and you should finndish with two coats fomm shelleck." He headed toward the window and noticed the radiator in passing. "Aha, the radiatiss you should silver op. And with the windiss, take loose puddy away, new puddy put in." Mr. Rudnick continued making notes as he walked from room to room. The Gross family trailed after him, and when he ran his fingers along the woodwork all of them followed suit and nodded discerningly.

The procession returned to the dining room. "O.K.," said Mr. Rudnick, snapping his notebook shut. "Mine paintners will come temorreh to fix it by you the apottment. Will be the place brannew. Will be a pleasure to live here." Again his glance encompassed the room, and he seemed to shudder. "Not like is now."

"What about the matter from the color?" asked Bella. "We haven't decided yet what should be the color of the apartment."

"A question!" jeered the painter. "What should be the color? Chotruse, uf cuss! Ye know what is chotruse?"

"Green," Bella said.

Mr. Rudnick pretended he hadn't heard her. "Chotruse is grinn." This was addressed confidentially to Pa. "Go to the best homes. Go to the finest flets on the Concuss, and is oney one color—chotruse! Mine apottment, where I'm living, is strickly chotruse."

"Well, it so happens I got diffrint idears on the subjeck," said Bella. "It so happens that what we want in the line of color is cream walls—"

"Crimm walls!" bellowed Mr. Rudnick. "Is no more stylish crimm walls! You know where you find crimm walls? In the chipp apottments where is living very common pipple. Feh! But go to the Concuss, go even to the Heights, and you know hommany places is chotruse? Plenty!"

"See here," said Bella, "it's our house. Do you mind

leaving us fix it the way we like, inasmuch as we are the folks living here and it so happens you are not?"

Mr. Rudnick eyed her steadily for several seconds. He then turned to Mr. Gross and, nodding in Bella's direction, said, "The boss, ha?"

The old man felt obliged to define his daughter's authority. "She's a single goil. When we fix the apottment like she says, maybe will come here some nice boyess—"

"Fa heaven's sakes, Pa!" Bella screamed. "What's his business that I'm single? Must you tell the whole world who comes here about your own daughter's condition?"

"Dope!" Mrs. Gross's shrill voice was also raised in protest. "Why you don't tell him hommuch money we not yet paying the butcher? Why you don't tell him fomm your gold watch in punnshop? Go on, tell your friend evveything fomm the femily, Mr. Tettletale!"

"Sha, sha, sha!" Mr. Rudnick's features now broke into a disarming smile. "O.K., so now I know how is. So will Rudnick make fa you crimm walls just like the dutter wants it. Now is evveybody serrisfied, and I'm seeing you in the munning."

He started for the hallway, but Bella's next question arrested him. "What about the woodwork?" she asked. "I want it should be a chawklit color."

"Ha?" Mr. Rudnick's baffled expression indicated he wasn't sure he had heard her correctly.

"I want the color should have two tones," explained Bella. "I want cream fa the walls and chawklit fa the woodwork."

Mr. Rudnick lifted his Panama hat and daintily scraped his scalp with his little finger. "Chucklit!" he murmured. Replacing his hat, he slowly and deliberately took out his notebook, scribbled something in it and then looked up.

"Excuse me," he said. "What kine chucklit you would like fa the woodwoik—Nestle's udder Hoishey's?"

"See here," said Bella, "I take that remark fomm whence it comes."

"Chucklit!" Mr. Rudnick replaced his book, tapped the crown of his gay Panama with his hand, and stalked to the door. As he was about to leave the apartment, he stopped, stared reflectively into space, and then turned around. "Listen, lady," he shouted at Bella, "Rudnick is gung to fix the place just like you say—two tunns, crimm and chucklit! And listen. If you not finding a nice boy after Rudnick is fixing the apottment, you know what you should put in the chucklit woodwoik? Ammints! You hear me—ammints!"

Bella Gross reached into her arsenal of invective for a particularly annihilating reply, but she was too late. Mr. Rudnick was out of the apartment, leaving behind the ringing echo of his voice shouting "Ammints!"

THE TERRIBLE VENGEANCE OF
H*Y*M*A*N K*A*P*L*A*N

By Leonard Q. Ross

Mr. Parkhill wondered whether he had not been a little rash in taking up Idioms with the beginners' grade. Idioms were, of course, of primary importance to those who sought an understanding of English: they were of the very essence of the language. At the last session of the class, Mr. Parkhill had spent a careful hour in explaining what idioms were, how they grew, how they took on meaning. He had illustrated his lecture with many examples, drawn from "English for Beginners." He had answered questions. And for homework, he had assigned what seemed a simple enough exercise: three short sentences, using an idiom in each sentence. But now Mr. Parkhill realized that he had been too optimistic. The assignment was not proving a success. It was, in truth, incredible.

Mr. Marcus, for example, had used the expression: "It will cost you free." That, to Mr. Marcus, was an idiom. Mrs. Tomasic had submitted only one sentence, as much as confessing that her imagination quailed before the magnitude of the assignment. The sentence was "Honestly is the best policy." Mr. Jacob Rubin was groping in the right direction, at least; he seemed to suspect what an idiom *was*; and yet, for one of his efforts, he had given: "By twelve a.m. the job will be as good as down."

And now, a full half-hour before the end of the period, it was time for the contribution of Mr. Hyman Kaplan. There they were, on the board: three sentences—under a heading which was like an illuminated marquee:

3 SENT. (& ID.)

by

H * Y * M * A * N K * A * P * L * A * N

(Mr. Parkhill had learned that trying to dissuade Mr. Kaplan from printing his name in all its starry splendor, on the slightest provocation, was just a waste of time.)

"Mr. Kaplan, read your sentences, please," said Mr. Park-hill briskly.

The briskness was quite intentional; it buttressed Mr. Parkhill's morale. The class had snickered several times while reading the sentences which Mr. Kaplan had written on the blackboard; now, with Mr. Kaplan to read them, there was no telling to what heights their emotions might ascend.

Mr. Kaplan rose, his smile that of an angel's in flight. "Ladies an' gantleman an' Mr. Pockheel. Tree santences I vas wridink on de board, mit idyoms. An' mine idea vas dat—"

"Please *read* the sentences," Mr. Parkhill broke in. Mr. Kaplan was congenitally incapable of resisting the urge to orate.

"I back you podden. De foist santence . . ." Mr. Kaplan read it. He read it distinctly, and with pride.

1. He's nots.

Mr. Parkhill took a long, deep breath. "That's *not* an idiom, Mr. Kaplan. That's—er—*slang*. No one who uses

English correctly, with taste, would ever use an expression like 'He's—er—nuts.' "

Dismay crept into Mr. Kaplan's face and wrestled with the great smile. "Is *not* a good axpression, 'He's nots'?" he asked, with a certain hurt. It was apparent that Mr. Kaplan had put his heart and soul into "He's nots."

"No, Mr. Kaplan. It's *very* bad."

Mrs. Moskowitz, large, serene, behemothian, shot Mr. Kaplan a pitying glance. "He's nots!" she crowed. It wasn't clear whether Mrs. Moskowitz was merely repeating Mr. Kaplan's words or was indulging in a little commentary of her own.

"But so many pipple are using dese voids," Mr. Kaplan protested, shooting Mrs. Moskowitz an injured look. "Honist, avery place I'm goink I hear, 'He's nots!' "

Mr. Parkhill shook his head, adamant in the face of the *vox populi*. "It doesn't matter how many people say it, Mr. Kaplan. It's an incorrect phrase. It has no place in good English. Besides, you spelled the word—er—'nuts' wrong. It's 'n-*u*-t-s.' "

Mr. Parkhill printed "N-U-T-S" on the board. He explained what "nut" really meant, distinguishing it from "not" with care. With much feeling, he drove home the point that "He's nuts" was outlawed by the canons of good usage. And Mr. Kaplan bowed to the hegemony of the purists. He seemed a little saddened. Something in Mr. Kaplan died with the death of "He's nots."

"Mine sacond santence." The second sentence was, if anything, more astonishing than the first.

2. Get the pearls. By hook or cook!

" 'By hook or cook,' " Mr. Parkhill repeated, very softly. " 'By hook or cook' . . . Mr. Kaplan, I'm afraid you've made another serious mistake."

This was too much for Mr. Kaplan to believe. "*Also* tarrible?" he asked, his voice charged with pain. "I tought dis vould be a real high-cless idyom."

Mr. Parkhill shook his head. "You seem to have an idea of what an idiom is, in this sentence." (Mr. Kaplan shot Mrs. Moskowitz a triumphant smile.) "But you've ruined the idea by your spelling." (Mr. Kaplan's smile scurried into limbo.) "You have confused two entirely different words. What's wrong with Mr. Kaplan's sentence—anyone?"

The beginners' grade glared at Mr. Kaplan's non-Spencerian hand.

Mr. Sam Pinsky answered first. "Should be 'by hook *and* cook!'"

"No!" Mr. Parkhill exclaimed severely. "That would only make it worse."

"I think it should better be, 'By hook or *crook*,'" suggested Miss Mitnick.

"Exactly! '*Crook*,' not 'cook,' Mr. Kaplan."

Miss Mitnick lowered her eyes and smiled modestly. This had a depressing effect on Mr. Kaplan.

"I tought dat 'crook' is like a boiglar, a robber, a chitter," he objected.

"It does mean that," said Mr. Parkhill. "But the phrase 'by hook or by crook' is something altogether different. It refers to—"

Mr. Kaplan was wrapped in gloom. To be both scorned by Mrs. Moskowitz, whom he regarded with condescension, and bested by Miss Mitnick—these were blows which a man of Mr. Kaplan's mettle did not take lightly. Mr. Kaplan sighed (it was the sigh of those who have seen justice fail), and searched for his gods.

"Your third sentence, please."

Mr. Kaplan seemed a little shorter, a little more rotund,

a little less bland and euphoric than usual. The disaster of his sentences had left its mark on Mr. Kaplan.

"I s'pose," he said wistfully, "dat mine toid santence vill be awful also."

It was a touching admission. Mr. Parkhill felt sorry for Mr. Kaplan. He felt worse when Mr. Kaplan read the third sentence.

3. Hang yourself in reseption hall, please.

There was a burst of laughter from Mr. Bloom, followed by peals of hilarity from Messrs. Rabinowitz and Weinstein, and reinforced by an unmaidenly guffaw from Mrs. Moskowitz. Miss Mitnick, a creature of more delicate habits, smiled shyly. Miss Kowalski placed her hands over her eyes and shook.

" 'Heng—your-salf—in—re-sap-tion—hall—plizz!' " Mr. Kaplan repeated stubbornly, clinging to the words with the love of a father for his own flesh and blood.

Mr. Parkhill waited for order to filter back into the noisy classroom. "Mr. Kaplan, you have made a rather amusing error." He said it as gently as he could. "If you will merely read the sentence carefully, and pay attention to the word-order—especially to the object of 'hang'—I'm sure you will see why the sentence struck the class as being —er—funny."

Mr. Kaplan nodded dutifully and read the sentence again, aloud. " 'Heng—your-salf—in—re-saption—hall—plizz!' " He pursed his lips, wrinkled his brow, closed one eye wisely, and stared at the ceiling. This exhibition of concentration completed to his satisfaction, he whispered the sentence to himself, all over again. Everyone waited.

"Aha!" It was Mr. Kaplan's first "Aha!" of the evening, and it rang with his old courage. "I got him!" This was

more like the real Hyman Kaplan, valiant, audacious.
"Ufcawss! Should be *kepital ladders* on 'resaption hall'!
Tsimple!"

The Mitnick-Bloom-Moskowitz *entente* was swept to
new peaks of rapture. This was a rare opportunity· at last
Mr. Kaplan seemed to have lost his magic talent for emerg-
ing triumphant from any predicament, however ominous.
Someone cried, "*Goombye*, Mr. Keplen!" A voice said,
"Oi! I'll die!"—and Mrs. Moskowitz retorted: "Yas! By
henging!"

Mr. Kaplan smiled bravely: it was heart-rending. Mr
Parkhill rapped on the desk with a pointer.

"No, Mr. Kaplan," he said kindly. " 'reception hall' is not
a proper noun, so it doesn't require capital letters. 'Reception,' by the way, is spelled 'r-e-c-e.' No, it's the meaning
of your sentence that's at fault. 'Hang *yourself* in the reception hall,' Mr. Kaplan? You don't say *that* to your guests,
do you?"

Apparently Mr. Kaplan did. "I'm tryink to make mine
gasts fillink at home."

Mr. Bloom's mocking laugh boomed across the room.
"Kaplan means 'Hang your *things* in reception hall!' "
The startled look which leaped into Mr. Kaplan's eyes
showed that Norman Bloom had hit upon the very word
which he had meant to use. "But 'hang yoursalf'? Kaplan
is som host!"

The gaiety was unconfined.

Suddenly a sedulous look shot into Mr. Kaplan's eyes.
He smiled. He rested his gaze first on Mrs. Moskowitz,
then on Miss Mitnick, and then—his eyes dancing with
meaning—on Norman Bloom. The noises vanished into
an expectant silence.

"Maybe isn't 'Heng your*salf* in resaption hall' *altogad-*

der a mistake," Mr. Kaplan murmured dreamily. "If *som* pipple came to mine house dat vould maybe be *exactel* vat I should say."

With ten minutes left after the exercise on idioms was completed, Mr. Parkhill put the class through a vigorous written spelling drill. (Spelling drills served admirably as "fillers.") He noticed that Mr. Kaplan did not seem to be participating in the exercise with his customary enthusiasm. Mr. Kaplan might just as well have been in a telephone booth: he was scratching little patterns, aimlessly, on a page torn out of his notebook.

"Restaurant," Mr. Parkhill called.

Mr. Kaplan seemed to have retired to some reverie of thought. The shame of those three sentences burned in Mr. Kaplan's soul.

"Carpenter."

Mr. Kaplan smiled, of a sudden, and began writing. His smile was lofty, supernal, with the quality of a private pleasure in some precious joke. Mr. Parkhill announced the next word as if it were a reprimand. "Confess!"

The final bell rang. The students handed in their papers and the room became a jumble of "Goodnights." Mr. Kaplan's farewell was almost light-hearted.

Mr. Parkhill took his attendance report to Miss Schnepfe, in the Principal's office, and started home. On the subway train he started to correct the spelling exercises. (Mr. Parkhill had a remarkable capacity for concentration.) Miss Mitnick had done very well, as usual. Mr. Bloom had managed to get an 80, his average mark. Mr. Scymzak had misspelled only six out of fifteen words—a splendid performance for Mr. Scymzak. Mrs. Moskowitz was still confusing English with some other, unrevealed language.

Mr. Parkhill frowned when he saw that the next paper was blank. Some student had made a mistake, handing in an empty page instead of his spelling drill. Mr. Parkhill turned the page over, to see if there was some mark of identification. He beheld a bizarre conglomeration of words, designs, figures, and strange drawings. There was an unfinished ear and a distinct four of spades. All these were executed in crayons of a gaudy variety.

Mr. Parkhill wrote a sentence on the page, "Mr. Kaplan: Please submit your spelling drill next time!" He was about to pass on to the next paper when something caught his eye. The scribbled words that were almost lost in the hieroglyphics seemed to *say* something. The writing appeared to be—it was!—*poetry*. Mr. Parkhill adjusted his glasses and read what some unknown Muse, in secret visitation, had whispered to Hyman Kaplan.

> Critsising Mitnick
> Is a picnick.
>
> Bloom, Bloom,
> Go out the room!
>
> Mrs. Moskowitz.
> By her it doesnt fits
> A dress—Size 44.

It was a terrible vengeance which Mr. Kaplan, mighty even in defeat, had wreaked upon those who had tried to cast dishonor on his name.

HAND IN NUB

By St. Clair McKelway

Mr. Mark Hunt, editor and publisher of the monthly digest magazine *Distillate, the Busy Man's Abridgement*, was looking out of his office window, thinking. When he was not at his desk, reading and shortening, if possible, the digests of articles, stories, novels, plays, biographies, poems, and other literary works which his staff has prepared for publication in *Distillate*, Mr. Hunt liked to look out of his window and think. He was a short, compact man (as, indeed, were all the members of *Distillate's* editorial staff) and by bending his knees a little, resting his elbows on the broad window sill, and putting his chin in his hands, he could make himself quite comfortable in this position.

The offices of *Distillate* were in the centre of a lovely Connecticut village formerly called Little Falls and now officially named Nub. With some of the profits of *Distillate's* first ten years, Mr. Hunt had bought the village outright and had made it over. He had had all the houses facing the old, elm-lined green torn down and had erected there the massive offices of *Distillate*, with rolling lawns and gardens all round. The *Distillate* employees, from the associate editors down to the printers, lived in handsome though somewhat constricted, semi-detached houses in the outlying sections of Nub. They never had to leave Nub.

They went to short Nub movies, played miniature golf
on the Nub course in summer, and went skiing on Nub
hillocks in winter; they married Nub girls, who had small,
neat babies in the Nub Foundation Hospital. It was a
happy community, dedicated to the single purpose of literary emasculation, and when Mr. Hunt was at his office
window, looking down on Nub, he not infrequently had
an inspiration. More than once, in just this attitude at the
window, he had thought of some celebrated work which
had not been cut down but could be. This morning he had
thought of one: the Holy Bible.

He had not been so stimulated by one of his ideas since
he had, two years back, suddenly realized that the works
of both Dostoevski and Tolstoy still existed in their original,
bulky forms—that neither author had ever been digested.
What a hit BROTHERS had been with all that muddled
introspection removed, all those tiresome conversations,
and how enthusiastic had been the reception of the short
short which he had called simply ANNA! On the whole,
he often told himself, he had got more real satisfaction out
of dealing with the Russians than he had on that unfor-
gettable day when he had seen, in a flash, exactly how to
bring Poe's RAVEN down to a quatrain.

And now the Bible. He would put Neff in charge of the
New Testament, Kapp in charge of the Old, he decided.
With, of course, some special work from Mott on the
Psalms. The whole thing could easily come down to about
fifty thousand words, perhaps forty thousand. It could be
presented in three installments as a supplement to the
regular monthly *Distillate*. To begin in the Christmas number. Mr. Hunt left his window, went to his desk, and rang
for his secretary, Miss Babb. "Send to Nub Hotel for copy,

Gideon Bible," he said to her crisply. "Required for conference."

When the associate editors of *Distillate*—Neff, Kapp, Mott, and three others named Cook, Boon, and Gross—came into Mr. Hunt's office a few minutes later for the daily editorial conference, Mr. Hunt was back at his window. They took their chairs around the conference table, and looked at one another with little smiles of eagerness and suspense, for they knew that when Mr. Hunt was standing with his back to them that way at the commencement of an editorial conference it invariably meant that he had an idea for them. Mr. Hunt turned around, left the window, and walked to his chair at the head of the table. "Morning, Neff, Kapp, Mott, Cook, Boon, Gross," he said, and sat down. The associate editors bowed and took their chairs. Miss Babb brought in the Bible and placed it in front of Mr. Hunt.

Mr. Hunt picked it up, turned it over in his hands, put it back on the table, and looked around at his associate editors. His expression was portentous. Instantly the associate editors grabbed pencils and stared tensely at the note pads in front of them, ready to set down their reactions to the chief's new idea.

"Have great thought," said Mr. Hunt solemnly. "The Bible. Propose we digest the Bi——"

Mr. Hunt did not finish, for something had slapped him sharply on the top of his head. The associate editors, who had distinctly heard the sound of a slap, looked up in astonishment.

Mr. Hunt was annoyed, then puzzled. He had certainly felt a slap, yet the idea that one of his own associate editors had reached over and slapped him on the head was absurd. He had been looking at them, moreover, and would have seen any such movement with his own two eyes. Miss Babb had left the room after handing him the Bible.

Mr. Hunt decided to ignore the matter.

"As was saying," he said. "Propose digest the Bi——"

Again something slapped him on the top of his head, rather more sharply this time.

Mr. Hunt looked at his associate editors and they looked at him. Then Kapp rapped his pencil on the table, which meant that he wished to speak, and Mr. Hunt nodded at him.

"Was watching that time," said Kapp. "Saw hand. Slapped you on head. Clearly saw, heard."

"Just hand or was also arm?" asked Mr. Hunt.

Mott rapped with his pencil and Mr. Hunt nodded at him.

"Just hand," said Mott. "No arm."

Gross now rapped with his pencil and Mr. Hunt nodded at him.

"I also," said Gross. "One large hand. Muscular, executive-type hand."

"Think hand of God?" asked Mr. Hunt. He pointed his finger at the circle of associate editors and rotated it, signifying that the discussion was now open and that any or all might answer.

"Think so," said Cook.

The others bobbed their heads up and down in agreement.

"Too bad," said Mr. Hunt. "Can't proceed, obviously. Must defer, perhaps abandon, idea. Conference adjourned."

Alone, Mr. Hunt walked over to his window. His mood was one of passionate exasperation, and he kicked the wall under the window twice with his small right foot. He started to take his familiar position, leaning on the window

sill, but drew back suddenly and walked to his desk and
sat down. That hand. He picked up a pencil and a pile of
digested literary creations and started to work on them
furiously, cutting and condensing. He felt the hand again
then, not slapping him but patting him reassuringly on
the shoulder. He shook it off irritably and went on with
what he was doing.

DOWN WITH THE RESTORATION!

By S. J. PERELMAN

DOES ANYBODY here mind if I make a prediction? I haven't made a prediction since the opening night of *The Women* some years ago, when I rose at the end of the third act and announced to my escort, a Miss Chicken-Licken, "The public will never take this to its bosom." Since the public has practically worn its bosom to a nubbin niggling up to *The Women*, I feel that my predictions may be a straw to show the direction the wind is blowing away from. I may very well open up a cave and do business as a sort of Cumaean Sibyl in reverse. You can't tell me people would rather climb up that Aventine Hill and have a man mess around with the entrails of a lot of sacred chickens when they can come down into my nice cool cave and get a good hygienic prediction for a few cents. So just to stimulate trade and start the ball rolling, here goes my first prediction: One of these days two young people are going to stumble across a ruined farmhouse and leave it alone. . . . Well, what are you sitting there gaping at? You heard what I said. That's my prediction.

Honest Injun, I hate to sound crotchety, and the last thing in the world I want to do is throw the editors of all those home-making magazines like *Nook and Garden* and *The American Home-Owner* into an uproar, but the plain fact is that I've got a bellyful. For over two years now, every time I start leafing through one of those excellent periodicals, I fall afoul of another article about a couple of young people who stumble across a ruined farmhouse and remodel it on what is inelegantly termed spit and coupons. Or maybe it's the same article. I couldn't be reading the same issue over and over, could I?

All these remodelling articles are written by the remodellers themselves and never by the ruined farmer or the man who didn't get paid for the plastering, which accounts for their rather smug tone. They invariably follow the same pattern. A young couple named Mibs and Evan (and if you checked up, I'll bet they were never married at *all*!) have decided to return to the land. I see Mibs as one of those girls on the short side, with stocky legs, a low-slung posterior, and an untidy bun of straw-colored hair continually unwinding on the nape of her neck. Before anyone ever heard of Salzburg, she wore a high-bodiced dress with full skirts, a sort of horrid super-dirndl with home-cooked hems that have a tendency to hang down in back. She is usually engaged in reading a book written by two unfrocked chemists which tells women how to make their own cold cream by mixing a little potash with a dram of glycerine and a few cloves. Evan is a full-haunched young man in a fuzzy woollen suit (I don't suppose there's any such thing as a fuzzy cotton suit, but you know what I mean) who is forever rubbing a briar pipe along his nose to show you the beauty of the grain. He smokes his own mixture of perique, Latakia, and Imperial Cube Cut, for the very good reason that nobody else will smoke it, and he has probably read more of Arthur Machen than any man alive.

Well, as I say, your average remodelling yarn begins with Mibs and Evan stumbling across the most adorable ruin of an eighteenth-century farmhouse. It doesn't *have* to be a farmhouse; it can be a gristmill, or a tobacco barn, or a Mennonite schoolhouse. It can even be an early Colonial hen house, with delightful hand-hewn beams and perfectly sweet old tar paper scaling off the sides. Apparently nobody previous to Mibs and Evan has realized its possibilities, but Evan takes one look at it and says in a guarded tone, "Two hundred dollars would restore that beautifully if you didn't go crazy putting in a lot of bathrooms you didn't need." "Oh, Evan!" breathes Mibs, her eyes shining above her adenoids and her brain reeling with visions of Cape Cod spatter floors. "Dare we . . . ?" That night, at dinner in the Jumble Shop, they put their heads together—Evan removes the pipe from alongside his nose, of course—and decide to jump at the chance. It involves giving up that trip to Europe, a choice the characters in these stories always have to make, but Mibs has always dreamed of a sunny garden filled with old-fashioned flowers of the type her mother used to read about in Max Schling's catalogue. So they bravely draw two hundred dollars out of their little hoard, leaving a hundred in case they ever want to take a really long trip to some place like Bali, and lay it on the line.

After considerable excitement, in which everybody searches the title like mad and Mibs discovers the quaintest old parchment deed describing their land in terms of rods, chains, and poods, they are ready to take the "Before" snapshots. Evan digs up one of the cameras used by Brady at the battle of Antietam, waits for a good cloudy day, and focuses across a mound of guano at the most ramshackle corner of the "manse," as Mibs calls it with irreverent mischief. The article generally carries several gray smudges captioned "Southwest corner of the house before work began," and you can't help wondering where those giant oaks came from in the "After" photographs. Maybe they sprang up from acorns dropped by the workmen while they were having lunch.

The first thing the high-hearted pair decide on is a new roof. This fortunately costs only eight dollars, as they use second-hand wattles and hire a twelve-year-old scab—all right, maybe he only mislaid his union card—to tack them on. The outside walls are a problem, but an amazing stroke of good fortune comes to their rescue. Opening a trap door they hadn't investigated, Mibs and Evan stumble across countless bundles of lovely old hand-split shingles which have been overlooked by previous tenants, like the hens. Two superb Adam fireplaces, hitherto concealed by some matchboarding, now make their appearance, in one of them a box of dusty but otherwise well-preserved pieces of Sandwich and Stiegel glass. "The attic!" shout Mibs and Evan simultaneously, suddenly remembering their resolution to look through it some rainy day, and sure enough, there they find a veritable treasure trove of pewter ware, cherry escritoires, Chippendale wing chairs, sawbuck tables, and Field beds, hidden away by survivors of the Deerfield massacre. "It just didn't seem *possible*," recalls Mibs candidly, up to her old trick of taking the words out of your mouth.

And now, suddenly, the place becomes a hive of activity. A salty old character named Lafe (who is really Paul Bunyan, no matter what *Nook and Garden* says) appears and does the work of ten men at the price of one. He pulls down trees with his bare hands, lays new floors, puts up partitions, installs electricity, diverts streams, forges the ironware, bakes porcelain sinks, and all but spins silk for the draperies. How this djinn ever escaped from his bottle, and where he is now, the article neglects to mention. The upshot is that in a little over two weeks, the last hooked rug—picked up by Mibs at an auction for ten cents after spirited bidding—is in place and the early Salem kettle is singing merrily on the hob. A fat orange tabby blinks before the fire and Evan, one arm around Mibs, is adding up a column of figures. "Think of it, lover," whispers Mibs with dancing eyes. "We did the whole thing for only *fifty-one dollars and eighteen cents!*" "Less than we'll get for that article in *The American Home-Owner*," murmurs Evan exultantly, reaming the cake from his pipe. "Tell me, does oo love its 'ittle—" . . . And now would you hate me if I stole out very quietly? I'm afraid there's going to be just a wee bit of baby talk.

KITCHEN BOUQUET

By S. J. Perelman

YESTERDAY morning I awoke from a deep dream of peace compounded of equal parts of allonal and Vat 69 to find that autumn was indeed here. The last leaf had fluttered off the sycamore and the last domestic of the summer solstice had packed her bindle and caught the milk train out of Trenton. Peace to her ashes, which I shall carry up henceforward from the cellar. Stay as sweet as you are, honey, and don't drive through any open drawbridges is my Christmas wish for Leota Claflin. And lest the National Labor Relations Board (just plain "Nat" to its friends, of whom I am one of the staunchest) summon me to the hustings for unfair employer tactics, I rise to offer in evidence as pretty a nosegay of houseworkers as ever fried a tenderloin steak. Needless to say, the characters and events depicted herein are purely imaginary, and I am a man who looks like Ronald Colman and dances like Fred Astaire.

The first reckless crocus of March was nosing up through the lawn as I sprang from the driver's seat, spread my cloak across a muddy spot, and obsequiously handed down Philomène Labruyère—colored, no laundry. Philomène was a dainty thing, built somewhat on the order of Lois De Fee, the lady bouncer. She had the rippling muscles of a panther, the stolidity of a water buffalo, and the lazy in-

424

solence of a shoe salesman. She stood seventy-five inches in her stocking feet, which I will take my Bible oath were prehensile. As she bent down to lift her suitcase, she picked up the car by mistake and had it halfway down the slope before I pointed out her mistake. She acknowledged the reproof with a glance of such sheer hatred that I knew at once I should have kept my lip buttoned. After all, perhaps the woman wanted my automobile in her bedroom for some purpose of her own.

"You—you can take it up with you if you want," I stammered, thinking to retrieve her esteem. "I've got plenty of others—I mean I've got plenty of nothing—I mean—" With my ears glowing, I attempted to conceal my *gaffe* by humming a few bars of "Summertime," but her cold, appraising glance told me that Philomène had me pegged.

"Whuh kine place *is* this?" she rumbled suspiciously. "You mus' be crazy."

"But aren't we all?" I reminded her with a charming smile. "*C'est la maladie du temps*—the sickness of the times —don't you think? *Fin-de-siècle* and lost generation, in a way. 'I should have been a pair of ragged claws scuttling across the floors of silent seas.' How well Eliot puts it! D'ye ever see any of the old *transition* crowd?" I skipped along doing my best to lighten her mood, carried her several hatboxes, and even proffered a reefer, but there was no doubt in either of our minds who had the upper hand.

That Philomène was a manic-depressive in the down-hill phase was, of course, instantly apparent to a boy of five. Several boys of five, who happened to be standing around and were by way of being students of psychopathology, stated their belief to me in just those words: "Manic-depressive, downhill phase." At the close of business every evening, Philomène retired to her room armed with a six-

teen-inch steak knife, doubtless to ward off an attack by
her Poltergeist. She then spent the best part of an hour bar-
ricading her door with dressers, armoires, and other heavy
furniture, preparatory to sleeping with the lights on. I say
"sleeping" utterly without conviction; she undoubtedly
molded lead statues of her employer and crooned to them
over a slow fire.

But if her behavior was erratic, there was no lack of consistency in Philomène's cuisine. Meat loaf and cold fried
chicken succeeded each other with the deadly precision of
tracer bullets. At last, when blood and sinew could stand
no more and I was about to dissolve the union, I suddenly
discovered that this female Paul Bunyan had grown to
womanhood under the bright skies of Martinique, and I
knew a moment of elation. I let it be bruited through the
servants' hall that I would look tolerantly on fried plantain,
yams, and succulent rice dishes. That afternoon the kitchen
was a hive of activity. The air was heavy with saffron, pi-
mento, and allspice. I heard snatches of West Indian
Calypsos, caught a glimpse of Philomène's head swathed
in a gay bandanna. With the care befitting a special occasion, I dressed negligently but with unimpeachable taste
in whites and cummerbund, mixed myself several excellent stengahs, and sauntered in to dinner for all the world
like an up-country tea planter. A few moments later,
Philomène entered with what might be called a smoking
salver except for the circumstance that it was stone cold.
On it lay the wing and undercarriage of an even colder
chicken, flanked by two segments of meat loaf.

After five minutes of reflection, during which, I am told,
my features closely resembled a Japanese print, I arose and,
throwing out my tiny chest, marched into the kitchen.
The malediction withered on my lips. Seated at the table,

my black hibiscus blossom was tucking in a meal consisting of *potage Parmentier avec croûtons,* a crisp *gigot, salade fatiguée,* and *pot de crème au chocolat.*

"You—thing," I said at length, and five minutes later Philomène was on her way back to St. Pierre.

Her successor was a chapfallen Australian cadaver who had reached his zenith as steward of a country club in Pompton Lakes and treated me and mine with the tired fatalism of a social worker. For some reason I never could fathom, unless it was that I occasionally wore a Tattersall vest, William persisted in regarding me as a racing man. He could recall every entry in the Cesarewitch Sweepstakes since 1899 and did, but faced with a pot roast, he assumed a wooden incomprehension that would have done credit to a Digger Indian. It was William's opinion, freely given, that cooked food was dead food and that I would triple my energy by living on fronds. He knew a hundred different ways of preparing bran, each more ghastly than the last. For an avowed vegetarian (or "raw-fooder," as he described himself), he spent his leisure in a puzzling enough fashion, polishing and whetting the superb collection of Swedish steel carving knives which was the one relic of his former magnificence.

William hadn't been with us long before I began to feel uneasy, but I attributed my disquiet to Edmund Pearson's admirable study of the Lizzie Borden case, which I was reading at the time. And then, on the sultry morning of August 4th—by an uncanny coincidence the forty-seventh anniversary of the Fall River holocaust—I came down to find awaiting me an exact duplicate of the breakfast which had been served on Second Street that fateful morning: warmed-over mutton soup, cold mutton, and bananas. I am not unduly superstitious, but there is no sense flying in

the face of history. I left the check and the usual reference
on William's bureau and hid in the woods until traintime.

The time had now come, I felt, for plain speaking. I inserted two and a half inches in the metropolitan press setting forth my special needs. I wanted something stout and
motherly, with floury hands and a hot apple pie cooling on
the window sill. What I got was an ancient Latvian beldam
named Ilyeana, who welcomed the idea of living in the
country with such alacrity I was convinced she must be a
fugitive from justice. Her cooking did nothing to contra-
dict the impression; three nights hand running she served
mulligan and coffee made in a tin and seemed strangely
familiar with the argot of hobo jungles. How near I was
to the bull's-eye was revealed a week later with the arrival
of a letter sent to Ilyeana by relatives in Canada. She ripped
open the envelope and a newspaper clipping fell to the
floor. I picked it up and was about to hand it to her when
I saw the sinister heading, 'Missing Man Believed Found."
The Mounties, idly dragging a lake near Moose Jaw,
Saskatchewan, had recovered some parcels which, laid
end to end, turned out to be the body of a man. "The victim's sister, whom the authorities would like to question,"
the account added, "is at present thought to be in Latvia."
Far from being in Latvia, the victim's sister was standing
at that exact moment peering over my shoulder in good old
Tinicum Township, Pennsylvania. I cleared my throat and
edged a little closer to the fire tongs.

"What do you make of this, Ilyeana?" I asked. I knew
damn well what she made of it, but you have to begin
somewhere.

"Ah, this happen every time I get good job," she said.
"Always pickin' on me. Well, I guess I go up there and
take a look at him. I know that head of hair anywhere."

At the station, Ilyeana bought a ticket to Savannah, which would seem a rather circuitous route to the Dominion, but nobody was surprised, least of all the passenger agent. What with people winging through to Martinique, Australia, and similar exotic climes, that little New Jersey depot could give cards and spades to Shepheard's Hotel in Cairo. And speaking of spades, could anybody put me on to one named Uncle Pompey, with a frizzy white poll and a deft hand for grits?

DENTAL OR MENTAL, I SAY IT'S SPINACH

By S. J. PERELMAN

———————

A FEW days ago, under the heading, MAN LEAPS OUT WIN-
DOW AS DENTIST GETS FORCEPS, The New York Times reported the unusual case of a man who leaped out a window
as the dentist got the forceps. Briefly, the circumstances
were these. A war worker in Staten Island tottered into a
dental parlor and, indicating an aching molar, moaned, "It's
killing me. You've got to pull it out." The dentist grinned
like a Cheshire cat—The New York Times neglected to say
so, but a Cheshire cat who was present at the time grinned
like a dentist—and reached for his instruments. "There
was a leap and a crash," continues the account. "The astonished dentist saw his patient spring through the closed
window and drop ten feet to the sidewalk, where he lay
dazed." The casualty was subsequently treated at a near-by
hospital for abrasion and shock by Drs. J. G. Abrazian and
Walter Shock, and then, like a worm, crept back to the
dentist, apologized and offered to pay for the damage. On
one point, however, he remained curiously adamant. He still
has his tooth.

As a party who recently spent a whole morning with his
knees braced against a dentist's chest, whimpering "Don't
—don't—I'll do anything, but don't drill!" I am probably

the only man in America equipped to sympathize with the poor devil. Ever since Nature presented me at birth with a set of thirty-two flawless little pearls of assorted sizes, I never once relaxed my vigilant stewardship of same. From the age of six onward, I constantly polished the enamel with peanut brittle, massaged the incisors twice daily with lolli-pops, and chewed taffy and chocolate-covered caramels faithfully to exercise the gums. As for consulting a dentist regularly, my punctuality practically amounted to a fetish. Every twelve years I would drop whatever I was doing and allow wild Caucasian ponies to drag me to a reputable orthodontist. I guess you might say I was hipped on the subject of dental care.

When, therefore, I inadvertently stubbed a tooth on a submerged cherry in an old-fashioned last week and my toupee ricocheted off the ceiling, I felt both dismayed and betrayed. By eleven the next morning, I was seated in the antechamber of one Russell Pipgrass, D.D.S., limply holding a copy of the National Geographic upside down and pre-tending to be absorbed in Magyar folkways. Through the door communicating with the arena throbbed a thin, blood-curdling whine like a circular saw biting into a green plank. Suddenly an ear-splitting shriek rose above it, receding into a choked gurgle. I nonchalantly tapped out my cigarette in my eardrum and leaned over to the nurse, a Medusa type with serpents writhing out from under her prim white coif.

"Ah—er—pardon me," I observed swallowing a bit of emery paper I had been chewing. "Did you hear anything just then?"

"Why, no," she replied, primly tucking back a snake under her cap. "What do you mean?"

"A—a kind of a scratchy sound," I faltered.

"Oh, that," she sniffed carelessly. "Impacted wisdom tooth. We have to go in through the skull for those, you know." Murmuring some inconsequential excuse about lunching with a man in Sandusky, Ohio, I dropped to the floor and was creeping toward the corridor on all fours when Doctor Pipgrass emerged, rubbing his hands. "Well, here's an unexpected windfall!" he cackled, his eyes gleaming with cupidity. "Look out—slam the door on him!" Before I could dodge past, he pinioned me in a hammerlock and bore me, kicking and struggling, into his web. He was trying to wrestle me into the chair when the nurse raced in, brandishing a heavy glass ash tray.

"Here, hit him with this!" she panted.

"No, no, we mustn't bruise him," muttered Pipgrass. "Their relatives always ask a lot of silly questions." They finally made me comfy by strapping me into the chair with half a dozen towels, tilted my feet up and pried open my teeth with a spoon. "Now then, where are his X-rays?" demanded the doctor.

"We haven't any," returned the nurse. "This is the first time he's been here."

"Well, bring me any X-rays," her employer barked. "What difference does it make? When you've seen one tooth, you've seen them all." He held up the X-rays against the light and examined them critically. "Well, friend, you're in a peck of trouble," he said at length. "You may as well know the worst. These are the teeth of an eighty-year-old man. You got here just in time." Plucking a horrendous nozzle from the rack, he shot compressed air down my gullet that sent me into a strangled paroxysm, and peered curiously at my inlays.

"Who put those in, a steamfitter?" he sneered. "You ought to be arrested for walking around with a job like that." He turned abruptly at the rustle of greenbacks and glared at his nurse. "See here, Miss Smedley, how many times have I told you not to count the patient's money in front of him? Take the wallet outside and go through it there." She nodded shamefacedly and slunk out. "That's the kind of thing that creates a bad impression on the layman," growled Doctor Pipgrass, poking at my tongue with a sharp stick. "Now what seems to be the trouble in there?"

"Ong ong ong," I wheezed.

"H'm'm'm, a cleft palate," he mused. "Just as I feared. And you've got between four and five thousand cavities. While we're at it, I think we'd better tear out those lowers with a jackhammer and put in some nice expensive crowns. Excuse me." He quickly dialed a telephone number. "Is that you, Irene?" he asked. "Russell. Listen, on that white mink coat we were talking about at breakfast—go right ahead, I've changed my mind. . . . No, I'll tell you later. He's filthy with it."

"Look, doctor," I said with a casual yawn. "It's nothing really—just a funny tickling sensation in that rear tooth. I'll be back Tuesday—a year from Tuesday."

"Yes, yes," he interrupted, patting me reassuringly. "Don't be afraid now; this won't hurt a bit." With a slow, cunning smile, he produced from behind his back a hypodermic of the type used on brewery horses and, distending my lip, plunged it into the gum. The tip of my nose instantly froze, and my tongue took on the proportions of a bolt of flannel. I tried to cry out, but my larynx was out to lunch. Seizing the opportunity, Pipgrass snatched up his drill, took a firm purchase on my hair and teed off. A mixture of sensation, roughly comparable to being alternately stilettoed and inflated with a bicycle pump, overcame me; two thin wisps of smoke curled upward slowly from my ears. Fortunately, I had been schooled from boyhood to withstand pain without flinching, and beyond an occasional scream that rattled the windows, I bore myself with the stoicism of a red man. Scarcely ninety minutes later, Doctor Pipgrass thrust aside the drill, wiped his streaming forehead and shook the mass of protoplasm before him.

"Well, we're in the homestretch," he announced brightly, extracting a rubber sheet from a drawer. "We'll put this dam on you and fill her in a jiffy. You don't get claustrophobia, do you?"

"Wh-what's that?" I squeaked.

"Fear of being buried alive," he explained smoothly. "Kind of a stifling feeling. Your heart starts racing and you think you're going crazy. Pure imagination, of course." He pinned the rubber sheet over my face, slipped it over the tooth and left me alone with my thoughts. In less time than it takes to relate, I was a graduate member, *summa cum laude,* of the Claustrophobia Club. My face had turned a stunning shade of green, my heart was going like Big Ben, and a set of castanets in my knees was playing the Malagueña. Summoning my last reserves of strength, I cast off my bonds and catapulted through the anteroom to freedom. I left Pipgrass a fleece-lined overcoat worth sixty-eight dollars, but he's welcome to it; I'll string along nicely with this big wad of chewing gum over my tooth. On me it looks good.

Index